*Two action-packed
novels of the
American frontier*

SIGNET BRAND DOUBLE WESTERNS:

WEB OF GUNSMOKE

and

UTE COUNTRY

Other SIGNET Westerns You'll Enjoy

- [ ] **CANYON COUNTRY** by Ernest Haycox.
  (#W7931—$1.50)
- [ ] **HEAD OF THE MOUNTAIN** by Ernest Haycox.
  (#Y7976—$1.25)
- [ ] **TRAIL SMOKE** by Ernest Haycox.
  (#W7797—$1.50)
- [ ] **A GUN FOR SILVER ROSE** by Ray Hogan.
  (#W7696—$1.50)
- [ ] **GUN TRAP AT ARABELLA** by Ray Hogan.
  (#W7930—$1.50)
- [ ] **THE IRON JEHU** by Ray Hogan.
  (#W7752—$1.50)
- [ ] **SIGNET DOUBLE WESTERN—THE RIMROCKER** by Ray Hogan and **THE OUTLAWED** by Ray Hogan.
  (#E7888—$1.75)
- [ ] **SIGNET DOUBLE WESTERN—THE SEARCHING GUNS** by Ray Hogan and **THE HANGMEN OF SAN SABAL** by Ray Hogan. (#E7657—$1.75)
- [ ] **TALL MAN RIDING** by Ray Hogan.
  (#Y7622—$1.25)
- [ ] **THE RENEGADE** by Cliff Farrell.
  (#Y7697—$1.25)
- [ ] **RIDE TO HELL** by Frank Gruber.
  (#Y7656—$1.25)
- [ ] **THE KILLER FROM YUMA** by Lewis B. Patten.
  (#W7796—$1.50)
- [ ] **THE KILLINGS AT COYOTE SPRINGS** by Lewis B. Patten. (#W7886—$1.50)
- [ ] **RED RUNS THE RIVER** by Lewis B. Patten.
  (#Y7623—$1.25)
- [ ] **SIGNET DOUBLE WESTERN—GUILT OF A KILLER TOWN** by Lewis B. Patten and **MASSACRE RIDGE** by Lewis B. Patten. (#E7751—$1.75)

THE NEW AMERICAN LIBRARY, INC.,
P.O. Box 999, Bergenfield, New Jersey 07621

Please send me the SIGNET BOOKS I have checked above. I am enclosing $_____(check or money order—no currency or C.O.D.'s). Please include the list price plus 35¢ a copy to cover handling and mailing costs. (Prices and numbers are subject to change without notice.)

Name_____

Address_____

City_____State_____Zip Code_____
Allow at least 4 weeks for delivery

Web of Gunsmoke
by WILL HICKOK

◉◉◉◉◉◉◉◉◉◉

and

Ute Country
by JOHN S. DANIELS

✶✶✶✶✶✶✶✶

Ⓢ
A SIGNET BOOK
NEW AMERICAN LIBRARY
TIMES MIRROR

NAL BOOKS ARE ALSO AVAILABLE AT DISCOUNTS IN BULK QUANTITY FOR INDUSTRIAL OR SALES-PROMOTIONAL USE. FOR DETAILS, WRITE TO PREMIUM MARKETING DIVISION, NEW AMERICAN LIBRARY, INC., 1301 AVENUE OF THE AMERICAS, NEW YORK, NEW YORK 10019.

Web of Gunsmoke Copyright © 1955 by Will Hickok
Ute Country Copyright, 1958, by Wayne D. Overholser,
© 1959 by Wayne D. Overholser

All rights reserved

Originally appeared in paperback as separate volumes published by The New American Library.

SIGNET TRADEMARK REG. U.S. PAT. OFF. AND FOREIGN COUNTRIES
REGISTERED TRADEMARK—MARCA REGISTRADA
HECHO EN CHICAGO, U.S.A.

SIGNET, SIGNET CLASSICS, MENTOR, PLUME AND MERIDIAN BOOKS
are published by The New American Library, Inc.,
1301 Avenue of the Americas, New York, New York 10019

FIRST PRINTING (DOUBLE WESTERN EDITION), MARCH, 1978

1 2 3 4 5 6 7 8 9

PRINTED IN THE UNITED STATES OF AMERICA

Web of Gunsmoke
by WILL HICKOK

Chapter One

He fell without knowing it, and he got up again without remembering, for he was a man from whom all but the deepest instincts had been beaten. The mind no longer ruled him; it had stopped caring. All his thoughts had retreated to a dim, distant place beyond the tortures of thirst and weariness or the dire pressures of fear. Only the unthinking fibres of his body kept fighting for survival, forcing him on.

He went down the rock-ribbed ramp of the hill, stumbling, sliding, without any certainty of direction, a head-down man who had, in his utter weariness, all but forgotten whom he was running from or why he was trying to escape.

The sun's blaze followed him, a constant torment. Cat claw and cholla picked at him with barbed fingers, but he was beyond feeling the sting of them. He bucked his way through a tangle of paloverde in full bloom, not once aware of the scurry of startled desert quail rushing up from the brush in full flight.

When he came to the low ridge of land he hauled in and pulled his head up, staring at this obstacle in dull concentration. He might have turned aside and found a way around the ridge, but he did not. Distance was time. Time was life itself. He was a man who could measure his future by the loss or winning of a few short yards.

. He went head-on at the ridge, climbing in slack-kneed stubbornness. He was a hard man to stop, this Curt Selby, and snubbed tight in the core of his mind was the knowledge that if he stopped now he was finished. He was dead.

He was a worked-down, saddle-toughened man, and when he topped the ridge there was nothing more left in him to carry him on. He lay where he fell, within sight now of the riverboat landing but too exhausted to get up, too tired even to think. But he knew he had to get up and keep going. He had to keep thinking.

He had to if he wanted to stay alive.

Far away and from low on the east shoulder of the mountain he could hear the baffled baying of the hounds still nosing the trail he had tangled for them last night in the cloudburst-flooded narrows of Cibola Canyon.

Lathrop and his damn hounds! Curt Selby shuddered, sick at his stomach from thirst and exhaustion. Sick from strain and the acid residue of panic. Yet he wasn't so much afraid of the hounds Dog Lathrop had turned loose on his trail, not now.

But he was afraid of the Indian tracker the county always hired in when someone was lost in the desert—or a killer had taken to the hills. The Indian wouldn't be baffled by the knots Curt Selby had tied in his trail. Not for long he wouldn't.

And behind the Apache would come Sheriff Jode Meeder and the posse of back-slappers and bounty hunters. A man had a right to be afraid when he had that kind of a crew dogging his trail, and he considered what they would do if they caught up with him. Curt Selby had reason to know. A killing was one thing. But the shooting of a towheaded boy was a crime that no man could forgive.

A thought touched him, thin and cold. *I dug my own grave the day I came home. They won't let me get away. I'm already dead.*

The cloudburst that had thundered and lashed the land yesterday had vanished during the night, and now the June sun blazed down on this far rim of the Arizona desert. Heat dwelt here where Curt Selby had fallen, and danger. He raised his head and shoulders up from the hot earth, and down the long slant of the ridge he could see the dark flow of the Colorado River. Thirst gagged him. Last night he had all but drowned in the flooded narrows of the canyon, but now it was water he needed to stay alive.

He kept staring through the heat haze at the river, refusing to let go of hope. *If I can get to the river, they'll never catch me.*

He got to his feet and stumbled on in that shuffling half trot that had carried him all these thorny miles ahead of Jode Meeder's posse of man hunters. The pace was hypnotic. Stride—suck air—stride. An eternity of running, falling, getting up, stumbling on again. He had the impression that he was not moving at all, that he was suspended in gray space. The river seemed to get no closer at all.

Then, all of a sudden, the river was there before him, its roiled yellowness flowing heavily past the bottomland cottonwoods and reed thickets. The landing would be somewhere downstream, not far now, but an edged wariness sharpened in him as he turned in that direction. *Better wait for the Cocopah to show up before taking the chance.*

He needed water, he had to have it. He slid down the cutbank, and the river's edge was cool and moist beneath his torn hands. He bent and drank, slowly and cautiously, with a desert man's hunger for water and his knowing fear of it. He was immediately sick. He turned and crawled into the shade of a willow, too done in to care what happened now. A man could stand only so much punishment, and Curt Selby had reached his limit.

He tried to remember when the *Cocopah* was due upriver from Yuma, bound for Ehrenberg, Hardyville, and the Mormon settlement of Callville, far to the north. The riverboat was his only hope for escape, and he thought he recalled gossip that the *Cocopah* would reach Ehrenberg on Wednesday.

But when was Wednesday?

He tried to remember, to reach back across the gray space through which he had fled. Monday was the day of the shooting. Of that he was certain. On Monday he had felt the Colt kick its heavy recoil against his bent elbow, and he had watched a man spin and die. And at the end of that harsh moment he had heard the voice in the street rise up against him in malice and hatred.

That's how you wanted it, Dad. You owned an empire, and I ripped it apart for you.

Curt Selby's memory reached back through the grayness, and in this moment of utter weariness he could reason out, above all other thoughts, the one relentless truth.

It was on last Monday, then, that he had started to die.

Chapter Two

Curt Selby was his name, and he rode into the town of of Signal with a hunted look on his face and a be-damned-to-you glint in his eyes. He was a towering man. A lean one. A two-day beard roughened his long jaw.

He had the stamp of a man who had seen more than his share of trouble in his time, and was either running from it or searching for more. The black-butted sixshooter he wore meant something, and the buscadero belt from which the weapon hung had not been designed for a Sunday man.

These were the surface signs that drew the first impressions. But there were others that had to be searched for—the pressure of the lips and the attentive quickness of the eyes. A touch of sardonic amusement was in the gaze, and beneath that lay the acid of memories that were not pleasant. It gave him a look of jaded truculence, of an old and weary anger that had been pushed deep into him by the three years since he had last seen this town but was yet to be answered and satisfied.

He turned his steeldust across Signal's pocked street and reined in at the hitch rail that fronted the Dollar Sign saloon. Hipping around in the saddle, he gave a long and thoughtful moment to his scrutiny of the street.

Signal had not changed. There were the same boundaries and wind-scoured buildings, the same men in the same old places, the same watchful malice measuring him from windows and shadowed doorways.

Curt Selby could feel these things as he could feel the steady pressure of the high sun against his back. He could taste the alerted malice of the town, a sourness that came out of three years ago and raised its gall in his throat.

It wasn't three years ago that I treed this town just for the hell of it; it was only yesterday. A fool kid with a hot temper trying to cast a big shadow, and a gun that was faster than any honest man's ought to be. Selby had memories of that day. He had put his mark on the town, and Signal had marked him. A man had to grow tall and look back to see his own smallness.

His gaze drifted, touching the front-flared buildings and the narrow alleys leading off toward weedy backlots. Abe Korbee's livery yard showed its wide archway at the yonder end of the street. His gaze pulled in again, and he saw the two bullet holes in the precise center of the golden bell that was the trademark of Lew Haverhill's saloon. Selby's faint nod was a sardonic salute. Damn good shooting for a half-drunk youngster on the back of a racing horse. He couldn't do better now, and he hadn't looked into a bottle for more than a year.

His gaze took in the red brick courthouse; he lowered it and saw Jode Meeder watching him from the shadowed doorway of the sheriff's office, an expression of puzzled uncertainty on his blocky face.

Full recognition had not yet come to Meeder, and that was not as Curt Selby wanted it. He still had his pride. He smiled thinly and cuffed back the brim of his hat with slow and deliberate disdain. He wanted no shadow across his face to obscure his identity. He wanted Sheriff Meeder and the rest of the town to know.

Lifting his leg across the saddle horn, he slid to the ground and looped the reins across the tie rail. An hour back on the trail he had watered and fed the steeldust, giving the animal a good rest before pushing on to Signal. This was the caution of a knowing man: never ride into a hostile town on a tired and hungry horse.

A nagging sense of incompleteness and dissatisfaction was working on him, and he had another look along the street. He had good reason to expect trouble from this town. But Signal was refusing to acknowledge him, hiding its curiosity beneath a sunlit serenity that was only a surface veneer.

Malice and danger traveled the silence of the street, sensed but not seen. Sheriff Meeder had not moved out of the doorway of his office. Orvie Shandrin and Clyde Melavin still sat on the liar's bench under the Emporium's board awning. Dog Lathrop squatted on his heels in front of the Golden Bell, idly scratching the ears of one of his hounds. Expressionless men. Watchful. Wondering and waiting.

Curt Selby's smile drew tighter, and he grunted softly, in slow anger. "These years never happened. Nothing at all has changed."

The thought stung him, and he was gripped by a rankled impulse to cross the street and put a little pressure against Sheriff Meeder, just to see if the man would bend. But he recognized the stupidity of that. If he had learned anything at all these last three years, it was the value of patience.

The day would come soon enough for him to buck Jode Meeder, and because he had smelled too much gunsmoke in his time he dreaded it.

Jode Meeder, he had reason to know, was a complicated man. He was all things to all men—or tried to be. He was sheriff and he was politician, friend of the rich and confidant of the poor. And deeper than those things lay cold and flinty qualities that few men ever saw, the hard and streaky temper of a killer.

He was making his way around the end of the hitch rail when he saw the boy come out of the Emporium and angle toward him through the street's dust at a jogging trot. The boy's voice caught at him as he started to turn away.

"Hey . . . mister?"

Selby drew up.

"C'n I watch your horse for you, mister?"

Selby turned slowly. Amusement broke through the moody truculence of his face as he gazed down at the boy, and he grinned faintly.

"You out hunting yourself a job of work, youngster?"

"Yessir. I on'y charge two bits for watchin' a man's horse for him."

"That's a lot of money," Selby observed thoughtfully, and heard the boy's prompt rebuttal.

"Another horse would cost you more, mister, if this here steeldust of yours was rustled while you weren't watchin'."

It made good sense, Selby nodded soberly. "That's right, for a fact," he murmured, and made his face grim as he eyed the street. "This looks like a town full of horse thieves, sure enough. Maybe if I could dicker your price down a notch or two. . . ."

The boy was tempted. Then his lips firmed. "Two bits

for an extra close watchin', and a dime for just keepin' an eye on him. That's my deal, mister."

Selby nodded, considering gravely. About eight or nine, he judged the lad to be, thin and stringy, so busy growing tall that he had no time for spreading out. The boy was scrubbing one dusty bare foot across the other as he waited, and from out of nowhere the memory of his own youth came into Curt Selby with a kind of bitter hurt. The cozy feel of hot dust beneath bare feet—it was a pleasure a man should pause now and then to remember, but seldom did.

Watching the lad, he said in a stone-sober voice, "I'll make a deal with you, friend. I'll pay your price if you'll point out the horse thieves so I can go down the street and kill them."

The lad's eyes rounded in startled alarm. "Now, mister, I didn't go to say. . . ."

Selby smiled faintly. "I guess that wouldn't be so good, would it?" he said. "If I did that, it would kill off your business, wouldn't it?"

"Yessir. Yessir, mister."

Selby grinned, and dug a silver dollar out of his pocket, put it into the boy's hand. "That pays for four of your extra-best jobs of watching my steeldust, friend. What are you going to do with all that money, now?"

The lad stood arrow-straight in the street's deep dust, and there was something in the high shoulders and thin face that echoed a memory across Curt Selby's mind. It was far away ghost-thought, dim behind all the rough trails he had traveled since he had last seen this town.

The boy's voice was firm; a man's words coming from the lips of a barefooted youngster. "Pop hasn't worked for a long spell, and there's a lot of things that my mom needs. . . ."

Selby's grin faded. The ghost-thought grew brighter in his mind, rising through the years. "I didn't catch your name, sonny."

"Bax Brighton."

That was the name. A towheaded toddler then, but now a stripling boy trying to act like a man. The memory rushed up through the years. The boy had his father's high shoulders and firm-boned features, but those clear gray eyes were his mother's. This, then, was young Bax Brigh-

13

ton, son of Amy. Son of big Sam Brighton, friend and neighbor of the Selby family and owner of the richest graze in the valley.

Curt Selby said quietly. "I want to hear the rest, Bax. What happened to your daddy's ranch?"

A look of hate threw its bitter shine across the boy's eyes. "It was took over by Buckle, mister. It was them damned Selbys done it. Them damned range-grabbing Selbys stole Pop's land!"

Chapter Three

Them damned range-grabbing Selbys stole Pop's land!
It was like acid hurled into Curt Selby's face. He stared down at the boy, seeing hate in eyes too young to know about such a thing.

But the hate was there, bitter and real. Years alone weren't the measure of a nine-year-old. It was the things he saw and heard that taught him how to hate. Young Bax Brighton had grown up before his time. He had a boy's face and a boy's stringy body, but in his eyes flamed the hatred of a grown man.

There was movement on the street. Selby raised his eyes and saw Jode Meeder stepping out of his office door, a blocky man with a blocky face that never revealed any more than he wanted it to. The sheriff was expressionless now as he came to a halt on the rim of the plank walk, waiting narrowly for events to shape his course of action.

The street was stirring, and Selby could feel its malice tightening around him. Dog Lathrop had stopped scratching the ear of his hound, and was looking toward Selby in sober concentration. A heavy-bore rifle was propped against the wall behind him.

Orvie Shandrin and Clyde Melavin were rising from the liar's bench in front of the Emporium across the street, and a quickening alertness whetted Curt Selby's thoughts. These were the ones to watch. Jode Meeder was deadly in a fight, but shrewd enough to leave the hottest irons for other men to grab.

A contemptuous thought bit into Curt Selby's mind: when a man owns a pair of good dogs, he doesn't have to do his own barking. That was the key to Jode Meeder.

Orvie Shandrin and Clyde Melavin were the ones to keep an eye on. Selby had reason to know. They knew all the quick ways and sharp turns of a gunfighter's trade.

Weather had darkened them, making their eyes pale by comparison.

They were remarkably alike in size and temperament, moving unhurriedly through the dust of the street toward the Dollar Sign saloon. Smiling faintly as they met Selby's gaze. Coolly sure of themselves. They would kill if the sheriff gave the word, knowing that Jode Meeder's office would protect them. A jerk of Meeder's head halted them in the middle of the street, and Selby breathed a soft sigh of relief. *Not yet, damn you. You'll wait for a better time.*

He was swinging his attention back to the boy when he heard the slapping of the Dollar Sign's batwing doors behind him.

A man's voice said, "What are you doing here, Bax?"

"Nothing, Pop. . . ."

"Have you been pestering this stranger to mind his horse for him?" the man said wearily. "How many times do I have to tell you, Bax? I won't have any son of mine begging chores in this town."

Curt Selby turned, a slow smile shaping his lips. "The boy's all right, Sam. He's done nothing wrong."

Recognition hit Sam Brighton like the blow of a fist as he stared at Curt Selby. He was a big man. He had Curt Selby's towering height, and there was weight in his shoulders that Selby would never possess. A shaggy bull of a man with the strength of an ore crusher in his long arms.

Selby murmured, "Long time no see, Sam."

The man didn't answer. Sudden temper flared through his face, and he sent his command harshly at his son. "Get away from here, Bax."

"But, Pop, I on'y . . ."

Sam Brighton spun, and the thrust of his arm sent the lad stumbling backward through the street's deep dust. Bax tripped and fell. He got slowly to his feet again, his thin face white and twisted as he fought to keep from crying.

Selby said quietly, "No cause to be so rough on the boy, Sam."

Brighton's big head jerked around, and hate was a livid flare in his dark eyes. He took a short lumbering stride toward Selby, and caught himself. He stood there, a shaggy bear of a man fighting visibly to keep a lid on his fury.

"By God," he said thickly. "By God, it's almost too much . . . too damn much for a man to stand."

Selby held to his smile, for once this big man had been a friend and he wanted to bring back the good things that had been between them.

He said gently, "What's eating you, Sam?"

He got no reply. He tried again, speaking patiently. "The boy didn't know me. I rode in, and he asked for the job of minding my horse for me. Nothing wrong in that, Sam. You ought to be proud of that boy of yours."

Sam Brighton's eyes were hot with fury. He brought up his massive shoulders in a slow rolling motion as if to ease some terrible pressure building up inside him.

He said savagely, "Don't give me any of your wind, fellow."

"We used to be friends, Sam."

"Damn you—shut up!"

"You're riding me too hard, Sam," Selby said gently. "I'm a friend, remember? You've got no jingle with me."

Brighton's mouth twisted, and he spat deliberately at Selby's boots. Selby stood motionless, feeling the slow heat of his own resenting anger.

He said, holding his tone quiet, "I guess that shows me, Sam. I ought to knock some of the hell out of you for that, but maybe you've got a reason to act like a crazy damn fool. Only don't do that again, Sam. I'm trying to stay your friend. Just don't push me any harder, man."

For a moment Sam Brighton stood balanced to come tearing at Selby with his huge fists and massive shoulders. Then, for the barest fraction of time, his gaze struck past Selby toward where Shandrin and Melavin and Jode Meeder stood watching. It did something to his rage, and he jerked abruptly around toward the saloon doors as though to escape.

It was Orvie Shandrin's mocking laughter that did it. It came through the street's silence, a laugh that was thin and brittle with derision, a blade that slashed all control out of Sam Brighton.

He spun back around, and there was no longer anything rational in his rage. His mouth opened as though to speak, to shout. But no words came, no sound at all, as he lunged violently forward and drove his fist into Selby's face.

Chapter Four

It hurt. The impact of the blow snapped Selby's head back and sent harsh waves of pain shuddering down his spine. Off balance, he caught Sam Brighton's second blow just above the buckle of his belt.

Once during a cattle drive he had been thrown and kicked by a bronc pony. Sam Brighton's sledging fist had the same effect on him. An explosion of exquisite agony slammed through his body, and instantly afterwards came an incredible weakness. He found himself down on his hunkers in the dust of the street without full understanding how he got there.

He stared up at Brighton, hurt and sick and goaded by a deep and dull core of resenting anger.

He thought he spoke to the big man coming at him through the street's dust, but he couldn't hear what he said. There was a huge roaring in his ears. In a dim and distant way he realized then that he had not spoken after all, but only intended to. His mouth was open, but he couldn't break the words out of him.

Then the paralysis that gripped his lungs vanished, and he sucked air deep into them. As the big man came lunging at him, he said in a thin, whistling tone of voice, "All right, Sam . . . all right, man."

Brighton's big hands reached down for him. He rolled back and away and came up to his feet, one chill voice crying out its dire warning through the uprushing heat of his own fury: *He's too big. You've got to get him quick.*

He was not quite ready for Brighton's rush. Stepping aside, he lashed a blow to the man's ear, but he wasn't braced to take the shock and the impact unsteadied him more than it did Brighton. He stumbled backward and hit the hitch rail as Brighton came veering around again.

As though from far away, he heard young Bax's thin-pitched cry of alarm. "No, Pop . . . Dad!"

But Sam Brighton was past all reasoning. Selby saw the start of the man's huge round-arm swing, and stepped forward with his own blow. He felt the shock of the impact clear up to his elbow. It slowed the big man, but did not stop him. A fist tore along the shelf of his jaw, and another ripped raw flame across his ribs. He twisted away from the big man, retreating in something close to panic.

The high heat of his fury and the thin chill of alarm held Curt Selby to a fine edge of prudence. This outraged bull of a man was one to be feared. The power to cripple and destroy was in those great arms and shoulders. In friendship Sam Brighton was a gentle man, but in this flame of unreasoning hate he could kill without knowing what he did.

Selby knew this. It warned him against the rakehell flare of rashness that wanted to send him head-on at the man. Sam Brighton had never been whipped in a roughhouse brawl. In this blaze of goaded rage he crowded Selby relentlessly, lunging and twisting as Selby retreated from him. Trying to catch Selby into the crushing power of his arms. Driven remorselessly on with the brute wish—to smash and maim and destroy.

A thought, sharp with real fear, dug into Curt Selby's mind: *A gun barrel is the only thing that'll stop him.*

And another thought slashed its warning through his brain. *Reach for a gun, and it'll give Jode Meeder's crew the excuse they're waiting for.*

He stepped in suddenly and rammed his knuckles into the big man's face and body; he stepped back from those clubbing arms, and then closed in for another swift attack. Hit and run. That was his only hope of dealing with a man of Sam Brighton's massive strength and unreasoning fury. A lobo wolf knew how—slash and dodge, and slash again.

It was vicious, it was brutal. He tore a redness from Brighton's nose and mouth, and he beat a dullness into the man's eyes. He kept driving in and falling back, striking and retreating. But to slow Brighton's head-on rushes he spent his own strength recklessly. A melting weakness was loosening his knees and taking the power out of his blows. Brighton's fist caught him as he retreated, and the impact of the blow sent him slamming backward against the hitch rail. He tried to straighten, but could not.

He stood there in cramping agony, unable to make himself move as Sam Brighton came slowly around. Everything seemed distorted and out of proportion— the shadowy shapes of townsmen ringing this corner of the street, the grotesque grimace of Brighton's face and the ponderous movement of his body as he came forward.

Pain cried out in Curt Selby's body; panic sent its shuddering waves through him as he hauled himself slowly erect and settled himself for another attack. *This time Sam'll finish me.* It was a frightening thought. *Got to stay away from him.*

He moved his foot in a slow, dragging step, feeling the tie rail scrape the small of his back as he shifted to one side. He saw Brighton turn heavily, realigning himself for the attack. Damned odd about Sam, he thought shallowly. The man had been hurt, his face a battered wreckage. Yet Curt Selby could not remember doing so much damage to the big man. Damned odd. . . .

Weakness came flowing back into him, and the street began tilting upward at a sickening angle. He had to grip the hitch rail behind him to keep from falling. He sagged there, tormenting his lungs with great gagging gulps of air. Breathing hurt. He couldn't get enough air into his lungs.

He saw Brighton shift his weight, rocking forward. A weary thought knifed Curt Selby's brain. *Now is your chance, Sam.*

And another echo, tormented and bitter, ribboned through his consciousness. *We were friends, Sam. Why are you doing this to me?*

The man seemed to gain momentum as he came closer, those huge arms lifting and hooking out in front of him. Curt Selby stared. That raging flame of hate was still in Sam Brighton's eyes, unthinking, unchanging.

Selby could not move away as the big man came bucking forward in that hard, mad-bull rush. Selby got his right boot up from the street and thrust it rigidly at the man. But that was all he could do. It was not in him to kick.

He felt the impact of Brighton's lunging weight hurl a sudden shock against the locked muscles of his upraised leg. An exquisite agony slammed through his hip and up into his back, and sharp echoes of pain went jolting along his spine. He heard Brighton's grunt, a belly-deep burst of sound.

He stared stupidly across that short space at the cowman, and in him there was no clear understanding of how he had halted that brutal rush. Only the fact mattered; Sam Brighton had been stopped.

An explosion of wind belched from Brighton's torn lips, and both big hands clenched the smear of dust Selby's boot had left on his middle. A look of pure agony was in his eyes. He pulled himself slowly erect, a powerful man refusing to let go of the hate that was in him.

"By God! You damned range-grabbing Selbys!"

"Listen to me, Sam. We were friends once. . . ."

"You sonofabitch!"

"Sam, give me a chance to talk."

"You bastard!"

"Sam—Sam!" Selby said. His voice was a groan. Beyond Sam Brighton was a white-faced boy seeing a thing too bitter for him to comprehend. A scared boy with eyes like wet glass.

"Think of your boy, Sam. Think of Bax. It's not right for a kid his age to see his pa in a mess like this."

Selby's voice was thick in his throat. He talked, but he couldn't reach the cowman with his words. He couldn't break through that craze of bitterness and hate.

"You sonofabitch!" Brighton said, and his voice was like the thin singing of taut wires.

"Sam, I can't keep taking that from you. It's getting too much, even from you."

The pain was letting go of Sam Brighton's middle. He raised his big hands and looked at them. Powerful, calloused hands that had built a rich ranch and then had let it slip away from him. Hands that had known rope burns and the scars of honest fights. He stared at his hands as though he hated them. And then he raised his eyes to Selby.

"These two hands," he said thickly. "These two hands of mine—I would have beat the fear of God into you. I would have killed you with them because you're another Selby come here to help tear the hearts out of the few honest men left on this range. That's what I wanted to do with these two hands of mine. You God-damned Selbys!"

Curt Selby took a slow breath. There was a pattern to this moment, a dark and dismal promise that echoed to him from many far places. The saloon in Tascosa . . . that night on the banks of the Red . . . the affair outside the Bird Cage theater, in Tombstone. Proud men with hot tempers and ready sixguns. He would never forget those fights. He would never cease regretting them.

Yes, the same relentless pattern. . . .

He was aware of many things. The white, pinched face of a frightened boy. The waiting of the crowd rimming the street, and all those faces honed sharp by morbid tensions. The alerted curiosity of Orvie Shandrin, and the shadows of dreary laughter pooled in Clyde Melavin's cloudy eyes.

And the sheriff, Jode Meeder, making no effort at all to halt this thing that was coming.

Selby gave care to his choice of words. A man driven by hot pride and raging temper was like a hair-trigger sixgun. There was always the unpredictable danger, the cocked violence. A man like Sam Brighton could read an insult in the most innocent smile, a challenge in a thoughtless word or intonation of voice.

Selby said, "We can go somewhere and talk, Sam. You and me. There are things I don't know about. About Buckle . . . and the ranch you used to have. I've been away for three years, Sam, but you can tell me. We were always good friends, you and me."

He spoke quietly, looking steadily at the cowman across that short distance. Nothing changed in the man's face, and the coldness sank deeper into Curt Selby.

Brighton raised his big hands higher, their palms turned up, showing the callouses and rope burns. He had not heard Selby at all.

"I wanted to beat some decency into you with these hands," he said thickly, and the one-track blackness of his temper was like the bore of a gun leveled on Selby.

"These two hands of mine—I would have killed you with them. A favor to the few honest men left on this range if I could have. But I couldn't. I tried, but I couldn't."

"You're out of your head," Selby breathed. "Listen to me, Sam!"

"If I can't do it with my hands, I've got to do it another way. Somebody's got to stand up to Buckle. You God-damned Selbys!"

Selby stopped breathing. His gaze slipped past Brighton, to Jode Meeder. The sheriff was faintly smiling. He didn't care that a man was soon to die. He didn't care at all. This was something he wanted.

Sam Brighton swore, low and hoarse. "You're wearing a gun. Then use it, damn you!"

Yes, the same wild and brutal pattern. But it had to change. A man rode many lonely trails before he learned that a gun was not the answer.

He shook his head. "No, Sam. Not against you."

Sam Brighton stood tall, his hate a black, towering thing. "I've called you everything. What does it take, man?"

"Nothing you can do, Sam," Selby said. "Nothing you can say. I won't draw on you."

"Yellow! Cur-dog yellow!"

"All right."

Brighton's voice raised, keening. "I'm telling you, man! If you won't draw, that won't stop me. I'll kill you, if I hang for it."

"I'm sorry, Sam."

He gazed quietly at the man through a long moment of waiting, motionless. And when he saw Brighton's hand lift from his gun, he thought the edge was gone. That was his mistake. He was turning away from the cowman when he heard Joe Meeder's quick shout.

"Watch out, Selby! He means it!"

Chapter Five

Yes, the pattern could be changed. A man did not always have to kill.

Selby spun, seeing the leap of the cowman's hand, as he threw himself forward. Mid-movement, he heard the explosion of the shot and felt the sting of burned powder against his face.

The momentum of his body carried Sam Brighton down with him. He struck at the gun, knocking it aside, and drew on some untapped reservoir of strength to drive a blow to the cowman's jaw. Brighton rolled over and over in a slack, witless way, and then sat up slowly in the dust of the street, gazing vaguely around him.

Selby crawled through the dust to the man. "I'll take that gun, Sam."

Brighton's head turned, a look of stunned defeat loosening the lines of his face and making them heavy.

Selby said, "The gun, Sam. I'll take it, now."

He reached out and took the gun from the cowman's hand. All fight was gone from Sam Brighton, and in that moment he was an old and weary man.

Selby pushed up to his feet, a sense of pity and bitter loss rolling through him as he looked down at the cowman.

"Give you a hand, Sam?"

You can beat a man down without ever humbling his pride or softening his hate.

"I'll see you in hell first."

"I'm sorry you feel that way," Selby said, and his voice was soft. "We used to have something together, you and me."

Brighton got his legs under him and shoved up from the street. Movement caught Selby's eyes, and he looked around. It was the boy, Bax, drifting closer, his face white and pinched with silent crying.

Brighton said, his voice flat and harsh, "I'll give you first shot, damn you. Hand me my gun back, and I'll give you first shot. That's all I ask—just one chance to settle with you."

"You hate me that much, Sam?"

The hate was there. "You're a Selby. You're the Buckle brand. You, your old man, or your brother—I don't care who or which. A gun is the only thing that will settle this, now."

Jode Meeder was tramping forward, flanked by Orvie Shandrin and Cylde Melavin. The memory of old rancors dug into Curt Selby, and he faced around toward those three with a tightening awareness.

He glazed coldly at the lawman. "Well, Jode?"

Jode Meeder drew to a halt, showing Selby a brief shadow of a smile. Then the smile faded, and he inclined his head in Sam Brighton's direction.

"I didn't think I'd ever see a man take Sam Brighton apart like you did. It was a good job of work, Mr. Selby, but it's my opinion you could've tied it up neater."

So now it was Mr. Selby! Selby's eyes slowly widened. He murmured gently, "How so, sheriff?"

Meeder's voice was a flat grunt. "You should've killed him."

The faintest of smiles pinched Curt Selby's lips as he stared at the lawman. "That looks like a sheriff's badge you're wearing. It's mighty strange advice, Jode, coming from you."

The townsmen were milling close, ringing the hitch rail. Meeder gazed stolidly around at them. He brought his eyes back to Selby.

"I'm a reasonable man and try to do an honest job for this badge the county pinned on me. I guess you know that, Mr. Selby."

There was acid in the memory. Selby's smile turned down at the corners. "Seems I remember leaving this town one jump ahead of you and your crew about three years ago," he murmured.

Jode Meeder shrugged his heavy shoulders. "That was just a kid stunt you pulled off. Get drunk and shoot up a town. I did the same thing when I was wearing fuzz instead of whiskers. I outgrew it, and so have you, Mr. Selby. No harm done, and I'm glad to see you back home."

Selby inclined his head in ironic acknowledgment. So now it was Mister this and Mister that, and the welcome carpet had been rolled out for his return.

He said softly, "Jode, I keep hearing the strangest damn things from you. It's going to take me time to get used to them."

Then he said, "So it's your opinion I should have killed Sam Brighton, here?"

Meeder reached into his pocket for one of the slim black cigars he chewed but never smoked. His gaze at Selby was one of friendly candor.

"I'd rather shoot a snake *before* it hits me, Mr. Selby."

"Preventive medicine," said Selby, and smiled dryly. "A rough cure for men."

Again Jode Meeder traveled his gaze around the ring of townsmen. His glance touched Orvie Shandrin and Clyde Melavin, and for a moment he was thoughtful. He was a lawman always attentive to the ingredients that kept his profession secure. The town's opinion was one important factor; the fast guns Melavin and Shandrin wore was another.

He gazed soberly at Curt Selby. "My job is to keep law and order in this town, Mr. Selby. I hate bloodshed as much as any man. God knows I've seen enough since I pinned on this badge."

A sourness rose in Selby's throat. A pretty speech. Plain talk from a God-fearing sheriff dedicated to run an honest office. But keep a pair of bounty-killers at your side while you do your orating. It was gall in Curt's throat. He said nothing.

"I've learned a few things in my time," Meeder said. "You stomp a snake before it strikes. If the snake is a man, it's just too bad. This is a rough range, here. Sometimes a rough cure is necessary. I'd rather see one bronc man killed than several honest men die with lead in them."

His teeth bit into the cigar, and he slanted a brittle glance at Sam Brighton. He swung his gaze back to Selby.

"This fellow is heading for a hang-rope," he said flatly. "He blames Buckle for his own failures. It's been working on him, and it's got to come out. He tried to gun you a minute ago when you started to turn away. It didn't come off, but that won't stop him. One of these days he'll find a nice safe cutbank, and when he's through shooting, your daddy or your brother—or you—will be dead. You should've settled with him when he asked for it."

Selby looked at Sam Brighton, standing head-down and defeated at the end of the hitch rail.

He said to the lawman, "But I didn't. I'll take my chances on Sam Brighton."

Meeder nodded slowly. "You're a generous man, Mr. Selby. I hope it won't prove fatal to you or your folks."

Selby said nothing.

Meeder hitched his belt up, grunting grimly, "Just the same, Mr. Selby, I'm going to chuck this tough nut into the cooler and give him a chance to think things over."

Selby raised his tone a notch. "Let the man alone, Jode."

Meeder reared up slowly, a look of affronted dignity on his blocky features. "I reckon that's not for you to say, Curt."

"Sam's got a wife and son to support," Selby said, and a note of weary anger was in his voice. "Give the man a break. He can't take care of his family in jail."

"Should've thought of that before he disturbed the peace in this town," Meeder grunted. Then his tone changed to one of friendly concern. "I don't like to go against Buckle. But the law is the law, Mr. Selby, and what I'm doing is for your own good. Brighton is going to the lockup."

He swung abruptly around, and bucked the cowman's shoulder with a stiff arm. "On your way, fellow."

Brighton spun with a sudden break of blind fury, and threw a wild blow at Meeder's face. The sheriff stepped back from it, untouched. Then Orvie Shandrin and Clyde Melavin swept past Meeder, moving with the sure swiftness of men who knew this sort of work and enjoyed it.

They caught Sam Brighton from both sides. Shandrin drove the heel of his hand to the base of the cowman's neck, a vicious blow. Melavin caught Brighton's arms from behind and yanked them back and up between the shoulder blades, kinking the cowman forward in wrenching agony. He drove his bent knee to the tail of the spine, jolting his man toward the jail at a shambling trot.

They were small men, Melavin and Shandrin. The weight of the two of them did not exceed Sam Brighton's powerful bulk by many pounds. But they were rawhide and barbed wire. They knew all the sharp and deadly tricks of handling a man.

Orvie Shandrin and Clyde Melavin—there were graves on the red earth hill above town that looked down on each of those two.

As Brighton went stumbling toward the jail, Shandrin swung about with that quick, easy grace that spoke so eloquently of the menace that was in him. His gaze sought out Selby, swift and questioning. It had the impact of a bullet. Selby stiffened under it. Then a bitten half-smile, thinly sardonic, bent the gunman's lips, and he swung sharply around and went trotting toward the jail.

Jode Meeder's gaze was one of jaded regret. "It had to be done, Mr. Selby. It's for the good of you and your folks."

Selby nodded dryly. "I'm obliged, sheriff. It's mighty nice to have you worry about my health for a change."

The crowd was breaking up. Selby watched those men as they turned away, remembering how they had stepped wide of a wild-headed kid three years ago. A kid? He had been twenty-four. But it wasn't years alone that made a man. Twenty-four years old, he had been, but still just a damn fool kid. He knew that, now.

He remembered the town's gossip about him. Spoiled rotten and headed for hell, for sure. Pampered when he should have had his britches warmed. Taught how to use a sixgun instead of a rope and branding iron. Always practicing with his gun, young Curt, and hungry to use it when he got a few drinks under his belt. Wouldn't be satisfied until he killed a man, and even then maybe not until he was in his own grave. Hamp Selby's kid was just plain no good.

Selby remembered the gossip, and he remembered the day he had treed the town and then headed for the hills only a short jump ahead of Sheriff Meeder and the bullets of that posse. He wasn't proud of that day. It took some men a heap of living before they grew up.

He watched the townsmen with sardonic amusement as they turned away, knowing this same memory of him was running strongly through them. Ed Newlin slapped him on the shoulder, a cordial gesture that overlooked the time Curt had shot the big wooden bathtub full of holes while Ed was in it. Naked and running down the street in panic,

Ed had made a picture no man in Signal would ever forget. Selby remembered. So did Ed. But Ed Newlin was keeping his memory buried.

Ben Padgett, who ran the gunshop next door to Ed's tonsorial parlor, paused to wish Selby well. A few of the others spoke in a friendly way as they went past. The wary guardedness and masked contempt was not in the eyes of these men now.

Signal had changed.

And now it was Mr. Selby when Jode Meeder spoke to him, and the sheriff was so concerned over his health that he censured him openly for not killing a man. For not killing Sam Brighton.

A sourness rose in Curt Selby's throat, a gall so bitter that it almost sickened him. Many stones had been turned over since he had last seen this town three years ago. There were too many changes in Signal that he could not understand.

Sam Brighton had been a friend. Now there was only hate in the man's soul, and the promise to kill.

He was Mister to Jode Meeder, who had hated him. And here were townsmen who had once feared him now treating him with goodwill and respect.

He raised his glance and saw the girl standing in the doorway of the pastry shop across the street. Effie Coombs. Tall and slim and inexpressibly more lovely than the picture he had carried in his mind across a thousand distant trails.

She had loved him, then, without ever telling him. He had known. But he had been too full of himself to care. Spoiled and selfish and hell-bent for the wild trails. *If I'd had a grain of sense three years ago, Effie . . .* The thought was in him, as strong as a voice crying out. But there was nothing behind it, only emptiness.

She was watching him. He raised his hand in a swift gesture to her, and took a quick step toward her. The mistakes of three tangled years could be forgotten. But he halted. A look of unchecked disgust swept through her face, and she turned abruptly, shutting the door behind her.

Yes, Signal had changed. His enemies were now his friends. His friends were now his enemies.

Slow movement drew his attention around. It was Sam

Brighton's boy, Bax, standing alone in the deep dust of the street. The boy's face was a twisted whiteness, his lips bitten tight against the tears that wanted to come.

Selby turned slowly, moving forward. A smile might help. Selby smiled.

"That trouble with your pa," he murmured. "Believe me, Bax, I wouldn't have had it happen for anything."

The boy suddenly shouted at him, a thin, tearing cry. "You damned Selbys!" And he threw his hand with sudden savagery.

The coin, the silver dollar, struck Selby in the corner of the mouth, bringing blood. It hurt.

Chapter Six

There had been a time in Curt Selby's life when his first need on reaching town was for a drink. If he had ridden a long trail it called for several drinks to loosen his joints and ease the weariness; if it had been a short trail it always took more than one drink to take the edge from his restlessness.

He was a man in whom many powerful currents flowed, strong pressures of energy and sudden impulse that he had never been taught to hold in check. When he felt good he wanted to down a few drinks and turn the town inside out just to prove that the world was his own private huckleberry.

When a mood hit him, he needed whiskey to drown his sorrows, knowing full well that next morning he would wake up with a howling headache and none of his troubles settled. Whiskey never helped. It had taken him a hundred headaches in a score of distant range towns to learn that.

Habit was strong; it was like a weight to be picked up and carried each time he saw a saloon, getting heavier and heavier each time. A year without a drink was a long time. . . .

He halted when his walking brought him up to the doors of the Cattlemen's House. It was in this saloon that he had taken his first drink. His father had brought him here, on his fourteenth birthday. It was one of the few times old Hamp had exerted his will on his motherless son.

Curt turned his head, looking at the saloon's winged doors. In there, that day, he had stood beside his father at the tall mahogany bar. He had hooked his boot heel across the brass rail, just as his father had done. Excitement had been in him, a hard hot flush of pride. A boy being ushered into a man's world. Wearing his first gun, and taking his first drink. Feeling tall as the sky, and strong as God Almighty.

"He's man-size, even if he ain't got the years yet," Hamp Selby said. "Bring out your best, Augie. Curt, here, is going to get drunk. All the way drunk. I want him to get educated about a bottle."

It was a thing to remember. There had been a painting above the back-bar mirror of a girl, unclothed, seated on the edge of a bed, combing her hair. Beautiful, glowing golden hair that flowed down across her bosom and across her legs. Curt still remembered that painting. He still remembered the man in the shadowy background, watching the girl through a partly open door.

He saw the girl and the man each time he drank, and then, suddenly and without any reason at all, a wild, blazing rage whipped through him, and he shouted a curse at the man in the painting and grabbed up the whiskey bottle and hurled it at him.

He remembered the startled look he had caught in his father's eyes. And the pinched alarm in Augie Bannon's. And the other men milling away from the bar, looking scared.

And the one who had not backed away, but stood grinning as he said in a voice that kept piling up inside Curt's brain until it became a huge, jeering roar, "The kid's had one too many, that's all." And the fellow's face spurting red as Curt clubbed the grin savagely with his gun barrel.

A kid on his first drunk. Some men never learned about a bottle. . . .

Selby stood there on the plank walk, feeling the hurt Sam Brighton had left in him. Sam Brighton, who once was a friend, had wanted to kill him back there. Effie Coombs, who once had loved him, had turned away in cold disgust.

The mood blackened in him, and he heeled sharply around and pushed through the winged doors into the saloon. Augie Bannon stood at the same place along the bar as he had been that first day. The same wet bar cloth in his hand. Grinning the same grin.

"A drink, Mr. Selby?"

"You didn't call me mister last time I was here."

The grin faded a little. "Why, I guess not. A drink Curt?"

"The best in the house."

Bannon reached under the bar and brought up a bottle. He set a glass down beside it. "The best, Curt. Reserved for Buckle alone."

Curt stared at the bottle. "That's not Dad's brand." He raised his eyes to the saloon man. "I ought to know."

Bannon's smile turned faintly uneasy, and he said in his most reasonable way, "This is Phil's favorite brand. Taste's different from old Hamp's, I guess. Since your brother took over Buckle I've kept this in stock. It doesn't seem to make no never mind to Hamp, though."

There was a wet ring on the bar near the bottle. Curt stared at it. A different brand of whiskey now for Buckle riders! That meant something. So old Hamp had stepped out of the saddle and turned Buckle over to Phil. Yes, three years had brought many changes to Signal's range.

He watched as Bannon poured the drink, filling the glass to the brim.

"Anything else, Curt?"

Selby raised his eyes. "Did I hear it right that Buckle took over Sam Brighton's land?"

The uneasiness dug deeper into Bannon's eyes. He put down the bar rag and rummaged in his pocket for a cigar. It took him time to find a match for it.

"I'm asking, Augie."

Bannon nodded slowly. "I thought you knew."

"I've had one letter from Buckle since I led Jode Meeder's posse out of this town three years ago. That was a month ago, Hamp asking me to come home."

Bannon said conversationally, "I guess the hardest chore for an old range dog like your dad to do is set down long enough to write a letter."

"Let's talk about Buckle," said Selby. "Seems that Phil has made a big thing out of Buckle since he took over."

Bannon struck another match for his cigar. Smoke boiled up around his face, hiding his eyes as he spoke.

"Your brother is the kind that thinks big, and does things in a big way. A fine man, Phil. No set-down-till-the-grass-grows in him. Not in Phil Selby. Yes, sir, a mighty fine man."

Selby gazed steadily at the saloon owner, building up a pressure.

Bannon said heartily, "I'll lay a few bets about that brother of yours. He ain't satisfied with Arizona being a

Territory, but he's the man who will do something about it. He'll keep working until Arizona is a State, and the first election will turn him out Governor, mark my words. Couldn't be a finer man for the job, either."

Selby said gently, "We're talking about Buckle, Augie. I know all about Phil. He's my half brother, Augie— there's a difference—and I know all about him. What I want to know about is Buckle and how many other outfits besides Sam Brighton's have been gobbled up."

Bannon's gaze drifted along the bar. At this hour, the place was empty. He didn't bring his eyes back to Selby as he spoke.

"You're taking it the wrong way, Curt. You're making it sound like your folks have turned Injun, hoggin' the range. It ain't so. The outfits Buckle took over sold out fair and square."

"Which ones, Augie?"

"Dee Wordley's spread, and the Cat Track, Bent Tree, Roman Four, and Charley Bell's brand."

"And Sam Brighton's. Six outfits in only three years! That's what I call spreading out fast."

Bannon's gaze jerked around, and his voice took on a sudden driven force. "Now look here, Curt. I like you, and I don't want you to take me wrong. But I ain't one to talk about anybody's business but my own, and that's how I want to stay. Don't ask me any more, Curt. What Buckle does is no affair of mine."

Selby looked at the barman, his smile one of slow irony. "Three years ago you liked nothing more than to swap gossip. You've changed, Augie. I can't help wondering— what scared you out of your old habits?"

He turned away.

"You forgot your drink," Bannon said.

"No," said Selby. "I didn't forget it."

He kept on walking.

Chapter Seven

At the rear of Ed Newlin's tonsorial parlor there was a small room furnished with a pair of benches, several wall pegs, and a huge wooden tub designed for bathing. The tub would hold two men at a time, or three if the festivities of some special occasion demanded it.

The tub was half full of water. Ed Newlin came in from another room, his face red from the strain of lugging a steaming copper boiler heavy enough for two men to handle. He dumped the hot water into the tub, tested the temperature and stepped back, a short, barrel-shaped man unused to such exertions.

"All ready for you, Mr. Selby."

Selby nodded. He walked around the huge tub until he located the plugged-up bullet holes, five of them evenly spaced in the thick wooden staves. Dry humor was in the glance he lifted to Ed Newlin.

A slow grin spread across the redness of Newlin's face. "You sure gave me a turn when you started shooting holes in that tub. Scared seven kinds of hell out of me, for a fact."

A residue of rankled shame lay deep and unforgetting in his eyes, and he tried to cover it with a rumbling laugh. "I should've knowed you were only funnin', Mr. Selby. Naked as a jaybird, and I went howlin' down the street in broad daylight. Signal sure enough got its picture taken that day. I had every widow woman giving me the eye for months afterwards. That was a day, all right."

Selby said, "You should have grabbed up a club and batted me over the head."

"You were only funnin'."

"I was drunk and looking for trouble."

Newlin said earnestly, "I never held it against you, Mr. Selby, not then and not now."

Selby looked at the man. "Ed," he said softly, "I'd think

36

a lot more of you if you'd stop being such a respectful liar."

He undressed and spent long minutes soaking up the heat of the water. It helped take the stiffness out of his joints, but he knew tomorrow would show a fine collection of livid welts on his face. He didn't mind. In his time he had been handed bruises by men of far lower caliber than Sam Brighton.

Sam had never before been stopped in a fight, and without that blind, hating rage he would have taken Selby's measure without even working up a sweat. Selby knew that, and counted himself lucky to come out of the brawl as well as he had.

He thought of Brighton, locked up in jail without anyone to care about his hurts, and a rankled restlessness started working on him again. He lathered himself with stinging yellow soapsuds, rinsed and stepped out of the water, afterwards rubbing himself dry with the coarse towel Ed Newlin had left for him.

He was a man of long lines and sharp angles, this Curt Selby, and the deeply weathered brown of his neck and face stood out in startling contrast to the whiteness of his skin.

He slapped the dust from his flat-crowned range hat, and put it on. He was struck suddenly by a mental picture of himself and he grinned faintly, thinking it odd that most range men thought first about their hats and secondly about their pants. Habit was a strange thing. It could help make a man strong, and it could reveal his weaknesses.

He dressed, slapping the dust out of each article of clothing before putting it on, afterwards returning to Ed Newlin's front room to get his shave. Stepping out of the chair, he reached into his pocket for money, and saw Newlin shake his head at this.

"No need for that, Mr. Selby. I'll put it on Buckle's bill."

Selby took the dollar out of his pocket. "I'll pay for my own, Ed."

Scrubbed and shaved, he felt more human than he had for days. Standing on the plank walk outside, he drifted his gaze along the wide, hoof-pocked street, seeing the wind-scoured, front-flared buildings and the homes on the treeless hill-slope beyond.

Signal was a composite of a hundred other range towns

Curt Selby had seen; it was like them all and yet it was different from all others, for this one he had seen grow out of a single crosstrails trading post. It was time and remembered events that gave a town its own identity.

The midday sun pressed a steady pressure of heat against Selby's shoulders, and for this hour there was only a thready current of traffic on the street. This was uncommon for a Saturday, and Curt pondered it moodily until he found the answer. Three years ago there had been a dozen or more small outfits back in the hills to send riders into town. Most of those layouts were gone now, swallowed up by Buckle.

Signal was a one-ranch town now, and not until Buckle's crew rode in would there be much activity. This shaped the answer of many things. Curt's smile was sour and without humor. No wonder Signal had bowed and scraped to him ever since he had ridden in, forgetting the rancors of the past.

He was a Selby, and the existence of this town lay balanced on the whims of the Selby family. Buckle was the pivot around which the lives of the town revolved. Buckle had become huge, sprawling, powerful. Its payrolls were Signal's only source of commerce, now that the small outfits had been gobbled up.

Buckle was rich, and money talked. When Buckle cracked the whip, Signal jumped. A town grew humble when it was forced to depend on a single powerful brand for its existence.

The thought rose sourly in Selby's mind. *Phil, you've got more in you than I ever guessd.*

It gave him a new appraisal of his half brother, a slim, quiet man who had seldom let out into the open the ambitions that goaded him.

They had never held much friendship for each other, Curt and Phil. They were as unalike as the mothers who had given them life.

There were hard currents of energy in Curt that made him restless and sometimes given to impulsive decisions. It had taken a score of senseless fights to teach him to curb his quick temper and give him a measure of stability. Even now he was aware of the tenuous line he traveled each waking day, and how easy it would be to fall back into the old wild ways. A *ladino* was hard to tame. The brittle temper and touchy pride were still in him, held in check by the thinnest of veneers, and he wondered if he would ever learn complete control.

Phil was out of a different mold. His currents ran deep and hidden, seldom breaking through to the surface. A man never knew what was in Phil's mind, and few ever bothered to wonder. Phil was that kind, quiet, unobtrusive, yet managing always to manipulate events to his own satisfaction.

Curt had always thought of Phil as a man too weak to fight and too cautious to gamble. He realized now how wrong he had been. Phil was ice; he was tempered steel; he was a razor edge concealed in a smiling sheath.

In three short years Phil had managed to get Buckle's reins out of old Hamp Selby's hand; in that short time he had extended Buckle's boundaries across six neighboring layouts and made it the most powerful ranch in the Territory. A man who could do that was one to be feared.

Standing in the heat of the high sun, Curt thought: *Hamp should have known better than let Phil take over.* But no one knew better than Curt about the blindness of Hamp Selby to the faults of his sons.

In the veins of the son flowed the blood of the father. Curt had inherited the wild streak that had once been in Hamp Selby; Phil had inherited the hard and heady ambitions. *Maybe Hamp knew what he was doing when he turned Buckle over to Phil. Maybe he wanted it this way.*

Restlessness pushed at Selby, and he went down the plank walk toward the hitch rail in front of the Golden Bell, where he had left his horse. Nearing that place, a sudden impulse turned him and sent him tramping across the street to Effie's bake shop.

He opened the door, hearing the tinkle of the overhead bell as he entered. He had not eaten since early dawn, and the warm aroma of freshly baked bread and pastries hit him like the blow of a fist.

Effie's voice came to him from the back room where she had her ovens. "I'll be with you in just a minute."

"Take your time, Effie."

"Who is it?"

"Curt. Curt Selby."

He went around the end of the glass showcase, and down the short hallway, feeling heat pile up against him as he entered the rear room. He saw Effie standing at a long table where she had been working with a great mound of dough. With her sleeves rolled up and the small smear of flour across her temple, she made a picture to be remembered. A fool never knew what he had lost until too late.

There was no break of expression as she met his gaze. Her eyes were cold.

She said remotely, "Well, Mr. Selby?"

He watched her a long moment, waiting for something that did not come. The feeling of futility and loss deepened in him, making him miserable.

He said, "Is that how it is, Effie? Nothing left between us?"

Her voice was flat, almost harsh. "There never was . . . never."

Selby's smile was soft, far away. "You liked me once. You never told me. You didn't have to. It was something I knew."

She turned away from the table to face him, slowly, deliberately. Nothing changed in her eyes. Her lips lost their fullness and turned thin with anger.

"If that is what you came here to talk about you're wasting your time, Mr. Selby. And mine. What I may have felt a long time ago is over and done with."

Selby murmured, "It's not with me, Effie. I wanted you to know that."

The anger rose into her eyes, and she flung her voice at him in swift, quiet spite. "There never was anything in you, Curt Selby, but yourself. All you ever thought of was wearing fancy clothes and riding a show horse through town like you were something special God created."

"I was just a fool kid, then. . . ."

". . . And getting drunk. Blind, staggering drunk, and then going into Greary's Alley to paw over some crib girl!"

"Drunk, yes," Selby said, and he held a lid on his own resenting anger. "But not the other, Effie. That's honest."

She jerked her head, her face pale with contempt. Her voice flattened out to a stony dullness.

"You will oblige me by leaving, Mr. Selby."

He watched her for a while, not moving. Then he said, "I'd hoped you'd give me a chance to talk, Effie."

"There is nothing to talk about, Mr. Selby."

He moved closer to her. The chill of her eyes brought him to a halt.

He said, "We could talk about the town. It's changed, and I'd like to know how, why. I've changed too, Effie."

She turned rigidly away from him. "I asked you to please leave."

He looked at her hair, at the slope of her neck, at the lines of her back. There was a memory in him of her warmth and softness, of the deep, surging needs he had once found in her. The memory turned cold in his mind, mocking him.

He said quietly, "I make no excuses for myself, Effie. I've done things I'm not proud of. A man has to learn. One drink, and I've got to go all the way. I learned that about myself. I haven't had a drink in a year."

She said nothing. Her shoulders were rigid.

"A kid gets crazy ideas, Effie. I grew up thinking I was God Almighty, and nobody was born who could stomp up a bigger cloud of dust. I've had that knocked out of me in the last three years. I rode a long way, and when I looked back I saw how small I was and how much I lost when I left here."

Her shoulders were trembling. She was crying, making no sound at all. He reached out and touched her arm, turning her. She didn't come to him.

He saw the blurred wetness of her eyes, and spoke gently. "Effie, Effie. Can't a man come back and make a new start?"

The bell over the front door tinkled, and the sound of a man's heel-hard walking came down the short hall.

The voice came with a hard thrusting arrogance. "What goes on here, Effie?"

There had been other such voices back along the trails Selby had traveled. Rash, demanding, insolent. Selby stepped away from the girl and heeled instantly around, feeling the stinging menace even before he saw the force of it.

The man was quite tall, but with a compactness of body that had a trick of diminishing his height. Weather had darkened his face to the deep brown of old leather, bleaching his tawny eyes so that they looked almost yellow. He could have been twenty or forty. Trail dust powdered his clothes and the black-butted gun he wore, tied low on his leg.

His voice hit Selby like a slap on the face. "Fellow, who are you?"

Effie said in swift alarm, "It's all right, Lane."

The man's attention did not shift. He held his brittle stare against Selby with the overriding insolence of one accustomed to being obeyed.

"I asked you a question, fellow."

Here, Selby knew, was a thoroughly dangerous man. The menace was to be seen, to be felt, to be feared, and it struck cross-grain against the touchy streak that was in Curt Selby. Yet he smiled.

"So you did," he said, and knew at once that his stubbornness was pushing him into a tight corner.

The man stood utterly without motion, saying, "Are you trying to make something, bucko?"

"Only a point," said Selby. "I don't recall being curious about you."

A ruddiness rose in the man's face, and his eyes took on a wicked glint. The insolence dropped out of his tone, and he spoke almost pleasantly.

"I don't mind telling you. I'm Lane Harragh. Ever hear name before?"

There were echoes from far places. Lane Harragh. Hired gunman with an unbelievable speed and skill. A legend with a sixgun, like that buck-toothed killer over in Lincoln County—the one they called Kid Bonney—Billy the Kid.

"The name is familiar," Selby said.

"I'll tell you something else," said Harragh in a thinning tone. "I never mess around another man's woman, and I don't hold a very high opinion of any jack who does. Does that set you straight, mister?"

"Not exactly."

"You've been trying to get cozy with the wrong girl. She's engaged to another man. A Buckle man. To Phil Selby."

Curt looked sharply around at Effie. Her face was quite pale, with no denial in it. He gazed at her a long moment while all doubt drained out of him.

Then he said, "I seem to be in the wrong place. I'm sorry, Effie."

He turned, giving no glance to Harragh, and made his

42

way toward the door. As he went past the gunman he heard the sharp and brittle arrogance of the command.

"Not so fast, fellow. There are things here I want to know about."

The tone of voice Selby coud have accepted. But not the hard grip of the hand on his arm. That was a challenge of infinitely greater malice—an expression of demanding insolence that tore all patience out of him and brought up that flaring wildness of temper.

He yanked his arm free and spun and slugged the man just above the buckle of his belt. Wind burst from Harragh in a high explosive whistle. He cracked the flat of his hand across Harragh's face, a blow that snapped the man erect and drove him back against the wall of the room.

Fury whipped its wild flames through Selby, and he flung a bitter glance over his shoulder to Effie.

"What gives this fellow leave to ride herd on you?"

Her face was utterly white, her voice barely audible. "He works for Buckle. Harragh is your brother's foreman."

Selby's mouth twisted. "Phil always had an eye for the best," he said. "The best of gunmen. The best of women."

Effie's lips parted, as if to speak. No words came. A thin whisper of sound brought Selby around, and he drove his fist to the meat of Harragh's arm as the gun cleared leather. The weapon fell to the floor.

The fury turned cold and relentless in Curt Selby, giving him a cruelty that, later, he always looked back at with a sense of shame. He drilled another blow to Harragh's middle, and snapped him erect again with a solid clout on the jaw.

Harragh started to fall. Selby caught the man, hauled him roughly around. He clamped one hand on the collar of the gunman's coat and the other on the seat of the pants, and sent him hustling down the hall to the front door.

He had the front door open when he saw the aggregation of men on the plank walk outside, Phil Selby among them. They looked around curiously as the door banged open, and amazement wrote itself baldly across all faces. It was Phil alone who held Curt's brittle stare.

"I've got something here that belongs to you," he said, and heaved Harragh bodily out the door.

Selby moved out on the plank walk. He stepped across

the unconscious gunman, gazing acidly at the man who now ruled the Buckle brand.

"This foreman of yours is something special, Phil," he said. "You ought to take better care of him."

He swung away from the gaping wonderment in Phil's face, and went tramping through the street's deep dust to his horse. He heard one of the Buckle riders flare out a heated oath, but he did not look around. If there was trouble to come out of this affair, it would not be now. He knew Phil well enough to be certain of that.

He mounted, swung the steeldust away from the tie rail, feeling the eyes of the town on him in silent wonderment as he went down the street.

He couldn't get Effie's face out of his mind. It was like the image of a pale light trapped in the retina of the eye after swift darkness. So Effie was engaged to marry Phil and now had Phil's pet gunman keeping an eye on her!

It hurt, knowing that. Another change three short years had made on this range, and the hardest of all to take.

Once out of town, he followed the wide swing of the road to the north, a lank, angular man sitting tall in his saddle, seeing nothing.

Chapter Eight

This, at last, was Buckle's home range, the nucleus around which a vast empire had been built in a time so short that it was almost impossible for Curt Selby to believe.

He had crossed what had once been Roman Four graze, and his route had taken him through a corner of the range Dee Wordley had owned. Dee's line fence was down now, only a few scattered posts remaining to tell about it. Half a mile or so yonder, he could make out the Wordley house and outbuildings through the growing dusk, empty now and lightless.

Selby rode on at a steady lope, the tightness of his lips giving him a look of taciturn toughness that fitted the mood which had been deepening in him these last few miles. Time brought changes to any range, the ruination of some and the growth of others. Nothing stood still, man or the things he created.

But it was not easy for Curt to find a place in his mind for all that had happened on this range in so short a time. The six good neighbors ringing in the original Buckle grass had not folded up and sold out without good reason. Somewhere along the line pressure had been applied in a very efficient and ruthless manner.

Crack the first man, and the resistance of the others would quickly weaken. That was fundamental, and something Phil Selby would know. A smart man, Phil. He had always been able to find ways to wrangle out the things he wanted for himself, without ever getting hurt in the process. Yes, damned smart. And now he had proved himself to be a dangerous one.

A thin wind was coming down from the massive wedge of Mogul plateau, bringing an abrupt end to the day's heat as it always did on this high-desert range. Mogul's wall was like a great arm curving around the vastness of the basin, shading to a deep indigo at this hour and stippled with pines along its high rim. In another few minutes the plateau would be a huge blackness shouldering the night sky. There was a sharpening bite to the wind, now that the sun was gone.

The road sloped down to the bottomlands of Saber creek, then rose up to the bench that gave Selby his first view of Buckle's headquarters, the old and the new.

There was no longer much room in Curt for surprise. It was as Ed Newlin had said in town: a man thinks big, he does big things. Like leaping Buckle's boundaries out to take in its former neighbors. Like building this fine new house with the mission tile roof and gleaming whitewashed adobe walls.

This house, Curt thought, was the kind to be expected of a ranch of Buckle's power and prominence. It offered comforts and beauty not to be found in the old one. The tall curtained windows were bright with lamplight. There was a big new barn off yonder, long, low equipment sheds, and a new bunkhouse for the hands. The entire area was surrounded by a line of white fence posts carrying taut strands of the newfangled barbed Glidden wire that Curt had heard about and hated with a free-range man's natural distrust.

Leaning out of saddle, he slid the lock-bar aside and with a thrust of his boot swung the fence gate open. He did not bother to close it, the rankled moodiness in him finding satisfaction in this rebellious gesture.

He rode up to the house and dismounted, leaving his horse ground-hitched a few feet out from the gallery steps. Tramping across the porch, an acrid thought touched him: maybe I ought to knock first and wait to be announced.

He twisted the knob, walked in. He halted just inside the door in pure wonderment. Here was finery such as he had never before seen, an elegance and atmosphere of genteel comfort that would strain a rangeman's grandest imagination.

A crystal chandelier gave a prismatic brilliance to the great room. Standing there, Curt gazed at the horsehair sofa and chairs, the gleaming treadle organ at one side, at the rich hues of the carpeting and the fine tapestries hanging on the walls.

This was not the headquarters of a working ranch with

furnishings designed to endure the hard usage of casual men. Buckle had indeed changed. This new house had been designed and furnished to impress all who saw it. This was the home built by a man whose ambitions reached far beyond the limits of a cattle empire—to the Territorial capitol and beyond. To the power centers of Washington and Wall Street.

Not until then did Curt sense the full depth and breadth of his half brother. All these things were not the result of hasty planning. Phil's plans had been shaped and modified and strengthened during years of careful thought, so that once he had command of Buckle he had been able to move swiftly and decisively, with no waste of time or effort. A man that shrewd and patient was to be respected —and feared.

Curt stepped deeper into the room, and he suddenly thought of his father, who had never felt comfortable in his clothes until they were mellowed by many sweats. An old mossyhorn like Hamp Selby in a place like this! Curt grinned at the thought, his humor sour in him. Amid all this finery, old Hamp would have about as much grace as a steer in a china store.

He looked around as the woman came into the room, and his smile took on a quick warmth. Here, at least, was one page of the past that had not been turned.

"Rosalita," he said, "how come you didn't get shucked along with the rest of the old outfit? There's mighty little left here for a man to remember."

The blood of the *indio* and the *Conquistadores* flowed in the veins of Rosita Trujillo. She was short and magnificently round. Her thick graying hair was coiled in a tight knot against the base of her neck, its taut, severely drawn lines accentuating the plumpness of her features. She squinted her eyes in the manner of the nearsighted, and an expression of genuine delight brought a quick glow into her face.

"*Madre de Dios!*" she murmured. "Señor Curt, it is you indeed!"

He grinned. "For a fact, *mamasita*. Buckle never whelped another pup as ugly."

She came to him with that remembered lightness of step that had never ceased to amaze him. She hugged him to her, half laughing and half crying, speaking the easy Spanish of the range.

"Always you have been in my mind. It is indeed so. Always in my mind and in my heart. Is that so much nonsense to you, Señor, now that you are no longer a little one but have the years of a man?"

He put his arms around her, and the overflowing abundance of her made him feel awkward in his lank height and maturity. To this Mexican woman he owed more debts than a man could ever hope to repay.

"As your own mother I raised you," she said. "As your own flesh, I loved you and feared for you. Your own mother could not feel such happiness as I have for your return."

There were things a man felt, but could not speak of. Curt said in a gentle drawl, "You trying to make me bust out bawling, Rosalita?"

Then he said, "If your Vascos looked through the window right now, he'd go running for his gun."

The woman released him. She stepped back, her expression one of haughty disdain. "My hombre would beat me if I did not welcome you properly."

"Vascos is a very generous man."

"Now you are teasing, Señor. Why do you make this joke to me? Like a great beast of a cow I have become with so much fat."

Curt said quietly, "You're beautiful to me, Rosalita. I'd have missed something mighty important if I hadn't found you here."

He leaned forward. There was a faint aroma to her that was about as near heaven as a hungry man could get. "Do I smell tacos?"

"You are hungry, Señor? But of course! *Si,* tacos filled with the tender meat of young goat. And the coffee is ready. This fine food I prepared for a fool of a husband who even yet has not come home. Come with me. We will eat together."

"*Momentito, mamasita.*" The grit of the mood Curt had carried with him out of town was still in him. Hungry as he was, there would be no pleasure in eating. Food could wait. Other matters, the dire and inevitable things, would not. There was a saying on the range below Mogul's rim:

the time for rest is when there's nothing more important to be done.

"There are things I've got to know, Rosalita. Where is Hamp?"

She looked up at him with mild reproval. "It is possible that you think your father could live—here?" She raised her hand in a disdainful gesture toward the room and its furnishings. "All these fine, beautiful things! So pretty to look at and so delicate to the touch. They are for women, Señor. Or for men who are not such as your father."

"Then Hamp is still living at the old place?"

"Of a certainty. Never does he come here, Señor. Only once did he come here. It is in my mind what he said. 'All this by-God foofaraw makes me want to spit on the floor just to make this camp look lived in.' In my mind your father will always be as a saint speaking a curse upon the devil."

Curt grinned tightly. "Sounds like the old walrus didn't trade everything to get his empire."

"Your father is old," Rosita said. "He is tired. He is sad. It is better that you be with him than have tacos with a fat, foolish woman."

He touched her arm. "Another time, *mamasita*."

He turned and went to the door. At the door, he turned and looked again at the room and its finery.

"Why do you not do it, Señor?"

He looked at the woman. A look of weary contempt was in her eyes. He didn't understand.

"Do what, *mamasita?*"

The spite was unmistakable in her eyes. "Do as your father himself once said. Spit on the floor of this so-beautiful, so-ugly room, just to make it look lived in."

Curt touched his hat in salute to the woman. Smiling thinly, he turned and went out to his horse.

Chapter Nine

In all of his fifty years in the saddle Hamp Selby had never learned how to accept idleness with any degree of complacency. Man and boy, he had always known toil before pleasure. It was something he was proud of.

Work had made permanent marks on him. It was on his hands and in the seams of his face. It had rounded his shoulders and shaped his legs to the barrel of a horse from which most of his labors had been done.

It was Hamp Selby's conviction that man was born to this life to work and to serve, and it pleased him to know that he had given his best to each chore and each responsibility. If he had failed anywhere down along the line, it was not for lack of trying.

And he realized there had been mistakes made. Perhaps many of them. The way he had raised his two sons, for example. He should have made them learn how to work, instead of spoiling them by shouldering all their chores.

It was almighty easy for a man to spoil his motherless sons. Playing up to Phil's self-centered whims was a mistake old Hamp would regret as long as he lived. Not that strictness and a few britches-warmings would have done much good. You couldn't wallop out of a boy what had been born in him any more than you could expect to tame a *ladino* steer by busting him a few times at the end of a rope. Phil's mother had been a far-thinking, ambitious woman. Only in Phil these qualities had taken a far more vicious turn.

Getting out of his chair, Hamp went to the stove and refilled his cup from the heat-blackened coffeepot, the strong chicory aroma momentarily sending through his mind the echo of many forgotten range camps.

He turned and went back to the pine-slabbed table and lowered himself again into the chair. For a while he sat there and watched his son eat. Beans, beef, and biscuits were fittin' food for any natural man, although it always tasted better when fixed over a fire of cow chips. Stove cooking, Hamp allowed, cut down a heap on the flavor of a meal.

He watched Curt bolt down his meal like a man who was empty to his toes. It gave Hamp a feeling of pleasure and satisfaction. Something was wrong with a man who couldn't take to honest-to-gosh range chuck.

Phil was one. Too all-fired finicky. Turned up his nose when he looked into a plate of plain beef and beans, which was rare these days of fancy goings on. Had richer tastes, Phil did. Give him his choice, and he'd have breast of pheasant or some other such by-God foofaraw he kept packing home for Rosalita to fix. Curt, now, had an appetite for grub that stuck to the ribs and growed hair on a man's chest.

He watched Curt shove back his plate and rummage through his pockets for a smoke. He couldn't find any. Hamp's coat was hanging over his chair. He dug the makings out of a pocket and tossed them across the table.

When Curt had his cigaret tapered and going, Hamp said, "You ready to talk now?"

Curt raised a slow gaze that Hamp found impossible to read. "I'm curious about everything that's happened around here," Curt said.

Hamp shook his head. "We'll talk about you, first."

A look of restlessness stirred through Curt's eyes. He said slowly, "There's not much to tell. I got drunk that day three years ago. Treed Signal, and then got chased out of town by Jode Meeder and his posse. I kept on riding."

"A man can make a lot of tracks in three years," Hamp observed.

"I made my share."

There was something Hamp had to know. "Leave anything you're sorry for behind you?"

"A lot of things," Curt said, and for a while was silent. "Little things, mostly. I gave the wheel a full turn, Hamp. All the way around."

Hamp said nothing.

"There was a fandango girl over at Tascosa. I'm sorry that night happened. A lot of fights in a lot of towns,

Hamp. I saw a man die. Maybe I could have side-stepped that. But he was drunk and in a temper, and so was I. He wouldn't have anything else, and neither would I. I guess we both wanted to know."

Hamp breathed quietly. "And now you know?"

Curt gazed into the blue smoke of his cigaret. His voice was soft. "Now I know."

There were old echoes in Hamp Selby's mind, and for a moment he listened to them. Then he said, "When a man hits the trail, he looks under a lot of rocks. All he ever finds is crawlin' things. I ought to know, because I had my look once, just like you had yours."

Some things a man did not like to remember. Hamp moved his shoulders, pushing the mood away from him.

He said, almost too casually, "I've got a bottle of Old Roanoke stashed away in the other room."

Curt looked up, his smile wry. "I've looked into a lot of bottles since that first time in Augie Bannon's saloon, Hamp. I never found anything in them but headaches."

It hit hard. Hamp's vision suddenly blurred. He turned his head quickly away, blinking. A man gets old, his eyes water up for no account at all. He was glad that Curt had not noticed.

There was restlessness working on him. The coffee had gone cold in his cup, and without much interest he pondered warming it with some from the pot. The thought slipped away from him.

He got out of his chair, grunting at the twinge of pain the abrupt movement sent through his lame knee. It took an effort to walk down the hall to the front room without limping, and it struck him that it was a damned odd thing, a man being too proud to admit to his own son that he was not what he used to be.

This room to which he had come had once been the entirety of the house, a log-and-adobe cabin built like a fortress at a time when the only security a man had was what he built with his own two hands. The Apaches were quiet now, except for a few bands of renegades raiding down around the Cherrycows. Times had changed. The dangers Hamp saw now were the ones that had sprung from his own loins and had been nourished by his own easy tolerances.

He paced restlessly around the big room, knowing that

Curt was waiting. He thought it strange how easy it was for a father to forgive, but how difficult it was to admit his own mistakes.

A father fearing the judgment of his son. Hamp had not wanted it like this. He had wanted Curt and himself to be two men. Two free and easy men who could talk over a tangle and square it off without fuss or restraint.

Curt was waiting.

Hamp halted his pacing and stood for a while, seeing this big plain room as a symbol of all that was in his mind and heart.

Nigh on to thirty years it was now that he had moved to this range, bringing with him a four-year-old son and the memory of the Indian raid that had killed Phil's mother. He had built his cabin, hired Rosalita to look after the boy while he rode a hundred and fifty miles to the nearest town to find himself another wife.

He reflected on that, a little shocked by the swiftness of the years. Alone, a man was not complete. That was fundamental. But on this untamed thorny range there were more practical essentials. Hamp had needed a wife to make a home and raise his son for him, and so he had ridden out to find one. There was not much nonsense in those days between a man and a woman. Things usually worked out for the best, regardless.

He had found Nola working in a honky-tonk, a pale girl with bitter eyes and no illusions left, and being a practical man his approach was direct and to the point.

"I am Hampton Selby, ma'am. Four days north of here I have a cabin, a few head of cattle, and plenty of good graze. I need a wife to raise my son and keep my house. I will promise two things to the woman who marries me: I will work hard for her, and I will always be respectful. Would those things be enough for you, ma'am?"

A jaded girl with dark, knowing eyes, and proud enough to make no excuses for herself. Her acceptance had been as simple as his proposal was direct.

"Most women settle for far less. I am grateful, Mr. Selby."

If she was not pretty, Hamp had not noticed. Looking back now, he found it odd that he could not remember for sure. There were many images in his mind, but not Nola's. All that remained were the important things. The gentleness of her voice and the many kindnesses she had given him. Holding up supper when he was out late on the range, and encouraging him when times were rough. Accepting the good things with gratefulness, and the bad without complaint.

Of such strong fabric was this woman who had been Hamp's second wife. Crying when he cried, and laughing when he laughed. Nola was like that. She had wisdom about men, and because of this she was all things that Hamp needed. Women like Nola were rare on any range. Hamp considered himself a lucky man to have had those few years with her, for she had given him many good memories.

She had given him another son.

He raised his head and looked around at Curt. "I was just thinking of your mother," he said.

"I allowed you were."

"Did it show through that much?" he asked gruffly, and saw Curt's slow knowing smile.

"Hamp," Curt said, "you always were the most obvious man alive."

There was an easy equality in this that drew a fine warmth into Hamp Selby. A gulf had been bridged, a barrier removed.

He said, "I reckon you'd like to hear about Buckle."

Chapter Ten

Curt sat in the old bullhide chair listening. Many of the things Hamp spoke about came as no great surprise. The pattern had been there for him to see.

Hamp spoke in a tone that offered no excuses. "I blamed myself for you going off the deep end that day three years ago. I taught you how to use a gun before you were old enough to button your own britches. Maybe that was good. Maybe it was bad. A man can lose his balance when he gets too fancy with a shooter."

There was a box of cigars on the table beside the chair. Curt helped himself to one. He got his smoke going, making no comment as he waited.

"Next mistake," Hamp said in his flat, soul-baring way, "was buying you that first drink in Augie's saloon."

Curt said, "I'd have yanked the tiger's tail anyhow, sooner or later. What's in a man, Hamp, has got to come out."

"Maybe," Hamp grunted. "Mebbeso."

He was silent for a while. Curt watched him. A big, shaggy man who had worked too hard and played too little, who had spoiled his two sons by carrying all the grief on his own shoulders. The sins of Hamp's many tolerances had come back to haunt him these late years, etching weariness into his face and laying a sadness across his eyes.

"I didn't want to make the same mistakes with Phil," he said. "He was a grown man, and I allowed what he needed was responsibility. He was always pushing at me. Not out in the open, but . . . ah, hell. He's your half brother, and you know him same as I do."

Curt's smile was a meager one. "I only thought I knew him," he said, and felt the quick impact of his father's eyes.

Hamp nodded slowly. "That hits it closer. I'm Phil's

father, but I never really knew how much he had in him. His mother was a lot like him. Never talked much, but always making plans. But there's a sharp streak in Phil that was never in his ma. I didn't know that until I turned Buckle over to him."

"When was that?"

"Just after Jode Meeder and his posse ran you out of town."

Curt's eyes were thoughtful. "Phil worked fast."

"He had it all worked out," Hamp said sourly. "Right down to the last spike in that fancy new house he built."

Hamp got his charred briar from the mantel over the big stone fireplace. He packed it with tobacco, scratched his match almost savagely. Anger lay deep in his eyes.

"All figured out fine and neat. Knew right where to go to get the new crew he wanted. Lane Harragh and all those other hardcases. Not one of the lot is worth a damn workin' cows, but they're all something special when it comes to guns. Phil always said he could make Buckle a big outfit." Hamp grunted bitterly. "That's what he sure as hell did after I gave him the reins."

Curt said nothing. The light from the table lamp cast a hawk's shadow across his father's craggy face.

Hamp said, "They moved on Bent Tree first. Nothing mean or tough. Phil knows how to put on pressure, and Tobe Faring got the idea quick enough. Tobe didn't want to sell, but that didn't stop Phil. Inside of three months Buckle was moving out on Bent Tree grass."

Curt looked down at his knuckles. "For what kind of money?"

Hamp said flatly, "Phil is no fool. He paid a good fair price for Bent Tree. Tobe's got no complaint on that score."

There was a cut on Curt's right hand, across the knuckles. He thought of Sam Brighton moodily.

"And the others?"

"Same deal all around," Hamp grunted. "Phil knows a few things. Pay a fair price, and folks soon forget that an outfit was pressured into selling by a crew of gunslicks. Money talks. Phil's got Signal in the palm of his hand. Hell of it is, the town likes it."

Curt raised his eyes. "And you don't?"

Hamp turned and looked at his shadow on the wall. It was huge, formidable, towering.

"You see that shadow? That's Buckle. I'm the one who started it, but that shadow is what it is now. Buckle has taken over the whole basin and it's ready to reach out for more.

"Buckle is the biggest outfit in the Territory. It'll get bigger if Phil has his way. Buckle has the best water, the best graze, the finest house, the tightest fences. It feeds the best food, pays the highest wages, and gets the best prices at the market."

Curt said, "I asked a question."

Hamp jerked around. "Hell no, I don't like it."

Curt waited.

Hamp's voice was harsh, savage. "I put thirty years of sweat into this range. I've got a wife and friends buried in this land. A man remembers. A man wants to be remembered. But when I go to town I'm nobody. I walk in Phil's shadow. He gives the orders and pays the bills and tells Augie Bannon what brand of whiskey Buckle will drink. Hell no, I don't like it. This outfit and all its by-God foofaraws—Curt, I hate it!"

Curt was silent. It took pride a long time to run down in some men. In Hamp humbleness would never come easily.

"But that's not all." The wrath flattened out in Hamp's tone, changing his voice to a drawn and weary agedness. "Maybe all that ain't even important. I'll show you something that is, Curt."

Curt got out of his chair and followed his father across the room. They went out on the long, low gallery that fronted the house. The rim of the bench sloped off a short distance out from the porch, looking out into the vastness of the basin. The night lay full and unbroken on all that range, the utter emptiness of it making a man feel small and alone.

"Look out there," Hamp said. "Not a light to be seen."

Curt's gaze pulled around. There was a heaviness in his father's face, a sadness echoing back to him from better days.

"Once was a time I liked nothing better than to sit out here after dark," Hamp said. "Off yonder was the lights of Faring house. Across there was Cass Lovelace's, with

57

Charley Bell's just a notch higher. Closer in was the lights of Sam Brighton's house. Mighty comfortable to sit out here and look at those lights, Curt."

Curt said nothing.

"When Sam or his wife would walk past the windows it'd look like the house was winking at me. That sound crazy to you, Curt?"

"No," Curt said.

"It was like Sam saying howdy to me. They were all my friends, every man, woman, and kid living in those houses. A man never felt lonely, those nights. He could look out at those lights, and it was like as if his neighbors were right here with him, visiting. You know what I mean, Curt?"

"Yes."

The air whispered close overhead, and a winged shape went cruising away against the night sky; later, the owl sent out its hunting cry, a thin, faraway sound.

"The lights are gone, Curt. I had good friends out there, and now they're gone."

"Tough, Hamp," Curt murmured.

They went back into the house. There was a chill to the room.

Hamp said, "I don't want to see Buckle grow by beating down other people. The right way is fine, but the wrong way I can't stomach. I always had it in mind that you and Phil would work together when I stepped out of the saddle. I made a mistake when I handed Buckle over to Phil. He's got it, and he'll keep it. He won't cut you in."

Curt moved his shoulders. It did not matter.

Hamp said, "I caught on to Phil, quick enough. That's why I had all the deeds made out in my name, when Phil crowded Sam Brighton and all the others into selling out."

Curt looked up in surprise.

"I'm signing those deeds over to you, Curt," Hamp said.

Curt smiled. "No call for you to, Hamp. I can make my own way."

Hamp shook his head. There was a tightness to his lips. "That's how I want it. Those six outfits Buckle took over —they're yours now."

Curt gazed thoughtfully at his father. "Those layouts

make a ring around Buckle. Is it your idea I can keep Phil from tromping down any other spreads."

"It occurred to me."

Curt's smile thinned out, turning bleak. "But that's not what you really want," he said slowly. "It shows through, Hamp. You'd like to see me deed those layouts back to the men who used to own them."

Hamp nodded slowly. Some of the fine color was gone from his face.

"They were my friends, and I want them back. Hand their land back to them, and they'll have some sense next time."

"Harragh and the rest—Phil put together a tough crew, Hamp," said Curt quietly. "It'll mean a fight. One side or the other will go down the hard way."

Hamp's voice turned suddenly harsh. "I want Buckle ruined. Ripped apart and wrecked. Phil is your half brother, but he is my son. I know well enough what I'm asking, Curt. I want this fine, fancy gun-powered ranch smashed down so honest people will respect it again, not fear it."

"Rough on Phil, Hamp. He's built up a world for himself, and he'll try to keep it. You can't stop him, and I won't matter. He'll fight, and hard. He's got everything to lose."

"Yes, everything to lose," Hamp said, and his eyes were bitter. "Rougher on you, though. You've got nothing to win."

Chapter Eleven

Curt was drawing water up from the well when he saw Phil approaching from the direction of the new house, half a mile to the west. He was mounted on a leggy black mare whose coat gleamed like polished jet in the sunlight just now breaking across the horizon.

Releasing the wet rope from the bail, Curt set the bucket aside. The water in it was like ice, clean and clear.

Turning, he watched the horse and rider with mild curiosity. Being a range man, the horse drew his first appraisal. The mare was a highstepping beauty. She was sleek, cleanly lined, and lifted her feet like a dancer. Curt smiled dryly. The black was a show horse, and therefore one not worth a damn as a worker. Put that mare to work chousing steers out of the brush, and she'd come apart in no time at all. A working horse had to have savvy on Buckle's thorny range, and that was something this showy black did not have. Still, Curt thought, the mare was a perfect choice for the rider.

Phil drew rein at the well and, after a brief glance toward the house, brought his gaze back to Curt. His grin was wide and easy.

"Thought I'd find you here if I got up early enough," he said. "You didn't give me much of a chance yesterday to say howdy."

Curt studied the man's eyes, but the grin was not there. It was a curve of the lips, nothing more.

He said in a drawl, "I kind of had my hands full, Phil."

The man on the horse chuckled amiably. "Not long, you didn't. You chucked all your problems at my feet, as I recall."

"Not all of them, Phil."

A soberness came into Phil's eyes, and he shook his head worriedly. "You always were a hotheaded one, Curt.

60

I've been worried. Tying into Lane Harragh like you did was a bad thing."

Curt smiled faintly. "Did I bang up your boy that much?"

"I was thinking about you."

"Obliged for your concern, Phil."

A nettled expression took hold of Phil's face. The suit he wore was of a fine fabric, excellently tailored. Dressed as he was in white shirt and dark string tie, he gave the impression of quality, of genteel softness. It was only an illusion.

His voice lost some of its easy warmth. "There's no sense in me telling you what Lane Harragh is. You know about his reputation. He's got a quick temper, and he's a devil with a gun. He doesn't like being manhandled."

"Neither do I," Curt murmured.

Phil's gaze narrowed slightly. "Are you telling me he got out of line yesterday?"

"He came busting into Effie's place like he owned it," Curt said flatly. "He saw me talking to Effie, and got the wrong idea. That was one thing. Laying a hand on me was another. It got him knocked around a little."

Phil shook his head. "I'm sorry it happened that way."

"Don't tell me," said Curt shortly. "Go tell your friend, Harragh."

Phil shook his head slowly, an expression of weary patience. "No need for you to jump at me. After all, we're brothers."

"That," grunted Curt, "is only half right."

"We've got the same father, the same blood in us." Phil's smile was easy, open. "No sense in you and me chewing at each other. What happened between you and Harragh is just one of those things. He didn't know you, and what you saw was only a sample of his loyalty to me and Buckle."

"For what price?" Curt asked acidly.

Phil let that pass. He said equably, "I've made Buckle into a big thing. It'll get bigger. I'm open and fair in all my dealings, but when a ranch gets big its troubles get big —squatters trying to grab off pieces of land, and rustlers nibbling on the herds. I need men like Lane Harragh to keep other hardcases scared away. You fight fire with fire when you run a layout this big, and I pay good money to keep Harragh and his crew on my side. You'll have no trouble from Harragh, Curt. After I've had a talk with him, he'll cool off."

Curt's nod was an ironic acknowledgment. "Then everything is hunky-dory again. Does that make you ready to cut me in on Buckle now?"

The man on the black smiled. His voice was pleasant. "In due time, Curt. But for the moment I've got to be free to work things out my own way. You'll have to play along with me for a while."

"For how long, say?"

"A year. Maybe less."

Curt was thinly sardonic. "Or a hundred years. Maybe more."

Phil's gaze tightened.

Sudden anger made its rough break through Curt. "Climb down from your ivory tower, fellow! I grew up with you, remember? Mud pies or busted toys—you've never let go of a thing you got your hands on. You'll never split up this ranch. Not with me, Hamp, or anyone. So stop pretending, man. You're talking to one who knows you."

A slow flush rose in Phil's face, and the grit of amused malice surfaced in his eyes. "You've been listening to the old man, I see."

And when Curt made no comment, he said thinly, "Those six outfits I took over—Hamp deeded them all to you, I suppose. It figures. Tie me down by clamping a ring around me. Is that Hamp's idea?"

Temper was in Curt's steady stare. It was a mature man's anger, diluted with disgust and impatience, but under firm control.

He spoke in a flat, even tone of voice. "I'll give you some advice, Phil. You own a good ranch you never had to work for, and you've got a fine fancy house. That's more than enough for any man. From now on you're finished hopping line fences just to make a bigger name for yourself."

Phil's gaze turned brittle. "You say!"

"One time is enough, Phil. Only once."

Rage congested in Phil Selby's face, but he was not a man to lose his grip on himself. He bottled up that rage with a low mocking laugh.

"It's too bad about you, Curt," he said. "I'll always remember you as a fool who tried to make big tracks with very small boots."

Phil reined the black around and sent it jogging toward the new house at an unhurried canter. Fury lay tight and frigid within him, so rigidly controlled that no shadow of temper broke through his steady composure. He was a man who knew how to contain himself, believing that rashness was the luxury of fools.

Approaching the house, he looked at the gleaming white walls, the arched windows and spacious gallery, the red mission-tile roof. Here was elegance never before seen in the Territory, a fitting house for a man destined to great things. The thought sat in Phil Selby's mind with the comfortable warmth of a long-concealed dream.

He liked fine things. Fine whiskey, fine horses like this high-stepping black. This great white house was as fine as any he had ever built in his imagination. But now that it was a reality, there were improvements that could be made. Stained glass would have increased the elegance. The patio could be enlarged, and a flowing fountain could be devised even on this thirsty land.

Phil was aware of this critical dissatisfaction that constantly nagged him. He considered it a symptom of strength rather than weakness. A man who refused to be satisfied with what he had would always reach out farther and higher for greater possessions.

He let himself through the gate and circled the house to the bunkhouse his crew occupied. Entering this long, low building, the rank odor of stale whiskey brought disgust into his eyes.

He went down the line of bunks, seeing the heaped clothing and the bloated faces of men sleeping off last night's drunk. He eyed those men with stony contempt. Blind, brainless fools who accepted each day as it came and never thought about tomorrow.

Hand them a month's wages, and all they thought about was getting drunk and bedding down with some blowsy crib girl in Greary's Alley, never remembering next day what they had experienced, good or bad.

Lane Harragh, though, was one of the rare exceptions. There was a rigid discipline in Harragh that held him within stern limits when he stood at a bar. Women seldom interested him.

Every man in this long, low room was dangerous to cross, which was why Phil Selby had hired them. But they were direct and uncomplicated, and therefore could be managed.

Harragh, though, was of different substance. The affair yesterday in Effie's bakery had been an accident that would never happen again. Curt had been lucky, and Harragh had learned a thing.

Harragh was that kind. If he stubbed his toe, he went back later and removed the obstacle. He was methodical in his cold, deadly way, as Phil was in his. In Lane Harragh were the hard, honed gears of a completely dangerous machine, smooth, practiced, passionless in the ultimate art of killing. Here was a man, Phil Selby told himself, to be reckoned with carefully and who, of all the others, was the one to be feared.

He reached down and touched the sleeping man lightly on the shoulder. Harragh was instantly awake, one hand snaking a gun from under his pillow. He glared up at Phil in unleashed fury.

"Haven't you got any sense at all?" he flared. "Man, don't ever pull a stunt like that again!"

"I want to talk to you, Lane."

"You picked a hell of a way to go about it." The gun in Harragh's hand was at full cock; he eased the hammer down to safety. A fine sheen of sweat was on his upper lip, and raw impatience was in his rankled stare.

"You were only a whisper from being splattered all over that wall, Selby. Next time you want to wake me up, sing out before you get close."

"I wasn't thinking, Lane."

"They dig graves every day for men who didn't think," Harragh snapped. He kicked his feet out of the blankets, and sat up on the bunk. Wearing only cotton underdrawers, there was a repellent beauty in the clean, smooth lines of his upper body.

There was no flabbiness, no softness. He was a man physically constructed to be exactly what he was. Efficient, dispassionate, ruthlessly practical in matters of deadly violence—a lean, compact man with enormous capabilities.

"Well?"

Phil motioned with his hand. "Some other place, Lane."

Harragh's lips twisted. Devils were laughing in his eyes. "The load this crew packed home last night, you could tear off the roof and they wouldn't know it."

Phil took a breath. "It's about my brother." It was not the right word. There was an intimacy in it that made this thing too calloused, too murderous, so that his conscience rebelled, demanding even the most marginal repudiation of kinship.

"It's about my half brother."

The devils in Harragh's eyes jeered at him. "So?"

"He can make too much trouble, Lane."

Harragh's smile was malevolent. "I got that idea straight from the big boy himself," he grunted. "That fellow has got it in him to make an almighty lot of trouble."

Phil waited, but Harragh offered nothing more. A sense of goaded impatience piled up in Phil until he could no longer bear it, and he suddenly swore out irritably.

"Good God, Lane! Do I have to tell you what to do?"

"You're the boss," said Harragh dryly. "I like to get my orders straight across the board."

Phil stared down at the man. "All right. All right, then. I want Curt put out of the way."

Now that it was out in the open, he felt a swift, hard surge of decisiveness and power. He had taken a long step. He would not regret it. There was no room for softness in his plans. What stood in his way had to be knocked aside or tromped under. That was a fundamental.

"Out of the way for keeps?" Harragh murmured.

"For keeps," said Phil flatly.

Harragh grinned slowly. "It can be managed," he said, and malice was in his soft laugh. "This job will be a pleasure."

"No," Phil said, and shook his head. "I don't want you to do it. You're my foreman. I don't want it to look like Buckle was behind this. Use one of the other men. Someone you are sure can do the job right."

"And make the thing look a little less official," Harragh said. The devils in his eyes laughed in silent mockery. "Maybe you're right, though."

He looked along the line of bunks, his gaze thoughtful.

Then he said matter-of-factly, "We'll give it to Pence Doane. He's been itching lately. He's fast enough. Way he's been shoving his weight around lately, I've been thinking maybe he's a bit too fast with a gun to stay on here."

He brought his gaze around to the cowman, and it seemed to Phil that a frigid wind suddenly blew against him.

"Might be I'll have to settle with Doane after he takes care of your brother," Harragh said. "A man can get too damn big for his britches."

Chapter Twelve

Pressing her horse unceasingly, Effie Coombs reached the southmost spur of Mogul plateau by midmorning. Here it was that she customarily gave her mount a breather after the long track it had covered from town.

This time, however, she did not. Instead, she put the animal at once against the steep, rock-ribbed slope, nagged as she was by an anxiety that was close to panic. Cresting the high spine of land, she gave the horse its first respite in four hard hours of traveling, halting in a stand of scrawny piñon. Dropping out of saddle, she snubbed the reins to a sapling, and made her way immediately to the fringe of the trees.

At this hour there was a prismatic clarity to the range below and beyond, the morning sun slanting just enough shadow to give depth and sharpened detail to the folds and furrows of the land. There was not yet enough heat to diffuse the air with haze.

Effie could make out each landmark along the trail she had followed from town. All the way from Signal she had been tormented by a sense of being followed. During those troubled hours of traveling she had halted many times to search her back trail for sound or the telltale drift of dust. Not once had she heard or seen anything.

Now, while her horse rested, she searched again, feeling the tightness of fear as her gaze retraced the trail that had led her here. It was a torn, twisted, upended land down there which had by its own nature forced devious traveling. Those ridges and miniature canyons had hidden her well during her riding, and she realized they could conceal other riders just as secretly. This knowledge was the core of her dread.

But nothing moved down there, either near or in the far distance. The range lay still and empty, giving no sound. She studied the black-laced tangles of the lava beds to the east, seeing only the diminished gray shape of a lone deer making its way to some hidden water hole or bedding place.

Nor was there any sign of life to the west of the divide where Buckle ruled its vast empire of grass. There was comfort in the emptiness of the range, and the fear eased out of Effie. It had been silly, she told herself, to be afraid.

This was Sunday, a day that Signal gave to its own interests and activities. By now the bell in the church tower would be ringing its call to the morning services, and Jode Meeder himself would be one of the first to go to worship.

He was a man of many extremes, Jode Meeder, and Effie had never found it possible to measure his real worth. She had once seen him grab up a shovel and beat a horse that had pitched him at Abe Korbee's livery yard, and later that same morning she had heard him quote scripture when he called at her bakery to get a contribution for the new parsonage.

He was a born politician, and in his way he was a good sheriff. Signal had been a quiet town during the three terms Meeder had held office. If Meeder was censured because of the pair of gun-toughs, Orvie Shandrin and Clyde Melavin, he used as deputies, there were those in Signal who felt that the sheriff was of the same caliber.

According to the gossip Effie had heard, Jode Meeder had come up from Galeyville and Tombstone, and from the worst of the Kansas rail towns before that. There were whispers about Hickok and the Earps and the rest. Meeder knew all the quick, violent ways. He was a man with a badge and a gun. Two times in the past Effie had seen men die before him, his eyes brittle and remorseless through the smoke of his gun. And on each following Sunday she had seen him at his pew in the church, a look of genuine devoutness on his blocky weathered face.

Yes, a strange and fearful man. Meeder would hound the trail of a wanted man relentlessly, almost savagely, but on Sunday he would be at church, insisting on Shandrin and Clyde Melavin coming with him.

There was comfort for Effie in this knowledge, for it was Jode Meeder and his deputies that she feared. The thought brought surety into her mind. Any other day they might try to follow her. But not on Sunday. Yet, this close to Buckle's range, there were other dangers, and when she mounted again she rode with unceasing wariness.

There was no trail, only the familiar landmarks to guide her. The lightning-scarred pine was a turning point. She slanted her mount down the granite-ribbed eastern slope of the ridge. The way leveled off, and she swung again toward the towering wall of the plateau. That great jutting thumb of eroded sandstone was a compass point. She angled further east, and at the end of another mile came to a badland of upended shale and gnarled cutbanks. She was too far north. She corrected her direction, drawing the angle down fine as she picked her way into the badlands.

Within a hundred yards she came to the hidden meadow. It was less than a quarter of a mile across at its widest place, green and lush in contrast to the gaunt, dreary wastes surrounding it.

Effie's gaze moved, searching. A week ago there had been a camp here by the rocks and forty head of Buckle cattle grazing out there on the meadow while the burned-over brands healed. Now the cattle were gone and she saw only the dead ashes where the campfire had been. Alarm dug into her, and she raised her voice against the smothering silence of the place.

"Ernie! It's me—Effie!"

The man's amused drawl gave her a tremendous start. "Right here behind you, Sis."

She jerked around in her saddle, a resenting anger whipping through her as she saw her brother slouching lazily against a shoulder of sandstone, a Winchester tucked under his arm.

He was lank, loose-coupled, young. His grin was one of bantering good humor. "Guess I ought to apologize for giving you such a scare."

Effie's nerves were taut wires singing in a wintery wind. She was thoroughly exasperated, and she wanted him to know it.

"You were there all the time. You knew it was me riding in."

"Uh-huh. Spotted you coming down the ridge, half an hour ago."

Effie tossed her head angrily. "Then why didn't you

let me know? Must you always play Injun when I come here?"

There was a glint of gravity, cool and grim, behind the man's easy smile, laying an acid against his humor. "It's a good habit to get into, now that I've taken up rustling for a living." He moved his shoulders as though shrugging off a thought he did not like. "Light down, Sis. I'll put a fire together and make some coffee."

She shook her head. "Not this time. I want to get back to town."

Ernie Coombs detected the worry in her, and instantly alerted. "Someone follow you this time?" he asked, his voice quick and sharp.

"No. I'm certain, Ernie. I was even more careful than the other times. It was just a feeling I had all the way out here."

She watched him throw his swift glance around the meadow, scanning the rimming rocks and cutbanks with an edged weariness that brought bitterness up through her. The Winchester was half up in his hands, and there was an outlaw look in his eyes that made a stranger of him.

He seemed to sense the turn of her thoughts and brought back his easy grin. "You're getting a case of nerves, Sis. Maybe you'd better stop coming out here."

She said in a low, troubled tone, "You're changing, Ernie. A year ago you were my brother. Now you're changing into someone I . . . I hardly know."

An irritable expression crossed his face, and he said shortly, "Do you think I like living in brush camps? I'm getting so I jump every time the wind blows."

Effie said swiftly, "Then come back to town. It's not too late yet, Ernie."

He grunted crossly. "And spend all my time loafing and sponging off you? Not any, Sis. When Buckle crowded out all the little outfits, guys like me were shoved into the brush. Phil Selby killed off all the jobs for cow hands. What do you want us to do, Effie—starve?"

There was nothing Effie could say. A rankled hopelessness was in her brother's eyes, and it was also in her. She felt a sudden stinging hatred for Phil Selby and the empire of grass he had built up under the Buckle brand. Much of that land Selby had torn from the hands of others. Therefore, right or wrong, there was a measure of justice in what her brother and the others who camped in this hidden place were doing.

Her brother had said it. A man had to live. When a man could not find honest work, he was forced into the brush. Some men became outlaws by choice; others, like Ernie Coombs, Dee Wordley, Charley Bell and the rest, were driven off the trail by conditions they could not defeat. In Effie's mind, Phil Selby's crime was far greater than that of the men who camped at this badlands meadow.

Ernie said, his voice flat and bitter, "All we're touching is Buckle stuff. We're not trying to get rich. We're taking only enough to square what we'd have earned on a job if Phil Selby had let us alone. That's straight, Sis."

Effie said, "Curt Selby is back. I wanted you to know."

For a long moment Ernie Coombs was silent considering that information narrowly. Then he murmured, "That could make this tougher. Curt's not like the others. Phil Selby and his crew of toughs don't know this range. Curt does. He can make a lot of trouble for us, that fellow."

Effie shook her head slowly. There was no clear shape to what was in her mind. It was a hope struggling within her, with nothing solid or tangible beneath it.

When she had seen Curt brawling in the street with Sam Brighton, who had been his friend, her first thought was that he had come home to claim a share of the wealth and power Phil Selby had brought to Buckle. But that had been changed by the way he looked at her when he was told she was engaged to marry Phil. It had been hurt in his eyes, and something close to pity.

The hotheaded wildness of a spoiled youngster had been curbed in Curt Selby. Effie could sense that. He had matured in the three years he had been gone, but the qualities she had loved in him were still there.

What hope that offered to her, Effie did not know. A man owed loyalty to his father and to his home brand. She understood that. But she had found greater depths in Curt Selby, an untamed, rebellious streak that could hold him stubbornly to his own beliefs. She could ask no more than that from him.

She spoke slowly. "I don't know, Ernie. I have a feeling that if we have a talk with Curt . . ."

She did not finish. Beyond her brother, behind him,

there was movement along the rim of the meadow. It was a shadow cast by the high sun. And then it was the man —Clyde Melavin—stepping into full view, swiftly. The gun was in his hand, up and ready.

The scream was in her throat; it was against lips suddenly frozen with horror. The scream went crashing through her mind and through her heart as the gun lined up for its shot.

Even then there was no real comprehension in Ernie Coombs. He was more curious than alarmed, and it was as he started his slow turn that Clyde Melavin's bullet hit him. The shock drove him up to his toes, and some spasmodic reaction locked him there, his back arched against the agony, his eyes raked by a swift and terrible thought.

The scream broke out of Effie then.

And she heard her brother's shout, hoarse, harsh. "Get away from here! Get going!"

Falling, his hand slashed the rump of her horse, sending the animal hurtling out into the meadow in a startled burst of speed. The reins, torn from her grip by that first panicked lunge, dangled free. She tried to grab them and missed, and heard the roar of another shot behind her.

She twisted around in the saddle, and as her horse went plunging into the badlands she had one final blurred glimpse of her brother, belly-flat on the ground, leveling shots into the arroyo where the killer had taken cover.

Ernie! O my God. . . .

Curt was crossing the pasture behind Dee Wordley's abandoned house when he saw the horseman beating in from the direction of the badlands that footed the plateau's easterly flanks. He drew rein, wondering what urgency drove a man to such recklessness on a range as rough and broken as this corner of the basin.

The rider rushed on, killing his horse. Curt recognized him, then—Effie Coombs' kid brother. When he saw that Ernie was going to overshoot him without stopping or even seeing him, Curt kicked his steeldust into a run that carried him into the path of the racing, lathered grulla.

His shout was not heard. Bending the run of his own horse, Curt swung in close to the grulla, grabbed the bit ring, and yanked the animal to a rearing, heaving halt. Curt saw the blood on the grulla's flank. He saw the ash gray of the rider's face as Ernie rocked unsteadily around in his saddle. The man's eyes were dull with shock, and there was no recognition at all in them.

"I've got to get to town," he said thickly. "It's that Clyde Melavin! My sister . . ."

The voice choked, a gagging sound. The eyes rolled, and Curt saw sickness contort the man's chalky features.

Curt said sharply, "What about Effie?"

Ernie's mouth worked and there was a harsh retching sound low in his throat. A nameless fear knifed into Curt Selby, ripping his patience.

"Damn you, man!" he said savagely. "What about Effie!"

Ernie was rocking slackly in his saddle. He started to fold forward across the pommel, and Curt caught him roughly by the shoulder and boosted him erect again. It did not last. The man sagged to one side, and his weight was more than Curt could manage. He fell.

Curt saw the blood then, and realized it was not the horse that had been hit by a bullet. The saddle was wet with the redness that had come from somewhere low in Ernie's back.

Cursing softly, Curt swung out of saddle and dropped beside the man. Ernie was face down on the ground, with his canvas jacket hitched up so that the bullet hole and spreading redness were wickedly exposed. Selby's lips compressed. He was looking at the clean, round wound made by a bullet entering the body, not tearing its way out of the flesh. The answer was brutally apparent: Ernie Coombs had been facing away, not fighting, when the slug hit him.

He turned the man over on the ground, knowing that this was death. The shock of his fall had knocked the stunned dullness out of the man, clearing his mind. His eyes were dim and watery, and recognition moved uncertainly through them.

"That you, Curt?"

"Yes. Who did this, Ernie?"

The man's lips moved, but no words came.

Curt said, "Clyde Melavin? Is he the one?"

Ernie nodded shallowly. He drew a slow, ragged breath. "Came up behind me. Didn't say a word. Just let . . . let me have it. God, Curt, but it hurts!"

"What about Effie?" Curt asked, his voice soft and quick. "I've got to know."

Ernie breathed again, and there was a thin, whistling sound in his throat. "He didn't have to do it that way," he said plaintively. "Melavin is fast enough. Could beat me any day with a gun, he could. You hear me all right, Curt?"

Curt nodded. "What about Effie?"

"He took the sure way, Melavin did," Ernie sighed. "A bullet in the back, and not even a howdy first. I tried to get a gun on him . . . tried to hold him off, but he dodged back into the rocks. Then he cut around and went after Effie. You listening, Curt? Melavin is out to get Effie."

Curt leaned closer. "Where did this happen, Ernie?"

He got no answer.

He shook the man gently, trying to rouse him. "In the badlands below Mogul? Is that the place?"

Ernie's eyes were closed. The breathing had stopped.

There were hard pressures crowding Curt Selby. This was a vast, tumbling range, and a man had to know where he was riding. The three-day growth of pale whiskers on Ernie's face spoke of a camp in some hidden place, but the dust on the clothes was indefinite, telling nothing.

He heeled sharply around and slapped the grulla behind the knee, raising its hoof. He found the answer he needed in the small chips of blue-gray shale imbedded in the hoof of the winded animal.

It verified what he had already suspected. It was somewhere in the badlands below Mogul Plateau that Clyde Melavin had made his kill and was now hunting for the girl who had witnessed it.

Chapter Thirteen

From his present position, Curt had two choices in laying out his route to the badlands. The logical one was to swing around the end of the lean spine of land tapering down from the plateau's rim, and hold to the comparatively level ground in making his run. That would get him to the badlands in the shortest possible time.

But there were times when a man had to take the intangibles into consideration and stack all his fears against one desperate gamble. It was a hard land that demanded reckless decisions, and if a man lost he carried the guilt and the regrets with him to his grave. Time was not always the deciding factor. On this thorny range it was often the impatient ones who lost everything.

The wind-packed, sandy bottom of a dry barranca afforded him three miles of fast traveling, at the end of which he came against the abrupt wall of the ridge. Checking the pace of his horse as it climbed was the hardest thing Curt Selby had ever done. Everything in him, the fear and the stark dread, wanted to make the frantic race against time.

A bleakly realistic streak in him warned him against killing his horse on this steep, rock-ribbed slope. Afoot, he would be impotent; by sparing his mount, there was still a chance.

His decision was not a completely rash one. This was a land that shaped the lives of its people to its own demands. There were conditions and compulsions no one could escape.

If Effie had been driven into the badlands, then those twisted, eroded tangles would also hide her well. It would take Cylde Melavin time to unravel the girl's trail. How much time, Curt would not permit himself to guess.

There were other things. Effie would be pressured deeper into the badlands, toward Mogul's towering wall.

It was instinct for the hunted to seek out the safety of high places. It was also instinct for the hunter to make for elevations that would give him a deadly advantage. So it was that Selby pointed his straining horse toward the upper levels, spending time to keep alive his one surviving hope to locate the girl before it was too late.

The ridge was a natural ramp rising toward the rim of the plateau, but it was a torment for rider and horse. There was not a ghost of a trail on this wicked spine of land, only the savagery of loose rocks and the thick tangle of buckbrush to be forced. A hundred yards up from the valley floor, the ridge pinched down to a knife edge no horse could travel.

Curt cut aside, dropping down the eastern flank, sacrificing elevation now for easier going. An angel was riding with him. He found an old game trail that led him along the flank of the ridge without costing him any more elevation.

He went cold inside when he heard the flat clap of a distant shot. Then he heard a second explosion, followed quickly by a third. There was an old saying passed down from the mountain men: one shot means meat; two shots, maybe you eat; three shots—nothing.

Curt kicked up the pace of his horse, and when the trail pinched out he forced his own, angling across the side of the plateau wall when the ridge petered out. The badlands were below him now, but he could see nothing down there. He was not high enough, and he could not gamble time climbing higher.

He caught a faint haze of dust at the rim of the badlands a quarter mile beyond and below him. Someone riding through one of those deep, slotty cuts. He lost the dust as he forced his way through a thick stand of piñon.

Out in the open once more, he located that telltale tawny haze again and didn't take his eyes from it as he crowded his horse across another hundred yards. A loose talus slope spilling down from the caprock high above halted him. He dropped out of saddle, bringing the Winchester with him.

Now there was only the waiting. The stark silence. The searching and the fearing. Then he saw her. Effie came out of one of those deep, slotty barrancas, and he saw the trapped desperation that was in her face as she turned toward the plateau's towering wall.

He wanted to shout to her, but he dared not. There were more urgent things. The girl located, he set all his faculties to the more critical job of finding the killer. This, he knew, might not be easy.

Melavin would know how to move through those arid gluches without kicking up telltale dust. It was part of the deadly game he played. Reveal his position to the girl, and she would be able to avoid him. This was a fundamental all killers understood and guarded against. Cylde Melavin was a man who knew all the sharp and murderous ways.

The land below Curt was torn and tumbled, and it was empty. It was not until he saw the black burst of the shot that he located the gunman, and even as he jerked his Winchester around he heard the slug scream from a rock near the girl.

He triggered his first shot with no thought at all of hitting, only to jar the killer's attention away from Effie. The man was not an easy target. He was stretched out flat on the rim of a cutbank to which he had climbed, forty feet above the floor of the gulch. The rim was undercut by erosion, and on that decomposed shale and rotted sandstone his position was a wicked one. Melavin realized that. He tried to scramble back to the less dangerous slope behind him. Curt halted that movement with a close bullet.

He sent his shout through the tumbling echoes of the shot. "You've had enough, Melavin. Throw down that gun!"

Melavin twisted violently around. He fired, and levered his rifle savagely, and he fired again. The bullets were murderously close. A splinter of rock bit into Selby's cheek, and he heard the wild cry of the glancing slug.

Selby drew the sights down fine, and in him was a terrible dread. *Please, God, not another man!*

He sent his shout down the slope at the killer. "Melavin! You fool!" A bullet snapped the sleeve of his coat. "Damn you, throw down that gun!"

But the man would not be stopped. He heard Melavin's gun roar out its hate at him, and he heard the wind of the close-passing slug.

A man did what he had to do....

He squeezed off his shot and felt the Winchester slam solidly against his shoulder. Through the dark burst of smoke he saw the gunman twist sharply around under the impact of the bullet, and saw him get his feet under him and come rearing up from the ground as though in a frantic effort to get away from the pain that was in him.

For a moment Clyde Melavin stood utterly motionless on that high ledge of marl, the rifle slipping out of his hands as he looked down at his own redness. Then he drifted unsteadily to one side, and the rim of the cutbank suddenly gave way under him. He vanished.

There was a low, grinding grumble of sliding earth, and dust came boiling upward to hide it all from Curt Selby's eyes.

He stood at the rim of the badlands, and felt the sickness take hold of him. Once before, in a faraway town that he would never forget, he had seen a man die and he had been hit by this sudden tearing knowledge of what he had done. It hurt no less now than it had that first time.

He said, his voice a muttered thickness, "I didn't want to do it, Effie. I didn't want it this way."

Effie was close to him, holding his hands in her own. He looked at her, and her face was a pale blur.

She said gently, "Clyde Melavin shot my brother in the back, no warning at all. If he had caught me, it would have been . . . worse. You know how he was with women. You had no other choice, Curt."

He knew that she was right, but the sickness kept hitting him in thick, turgid waves. He had held a gun in his hands, and he had fired the gun, and he had killed a man.

Effie's hands were a pressure drawing him to her, drawing him against her. She held the softness of her body close to him, and it was what he needed.

She spoke quietly to him. "I remember all the things Signal used to say about you. They said you were spoiled, and maybe they were right three years ago. But not any more. The said you've got a wild, mean streak in you, but if you did that's gone now."

She was crying softly as she spoke. "You're tough, Curt, but you're not hard. It would be easier for you now if you were. Let go of yourself, Curt. Cry, if you can. It would help."

He couldn't cry. It wasn't that way with him. He broke away from her and went stumbling down the rocky slope into a gulch. The eroded walls thrust high and naked above him. He stopped walking and let the sickness come out of him, and after a while he turned and went back to where Effie waited.

He sat down beside her, saying nothing, waiting for the numbness to leave him. He felt her hands in the pockets of his coat. She brought out the tobacco and papers, and laughed softly at her own awkwardness as she shaped the cigaret for him.

"I've tried this before," she said. "I guess I will never learn."

She put the cigaret between her lips, touched a match to it and got it going. She gave it to him, saying: "Talking might help, Curt."

He raised his eyes and looked off toward the settling haze of dust. What was there for him to say? That he was sorry he had killed Clyde Melavin? He regretted it, but he was not sorry. There was a difference. This was a thorny, hard-knuckled range that forced its people to take harsh measures. A man did the things he had to do. He tore out cactus so there would be more graze for his cattle; he stomped rattlesnakes that threatened him; he shot down a killer when there was no other choice. This was the edict of a land that gave mercy only to those who earned it.

He was not aware of his brooding silence until Effie spoke again. "May I say something, Curt?"

He nodded. He sat there on the hard ground, thankful for her nearness, thankful for the sound of her voice.

"When I saw you fighting Sam Brighton yesterday, I thought you'd come back only to get a share of what Phil Selby built up these last three years," she told him. "I was wrong about that, wasn't I?"

He looked down at his hands. They were big, strong hands that had learned how to work and how to fight. "All wrong, Effie."

"Why did you come back, Curt?"

"Dad sent for me." It was only half of the truth, and not enough for this girl. He knew he was going to hurt her, but he said flatly, "Hamp is fed up with what Phil has been doing. He wants me to tear Buckle apart, and that means smashing Phil. I'm sorry, Effie."

"And I'm glad, Curt."

He looked around at her in swift surprise. There was a touch of sadness in her smile.

"I saw a lot of Phil after you left," she said. "For a while I thought he was the right one. He's a big man, and he will get bigger. I kept telling myself that the wealth and position he could give me were all that mattered, and it made no difference how he got them. I kept telling myself that, Curt. But I could never make myself believe it."

He stared at her.

Her smile tightened. "I made no promises to Phil. He *told* me, Curt. That is Phil's way of doing things."

There was a rising awareness in Curt, a deep, quickening warmth. He hitched himself around on the ground so that he could look more closely at her, and all the things a man could ever want were promised in her eyes.

He said in slow wonderment, "Why, Effie, I'm just now learning to see!"

He put his arms around her, and she laughed softly and sank backward to the ground, drawing him with her. It was the oddest thing; it was as if he had lived this moment a thousand times in his mind and in his heart. The dream had always been in him, unseen until now. Yes . . . the oddest thing. . . .

Somewhere up the slope a hooded oriole was singing, and then that sound faded away and was lost in a world of nearness and warmth and touch. Nothing else mattered. . . .

Chapter Fourteen

Jode Meeder was having himself a lazy hour in his office, enjoying the fine cigar he always favored himself with each Sunday afternoon at this time of day.

It was a quiet hour, with only a thin current of traffic on the street. His Sunday routine had become almost a ritual during the years he had worn Signal's law badge. When his smoke was finished, he would go over to the Golden Bell and let Lew Haverhill buy him a shot of the saloon's best, and at sundown he would go to the restaurant and treat himself to some of Ma Elkins' excellent cooking. It was good, he thought, for a man to pamper himself once a week.

He was glancing idly through the window when he saw the two riders angling down the long slope of the hill north of town, leading a third horse by the reins. At first he was only mildly curious.

It was easy, even from this distance, to recognize Effie Coombs's slim shape. Jode Meeder always found it a pleasure to watch a woman ride. They had a pliant grace in the saddle that no man ever achieved, and Effie Coombs was something special. She made a picture a man carried in his mind long after she was out of sight.

The recognition of Curt Selby riding with the girl nudged some of the easiness out of Jode Meeder's mind. The events of yesterday, when Selby had dumped that hotshot Lane Harragh at the feet of the Buckle crew, had left troubled thoughts in the sheriff's mind. Things had been moving along fine for Meeder these last three years, and he wanted no knots tied in the plans he had made for himself.

When they made the swing toward Ute Street, Meeder had his first unobstructed look at the horse Curt Selby was leading. In his time, he had packed enough dead men into town to know what one looked like. He grunted softly and bent closer to the window, squinting. The brittle glare of the afternoon sun brought water to his eyes, and he called sharply to the man napping on the cot in the next room.

"Orvie, come in here!"

There was something feline about a man who could snap awake and be on his feet with immediate control of all his faculties. Orvie Shandrin was like that. He appeared in the doorway, lank, lean, a smiling malice in his tawny eyes.

"That cigar bite you, Jode?" he drawled.

"Always the funny man, ain't you?" Meeder snapped, and pointed through the window. "What do you make of that?"

Shandrin bent to the window, his eyes narrowing against the street's brilliance. He didn't appear bothered by the shaft of sunlight that hit him full in the face. Shandrin could look at the sun itself without blinking, Jode Meeder thought. The man had the eyes of a cat—a killer's eyes.

Shandrin straightened, grinning faintly. "Looks like young Ernie Coombs got cured of running off Buckle cattle," he observed.

It verified what Meeder had guessed. Another thought came plunging into his mind. "If Curt Selby did the shooting, that girl sure as hell wouldn't be riding with him."

Shandrin shrugged his compact shoulders. He picked up the makings from the desk, and gave his attention to shaping a cigaret.

The thought kept piling higher and higher in Jode Meeder's mind. "It wasn't Selby killed young Coombs. It was someone else did that job." He stared up at his deputy. "Where is Clyde Melavin?"

Shandrin took his time with the cigaret. He struck a match, and looked through the flame at the sheriff. He smiled. His voice was cool, unruffled.

"Why ask *me*, Jode?"

Temper was kicking around inside Jode Meeder, and he was not a man to hold it in check for long. "Because you and Melavin are thick as thieves, that's why," he snapped harshly. "He can't go to the backhouse without you knowin' it."

Impatience brought Meeder up to his feet, and he kicked his chair across the floor behind him. He did not have Orv Shandrin's lank height. He stared up at the deputy, his blocky face tight with anger.

"I know a few things about Melavin. He can't let a woman alone, and he's been doin' a lot of thinking about Effie Coombs. He's been waiting for a chance to try to push her over, and he'd like nothing better than to shine up to Buckle by putting a crimp in the tail of Ernie Coombs and the crowd who've been nibbling at Phil Selby's herds."

Meeder's tone bit tighter, turning savage. "Melavin wasn't at church this morning. He hasn't been in town all day. You hear me, Orv. I want to know where he went."

An uneasiness came into Shandrin's eyes, and he looked away. "I wouldn't know, Jode."

Meeder's temper sharpened to a sudden wicked edge. He put his hand flat against Shandrin's chest and pushed him back against the wall.

"You're supposed to be a bright boy, Orv," he said, and his tone was dangerously soft. "Maybe you think you're sudden with a gun, but you'll never see the day you could fill my boots. I can tie a can to you, Orvie-boy. I know enough to put you out of business for keeps."

Shandrin breathed shallowly. "Now, Jode. . ."

Meeder's voice jumped harshly at the man. "Where is Melavin?"

Shandrin ventured a smile, but it didn't quite come off. He said thinly, "Nothing for you to get all het up about, Jode. Clyde tailed the girl out of town this morning, that's all. He wanted to get a line on her brother and the rest of the outfit that's been running off Buckle cows."

"The poor damn fool!"

"Clyde can take care of himself," Shandrin said.

Meeder's mouth twisted. "When did he ever get in a tangle with one like Curt Selby, I ask you?"

Shandrin's lips were dry. He ran the tip of his tongue along them. He looked around uncomfortably. "What are you getting at, Jode?"

"You don't see Melavin riding in, do you?" the sheriff demanded acidly. "Add it up for yourself, Orvie-boy. Curt Selby didn't gun young Coombs. Melavin did that. He tailed Effie to her brother, and he gunned the kid. What do you figure he'd do about the girl, after that?"

Shandrin frowned. "He'd try to get to her. He always had an eye for that filly."

Meeder spat on the floor. "You just had a good look at her. Did she look like Melavin got to her, Orvie-boy?"

Shandrin shook his head slowly. "Guess not."

Jode Meeder's rage became a black, withering thing, and he said harshly, "I fired Clyde Melavin yesterday. You hear me? I don't aim to get smeared by any man's damn foolishness. Melavin got too biggety, and I fired him. What he did today was no skin off my nose. We'll bury him just like any other idiot who bit off more than he could swallow."

Orvie Shandrin was slow to understand. He eyes gradually widened. "Bury him?" Then his eyes narrowed and took on a vicious glitter. "You think that Curt Selby got Clyde?"

"You're a real bright boy, Orvie," said Meeder contemptuously. "When you get it figured out, you can forget all about Selby and that gun you think you're so fancy with. I'm telling you, man! I don't want any one else from my office added to Curt Selby's list."

They drew rein in front of the gunshop, for Ben Padgett served also as the town's only undertaker. He repaired and sold guns, and it was his job to help bury the men those guns killed.

Hipping around in his saddle, Curt looked at the girl beside him. It had been a long ride, and a sad one for Effie Coombs. Fine lines of weariness were etched in her face, and she carried her grief deep inside her, showing it only in her eyes.

Looking at her, Curt remembered that moment at the rim of the badlands when he had been sickened by the killing. *She helped me to forget, and all the time she was crying for her brother.*

He said gently, "No need for you to stay, Effie. I'll make all the arrangements. I'll see that Ernie gets the best."

She thanked him with her eyes, and he watched her as she rode on down the street to Abe Korbee's livery yard. There rode a girl who would give love and comfort to a man, but would never be a burden to him. This was how Curt rated Effie Coombs. She was warmth and she was softness, but in her also were the strength and courage this range demanded of its people. Effie had seen her brother murdered, but not until she was alone would she let the tears come, for she was a girl who would permit no one to share her grief.

As he stepped out of saddle, Selby saw the crowd of men gathering in morbid curiosity around Ernie Coombs' body, and anger plunged bitterly through him.

"You've seen dead men before! Get the hell out of here, all of you!"

There was a sting to his temper that broke up the crowd and sent the men on their way. He turned and found Ben Padgett watching him from the doorway of his gunshop.

"Why is it they have to crowd around and stare when a dead man is brought in?" he asked bitterly as Padgett came up to the hitch rail.

"It may be," Padgett said slowly, "that they're seeing themselves, except for a lot of luck."

Selby's gaze moved to the body lashed across the horse. "Luck is a damn strange thing," he said. "For some men it can be mighty sweet, but for Ernie Coombs it went all sour. I want you to give him your best, Ben."

Padgett held all expression out of his face. "As you say, Mr. Selby." He cleared his throat, and he was thinking of Effie Coombs's modest earnings from her bake shop as he murmured, "It might run into a sizable bill, though."

"Buckle is good for it."

Ben Padgett was a small graying gnome of a man for whom the world no longer held many surprises. He was surprised now. He reflected it in his eyes.

Selby spoke shortly. "Ernie's luck went sour when Buckle's luck turned rich. If anyone's to blame for that kid being tied across that horse, it's the Buckle brand. You know that as well as I do, Ben."

Pedgett moved his feet uncomfortably.

Selby let out his anger a notch. "And stop handing me all the Misters," he said flatly. "I didn't get 'em three years ago, and I don't want them now."

He heeled around and saw Jode Meeder and Orv Shandrin angling across the street toward him. He answered the sheriff's nod with a short-clipped grunt that was anything but civil. He didn't like the lawman, and there was no patience in him for concealing it. Meeder accepted Selby's curtness without any show of resentment, slanting his head in the direction of the body on the horse.

"Looks like you brought in a cured cow thief, Mr. Selby."

"I brought in a shot-killed man—Ernie Coombs."

The sheriff smiled mildly. "Same difference, as I see it."

Selby stood thin-lipped before the two lawmen, his gaze flat, cold. "Have you got any proof of this kid stealing Buckle cows?"

Meeder shrugged, his smile unruffled. "Ernie Coombs was only one of the bunch. I could name the others— Dee Wordley, Charley Bell, some of the hands that usta work for the outfits Phil bought out after he took over. They've all been nibbling at Buckle herds. It's common knowledge, Mr. Selby."

"I asked what kind of proof you have," Selby snapped.

Some of Jode Meeder's amiableness withdrew, and he said frankly, "I never caught them with running irons in their hands, if that's what you mean. Haven't even been able to get a line on their camp, for that matter. But the fact that they've all been spending so much time in the brush ought to prove something."

"Until you've got something that will stand up in court," Selby said coldly, "don't call this kid a cow thief."

Meeder took a slow breath, and brought his smile back again. "It's a mighty generous attitude to take, Mr. Selby. It suits me, if it suits you. Mind telling me how this boy was killed."

"A gunshot. In the back."

Jode Meeder's eyes slowly widened. "That makes it murder."

"Nice of you to see it that way, sheriff."

"One of Ernie's crowd do it?"

Selby said thinly, "You could look closer, Jode. One of your men did it."

A trace of irritation ran through the sheriff's blocky face. "You're not talking sense, Mr. Selby. I've been in town all day. So has Orvie, here."

"Clyde Melavin wasn't."

Meeder's lips pinched together. "You telling me Melavin did this job?" he asked.

Selby nodded stonily. "One shot—the sure way—in the back."

Meeder swore with sudden force. "By God, Mr. Selby, don't tie this killing to my office. Clyde Melavin wasn't my man. I fired him last night. He was getting too biggety, and I fired him." He hitched his head around toward his deputy. "That right, Orv?"

Orv Shandrin was a man carved from stone, with hate in every line of him. He nodded slowly. His voice was a dry, chipped sound. "That's right."

Selby's smile was bleakly contemptuous. "Glad to know you're running a clean office, sheriff."

"Any man who doubts it has got me to settle with," Meeder said in a rough, blaring way. "If Melavin did this job, he'll pay for it. You know where I can find him, Mr. Selby?"

"Yes."

He looked at Shandrin. He said thinly, "North side of the badlands, close up to Mogul Plateau. There's a high place shaped like a Mexican hat, only flat on top. It's a likely place for a killer to stretch out and try to put a bullet in a girl he couldn't catch and do God knows what to. Whole side of the hill is caved in. You'll have to dig deep to find your former deputy, Meeder. When you dig him out, you'll find my bullet hole through his left shirt pocket."

It was challenge; it was ultimatum handed with stony contempt to the two lawmen. Orv Shandrin's mouth was a purse that contained the rankled malevolence that was working roughly on him as he stared across at Selby.

Jode Meeder was more complicated. The sheriff's thoughts withdrew into secret depths, and he moved his blocky shoulders in a gesture of weary finality. His voice was slow, without condemnation.

"Clyde Melavin tried to play a devil's game, and now he has paid the devil's dues. It's tough on you, though, Mr. Selby."

"On me?"

"A man is never quite the same after he has killed a fellow human," Meeder said, his expression one of jaded regret. "I ought to know, Mr. Selby. I've had to do it enough times—too many times."

Selby's contempt was hard to restrain. "Your sympathy and understanding," he said in thin bitterness, "is a great comfort, Jode."

A slow flush deepened in the lawman's face, and for

the briefest space of time a thorny malice surfaced in his eyes. It vanished at once, however.

Movement alerted Selby, jerking his gaze around to the deputy. "You keep fiddling around that gun handle, Shandrin. You got something special on your mind?"

Jode Meeder heeled sharply around, a turn that had a rough and ready violence in it. He stared flatly at his deputy. He asked shortly, "Something chewing you, Orvie?"

Orv Shandrin stood utterly motionless. The will to kill was in his eyes, and he could not drive it out of them. His hand lowered to his gun. His hand raised; it lowered again. He couldn't keep his hand still.

Staring at his deputy, Jode Meeder's voice turned curiously soft. "Well, Orv?"

Shandrin swore in a thick, choked way. "What's this jingle all about, I'd like to know? Melavin and me split up when he checked in his badge last night. He's dead. It's nothing to me."

He heeled abruptly around, kicking up small clouds of dust as he went tramping back toward the jail office. Jode Meeder's grin returned.

"That satisfy you about Shandrin, Mr. Selby?"

Curt shrugged.

"They were close, Melavin and Orvie," said the sheriff easily. "It may take him some time to get over this, but he'll be all right. He's my boy, Orvie is, inside and out."

Selby smiled meagerly. "Is that supposed to make me feel better?" Then he said, "Sam Brighton has spent enough time in jail, sheriff. I want him turned out."

Meeder frowned. He lifted his shoulders, let them drop. "All right, if that's what you want."

"It's what I want," Selby murmured.

Meeder said forcibly, "I'll turn Brighton loose, but I feel obligated to warn you. He'll join up with Dee Wordley, Charley Bell and the rest. All you'll ever get from that crowd is trouble for the Buckle brand."

A glint of saturnine humor ignited in Selby's steady gaze. "That's what I know, sheriff. That is exactly what I want."

Chapter Fifteen

The house Sam Brighton had taken for his wife and son was a rough-sawed plank dwelling standing on the bare flats on the south rim of the town, with no tree to protect it from the westerly sun that blazed down its heat without mercy.

Approaching the house Selby heard a man's flare of bitter temper, followed by the more mollifying tones of a woman's voice. Dropping his cigaret into the dust, he ground it under his heel with a rangeman's habitual wariness of fire. He knocked on the door.

Amy Brighton was a woman who had once known a fine home and fine things. Now they were gone and she had only a shack on the seamy side of the town. It had not humbled her. She was small and had the rounded matureness a man liked to see in a woman. If her face did not possess vivid beauty, a man was not aware of it. It was her steadfastness, the memory of her quiet gentleness that he always carried away with him.

"Well, Amy," Selby said as she opened the door. He saw her troubled smile and read the fear that lay behind it. He said, "I was hoping Sam would talk with me, Amy."

Behind her, Sam Brighton's voice jarred harshly. "Get away from here, Selby. I'm warning you, man—get away from here!"

It was her husband's bitter anger flaring out against Selby's polite manners that decided her. She was a gentle woman who believed that mannerliness should be accepted with equal courtesy. She had her pride, and her patience its limits.

She held the door open for Selby. "Please come in, Curt." Closing the door against the blaze of sunlight, she turned and spoke to her husband with a quiet force of will that Selby had never suspected was in her.

"Like it or not, Sam, we have a guest and you will mind your manners. I will have no brawling in my house."

Selby thanked her with his eyes. It was a small, cramped room with an oval rag rug giving faded color to the rough floor. There were two ladderback chairs, and a rocking chair near the table in the corner. At the end of the room there was an old horsehair sofa, with a pair of unframed lithographs tacked to the wall above it.

Sam Brighton stood across the room, the marks of yesterday's fight swollen and discolored on his face. His eyes were rigid with rancor, and propped against the wall, within easy reach, was a Henry rifle.

Selby said quietly, "Howdy, Sam," and heard the man's low, smothered oath. He let that pass, speaking amiably, as though their trouble had never happened. "Mind if I sit down?"

Brighton took a deep, ragged breath, and the rage built up in his stare to an explosive congestion.

Amy said swiftly, "Sam!"

Her voice, quiet as it was, brought a measure of control back into him. He said harshly, "Why not? Go ahead, Selby. Have your look at the house the white trash live in. Then go back to your brother's fancy mansion and have your laugh. That's why you came here, I guess."

Sadness was in the weary shake of Selby's head. "Sam, Sam," he said softly. "Do you hate me that much?"

"Is there any reason I should love any Selby?" the man demanded bitterly.

"There are culls in every herd. You know that, Sam."

He was getting nowhere with this kind of talk. He knew that. Yet he didn't know how to open up his mind to this embittered, angry man. Sam Brighton was a ruined, defeated man, but he still had his pride. It was that steel-edged pride that made him all the more difficult to deal with.

Selby said, "I've got something for you, Sam," and as he reached into his pocket he saw the man instantly grab up the rifle.

Selby smiled thinly, brought the packet of papers out of his pocket. He tossed them across the room to the man's feet.

"Top one is for you," he said. "The rest are for Dee

Wordley, Charley Bell, and all the other outfits Buckle bought out."

Wariness stood rashly in Brighton's eyes as he stared across at Selby. Then he propped the Henry against the wall, and picked up the papers. He untied the string that bound the packet, and opened the paper that bore his name. His eyes widened. His gaze snapped to Selby, brittle, bitter.

Selby said evenly, "Those deeds hand back the land Buckle bought from you and the others. You're back in business, Sam, you and all the rest."

"What kind of a damn trick is this?" the man flared.

"It's not a trick," Selby murmured.

Brighton's mouth twisted. "The sun never rose on the day Phil Selby would let go of anything he ever got his hands on," he said harshly.

"That's right," Selby said, and smiled faintly. "Only Phil never got his hands on any of those outfits. If you'll think back, it was old Hamp those deeds were made out to. There's a difference between the wolf and the pup."

Sam Brighton stared. His wife came across the room and stood beside him. Her face was pale, a glistening wetness standing in her eyes.

Selby spoke slowly. "Phil is one man; Hamp is another. Phil has some high and mighty ideas that Hamp never did have. Does that make any sense to you, Sam?"

Brighton looked down at his wife, and she was crying softly. He brought his gaze back to Selby.

"A man can make mistakes when he raises his sons," Selby said. "When he sees the wrong turns he made, he wants to go back and try to straighten them out."

Brighton said thickly, hoarsely, "Bring it out in the open, fellow!"

"It ought to be plain enough," Selby said. "Hamp is sorry about what has happened here. He is giving you and all the others back your land."

Unchecked rage rushed through Sam Brighton's face, and he sent the deeds hurling across the room with a savage throw of his hand.

"We'll accept no charity from a range-grabbing Selby!" he flared.

Selby sat still in his chair, breathing slowly, warned by the uncontolled fury that was in the man's eyes.

Brighton's contempt came ripping at him, like the blade of a knife. "That would make a mighty fine gesture now, wouldn't it?" he sneered. "The Selbys force their neighbors to sell out, then make a big show by giving the land back! Every newspaper in the Territory would print the story about the kindness and generosity of the Selbys. A story like that would get Phil Selby elected Governor, and after that there'd be no range too small for him to steal."

He jerked around and yanked the rifle up, swinging it savagely on Selby. "Get out of here, man!" he said thickly. "Get out of here before I kill you!"

Selby stood up slowly. "All right, Sam." He turned and went to the door. At the door he hesitated, then swung slowly back, careful how he moved against that leveled rifle.

He looked at the whiteness of Amy Brighton's face, and he looked at the raging bitterness that was in her husband's eyes. There was danger in Sam Brighton. He was a man who had worked hard for his land and then lost it, who had fought in the dust of the street and had been beaten and thrown into jail. The rifle was rigid in his hands, the hammer eared back to full cock. It would not take much—only a shard of a thought—to make him kill.

Against the cowman's hating blaze of temper, Selby spoke softly, slowly. "Last night I went out on the porch with Hamp. He's still living in the old house, you know. He won't have any part of the fancy new one Phil built.

"Hamp stood there on the porch and looked out across the basin. He's an old man, Sam, and all he could see was things the way they used to be. The basin was dark, from one end to the other. Used to be there were lights where you and Wordley and the others lived."

Selby looked at the rifle leveled on him, and he raised his eyes to Brighton's rigid face.

"Hamp asked me to bring the lights back to the basin," Selby said.

Brighton's eyes drew narrow.

"That's how it is with Hamp, Sam. He's fed up with the way Phil has run things on Buckle. He's sick of the new outfit. Fancy trimmings and a crew of gun-toughs to grab a lot more. That's why he wrote for me to come home. He wants me to help him bring back the old days."

Brighton's mouth twisted. "Too late for that."

Selby bent his head toward the papers on the floor. "You own your land again, you and the others. You can move back into those houses out there. You can bring the lights back into the basin for Hamp to see."

Brighton said harshly, "And how do you think Phil and his crew of gun-sharps would go for that?"

"They'll put pressure on you again."

"They wouldn't talk much next time," Brighton said thickly. "Not Lane Harragh and his killers."

"Then you and the others will have to get together. You'll have to fight, Sam."

Brighton's snort was an oath. "What are you trying to do, Selby—get us to pull Hamp's chestnuts out of the fire?"

Selby stared at the man.

"Hamp gave his ranch to his son, but he's not man enough to take it back. Me and the others won't grab the dirty stick for him. Hamp made his own bed; now the old fool can lay in it."

Selby's eyes turned cold. "All right, Sam."

He opened the door. Brighton's temper blared at him. "If you want Hamp to have Buckle back, then take it away from Phil yourself!"

Selby smiled thinly. "I'm going to try."

"You against Harragh and his crew?"

Selby gave no reply. He closed the door against Brighton's sneering derision, turned, and walked away. He didn't look behind him. He came to the street and a man spoke to him and he did not answer. He didn't even see the man.

Chapter Sixteen

This was Monday, dawning clear and cool, turning hot and muggy as the hours wore on, with great piles of thunderheads building darkly above Mogul Plateau's massive wedge. The smell of rain was in the air, and at midafternoon the sky took on a wicked, brassy tinge. Thunder grumbled distantly, and gusts of wind sent dust devils romping along Signal's main street.

All that day Curt Selby felt the temper of the town change. At first he had been met by the fawning deference of townsmen who were knuckling aside old rancors in order to preserve the good will of the powerful Buckle brand that Selby represented.

But during later hours he felt those men change toward him. At first it was an indefinable thing. Then as the day wore on he saw the coldness grow tighter in men's eyes, saw contempt pinch their lips and turn their faces hard and remote. The hostility of the town was a growing pressure clamping him from all sides, and he could not understand it.

Hamp, too, felt the silent sting of the town's rising malice. He came racking into town shortly after noon, and habit sent him into the Cattlemen's Rest for his drink. He did not stay there long. He came tramping out shortly later with a brooding thoughtfulness on his craggy face, his voice short-clipped and irritable when he located Selby at Abe Korbee's livery yard. He stared crossly at the steeldust Selby had saddled.

"Where were you headin'?"

"Figured I'd ride out for a confab with you," Selby said. He studied the truculent moodiness of his father's face for a moment. "What's eating you, Hamp?"

"This damn town, that's what."

Selby smiled meagerly. "So you feel it, too!" he murmured.

"Feel it!" the cowman grunted. "I can smell it, taste it, see it. What's happened in this town, anyhow?"

Selby shook his head slowly. "You tell me, Hamp. I sure don't know."

Leading the steeldust by the reins, Selby went through the livery yard's wide arched gate, Hamp tramping heavily beside him.

Hamp walked in head-down moroseness, a soured anger in his voice. "After I turned Buckle over to Phil, I stopped counting in this town. I was a nobody walking in Phil's shadow. All of a sudden now, I'm not even that. I'm treated like dirt to be spit on."

He wagged his head around toward his son. "What's happened, I want to know? I met up with Sam Brighton and Charley Bell in the Cattlemen's a while ago. Did you tell them about their land?"

Selby nodded slowly. "I turned their deeds over to Brighton yesterday."

"They sure as hell didn't act very grateful," Hamp grunted.

"They've got the idea you're trying to get them to pull your chestnuts out of the fire," Selby said dryly.

"How's that?"

"They figure you're trying to get Buckle back from Phil. It's their idea you're not man enough to whittle your own stick and want them to do it for you."

"By God, Curt!"

"Can't blame them much, Hamp," Selby said softly.

"Hand over six good layouts free for nothing, and this is the thanks a man gets!" Hamp bit out acridly.

A gust of wind whipped past them, spinning dust up from the street. Dog Lathrop came around the corner of the the hay barn behind Ross Ellender's Feed Store, a pair of redbone hounds straining on their leashes. Always a taciturn man, there was something plainly malign in the way Lathrop strode past without speaking or even looking up.

Sudden anger yanked Hamp around. "Hold on a minute, Lathrop!"

The man came to a halt, turning slowly. The hounds swung around, sluffing the ground and stretching out Lathrop's arm as they strained restlessly against the leashes.

95

"Since when did you get so uppity you can't give a man a civil howdy when you pass him on the street?" Hamp demanded caustically.

Lathrop raised his head slowly, looking at Hamp without any readable expression. There was something canine about the man that always made a distinct impression on Curt Selby when he saw Dog Lathrop. It was because of the lank, loose-jointed height, he decided, the undershot jaw and the shoulders bent from reading trail signs and holding in check his pack of leashed hounds when he was on a hunt. Get close enough to the man and he even exuded the odor of his dogs, Curt remembered.

Lathrop's gaze was long and deliberate. His eyes didn't change. When he spoke it was with such overbearing pleasantness that each word was a whiplash of insolent malice.

"Why, howdy-do, Mister Selby. Both of you."

Temper rushed darkly into Hamp's face, and Curt clamped a quick grip on his father's arm.

"Let it ride, Hamp."

He heard Lathrop's snorting laugh, and felt his own anger heat up as the man swung away with his hounds. He pulled Hamp forcibly around.

"It's not worth making a ruckus about, Hamp."

"By God, it's almost more than a man can stand," Hamp said bitterly. "He smells like a cur dog, that fellow, and he treated me like I was something his hounds dug up. It's too damned much, Curt. I recollect the winter I kept that ingrate alive on Buckle beef when he was too hard up to buy his own grub."

"Forget it, Hamp."

They walked on. Wind shoved at them in rough, fitful gusts. Dust clouded the air. The thunderheads still grumbled above Mogul Pleteau, but the storm seemed to be moving off to the west.

They came to a halt in front of the Cattlemen's Rest where Hamp had left his horse. Curt's gaze was restless on the street, feeling the malice of the town crowding against him. He stood there beside his father, and the scant attention they got from passing townsmen was thorny with spite and wary contempt. A picture was beginning to shape in his mind.

He said, his voice thin, bleak, "Sam Brighton and the

others think you're trying to hand them a dirty stick. They think you're trying to set them up against Phil and his crew of gun-toughs—a job too mean for you to handle yourself."

Hamp spat savagely into the dust of the street.

"The town has got a different itch against you," Selby said. "Everyone on the street is worried about his pocketbook. They figure they've had a good thing in the Buckle that Phil built up. Phil played it smart. He never haggled prices here. Money talks. Signal likes being a one-ranch town. When there's a bunch of small outfits doing business, there's always a lot of dickering on prices. Signal likes things the way they are, Hamp."

The cowman swore bitterly. "The poor damn fools! They're too blind to see past their next meal, and too scared to think past tomorrow. Let Phil get any bigger, and he'd kill this town any time the notion hit him."

Selby smiled sourly. "Just try to tell the town that, Hamp."

Temper congested darkly in the cowman's craggy face. "Hell with this town," he bit out, and yanked the reins loose from the tie rail. He swung into the saddle. Leather creaked under him. "That highfalutin' whelp of mine is the one to tell," he said savagely. "I'm going to square him off about some things, once and for all!"

"Hamp, you watch out!"

The man reared up in his saddle, glaring his wrath down at Curt.

"Watch out for Phil?" he snapped. "I spawned that pup, and I ain't about to be afraid of him."

"I was thinking of Lane Harragh and his crew," Selby said, and heard the old man's derisive grunt.

"Harragh won't climb out on any limb," Hamp growled. "It's Phil I'm going to jump. It won't do any good, but I'm going to give that pup the whaling he should have got twenty years ago."

Hamp hauled his horse around and went racking down the street, into the wind. Worry dug into Curt Selby and sent him heeling around to the steeldust. He halted abruptly and let his boot slip out of the stirrup.

Hamp was right. Lane Harragh was a deadly man, but a careful one. In his temper, Hamp was capable of giving Phil a trouncing, or trying to, even if Phil was a full-grown man. Harragh would keep hands off, nor was Phil apt to be dangerous. Phil was no fool, for if Hamp was killed the empire he was building up around the Buckle brand would collapse in ruins.

Knotting the reins around the tie rack, Selby moved restlessly along the street. Effie was standing in the doorway of her bakery, and as he paused at the foot of the low steps a deep and grateful warmth rose through him. Here, at least, was one who did not hate him.

Smiling, he said, "Effie, you're what a man dreams of when the world is turning upside down under him." Then he said, "I had a talk with Ed Newlin first thing this morning. The services for Ernie will be held tomorrow."

"Thank you, Curt."

There was an aroma coming from the open door behind her. Selby sniffed the air. "Would that be apple turnovers I smell?"

A smile broke through the strain that was in Effie Coombs's eyes. "I remembered how much you like them. Come in, Curt."

He started up the steps. He halted, shaking his head slowly. "Guess I'd better not."

She stood tall and slim in the doorway, looking out at the street in a kind of defiance. There was a touch of anger in the gaze she dropped to Selby.

"Why should you care about what this town thinks?" she demanded.

"I don't, Effie. But I do care about the trouble I might bring down on you."

Her lips lengthened and drew thin. "I made no promises to Phil Selby. He has no claim on me."

"He thinks he does. So does Lane Harragh."

The anger livened in her eyes, becoming real. "Curt Selby, you make me feel like . . . like swearing!"

He looked up at her, amused. "Don't recollect ever hearing a lady cuss, Effie. It wouldn't sound seemly."

"I don't care!" The flush deepened in her cheeks, and in anger she was truly beautiful. "I don't give a damn about what this town thinks. Or a damn about what Phil thinks. Or a damn about what Lane Harragh and the rest of those toughs think. Do I make myself clear, Curt Selby?"

He grinned. "Tolerably."

"Then you march right in here and eat those turnovers

I baked for you," she told him distinctly.

He was properly meek in his reply. "Yes'm."

He went inside and he ate, and she brought him a glass of cool milk and he drank. He brought her to him and held her close and kissed her, thinking that in this girl were all the depths of warmth and comfort that any man could ever want or dream of. The pressure of her hands against his chest drew them apart, and he saw the shadows of worry again in her eyes.

"I heard about Sam Brighton and the others," she said. "How can men be such blind fools?"

"Easy," Selby murmured, "when a man has been hurt as bad as they were. "

"They were paid a good price for their land," Effie protested.

"Their land was mortgaged, and after the money was gone there were no jobs. It's a tough thing, Effie. That's what they're holding against Buckle."

She flung her voice at him bitterly. "But they've got their land back now! Hamp gave it to them, Curt—free, clear, no strings attached."

"Except for Phil," Selby said. "Except for Lane Harragh and his crew."

"What do you mean?"

"Phil hasn't changed. He'll go after those outfits again. Next time Harragh and his men will go after them the hard way. Phil paid off once. He won't pay again."

Effie said flatly, "Then Sam Brighton and the others should stand behind you and fight!"

"They don't see it that way," Selby said, and his smile was thin, sour. "They figure it was Hamp who turned loose all this trouble. They figure it's Hamp's place to put a stop to it."

"But what can he do?" the girl cried out in quiet despair. "What can you do, alone?"

"I don't know," Selby said, and a sense of weary hopelessness came crushing down on him. "I just don't know, Effie."

The storm clouds rolling off to the west were bringing an early end to the day. Here in town the wind had died down a little, but in the direction of the basin there was a wicked yellowness scudding low across the range—a sandstorm raging on the Cache Rock flats.

Selby was going past the red brick courthouse when Sheriff Meeder's voice caught at him roughly from the door of the jail office. "I want a word with you, Selby."

Selby halted and turned, waiting in saturnine amusement as the lawman came tramping toward him. Yesterday Jode Meeder had been mealymouthed, eager to please. Now that was gone. His face was hard, his gaze brittle, his voice cold.

"There's a man in town looking for you, Selby."

There was no deference at all in Meeder's tone of voice; it was like the impact of a fist, and Selby thought: *So you're another one who is going to back Phil and Harragh in this fight.*

He said dryly, without much interest, "I'm not hard to find, Sheriff."

Meeder's mouth thinned out, and his insolence took on a wicked edge. "That's why I took the trouble of telling you. I'm giving you a chance to get yourself lost." His shoulders reared higher, giving a forward thrust to his head, and he spoke in a flat harshness. "I don't want any shooting in this town."

A cold wind blew against Selby. "Do I know the man?"

"He seems to know you well enough. Fellow's name is Pence Doane."

Selby leafed back through the pages of three long years; there were many towns and many faces in his memory, but no Pence Doane. He shook his head slowly, troubled by a thought. The name had come easily to the sheriff, like one long familiar.

Selby spoke mildly, almost pleasantly. "Friend of yours, is he, Jode? A Buckle man, maybe?"

He knew at once he had hit a touchy spot. Meeder's face took on a florid darkness, and temper rushed into his voice.

"I've had about enough of your cheek, Selby. All I know about Pence Doane is that he worked for Buckle until he heard you were in town. Quit his job this morning and rode here to find you. He's got a score to settle with you, and I want to know what it is."

Selby's gaze was cold, remote. "I wouldn't know." A

100

moroseness tightened in him. "Maybe he rode here to do a Buckle chore."

"I allowed you'd air something like that," Meeder said contemputuously. "All you can think of is making trouble for your half brother, ain't it?"

Selby smiled.

There was a wicked thrust to the lawman's stare. "Are you going to leave town?" he demanded.

"Is Pence Doane?" And when Meeder refused to answer that, Selby said softly, "I'll be around, Jode. You want to know something, sheriff?"

"I'm listening."

"Buckle is not so big that it can't be ripped down to an honest size. It took a Selby to build it up; it'll take another Selby to knock it down."

Chapter Seventeen

The sun was lost behind the thunderheads rolling off to the west, and the day had taken on a gray and dismal hue, with dusk still a full hour away.

In his room at the Territorial Hotel, Curt Selby washed at the cracked bowl and put on a clean shirt, wondering wryly why he bothered to do so. How he looked, good or bad, did not matter in this town, for the pressures of rancors old and new were crowding relentlessly against him. He was a man alone, and he was a lonely man.

He had never felt more shut off from the world. It was like a web tightening around him—an inexorable web of gunsmoke. And because he knew the dire things a man could do with a gun, he hated the town and the Buckle brand and the brutality it was shoving against him.

He turned and bent to the window, searching the street below until he saw the man idling at the hitch rail in front of the Golden Bell. That would be the one—Pence Doane. There was always this pretended indifference when a gunman waited to make his kill. There was always this veneer of guilelessness to mask the venom and deadly flame.

Is this the one you sent to get me, Phil? The thought ran thin and thorny through Selby's mind. There was no uncertainty in him. The design of the man was unmistakable—the low-laced gun, the pressured lips, the restlessness of the eyes that never strayed far from the hotel.

There was an ache in Selby's throat. *God in Heaven, will there always be another man to meet?*

He straightened, turning away from the window. He was gripped by a sudden impulse to go down the back stairs and put this town forever behind him. The thought rose strongly through him, and then it faded.

Hamp was right. Buckle had to be stopped. If it was not stopped other good men would be thrust aside or tromped down, just as Sam Brighton, Charley Bell and the others had been smashed under.

Phil Selby had that kind of unrelenting hunger. He was goaded by ambitions that could never be satisfied. He would keep on grabbing and cheating and hurting until the hatred of all men rose up to destroy him, and that was a thing Hamp did not want. It was a thing he would not have, a prideful man who rooted his dignity in one harsh edict: when a Selby went cultus it was for another Selby to deal with him.

So this is how it is, Curt thought in a cold and weary way. He went out of the room and down the stairs, feeling the weight of the gun sagging from his belt. A board creaked in the floor of the lobby, a startling sound. Whitey Simms was watching emotionlessly from his desk across the room. *You hoping it's me who'll get it, Whitey?* The voice was an echo rocketing bitterly through Selby's mind.

He came to a halt at the rim of the porch. The street was empty except for the man at the tie rail in front of the Golden Bell. The fellow turned slowly, showing a lean, malice-ridden face and coldly mocking eyes.

How much did Phil pay you for this, Doane?

Pence Doane stepped away from the tie rail, waiting. The thoughts kept ribboning through Selby's mind.

What will the money buy for you if you win out, Doane? Some whiskey and a woman? And what will you have left when they're gone?

The town was waiting.

He looked toward the sheriff's office in the red brick courthouse building, expecting no interference from Jode Meeder and seeing no sign of any. He did not care. *Hell with you and your one-sided law, Meeder.*

His eyes moved and he was looking at the bakery, thankful that Effie was not watching this. She knew about things such as this. There was room in a man for only one thought, only a single bleak speculation, when he walked out to face a killer. A woman could weaken him with her presence, or she could strengthen him by not intruding on a thing too inexorably brutal for her to prevent.

I'm sorry, Effie; it's tougher on you.

Pence Doane was moving out to the middle of the street, his slow pacing itself a jeering challenge. He came to a halt, firming his boots in the dust of the street.

Selby stared across at the man, feeling the tightness take hold of him. His thinking turned quick and sharp. Anger raked him. Challenge stung him. Decision hardened him.

All right, Doane! All right, damn you!

There was a stone under his right boot. Pence Doane shifted his foot, scraping the stone aside so that there was nothing to disturb his stance.

It was the minute details that counted most. Pence Doane had learned this from that buck-toothed special who had filled so many graves over in Lincoln County, the one they called Billy the Kid. He had learned all the fine points of his trade by studying the best—Wes Hardin and Longley, Curly Ringo and Lane Harragh.

He watched Curt Selby come down the hotel steps and into the street, and a gritty thought rose up through the keened virulence that was in him. *Two hundred dollars on the hoof! Come on, man; this is my payday.*

Moving hurriedly through the gray light, Orv Shandrin crossed the weedy backlot behind Ellender's hay barn and approached the street through the slotty lane between the feed store and Hub Wintner's saddle shop. The eyes of the town, he knew, were on the street. This hour had been made to order for him, and a streaky satisfaction was in him as he came up behind the water barrel blocking the space between the two buildings at the edge of the plank walk.

From this point of vantage he could survey the street where Pence Doane waited and Curt Selby walked. Age had rotted the barrel and warped its staves so that it neither held water nor offered protection against bullets. That did not matter. Selby would not live long enough to send any shots this direction.

Shandrin drew his .38-40, earing back the hammer to full cock. Smiling shallowly, he laid the Colt across the rim of the barrel, lining up its sights with bleak precision on an imaginary target between Selby's shoulder blades.

Selby had come to a halt. Beyond him and some distance across the vacant lot a boy was hoeing a small garden patch beside some poor man's shack. The boy did not matter. Only the place between Selby's shoulders where the bullet would strike mattered.

A honing malice chewed savagely on Orv Shandrin's

patience as he gazed down the gun sights. *This will be for Clyde Melavin. Too bad you'll never know about it, Selby.*

They stood facing each other across that gray space, and the town watched and the town waited, unmoving and morbidly silent. The hush piled up and thickened on the street until it was a pressure that no man could bear, and it was Pence Doane who broke it, his voice a harsh, slashing burst of sound.

"You should have known I'd catch up with you sooner or later, Selby. You must have known you couldn't get away."

Curt Selby's smile was a small, bitten expression, edged with contempt.

"Why try to make something else out of this, Doane?" he asked coldly. "We've never met before and you know it. This is just a job you were paid to do. Why try to make it look like something else?"

Doane's mind was grooved to a single bleak channel that he could not change. "I swore I'd settle with you for that stunt you pulled last year in El Paso, damn you." His voice was a whip lashing savagely through the silence of the street.

Selby's smile did not change. "I've never been in El Paso. I could prove that."

"You and your lies!"

"Why keep talking, Doane?"

The pattern was in Doane's mind and he had to follow it through. It was the thing on which he was building up his rage to kill.

"You carried on with my sister, then walked out on her. She was a good girl, and you ruined her."

"Are you talking about Rose Stevens?"

Doane's rage was a black, unthinking pressure crowding him recklessly on. "You know damn well I am!"

"Your sister, you say?" The amusement in Selby's gaze was a dried out, sardonic thing. "I only made up the name. I thought yours is Doane."

It shattered the gunman's deception, for a moment striking him dumb, his mind too grooved to one bleak channel to move quickly into another. He stared at Selby until the full realization of his error hammered a hating wildness into his eyes. Then he slapped for his gun, savagely.

The man was murderously fast. Even as he faded to one side, Selby saw the weapon whip upward. He saw the black thrust of smoke and heard the blast of two shots, one from Doane and another from somewhere at the rim of the street behind him.

He heard the driven anger of the close-passing bullets, and laced his own shot at Doane, into the body. He knew where that slug went. He threw himself backward as another gunshot slammed at him from behind.

He hit the street and rolled in dust, twisting himself around toward the haze of smoke clouding the air between the saddle shop and Ellender's feed store. He could not see the man. He fired once and again and a third time, spacing each slug across the bulge of the barrel.

He heard a man's choked cry of agony. The barrel was jarred by a lunging weight, and then it fell apart as Orv Shandrin reared up and stumbled forward against it, triggering spasmodic shots at a target he could no longer see. His legs caved under him, and he fell.

Selby stood up, and now the street was again silent with the hushed malevolence of men who could not believe what they had seen. A voice came across to Selby in awed anger.

"Anyone that good with a gun couldn't be honest."

Somewhere off the street a woman suddenly screamed, a thin throat-torn cry. "They shot my boy! They've killed my Bax!"

Shock hit Curt Selby and became a self-blaming sickness damning him for what had happened. A man and his gun! A man using a gun in anger and shooting a boy who had stood in the path of a wild bullet.

The sickness kept tearing at him until it became an unbridled, overpowering torment that ripped out of him everything but a frantic, unthinking desire to escape.

He started running for his horse. A man shouted harshly and came in front of him, and he knocked the fellow aside with a clubbing swing of his arm. He kept running in a blind, senseless way, with no clear thought in his mind except to get out of this town and away from the violence it had hurled at him.

He yanked the reins free and threw himself into the saddle, and now over the steady screaming of Amy

106

Brighton he heard the deep, swelling roar of a mob's brutal voice.

"Stop that fellow! Get him—get him!"

A gunshot beat out its harsh report.

"Get your posse together, Meeder! Go after Lathrop and his hounds, somebody! Round up the horses and don't forget to bring enough rope to lynch that gunslick!"

It was a witless thing, and in a dim and shattered way Curt Selby knew that. But he couldn't stop himself. The after-echoes of the violence kept shocking through his mind, and the sickness in him changed to an overwhelming panic to escape the town and what it had forced him to do. There was no other thought.

He sent his horse plunging out of the town, pointing it toward the desert and the black towers of the thunderheads, and when the animal ran its heart out that night, Selby went ahead on foot, stumbling through darkness. . . .

Chapter Eighteen

Late that afternoon Selby came out of his stupor and found a backwash where the water was reasonably clean. He bent and washed the sourness from his mouth, afterwards sloshing his sunburned face with the water. It helped.

He stood up, and through the willows he could see the silt-heavy yellowness of the Colorado River. Yonder was the California shore line, the muddy banks drying out within a few short yards and becoming the rim of a desert as stark and deadly as the one he had just crossed.

Yonder was escape from Jode Meeder's posse; it was the end of his running. Or he could board the *Cocopah*, if the riverboat had not steamed past him while he was unconscious, and escape northward to Hardyville or the Mormon settlement of Callville. There would be more security for him in that direction, for he had heard of Jode Meeder crossing the river into California more than once with his posse to bring back a wanted man. Meeder was a hard one to stop.

He was a gaunted, bone-weary man, this Curt Selby, and it took an effort to untangle the numbness from his mind. He had no clear memory of his flight across the desert. At dusk on Monday he had shot down two men who had tried to kill him, and he had heard Amy Brighton's throat-tearing scream of horror about the boy who had been hit by a wild bullet.

That was Monday, and this was Wednesday; that was in Signal, and this was the bank of the Colorado, a hundred thorny miles away. He had only a blurred memory of the tortures between—his horse running its heart out, the cloudburst that had sent its torrents plunging through Cibola Canyon, the crazed bitterness and self-blaming regret that had forced him on and on in a madness to escape.

He knew now that he had been a fool to run, for it

was not his bullet which had hit Bax Brighton. It couldn't have been. Only Orv Shandrin had fired in the direction of the Brighton house.

But by running away he had made Signal believe the worst. By his own unthinking folly he had ignited the malice of the townsmen, changing them into a mob howling for his capture and a rope to lynch him. He swore softly, in weary bitterness. *When I jumped town I tied Phil's noose around my neck. He sent the killer, but I dug my own grave.*

The sun was low over the river, and he knew that Jode Meeder and his posse of bounty-hunters could not be more than an hour or two behind him. Too late now for rest; too late even for fear. He turned back through the willows, setting a dogged pace as he swung off to the south. He came to a gutted area of old placer workings, and knew that La Paz was somewhere not far ahead, to the east of the river.

The numbness was returning to his legs, and he knew this final reservoir of strength could not carry him much farther. He played a game with himself to keep going. If he could make it to that high hogshead of granite he would allow himself enough time for a quick smoke. He made it to the rock and had his smoke.

He set his mind on the next goal. *If I can climb that next ridge before sundown I'll give myself a rest.* He topped that rock-ribbed height as the sun was dropping behind the horizon, but he did not rest. Not far ahead he saw the cluster of adobe huts and sagging shacks of a dying town. That was La Paz. He stumbled on, down the gaunt flanks of the ridge and across the gutter rubble of worked out placers.

The aroma of wood smoke sent him across to a rough-sawed plank shack at the east side of the town. Just short of the place, he stumbled and fell, and when he climbed back to his feet he saw the man eyeing him narrowly from the doorway.

He was a towering man with massive shoulders and a sun-reddened face and a miner's dingy pants stuffed into the tops of heavy boots. The shotgun looked like a toy in his huge hands. He grinned slowly and propped the gun against the door.

"Mister, you don't look to me like no claim jumper."

Selby shook his head, suddenly too tired even to speak, hearing the chuckle rumble in the miner's deep chest.

"Wouldn't make no never-mind anyhow," the man said. "All's left in this diggins is bean money. Mister, you look mighty done in." He jerked his head toward the room behind him. "Come on in and set. I've got enough grub on the fire for us both."

Selby shook his head again. His voice was a cracked, hoarse sound. "Got to keep moving."

The miner smiled placidly. He looked at Selby's scarred, seam-split boots, at the grayness of exhaustion that underlay the burned redness of Selby's face.

The miner spoke with a knowing mildness. "There's times when a man can travel faster by takin' it slower. You could set long enough to get some food in you, friend."

An irrational anger rose through Selby, giving his voice a kind of singing thinness. "Damn you, I'm not asking for a nursemaid." He was instantly shamed by his flare of anger, and he said with hoarse contriteness, "Look, I lost my horse yesterday and I've been walking ever since. I'm tired, and I've got to have another horse. Have you got one you'll sell me?"

And when the miner shook his head, Selby's tone turned thick with desperation. "Is there any in town for sale? I've got money."

The man studied Selby for a moment, his gaze grimly thoughtful. "I know of a mule you could buy, maybe." Then he asked slowly. "On the jump, are you?"

Selby took a breath. His throat ached. "Yes."

"Allowed so," the miner said, and some of the easiness went out of his tone. "Stick-up, was it?"

"No."

The man glanced around at his shotgun. He brought his gaze back to Selby. "Mind telling me why they're after you?"

It seemed to take something out of Selby even to speak. "There was a fight. A boy was shot."

The miner's eyes narrowed, hardened. "You the one who shot him?"

Selby jerked his head. "No."

The man stared at him for a long while, then he moved his massive shoulders. He said, speaking slowly. "I haven't been inside a church for years. Out here a man has to make his own religion or go without, mister."

He dug tobacco out of his pocket, stuffed it into an ancient briar, watching Selby steadily. "Last month a killer showed up here I'd heard about. Snake mean, that fellow was, and tried to throw a gun on me when I wouldn't hand over my grub sack. I walloped him on the head and tied him up. Kept the cuss here until a posse from down Yuma way showed up and took him back to the jail he busted out of."

Gazing at Selby, he scratched a lucifer and got his pipe going. "But what little religion I've got works both ways. When a jigger shows up who needs a hand, I like to give him one. Was I to get a riding mule for you, where would you head, mister—for Californy?"

Selby pushed his head higher. His eyes were hard. Flat-lipped, he said, "I'd go back to the town I ran away from." He wanted to make it plain. "One way or another, muleback or on foot, that's where I'm going. Now are you going to tell me who to see about that mule, or do I have to find out for myself?"

The miner grinned faintly in his beard. "You're a salty one, ain't you?"

Anger broke through Selby again, and he started to stumble on. The man's mild drawl halted him.

"Cobby Wain would bleed you dry for a critter that ain't worth more than twenty-five dollars. Give me your money, friend, then go inside and get some food in you. I'll buy the mule for you. It'll give me a pleasure to dicker that old skinflint down to an honest price."

And when he came back leading the mule, he said mildly, "If a posse was to show up askin' questions, I'd likely tell them the sun was in my eyes when you rode off."

"No," Selby said, his voice softly bleak. "Tell them Curt Selby went back to the town of Signal. I want them to know, amigo."

He put the night behind him, and all of the next day, camping only long enough to eat the food the miner had packed for him and to get a few hours of needed rest. There was a constant ache in his joints that only time could repair, but the sleep, brief as it was, had taken the numbness from his brain.

He had no clear plan in mind, nor was it possible to

shape up any definite course of action. There were too many conditions over which he had no control: the temper of the townsmen, and whatever action Phil Selby might have ordered Lane Harragh and his crew to take.

If the town still blamed him for the bullet that had struck down the Brighton boy, he would fight that accusation as best he could. He gave no great thought to that danger. The men of Signal had eyes, and now that they'd had time to cool off they would reason out the truth of that wild bullet Orv Shandrin had fired.

It was what Phil Selby might have ordered Harragh and his crew of gun-toughs to do that bit bleakly into Curt's mind. Phil had paid good money to Sam Brighton and the others once. He would not do it again. Next time he would use guns to take over the land that Buckle needed to round out an empire.

And it was what Hamp might have done after Monday's shooting that etched a coldness of dread into Curt Selby's mind.

Hamp knew only one way to handle a fight such as this: sand, guts, and guns. Hamp blamed himself for the ruthless giant the Buckle brand had become, and he blamed himself for the crimes of his own son. This thing had outgrown the ties of blood. One son had schemed violence against another son, and that was a crime no father could tolerate. Hamp would understand what he had to do: Phil had to be stopped. Phil had to be destroyed. To do that, Lane Harragh and his crew of hired gun-toughs would have to be destroyed.

That was the core of Curt Selby's dread as he approached the town in the dim hour of early dusk. There was violence in his father, for old Hamp had fought Indians and renegade whites to carve out his Buckle brand. Hamp had earned his land with the flame of his own anger and the quickness of his gun.

But Hamp was no longer young. The years had slowed his body, if not taming his anger. It was no detraction from the shadow of greatness he had once cast in his most competent days that he had never been the equal of Lane Harragh in a trouble of this kind.

His chances were infinitely more dire in this fight, for any stand Hamp might make against the Buckle brand would have to be made alone, without the support of friends. Hamp would know that. Curt, himself, understood it. But he knew his father would not be restrained now that Phil had taken the final irrevocable step by ordering the violence of guns used against his own kin. Hamp would do what he had to do against Phil, fearing failure more than his own death.

Selby approached the town from the south, following a sandy barranca without fully understanding the reason for this act of caution. It was the quietness of the town as much as anything that disturbed him. It was not a normal thing for this early hour of night. There should be men on the street, but when he peered out across the screening thickets he could see none. The darkened street was ominously empty, the silence of it tightening Selby's nerves with an acute uneasiness.

The barranca tapered off on the weedy backlot behind the Golden Bell saloon. He approached the rear of the building, nagged by the sensitory warning that violence waited in this silent town behind closed doors and in the minds of men.

He tried the door, and it opened easily. Stepping warily forward, he heard the small clattering sound of metallic objects kicked by his foot. He stooped, groping. They were empty shell cases. Some man had paused here at the door to reload his gun before leaving the building.

Selby moved guardedly ahead, his own gun drawn now and held at ready. He picked his way through Lew Haverhill's storeroom and down the short hallway. The saloon's main room was there before him, dimly detailed by the starshine fiiltering through the front windows.

One of those windows was shattered, only a few jagged shards of glass remaining in the frame. The acrid aroma still hanging in the air brought certainty into Selby's mind: there had been recent gunfire in this town.

He moved deeper into the room, drawn by the sprawled shape on the floor near the end of the bar. There was enough light to show him Lew Haverhill's habitual silk shirt with the ladies' garters banding the sleeves above his elbows. The bullet had caught Haverhill full in the face. There wasn't much of it. He hadn't know what hit him.

Selby straightened, the dread biting deep and cold into him. There was an overturned poker table near the shattered window, and near it was a smashed chair with the

113

body of another man folded over it, head down against the floor.

Selby squatted on his heels beside the dead man, with his back to the window. He struck a lucifer, holding the flame tightly cupped in his hands, and saw the brief flare of light strike obliquely across the dead man's face. One look was enough.

He killed the match, picked his gun from the floor, and stood up. Recognition was a certainty. The dead man was one of Lane Harragh's crew.

The answer stood bleakly in Curt Selby's mind. *This time you went all the way, Phil. This time you turned Injun.*

Chapter Nineteen

Selby stood in darkness near the shattered window, trying to piece together what had happened here. There were only a few small fragments of glass on the floor beneath the window. This meant something. And the position of the dead Buckle gunman fitted the pattern of ruthless brutality that was shaping up in Selby's mind.

There had been nothing halfway in the orders Phil had given to Lane Harragh. A Buckle gunman had been stationed at this window with orders to watch the street and be ready to kill. This much was plain to be seen, and because Selby understood the thoroughness of Phil's mind he knew other Buckle gunmen had waited at other windows along the street. For what purpose, Selby could only guess. The answer was not difficult to find. Phil would not pay twice for the outfits he wanted under the Buckle iron. The targets for his crew, therefore, had been Sam Brighton, Charley Bell and the others.

"Harragh staked out a man at this window," Selby thought bleakly. "Lew Haverhill couldn't stomach the setup, and tried to stop it. Harragh's man shot Lew. Haverhill's shotgun finished off this fellow and blew out the window behind him."

And with that understanding another thought pinched its bitter knowing into Selby's mind. *Hamp is dead, or Phil wouldn't have jumped this far.*

He went out the rear door of the saloon, out into the brooding night. The silence of the town gave a feeling of suspended violence, as though the lightning had already struck and now Signal was waiting for the thunder.

He moved guardedly through the weeds of the backlots, then turned and picked his way along the narrow lane between Ed Newlin's barber shop and the Odd Fellows' Hall. He halted at the rim of the plank walk, holding back in darkness that was untouched by the moon's rising light.

From this position the street was more clearly to be seen. There was a body face down in the middle of the street, and another sprawled closer in to the walk, with the legs drawn under it as if the man had been shot down while at full run. There was a look of frantic flight in the position of that body that death had not erased. Moonlight was pale on that rigid face. Tobe Faring, who had owned the Cat Track brand on the east side of the basin.

Selby turned back through the narrow lane, a harsh and bitter anger pumping through his blood. A cold rage that made him want to stride out into the street and send his shout through the town, to draw the men who had committed this brutality out of their hidden places and smash them with his hands and with his gun. But he clamped a lid on that rakehell impulse, realizing how completely suicidal such an act would be. There were too many things yet to be learned. Too many questions to be answered. Too many men to be searched out and identified, for there was nothing more murderously false than the apparent emptiness of the town.

He drew further back from the street, cutting a wide circle through the night. He came to Abe Korbee's livery corral, and followed the rails back to the street. There were no lights here. He went across the street at a low-bent run, and slowed to a wary trot as he circled across those backlots and came at last to the rear door of Effie's bakery. He rapped lightly on the door, and heard the muted shuffle of movement inside. And then Effie's guarded question.

"Who is it?"

"Me, Effie—Curt."

The door at once opened and he stepped swiftly into the room, hearing the click of the door locking immediately behind him. The room was without light. The darkness was impenetrable. Close beside him, he heard Effie's soft sob of relief.

"Curt! I was so afraid . . . ."

"I'm all right, Effie. What's happened here?"

"Don't you know?"

"Only that four men have been killed." Curt named the four men.

"Five, Curt," she said shallowly. "Jode Meeder is dead in his office. Lane Harragh killed him."

Selby was jolted by thorny shock. Effie seemed to sense

it. She put her hand on his arm, speaking in a voice drained of all emotion.

"Sheriff Meeder got back to the town this afternoon with his posse, just after Tobe Faring and the Roman Four man were killed. It was horrible, Curt. The sheriff closed his eyes to a lot of things Phil did, but this was too much. He ordered Buckle out of town, and Lane Harragh shot him."

Selby said in a soft and savage fury, "I've got to know everything that's happened, Effie. What brought all this to a head?"

"Anything—everything—nothing in particular, Curt." Her voice was a softly despairing cry rising up to him through the darkness. "Your father rode out to Buckle— it was just after noon on Monday, wasn't it?—and ordered Phil to get rid of Harragh's crew and stop hogging range. He didn't get anywhere. Phil only laughed at him."

She was silent for a moment. He could feel her fingers biting into his arm.

"But when Hamp learned that Phil had sent one of Harragh's men to force you into a fight and kill you— it set Hamp wild, Curt. He went at Phil with his fists— that was two days ago, I think—and then he came here to get Sam Brighton and the others to help him. They wouldn't listen to him.

"I think Hamp must have gone out of his head, Curt. He went back to Buckle while Phil and his crew were here in town. That was last night. He ripped down the new barbed wire fences, and set fire to the new bunkhouse. That wasn't enough for him. He went to Phil's big new house and smashed the windows and furniture. He burned the house down, Curt. There's nothing left of it now."

Selby smiled bleakly. Such was the tremendous fury of old Hamp when he was crowded too far. It was a satisfaction.

Effie was speaking in thin anger. "When Sam Brighton and the others heard what Hamp had done they saw how foolish they'd been. They got together the hands who used to work for them, and offered to back Hamp in his fight against Buckle. That is when Phil ordered Harragh and his crew to clean them out."

The rest Selby could guess. There were dead men in Lew Haverhill's saloon and in the dust of the street to give him the picture.

"They didn't stand a chance against Harragh and his specials," he said savagely.

"They haven't stopped trying, Curt," Effie said.

He stared sharply around. The darkness concealed the girl. She was an image seen only in his mind.

"They're all in Augie Bannon's saloon," Effie said. "Phil and Harragh took over the courthouse. Tomorrow they will finish this, Curt. There's enough of them."

A question was in Selby's mind, too long restrained. "And Hamp?"

"He was hit. Not bad, I think. He's in Bannon's place with the others."

A tremendous relief surged through Selby. He had not come too late. Hamp had paid a bitter price for his misjudgment; he had suffered his share. Death would have been an unbearable injustice after what Hamp had done.

There was a sound out back, beyond the locked door. The voice was only barely audible.

"Damned right, I saw someone! Don't know who— just a shadow of him, heading in this direction!"

Another man grunted irritably.

Then that blade-thin voice again, malignantly brittle. "This is that Coombs filly's place, ain't it? If it was Selby I saw, then here is where he came."

Selby reached through the darkness and caught Effie's arm, turning her and pushing her toward the front of the building. He drew his gun.

Someone tried the door, gently. A man's weight put thrusting pressure against the locked door. Selby lifted his gun and spaced two bullets through the panel, hearing a man's broken cry through the double blast of the shots.

He spun immediately, running through the blackness as gunfire came crashing through the door behind him. Effie had the front door open and was waiting.

"To Bannon's place," he said. "Run!"

He went along behind her at a fast lope, half turned to keep an eye on the side of the bakery. He saw movement there. Gunflame laced the night, and he felt the windy flurry of the close-passing bullets. He hauled sharply around and fired two swift shots at that shadowy shape, holding himself low. A body twisted around and fell.

Gunfire broke at him from a window of the courthouse, and he veered off at a tangent to draw the danger away from the girl. The cadence of the firing became a cannonading slam of lead raking the darkness around him. Bullets plowed the dust of the street, squalling viciously, and slugs slammed the saloon's siding as he went running along the plank walk. He lengthened his strides. An explosion of splinters needled his face as he hit the saloon's batwing doors. The racket of shooting dropped off, the silence so abrupt that it hurt his ears.

There was a man pulling Selby roughly down to the floor. A close voice said, sharply, "That you, Curt?"

The man was Sam Brighton.

"Yes," Selby said.

"Man," Brighton grunted, "you used up more than your share of luck when you came through that barrage."

Selby looked around. "Your boy, Sam—how bad was he hit?"

"He'll be up and around in a week," Brighton said, and wagged his head bitterly. "A lot of things happened I'm sorry about. There's times when a man can't think straight."

"No fault of yours, Sam." There was just enough skyshine coming through the saloon's wide windows to give shape to the room and its occupants, but no clear details. "Is Hamp here, Sam?"

"Yonder by the wall. Hit, but still cussing. That old walrus bleeds vinegar and vitriol," Brighton said with crusty admiration.

Selby touched Effie's arm, and they made their way across the room. Hamp lay face down on a pair of tables that had been drawn together against the wall. There was a look of pure outrage etched across the pain that had bleached his craggy face. He lifted his head at Selby's approach, blinking.

"That you, Curt?"

"Yes. How bad is it, Hamp?"

"Never you mind!" Hamp snapped, and pivoted his glare between Curt and the girl, his face abruptly congesting. "Damn it all," he said peevishly, "get that female away from here. Can't a man suffer in privacy?"

Uncomprehending resentment rose warmly in Selby. "Don't try to take your hurts out on someone else, Hamp," he said softly.

The cowman snorted. "Damn it, you don't know," he grunted. "I've got nothing against Effie. It's just that I caught a bullet in a mighty bashful place."

Charley Bell was squatting near the table, a short gray man who seldom smiled. He was not smiling now as he looked up at Selby.

"He'll be sitting one-sided for the next month," he said. "Any other time this would be worth a laugh. Right now it ain't. You see anything outside, Curt?"

Selby shook his head. "Only the dead ones."

"What about that shooting over at Effie's place?"

"A couple of Harragh's men had ideas. I hit one. Maybe both."

"Bad enough to check them out of this?"

"I don't know."

"Makes no difference," Charley Bell said with weary anger. "Harragh has got enough guns left to finish this any time he takes the notion, now or tomorrow." He turned and walked away, saying to Effie, "There's a man over here you ought to look after, young lady."

Selby picked up an overturned chair and set it right. The room was a shambles of upended tables and chairs that had been chucked aside during the heat of the fight. The backbar mirror was no more, and the front windows had been raked out by savage lead. The acrid stench of burned powder still laced the air, and across the room where Effie had gone a man was groaning softly.

"That's Howie Jackson, over yonder," Hamp said with quiet bitterness. "Wrangled for Tobe Faring. You remember him? Howie took one in the belly. Not a chance—not a chance."

Selby closed his eyes. Too many had died. Tobe Faring lay dead out there in the street, and in this room a man who had worked for him was dying. Too many dead. Too many yet to die.

"I sure played hell with things," Hamp said, his voice low and raw with self-accusation.

Selby opened his eyes. He looked at his father. "All you did was bring this to a head," he said shortly. "It had to be done sooner or later. Phil had to be stopped sometime."

"Does this look like he's stopped?" Hamp demanded bitterly. "Eight men in this room, and one of them dying with a gunshot belly! Harragh's got twice that many out

120

there, and all them the best that Phil could buy. Does this look like I've stopped anything?"

"Don't ride yourself, Hamp." Then Selby said quietly, "A drink?"

"It might help."

Selby got out of his chair and went around the end of the bar. The glass of bullet-smashed bottles crunched under his boots like brittle gravel. The air back here was rank with the smell of spilled whiskey. He took a bottle down from the shelf, carried it back to the man on the tables, twisting the cork out as he walked.

Handing the bottle over, he saw the silent question in Hamp's eyes and shook his head wryly. Hamp shrugged, and drank alone.

A gunshot suddenly punctured the silence of the night. There was the sound of breaking glass and a man's hooting cry from across the street. Hamp cursed with soft savagery.

"They've been doing that for two hours now. Potshooting just to keep us jumpy. Why the hell don't they come on across and get this over with?"

Selby said quietly, "What about Phil, Hamp?"

It was a question Hamp had asked himself many times, always closing his mind to the answer. There was misery in his eyes. What did a father do about a son who had turned wolf? Use a gun on him, or turn aside and leave it for someone else to do? The demands of justice could be a terrible thing. The commandments of a man's own blood could be infinitely more cruel.

"I don't know, Curt. I just don't know."

A man was crouching at the window. He jerked around, his warning a thin, strangled sound through the darkness.

"They're coming out! God A'mighty, couldn't they wait until tomorrow?"

Chapter Twenty

Through the empty window Selby saw them come out of the courthouse and into the street. Shadows moving in the darkness, not men. But shadows that knew all the quick and violent ways of killing. They moved unhurriedly, spaced apart from each other in the manner of men wise to all the facets of this kind of work. Men bending low behind drawn guns, awaiting only the signal that would send them plunging forward to smash and destroy.

This was the end of the waiting. Selby could feel the pressures crushing down on the men around him. Those same compulsions were tearing at his own nerves and mind. Fear was a sourness in his throat, but it was the controlled fear of a mature man. No panic. Only the regrets that this thing had to be.

His gaze kept picking at those advancing shapes until he found Phil, with Lane Harragh moving close at Phil's side. He knew then what he had to do.

He sent his command flatly through the darkness of the room. "No guns. No shooting."

Sam Brighton was at his side. Astonished, half rankled, Brighton jerked around. "What else is there, man?"

"No guns!" said Selby harshly.

A man caught at him as he turned and went to the door; he thrust that fellow roughly aside and strode on. Out the doors, hearing them slap shut behind him on their spring hinges. Hearing Effie's agonized cry of protest.

His appearance brought the Buckle gunmen to an abrupt halt, staring at him. A man grunted with harsh amazement.

"By God! That's the big fellow himself!"

Selby thrust his voice flatly through the street's sudden hush. "I've got something to tell you, Phil."

And he heard Phil's brittle refusal, a cold and completely passionless denial.

"Not to me, you haven't. Harragh will deal with you."

Selby stared in silent wonderment. This, then, was Phil's final repudiation of blood, his uncompromising rejection of family. He had built a wall around himself with ambitions that were relentless, unrelenting, and now he stood alone and aloof, owing nothing, demanding everything.

"It would be easier now if I could hate you," Selby said with quiet regret. "But I can't. I can only pity you, Phil."

Lane Harragh spoke out in his thin, overbearing way. "Any talk you've got to make, fellow, you can make to me! We're tired of waiting. Speak out, man!"

Selby shifted his gaze to Lane Harragh. There was finality in the gunman's stare, the pitiless demands of a man tremendously aware of his competence with a gun. Violence was the tool of his trade, to be used as needed without compuction or conscience. He would not care.

Selby said slowly, "What is it you want?"

Harragh grinned savagely. "Get out of this town. Out of the basin, you and all those others holed up behind you. One price, fellow—that's it!"

There was movement on the far ends of the street. Men were coming forward through the darkness. Selby was puzzled. Danger was here, restrained by the thinnest of margins, and on this street curiosity could be swiftly fatal. Yet the men kept coming forward.

Selby put them out of his mind, saying steadily, "And if we don't?"

Harragh was malignantly pleasant. "We'll give you a good burial."

The street was filling up on both sides. Masses of men moving in silence. There were women among them. This was a thing Selby could not understand. These were people who hated him as the man who wanted to rip apart the power of the Buckle brand and bring an end to their easy ways. Buckle was their patron. They were supported by Buckle's benficence, humbling themselves to the will of the iron.

Selby set those people out of his mind. They hated him. They did not care.

He looked steadily at Lane Harragh in whom such a world of virulence lived. "What happens to this town?" he asked slowly.

Harragh's malevolence tightened. "What the hell does that have to do with you?" he demanded insolently.

"Several things," Selby answered. "Important things, Harragh."

He slanted his head toward the saloon behind him. "Those men in there aren't thinking only of their land. This is bigger than that, Harragh. They want a town that the Territory will respect. Not just a one-ranch town, but a town where the little people will have a chance."

Harragh snorted sardonically, a corrosive sound.

"They want a town where a man won't have to get permission from the ruling ranch before he can go into business. They want to be their own men, and have schools for their kids and churches . . . ."

Harragh's temper suddenly blared. "I've heard enough of this hogwash! You and that bunch behind you—you've got just one minute to get out of this town!"

There was a shifting of the masses. A slow and heavy stirring. Out of them a man's voice rose clearly—not much out of normal pitch—strongly.

"We like the way he tells it, Harragh. These men are staying."

Lane Harragh jerked violently around. His men readied themselves, alerted to a new danger, disturbed but not yet afraid.

Deadliness was in Harragh, his temper spiring to a terrible pitch. His voice was a savage, whiplashing sound.

"Clear out, all of you! I'll give you the same sixty seconds to empty this street!"

No man moved. The masses stood motionless. Men who wore guns. Men who knew the quickness of honest dread, but in whom rode the strong, steady currents that could thrust aside fear itself. Signal had planted its feet on the ground, and if there was to be death here there would be a far richer life on the street tomorrow. Signal was claiming its own place under the sun.

There was no longer that towering surety in Lane Harragh. He did not have enough guns to fight a thing like this. Guns were not enough, and he knew what a town could do with its hands when it was crowded too far. The decisiveness in him was no longer cold rock. It changed to clay. It changed to sand running swifty out of him.

Phil saw this and shouted in a wild, insensate way at

Harragh. "Kill that man!" He pointed a rigid finger at Selby, his face livid with a madness of rage. "Harragh, kill that man, I said!"

And when Lane Harragh did not move, the rage swept all sanity out of Phil, and he shouted in a completely berserk way and went running head-on at Selby, firing in savage fury.

The bullet came from one of the townsmen. Or it came from some man inside the saloon. Or it came, driven by bitter malice, from one of Lane Harragh's defeated crew.

No man on the street could say for certain who fired the shot that put an end to Phil's murderous run. Only the fact mattered. There were no questions to come afterwards, only acceptance. There were many shapes to the justice of a harsh range, and out of the ashes of violence grew things that would endure. It had always been so.

The bullet slammed Phil to an abrupt halt, and he loosened, and he fell. One of Harragh's men shouted and fired at Curt Selby, his slug missing by the narrowest of margins. Then Harragh's guns were leaping and flaming.

The street roared. The gunswifts of the Buckle brand stood in knotted malice against the fury of the town, and then those men were down in the dust of the street, and Harragh alone remained untouched. He fired, and Selby felt the sting of the bullet against the flesh of his shoulder. Selby twisted aside and sent his shot at the man, hearing the wind of Harragh's second bullet against his ear. He fired again, and moved forward through the black haze of powder smoke, the hammer eared back at ready. Then he let the hammer roll forward under his thumb, sparing that bullet.

A look of shocked wonderment was in Lane Harragh's face as he gazed at Selby. His voice was a slack sound.

"Didn't allow you were this good, Selby."

There were bitter regrets that came to a man at times like this. "I'm sorry this had to happen, Harragh."

The gunman didn't hear him. The words came drifting through his parted lips. "It's the only time I ever misjudged a man. In all my time, it's the only mistake I ever. . . ."

His legs let go, and he slowly fell.

It was much later before Selby and Effie were given a moment to themselves. The street had emptied, and quiet had returned to the town.

She came to him and put her hand on his arm, for a while not speaking. She had this ability to accept silence without protest, giving a man his own thoughts and time for aloneness.

Presently she spoke quietly, "You're thinking about Phil?"

"Yes. And about Hamp."

"Hamp will forget all the bad things," Effie said softly. "He'll remember only the good. It's always that way, isn't it?"

"I don't know, Effie. That's what I was wondering."

"It is, Curt. Believe me, it is!"

Suddenly the uncertainty was gone out of him. Suddenly the weight was lifted, and in him there was the buoyance of the promised tomorrows rising strongly through him. He turned to the girl and drew her to him, a little impatiently.

"There are a million tomorrows waiting for us, Effie."

"There is only tonight, Curt," she whispered.

THE END

Ute Country
by JOHN S. DANIELS

One

CLAY MAJORS ROSE EARLY as was his habit, a habit that controlled him as completely in his hotel room in Gunnison on this June morning as it did on his ranch in the Ute reservation. He shaved, went downstairs for breakfast, and, returning to his room, packed the small bag he had brought with him and for a moment stood in front of the mirror vainly trying to comb his dark, unruly hair so it would stay in place.

He was afraid, an emotion he recognized for what it was. Funny, he thought, what scares a man. He was never frightened by a problem he could solve with his big, capable hands. Or with a gun or rope or ax, for these were tools which he used often and well. But today he faced another kind of situation, one which required finesse instead of strength.

In half an hour the train from Denver would pull into the depot and Margaret Trent would step down. What he said and did in those first few seconds could well determine his future, his and Margaret's. They had been engaged for a year, but he had been in love with her longer than that.

Oddly enough, he was never ill at ease when he went to see her in Denver, but he was now, and he would be when he saw her. The difference, he knew, lay in the fact that Margaret had never been west of Denver, and he wasn't sure she could live in this new, raw country. He was sure of only one thing. He could not live in Denver. That left one alternative. He had to convince Margaret she could live here.

Turning to the bed, he picked up his gun belt and buckled it around his middle. Margaret had never seen him wear a gun. He wondered what she would think when she saw it. He had pleaded with her to come, assuring her there was no danger from the Indians. There wouldn't be, he thought, but he hadn't told her there might be danger from white outlaws. Well, one thing was certain. The gun on his hip was the best way to insure her safety.

He picked up his bag and went downstairs. Forcing his way through the crowded lobby, he paid at the desk and, as he turned toward the door, he heard a man say, "Why, by God, it's Clay Majors."

Larry Casteel! Just to hear his voice was enough to make the short hairs on the back of Clay's neck stand straight out. He stood motionless as he fought his temper. This was one day when he wanted no trouble, not even with Larry Casteel.

Blood pounded in his temples; one hand tightened on the handle of his bag, the other clenched at his side. He turned slowly, and said, his tone as courteous as he could make it, "Hello, Casteel. I didn't know you were in Gunnison."

Casteel was a gambler and a showman from the mining camp of Ouray on up the Uncompahgre from the Los Pinos Agency. He was in his middle thirties, five or six years older than Clay, a big man not quite as tall as Clay but heavier in the shoulders.

Handsome, if you like a man who waxed his mustache and wore expensive clothes and a diamond ring and a pearl-handled gun and smelled as if he had just taken a bath in cologne. Clay didn't, but he grudgingly admitted that the man had an appeal to women, a fact which Clay could not understand, because he knew Casteel was predatory and vicious and had only one measurement in his judgment of women—their capacity as bed partners.

Clay didn't make a habit of hating people, but he had plenty of reason to hate Casteel. He had tangled with him the first week he had come to the western slope six years before. With a couple of partners, he had staked out a townsite above the Los Pinos Agency just east of the reservation. Casteel had bucked it and had started a rival townsite where there was room for only one. In the end both men had withdrawn and the townsites had been merged, but the feeling between the two that had started then had grown with the years.

Clay would never forget the night he had played poker in Casteel's Gay Lady Variety Theatre and had lost heavily. He knew he had been cheated, but he couldn't prove it. He would not forget, either, another occasion when he'd quarreled with Casteel about the Utes, and Casteel had called him an Indian-lover and said Clay must be sharing the blanket of some Ute squaw or he wouldn't like them so much.

The fight he'd had with Casteel after that was one he'd always remember. It was the most bitter of all the brawls he'd had, and ended only because both men had been so physically exhausted they couldn't continue.

Now there was a short moment of silence, Casteel's bold gaze raking Clay's face, his expression truculent, and Clay, remembering the other fight, knew he had to avoid one this morning or he would lose Margaret before he got her out of Gunnison.

"I've been in town a couple of days on business," Casteel said, then he raised his voice so everyone in the lobby could hear. "What do your Ute friends say, Majors? Are they ready to move?"

The lobby was jammed with mining men, drummers, cowboys, railroad men, and pilgrims waiting to settle on the reservation. Gunnison was a boom town, the center of a prosperous mining area, and for the time being the end of steel. Outlaws might be in the room, too, for law was slack and fortunes constantly changed hands over the gambling tables or in dark alleys or on the lonely trails that radiated out from Gunnison to every point of the compass.

Possibly the room was filled with Casteel's friends. Clay didn't know and didn't care. All he wanted was to get out of the lobby without a fight, but it wouldn't be easy. With the feeling as tense as it was in Gunnison, all Casteel had to do was to brand him a "Ute-lover" and somebody would talk about finding a rope.

"I haven't heard a thing," Clay said, and started toward the door.

"Hold on," Casteel said loudly, taking him by the arm. "It's Ute-lovers like you who have kept the damned savages in Colorado. You ought to have something to say to these boys."

Clay jerked free from Casteel's grip, aware that the lobby had become ominously silent, that every man in the room was staring at him. He knew exactly what Casteel was trying to do. This crowd could be turned into a mob in a matter of minutes. When it got done with him, he'd be laid up in bed for a week, Margaret wouldn't know why he hadn't met her, and Casteel wouldn't even have his white silk shirt soiled.

"The moving of the Utes is up to the commissioners and the cavalry at the cantonment," Clay said. "It's none of my business."

"I figure you've got your hand in the pie, Majors," Casteel said. "After all, you were big chief Ouray's friend and that's why you've got the only ranch inside the reservation. I can see men in this room who have been waiting for a piece of that good land like you've got. All we've heard for months is that the Indians are going to be moved to Utah. Well, we've got a right to know when."

A growl rose from the crowd, ominous, animallike. Casteel wouldn't have to say much more to fan into flame the fire that smoldered inside nearly every man in Gunnison. Hatred for the Utes had existed since the Thornburgh fight and the

Meeker massacre almost two years ago. Once the Utes were gone, the hysteria would die down, but it was here now, ready to erupt into violence, and Casteel was working on it like a master.

Without another word, Clay wheeled and rammed his way through the crowd toward the door, shouldering and elbowing men out of his path as though they were ninepins. Someone cursed him. One man yelped in pain as Clay's elbow caught him in the stomach.

Above the sudden fury of sound that rose from the crowd, Casteel's voice was easily heard, "Gents, there goes the Number One Ute-lover in Colorado. I've often wondered how many breed kids he's started among the Uncompahgre Utes."

A man yelled, "Don't let him get away. Let's work him over."

Another said, "I wish I had that ranch he's got."

And a third, "He looks like rope bait to me."

Clay reached the door as one man put out a hand to grab him. Clay shoved the hand aside, but another one gripped his shoulder. Suddenly furious, so furious he lost his self-control for a moment, he whirled on the man and hit him squarely on the jaw, sending him reeling back into the arms of a man behind him.

Clay backed against the wall beside the door, right hand on his gun butt. He shouted, "If any of you want to make me the goat this morning, you can do it, but it'll cost some lives."

His gaze swept the room. He felt their hate pushing at him, saw it in their eyes, in the way they stood, tense, excited, wanting to take their anger out on him, but now that they faced him they found him too formidable. So the seconds ticked off, Clay hearing his own breathing and feeling the pound of the blood in his temples. Whatever happened, he wasn't going to take a beating from these men even if he had to kill some of them. They must have sensed the brittle quality of his temper, for they stood motionless, staring at him.

A man near the foot of the stairs slowly dropped his hand to the butt of his gun, standing with his left side to Clay so his motion wouldn't be seen, but Clay caught it. A couple of drummers between him and Clay almost fell down getting out of the way when Clay drew his gun and lined it on the man at the foot of the stairs.

"Go ahead, mister," Clay said. "I don't know you and I sure don't want to, but if you pull that gun, you'll be in hell quick and sudden."

The man's hand fell away. Clay nodded at Casteel. "You're

the gent that kicked up the dust. You want a try at me again?"

It was a risky gamble and Clay knew it, but he was going on the assumption that Casteel didn't want a fight himself or he wouldn't have worked on the crowd as he had. He was right, for Casteel shook his head.

"Not today. I said I was in town on business. Very pleasant business, too. I'm meeting the train."

Clay edged toward the door. He said, "Stay inside. Poke your nose outside within the next three minutes and you'll get it shot off."

He backed through the door, gun still in his hand, and waited a moment. An explosion of talk broke out from inside the lobby, but no one came through the door. Turning, Clay worked his way through the heavy traffic of ore wagons and burro trains and men on horseback that clogged Gunnison's Main Street from early morning to darkness. He reached the opposite side and strode on toward the depot, walking fast because he had to do something to blunt the edge of his temper.

He had been lucky and he knew it. If someone else had picked up the quarrel after Casteel had dropped it, he'd have been in trouble. Not that he'd settled anything. Sooner or later he would kill Casteel or Casteel would kill him. That was written in the book, but at least he had avoided a showdown today. Later, after Margaret had gone back to Denver, he would welcome a finish fight with Casteel.

When he reached the depot, he saw that the Agency stage stood waiting on the opposite side of the platform from the tracks. The driver, Slim Galt, nodded at Clay as he came up. He was a splinter of a man about Clay's age with a melancholy face and a tired, tobacco-stained mustache. He had been in the country for years and, like Clay, understood and sympathized with the Utes, which was one reason he was Clay's good friend.

"You bucked the tiger, lost your shirt, and now you're ready to go home," Galt said.

Clay shook his head, and then, because he had to blow off to someone, he told Galt what had happened in the hotel lobby.

Galt nodded as he fished a match out of his vest pocket and began to chew on it. "You were lucky to get out of it that easy. This town's ready to pop. If a Ute rode in here, they'd hang him the minute they spotted him."

"I know that," Clay said, "but nothing would have happened if Casteel had kept his mouth shut."

"Sure, and if he's alive the day they bury you, he'll dance

on your coffin." He tipped his head back and squinted at Clay. "You'd better get used to the idea of riding back with him. He's meeting a girl here and taking her to Ouray just like he's been doing for years. By God, he uses women up faster'n a hog eats slop."

Clay cursed bitterly. "Who is it this time?"

"Judy Allen. You know her, don't you?" Clay nodded, and Galt went on, "Used to sing in the Palace right here in Gunnison, then she went to Leadville. Denver, too, I hear. Anyhow, Casteel's given her a job singing in his Gay Lady in Ouray. Same old story." Galt's temper exploded as he spit the match out of his mouth. "Clay, if you don't kill that son of a bitch, I will."

Clay heard the hoarse whistle of the train above town; he heard the steady clanging of the bell, but the sounds seemed to come from a great distance. He cried out, "If I'd known about Judy, I'd have killed him in the hotel."

"Would have been the wrong place." Galt's sour expression remained unaltered. "Maybe you'll get a crack at him tonight."

Clay nodded absently, thinking of Judy Allen. He had known her when she was here, an attractive, statuesque girl who had the best soprano voice he'd ever heard. He had taken her to supper twice, enjoying her company as any lonely man would when his own girl was a long ways off. At the time it had been common gossip that several of the wealthiest men in town had propositioned her and she'd turned them down.

Now, thinking back, he realized how much he had admired her, how perfect the hours had been he'd spent with her. She was a direct, straightforward woman who didn't dissemble. He remembered how thoroughly at ease he had been with her, not having to watch every word he said as he did with most women. If it hadn't been for Margaret, he would have kept in touch with her. But for her to go to work for Larry Casteel was . . .

"You remember Geneva?" Galt was saying. "A little blond dancer who was at the Palace last winter?"

The train was coming in, brakes screaming, the bell still clanging. Clay had to step closer to Galt to hear. "I remember," he said. "Casteel took her to Ouray last March. They stayed overnight at my place."

Galt nodded. "I ain't likely to forget it. I was driving that run. I sure cottoned to Geneva. Never missed a show when she was at the Palace if I was here. The way she twisted around up there on the stage and threw her butt at you was enough to make a man forget home and mother and everything else. I told Casteel I'd kill him if he done her like he done the others. He just laughed in my face."

Galt stared down at his big-knuckled hands. "I'm scared of him, I guess. I sure ain't no gunslinger and they say he is." He took a long breath. "Maybe I'll plug him yet. You heard?" Clay shook his head. "Casteel took her in for a couple of months, then throwed her out. Now she's doing business in a crib along the river. Looks ten years older'n she done last March when you seen her."

The locomotive coasted by with a great charging and hissing of steam, the bell adding its clanging to the racket. Two baggage cars clattered past; then, as the train jerked to a stop, the crowd surged toward the passenger cars and there was a hubbub of shouting and people shoving and waving at one another.

Men piled out of the cars as the locomotive stood panting on the track. Some of the men were miners, others pilgrims who would join the crowd waiting for the reservation to open. Later the women and children got down, families joining husbands and fathers who had come on ahead to find places to live.

As Clay walked around the platform, he saw Casteel a couple of cars up the track. Judy Allen stepped down, tall and graceful and to Clay's eyes altogether lovely. Casteel greeted her and took her valises.

Fury burned through Clay as he watched. He told himself that if Casteel ruined Judy the way he had Geneva and so many others, he would kill him. He wasn't like Slim Galt. He would do it. Larry Casteel had been permitted to live far too long. He should be removed like any monster that preyed upon the weak.

But Clay held back, knowing he couldn't jump the man now. He'd hunt him up in Ouray after Margaret had gone home. He didn't know how fast Casteel was with a gun, but the man had at least three killings to his credit. Maybe more. Well, it didn't make any difference. He'd——

Then he saw Margaret getting down from the same car in which Judy had ridden, slender and pretty just as he had remembered her from the last time he'd been in Denver. He had never noticed until this moment how delicate her features were, how small she was, fragile-appearing among the big-bosomed, wide-hipped women who belonged in this country, and suddenly the familiar fears and doubts were in him again.

He bulled his way through the crowd, yelling, "Margaret," loud enough for her to hear over the racket that was being made by a hundred people. Then he reached her and she smiled and said,

"Clay, Clay, it's been so long."

He swept her into his arms and kissed her. She clung to him, hungry for his kiss and returning it with a fire he had never felt in her before, and in that moment all the doubts were gone.

Two

CLAY TOOK THE LEATHER VALISE from Margaret, saying, "The stage is on the other side of the depot. I'll take you to it and then I'll get the rest of your luggage."

"There isn't any more, Clay," she said. "This is all I brought."

He glanced down at her as they made their way through the scattering crowd. Again a small doubt stirred in him. It wasn't like Margaret to travel light, so she didn't intend to stay long.

He said impulsively, "Margaret, let's get married here in Gunnison. Today. We can take the stage in the morning."

She looked up at him, smiling tolerantly as she did when he suggested something that was boyishly foolish. "I'd like to, Clay, but I promised Mamma I'd bring you back to Denver with me and we'd have a church wedding."

Her small hand was on his arm, her chic straw hat with the red feather coming barely to his shoulder. He looked at her and then glanced away, swallowing his disappointment. Not that he had expected her to say she'd get married today, but he knew she had been counting on a church wedding, and it bothered him that she would use her mother as an excuse.

She was wearing a gray traveling suit that fitted her perfectly and went well with her blond coloring, and it came to him in a flood of hopelessness that these were the kind of clothes she should always wear, that she belonged in Denver, not out here where she could expect nothing but hard work and privation and even danger, danger that he had lied about when he had written that it did not exist.

Actually it didn't exist in Clay's mind, for physical danger never bothered him. He had lived with it most of his life and he expected it. He had not realized he'd lied, but he knew now he had, and he sensed she was afraid by the way she clung to his arm, the way she held back. Her gaze swept the crowd that was moving toward Main Street, then fastened upon the stage and the horses and Slim Galt.

"It's wild and primitive, isn't it, Clay?" She sighed. "Living in Denver and looking at the mountains is one thing, but riding on a train with the track hanging on the side of a cliff and the world dropping off below you is something else."

"They don't have any trouble except sometimes in winter," he said.

He loved her too much, he thought, so much that he had worked and planned and schemed to get his ranch up Cimarron way, to make a home for her that would be his, once the Utes were gone and the reservation was thrown open to settlement, loved her so much that he had not fully realized he belonged here but she didn't.

She kept looking around, eyes flicking from one thing to another, then she sighed again as if relieved. "I don't see any Indians, Clay."

"You wouldn't here," he told her. "We're not on the reservation. If you want to see them, we can go on in the morning to the Los Pinos Agency."

"No, no," she said quickly. "I never want to see an Indian. Especially a Ute. When I think what happened to that poor Mr. Meeker, and the others who were there, and the women . . ." She shuddered. "I heard Rose Meeker speak in Denver after the massacre. It's too terrible even to think about."

There was no use to tell her that Nathan Meeker had brought the trouble on by his lack of understanding, that there were many good Utes. Ouray when he had been alive. His wife Chipeta. Sapinero who had become head chief after Ouray's death. Santo. No, he had better remain silent, for Margaret's sentiments were those of probably 99 per cent of the white people of Colorado, and from the tone of her voice she wasn't likely to change her feelings.

When they reached the waiting stage, Clay said to Slim Galt, "Slim, I want you to meet my future wife, Margaret Trent. Margaret, this is our driver. He's the best whipster on the western slope."

Margaret gave Galt her hand as he took off his hat. "I'm pleased to meet you, Mr. Galt. I hope you will get us safely to Clay's ranch."

"Ma'am," Galt said with exaggerated gravity, "I always

get my passengers safely to where they're going. Last week we had to fight our way through a herd of cougars. The week before it was rattlesnakes. The week before that it was the Injuns. Five thousand howling, painted hostiles attacked the stage going down Cedar Creek. I drove 'em off single-handed, killing 2,301, and didn't lose a single passenger."

Galt strode away, his lips holding no semblance of a smile. Margaret whirled on Clay. "You wrote to me there wasn't any danger . . ."

"Hold on, honey," he said. "Can't you tell when you're being joshed? Slim never has any trouble."

She stared at him a moment, then tried to smile, and failed. He put an arm around her slim waist and hugged her. She looked up at him, the corners of her mouth working. "It was such a long ride. I thought I'd never get here. I . . . I guess I'm just tired." Tears rolled down her face. She wiped them away impatiently, her hand streaking a cinder down one cheek.

Clay said, "Sure you are," and thought of the day-long trip in the stage that was ahead of them.

Trying to take her mind off what Galt had said and mentally castigating him for his brand of humor, Clay patted the body of the stage, asking, "Ever ride in a coach?"

She seemed to see the vehicle for the first time. For a moment her eyes were on the intricate scrollwork, then she glanced at the whip with its silver ferules, the big brass side lamps, the body painted a rich red, and finally at the horses with their shining harness buckles and ivory rings. She murmured, "It's very pretty, isn't it?"

"Slim takes a lot of pride in it," Clay said. "Stage drivers are a breed by themselves. Like captains on a ship. When you're a passenger, you take orders. They're good because they have to be, and Slim's the best."

She turned from the coach. "Let's walk, Clay. I was on the train so long I'm not sure I can."

They moved past the platform and along the cinders beside the track, deserted now. Suddenly she burst out, "Come back to Denver with me, Clay. Dad will take you into the hotel as a partner. We'd be comfortable living there. And happy."

"Comfortable but not happy," he said gently. "I've tried to make you understand how it is in my letters, but I'm not a very good letter writer."

"Oh, but you are, Clay. And we would be happy. You'd see."

He shook his head. "It would have been different if I'd been a fifty-niner like your dad was. He went up Clear

Creek and made a strike, then he built his hotel and it's made a good living for you and your mother ever since. But he did it himself, Margaret. He didn't depend on his father-in-law."

She looked up at his angular roughhewn face. "You're a good man, Clay, or I wouldn't love you, and you're so strong you can twist and shape things and people the way you want them." She shook her head. "But you're stubborn, Clay. Terribly stubborn."

They stopped, Margaret facing him, and he wondered bleakly if love was enough to give two people happiness. He said slowly, "I know what I can do and what I can't. Living in town is something I can't do. That's why I wanted you to come here and see my place. I've worked hard to make something out of it for you and our children."

"Of course you've worked hard, Clay," she said, "and I want to see your ranch. I've got a problem, too. I have to find out if I can live in your country. If I can't . . ." She stopped and turned away as if that was a possibility she could not face, then she added a little bitterly, "Must it be the woman who has to give, Clay?"

"I think so," he said. "At least my woman has to because I can't." He put his hands on her shoulders. "I love you, Margaret. I'll make a good home for you. I promise."

She smiled wearily. "I know you will. I'll try to like your country. I really will."

He glanced at the stage. "Looks like Slim's ready to load. We'd better get back."

They returned to the coach, Clay more troubled than he wanted Margaret to know. All of his fears were justified, he knew, and he knew, too, that many of the same fears had been in Margaret's mind. He should have been more honest with her. He was thirty, she was twenty-three. They couldn't go on putting off their marriage. That was why these next hours were so important. Decision must come of her visit.

He gave her a hand up into the coach. She moved across the seat to the opposite window, he sat in the middle, and a boy got in beside him, a boy not more than eighteen. He carried a gun, Clay saw. He had an old young face, and a tough one, hardened by life far beyond his years. A middle-aged man got in and sat facing Margaret. Judy Allen followed, then Casteel.

Slim Galt climbed to the box and cracked his whip, and the coach rolled. The boy next to Clay leaned forward, looking out of the window, and it seemed to Clay he gave a signal to someone outside, a bare lifting of the hand that might have meant something, or nothing.

Clay leaned forward and looked out, thinking that only a moment before no one had been there. But there was now, two horsemen whom he knew only by the names of Julio and Grat, hardcases who hung around the Gunnison saloons and had been in jail at least twice for disturbing the peace.

Julio was forty or more, a slender man with a hooked nose and a long scar down his left cheek that might have come from a knife fight years ago. Grat was younger, short and heavy-set, with a pair of eyes as brittle and hard as obsidian.

Clay glanced at the boy, but he was staring straight ahead, his face telling Clay nothing. The stage swept on past the two riders, who paid no attention to it. He was imagining things, Clay told himself. He was just worried about Margaret, hoping nothing would happen that would disturb or upset her.

He settled back against the seat, suddenly aware that Judy Allen was looking at him. She said, "Why, Mr. Majors, I didn't realize who you were, getting settled and all."

He touched the brim of his hat, uneasy because Margaret would probably ask how he happened to know a variety-theater singer. He said, "How are you, Judy?"

"Oh, I'm fine," she said. "You know Mr. Casteel, don't you?"

"I know him," Clay said.

"Sure he knows me," Casteel said, laughing, his white teeth much in evidence. "And I know him."

"I'm going to Ouray with him," Judy explained. "To sing in his Gay Lady. I have a sixty-day engagement."

Clay glanced at Casteel who nodded and smiled, his face a mask of good humor. Clay turned his eyes away. If he had trouble with Casteel today, it would be because the man forced it upon him.

"We're going to be cooped up in this shebang all day," Casteel said. "Tomorrow, too, for most of us, so we might as well get acquainted. I'm Larry Casteel. I own the Gay Lady in Ouray and I came to Gunnison to meet my new singer, Judy Allen."

Judy nodded, smiling. "I'm pleased to meet all of you. I hope you'll come to Ouray to hear me."

She was tall and strong-bodied with brown eyes so dark they were nearly black, and a great love for life that Clay admired in any woman. She was handsome with natural coloring in her cheeks, and Clay remembered he was surprised the first time he had been close to her. Unlike most entertainers, she used very little make-up.

"Your turn," Casteel said, motioning at Clay.

"Clay Majors. My ranch is an overnight stop, so I'll be your host tonight." He motioned toward Margaret. "My fiancée, Miss Trent."

Casteel tipped his hat, and Judy said, "How nice, Miss Trent. I remember seeing you on the train. You're fortunate, marrying a man like Clay Majors."

"I'd say it was the other way around, Judy," Casteel said. "I don't understand how Big Ugly here managed to have a beautiful woman like Miss Trent fall in love with him."

"He's not Big Ugly," Margaret said spiritedly, "and I resent your . . ."

"Forgive me." Casteel raised a defensive hand, laughing. "It was just a figure of speech. All of us who know Clay Majors appreciate his many . . . shall we say, virtues. And his faults, too. I envy a man who is loved by a woman who rises to his defense." He nodded at the middle-aged man on the other side of Judy. "And you, sir?"

"Jason Brimlow, from Denver." He sat bolt upright, a pudgy man with the pale cheeks of one who seldom saw the sun. He clutched a leather satchel as if he were afraid it might become alive and leap off his lap. He licked liver-brown lips and glanced past Judy at Casteel. "I'm going to Ouray on business."

"I'm at your service," Casteel said, "if I can do anything for you while you're in Ouray. I'm well acquainted there."

"Thank you," Brimlow said, and looked out of the window, fingers tightening on the satchel, plainly indicating he wished to be left out of the conversation.

"You," Casteel said, nodding at the boy next to Clay, his tone curt.

"None of your Goddamned business," the boy snarled.

Clay's elbow slammed hard into the kid's ribs, jolting breath out of him. "There's ladies present," he said.

"I'm sorry, ma'am," the boy said to Margaret. "I ain't been around decent women lately and I clean forgot my manners. I'm Pete Shannon. I've got a job in a mine above Ouray."

"What's the name of the mine?" Clay asked.

"I forget," Shannon said, and, as Brimlow had, turned his head to stare out of the window.

After that they rode in silence for a time, Judy's cheeks feverishly bright, her eyes fastened on the reticule in her lap. They crossed the river west of town, hoofs drumming on the heavy planks, then Galt let the horses out, and the town fell behind and was lost to sight, dust dripping from the wheels and drifting into the coach.

Casteel took a cigar out of his coat pocket, glanced at Margaret and replaced it. For a time there was no sound but the rhythmic pound of hoofs in the dust and the groan of the leather braces. Then two riders galloped by between the coach and the river. Glancing at them as they passed, Clay saw they were Julio and Grat. He pondered this for a moment, Margaret's head resting on his shoulder, and worry grew in him.

They were tough hands, but whether they were the kind of cheap hardcases who were capable of nothing worse than rolling a drunk in an alley behind a saloon, or whether they were road agents who could hold up a stage, was a question in Clay's mind. Both kinds were plentiful in Gunnison these days. Again, Clay thought, he wouldn't have been giving it the slightest worry if Margaret hadn't been in the coach. If he had any chance to persuade her to stay, it would be by proving that this land which seemed so violent to her was in reality a peaceful one.

Clay glanced at the boy, who was staring out of the window. He asked in a low tone, "Shannon, you know those men?"

"Hell no." The boy swallowed, his thin face turning pale as he glanced at Margaret, then at Clay. "I'm sorry ma'am." He swallowed again. "No Majors, I never seen 'em before."

Quickly Shannon swung his head to look at the river. Clay, glancing at Judy, saw that she was still staring at her reticule. She was as decent as any woman, Clay knew, but the kid had quickly condemned her. So would Margaret and Jason Brimlow. Clay felt a deep sense of compassion for her, and then he wondered how long she would be decent, once she started her engagement at the Gay Lady.

Turning his gaze to Casteel's bland and guileless face, he told himself that he would kill the man if he ruined Judy as he had Geneva and so many others. Hating did not come easy to Clay Majors, and he wasn't entirely sure why he felt so strongly about Casteel.

Now, staring at Casteel, Clay caught the sudden eagerness that crept into the gambler's face as he looked at Margaret. Then Clay knew exactly why he hated him. Margaret or no other woman would be safe if she was alone with Larry Casteel.

Three

FOR A TIME the road lay north of the Gunnison River, running parallel to it. High with the spring runoff, the river spilled over the road in a few places, an angry stream that made a sullen rumble as it chewed at its banks and piled driftwood against the rocks.

The waterproofed curtains of the stage were rolled up and buttoned to the flat roof. The air, scented by the smell of sage, was heavy with the dust that was stirred by hoofs and wheels. As the minutes passed, the sun worked higher into the clear sky, laying a steadily increasing heat upon the land.

Slim Galt held the horses at a steady ground-eating pace, swinging around curves, wheeling up over steep slopes and back to the river level, dashing through brief shade from the tall cottonwoods along the bank and back into the harsh sunlight again. Galt seldom said a word, he rarely used his whip, for he was a master reinsman, communicating silently to the horses through his lines.

So the minutes piled up into an hour, then two, and Margaret, worn out by the long train ride from Denver, dozed with her head on Clay's shoulder, finding assurance perhaps in his presence. At least that was the way he hoped it was.

Now and then Clay's eyes met Judy Allen's. When they did, she smiled at him, her full-lipped mouth holding a sweet expression which was entirely unaffected with her. She sat with her shoulders back, her head high. Clay felt like shaking the kid beside him for the way he had inadvertently insulted her, yet it was to be expected, and Judy should be used to it by now.

Clay tried to avoid looking at Casteel. Even in silence the gambler had a way of appearing superior to the other men in the coach, and every motion he made from caressing his waxed mustache to turning the diamond ring on his finger honed Clay's temper to a finer edge. He knew he was being unreasonable, perhaps childish, but he wasn't sure he could sit here all day with Casteel without blowing up, yet he knew it was something he had to do.

Now and then Clay glanced at Pete Shannon, who sat on his left. Usually the kid was staring out of the window, and Clay could tell little about him from the back of his long neck except that he needed a haircut. He had a rank smell of one who seldom changed his clothes and never bathed. The only time he looked around was when he turned his head to pin his green eyes on Jason Brimlow, and then they narrowed and became coldly speculative.

Clay wondered about the boy, where he came from and who he was, and whether he had given a signal to Grat and Julio back there in Gunnison. Clay felt sure of one thing. The kid didn't have a job waiting for him in a mine above Ouray. He had probably never been in a mine in his life.

It was Jason Brimlow who held the most interest for Clay. He was about fifty, Clay judged, with the round belly and soft hands and paper-white face of one who never did any work that required more physical effort than dipping a pen into a bottle of ink. Now and then he removed his black derby and wiped his head, which was shiny bald. A businessman of some sort, Clay decided. Perhaps a banker.

Brimlow seemed unaware that anyone else was in the coach, and he certainly didn't realize that Clay was watching him. Except for the times when he wiped his head, he sat frozen as if he were in a cataleptic trance, his arms around the leather satchel which he hugged against his belly. He was a badly frightened man, Clay decided, so frightened that he was physically sick.

The stage made a wide swing and crossed the river on a narrow bridge, the horses' hoofs striking with sounds that were pistol-sharp in the thin air. Margaret woke with a start, glanced out at the angry water lapping against the ends of the planks, shuddered and turned her head so that her face was buried against Clay's shirt.

"Nothing to worry about, honey," he said, putting his arm around her. "This bridge has been here a long time."

"Three or four years," Casteel said, his eyes showing faint amusement. "I feel exactly the way you do, Miss Trent. If the river keeps coming up, this bridge will go out."

Only by a great effort was Clay able to remain silent. He knew that Casteel was trying to bait him, and that nothing would be gained by taking the bait.

Margaret kept her face hidden until they were across, and the stage had swung west along the south side of the river, then she straightened and sank back into her corner as Clay removed his arm.

"I'll never cross that bridge again," she said determinedly. "You wrote to me that this country wasn't dangerous, but that bridge isn't safe."

The accusing way she looked at him irritated him. He said, "There's danger anywhere if you look for it. I read the other day about a Denver man who fell down a flight of stairs and broke his neck."

"They have floods in the eastern part of the state," Judy said. "A man was drowned by a cloudburst in Turkey Creek canyon not long ago."

Clay gave her a grateful glance, thanking her for coming to his aid. In a way what she had said balanced Casteel's remark.

"I know," Margaret said, and sighed. "Are we in the reservation yet?"

Clay nodded. "Been in it quite a while."

Margaret glanced out of the window as if expecting to see a band of Indians ride up out of the river.

Casteel said, "You won't see any Utes here. Too close to Gunnison. They're a cowardly, scurvy lot. More scared of the whites than the whites are of them." He glanced briefly at Clay, a cynical smile on his lips.

Margaret said, "They may be cowardly, but they're vicious, too, the way they massacred the men at the Meeker Agency."

"I don't think they were cowardly," Judy said. "They gave the soldiers a beating."

"Now, now," Casteel said as if gently reprimanding her. "You could hardly call it a beating, pinning down a little bunch of soldiers for a few days." He shook his head. "If it had been the Sioux, we'd have had another battle of the Little Big Horn, but the Utes were content to hide on a cliff and fire a few shots."

"It's the Meeker women I keep thinking about," Margaret said. "The way they must have suffered. Not that the Indians can be forgiven for murdering Nathan Meeker and the others. I remember a letter his daughter Rose wrote to the Denver *Tribune*. She said something about the life of one white man being worth more than the lives of all the Indians from the beginning of time."

Casteel leaned forward, thoroughly enjoying this. "Yes, I remember that letter very well. I copied it because she stated my sentiments perfectly. At the end of the letter she asked who can pay for this mighty woe. The blood of the martyred ones cries out for vengeance, she said. But there has been no vengeance. The whole bunch should have been strung up. Instead, they're free as birds."

"You do remember her letter," Clay said.

"You bet I do. The Utes are animals." Casteel pounded a fist into an open hand. "Animals, I tell you. I've watched them. How they live and how they eat. Worse than savages. Just like animals. I'm surprised the Meeker women didn't commit suicide after what happened to them."

"I was with General Adams when they were rescued," Clay said. "I didn't think at the time and I still don't that they were harmed in any way."

Casteel laughed shortly. "Of course you would say that." He looked at Margaret. "I cannot understand how any white man can consider himself a friend of the Utes. It's like saying you're a friend of a pack of wolves. Ouray was the best of the lot, and that's not saying much."

Clay's hands fisted on his lap; he felt the blood in his temples pounding as if it were about to break through his veins. He said with forced calm, "Ouray is dead, Casteel. He can't defend himself."

"I apologize to his sacred memory," Casteel said sarcastically, "but there are plenty of others who are alive and can defend themselves. Colorow. Sapinero. Piah. Santo. I say they are all animals. Of course when a man is paid enough to be their friend, I guess it's understandable that he would publicly say he was."

Clay took Margaret's hand. "He's talking about me. I sympathize with the Utes. That's all. What they did on White River was wrong, but any human being can be goaded into doing the wrong thing. The massacre wouldn't have happened if the troops hadn't been called in."

"Human beings, you say, Majors?" Casteel jeered.

"I knew Ouray well," Clay went on, ignoring Casteel. "He was a fine man, better than most of the whites he dealt with. In a way it's a good thing he's dead because he would have been badly hurt to learn that the whites are breaking their word again and the Uncompahgre Utes are to be moved to Utah instead of to the junction of the Grand and Gunnison Rivers, which is what the last treaty said."

"It also said 'Lands adjacent to,'" Casteel cut in. "There's no breaking of a treaty there."

Clay dropped Margaret's hand. He placed both of his on his knees, his eyes meeting Casteel's. He was possessed by an almost uncontrollable desire to reach across the narrow space and grab Casteel and beat his face into a bloody pulp. Casteel, seeing how Margaret felt, had built upon her hate. Out of sheer perverseness, he sought to drive a wedge between her and Clay.

Margaret apparently did not sense what was happening.

Neither did Jason Brimlow, but Pete Shannon was watching, the eager expression on his thin face of a jackal anticipating a fight between two great jungle animals so that later he might move in and feast on the carrion after the fight was over.

But Judy Allen understood. She said quickly, "I'm hungry. Isn't it about noon?"

Clay took a long breath, the spell broken. He realized how close Casteel had come to provoking the fight he had sought since early morning. Yet there could be no fight here in the confines of the coach with two women in it. Perhaps he didn't really want a fight, perhaps he sought only to bring Clay to the verge of it, prodding him and goading him for the pleasure it gave him.

Now Casteel smiled pleasantly. "I think it is, Judy. Don't we have a noon stop soon, Majors?"

Clay nodded, his body still rigid, veins standing out boldly on the backs of his clenched hands. As if in answer to Judy's question, the stage wheeled off the road and braked to a stop beside a tall, square house made of cottonwood logs. Galt swung down from the high seat, calling, "Noon stop. Thirty minutes to eat."

The passengers stepped out and stretched, Margaret stumbling and Clay catching her before she fell. She shook her head at him, smiling ruefully. "I'll be all right in a minute. There just wasn't much room in there to move around."

"No," Clay said, and led her toward the house.

The meal was a poor one: the biscuits hard, the coffee as black and unpalatable as tar, the salt pork half-cooked. Margaret tried to eat, but finally pushed her plate back.

"We'll have a good meal tonight," Clay assured her. "When we get home." The word home did not strike a chord in her, he saw, and added, "I was glad to hear you say you wouldn't cross that bridge again. You'll just have to stay with me."

She said nothing. He wasn't sure she even heard what he said. He glanced at Pete Shannon, who was wolfing down the food, and Jason Brimlow, who wasn't eating but sat hunched over his leather satchel. Galt and Judy were both eating, and now, as Clay glanced at Casteel, the gambler put a cigar into his mouth and rose and went outside.

Clay said in a low voice, "Don't pay any attention to what Casteel says. He's no good."

He sensed the temper that rose quickly in Margaret. She said, "He's very much a gentleman, it seems to me."

There was no way to get through to her, no way to make her understand the total depravity of the man. Clay doubted that even Judy with her experience had any real understanding of Larry Casteel.

"He's a gambler," Clay said, "and a crooked one at that. He runs a variety theater in Ouray, but gambling is his real business."

Margaret glanced around at the bare log walls, the long table with its oilcloth covering, the tin plates and tin cups, the food still on her plate, then at the slovenly woman who sat at the head of the table and who had waited on them when they first came in. She was eating with one hand, the other arm holding a mewling, dirty-faced baby that was trying to nurse.

"I should think that in a country like this," Margaret said, "populated with heathens and savages, a crooked gambler would be following an honorable profession."

Clay rose and went outside. More than anything else in the world he had wanted today's ride with Margaret to go well, wanted to give her a pleasant introduction to this country which he loved, wanted her to see its beauty and charm and rugged grandeur, but already she was set against it, too frightened to see anything but the violence of it.

He might have succeeded if it hadn't been for Casteel, but now he was possessed by a hopeless feeling of defeat. He knew he loved her and he was sure she loved him, but he asked himself again if love was enough, and he was depressed by a conviction that it wasn't.

He walked around the building and saw Casteel leave the outhouse, the cigar tipped jauntily from his mouth. Clay walked directly to him and grabbed a fistful of his shirt. He said, "Casteel, you'll keep your mouth shut in front of Margaret for the rest of this trip, or by God, I'll beat the living hell out of you."

"With the help of your cowboy, Lew Fisher, and maybe Slim Galt," Casteel said, grinning around his cigar. "It'll take three of you to do the job."

"Just one," Clay said. "Me."

"Let go," Casteel said. "I don't want your dirty hand soiling the front of my shirt. It was clean this morning."

Clay released him. Larry Casteel was not a man who could be bluffed. There was nothing Clay could do short of giving him a beating. He said, "Remember what I told you."

Casteel flattened out his rumpled shirt front with a few pats of a well-manicured hand, and, taking the cigar from his mouth, blew out a cloud of smoke. He said, "Majors, you don't deserve a beautiful woman like that and you'll never get her. It's like an ugly mustang trying to mate up with a thoroughbred mare. She'll never have you."

He stepped around Clay and walked toward the house. When Clay turned, he saw that Slim Galt had been watching. The driver spit a brown stream into the grass and wiped a shirt sleeve across his mouth.

He asked, "Why didn't you bust him, Clay?"

"Not yet, not yet." Clay said, then asked abruptly: "You know a couple of hardcases named Grat and Julio?"

Galt nodded. "Them hombres that passed us after we left Gunnison?"

"They're the ones," Clay said. "They were giving us the eye before we left the depot."

"I've seen 'em around Gunnison," Galt said. "Mean and ornery as they come. They've been suspicioned of a couple of killings and a robbery north of town, but nothing could be proved on 'em. No need to worry about 'em, though. Too yellow to make a play against a stage that's got you'n me on it. Casteel, too, damn his soul."

"Casteel wouldn't be in cahoots with 'em?"

"Naw, that ain't his size. He'll cheat you out of your eyeballs in a card game and plug you in the guts if you make a squawk, but he ain't no road agent. Funny 'bout a bastard like that. There's some things even he won't do." Galt glanced at his watch. "Time to roll."

Clay followed Galt to the coach, not at all sure he was right. One thing was certain. White outlaws were to be feared far more than the Utes, but that was something he could not tell Margaret. Then he thought of Jason Brimlow and wondered what was in the satchel he guarded so jealously.

Four

IN LESS THAN HALF AN HOUR after the noon stop, the stage dropped into the gorge of the Lake Fork of the Gunnison, following a ribbon of a road that seemed too narrow for the wheels of the coach.

Margaret looked out of the window, shuddered, and put her face in her hands. Clay slipped an arm around her, but she held herself stiffly away from him, refusing to speak to him or even to look at him until they had crossed the narrow bridge over the swift-running stream and had climbed out of the canyon on the other side.

"It's quite safe, Miss Trent," Casteel said, amused eyes on Clay. "From where I sit, I'd say that half the tire of each outside wheel was hanging over the side, but that's all Slim Galt needs. You could drop a dime on the road ahead of him and he'd hit it dead center."

Margaret kept her face hidden until the stage was wheeling through the spruce timber. Clay withdrew his arm as he said, "We're out of the canyon now."

She sank back into her corner, her hands on her lap. She forced her white lips into a half smile as she asked, "Clay, do people cross there all the time?"

He nodded. "You don't think anything about it once you've been over it a few times. Stages use it. Freight outfits. All kinds of rigs. With Slim Galt handling the reins, you're just as safe in the stage as you would be riding a horse."

"Safer, Miss Trent," Casteel said. "Unless you're a good rider, like Majors."

Why couldn't he keep his damned mouth shut, Clay thought angrily? Casteel had a way with words just as he had with women, already convincing Margaret he was a gentleman. By a mere inflection he made it seem that Clay belonged on a horse, not riding in a stage beside a beautiful woman like Margaret Trent.

Perhaps Casteel was right, Clay reflected. He should never have asked Margaret to come. He had built his dreams around her and had let them grow until they had gone far beyond the bounds of reality. Now, he told himself dismally, they both faced disappointment.

The stage was climbing steadily, the great peaks to the south cut off from sight by the heavy timber. It was not far to Clay's ranch, but they would not get there until late afternoon. Galt had made good time during the morning, for in general the road had followed the level of the river, but from now on the grades were steep and even in dry weather the road was slow. It had cooled off here in the shade of the thick-growing spruce, and it seemed to Clay that Margaret had relaxed.

Judy was dozing, unperturbed by the crossing of the Lake Fork. Pete Shannon was more tense than ever, keeping his face to the windows, his eyes restlessly searching the timber. Jason Brimlow had not moved from the time they had started after the noon stop except for the turning of his body as the coach swayed on its leather braces. He sat with his chin extended over the top of his satchel, both hands gripping the sides tightly. He'd be more comfortable if he relaxed, Clay thought, but it was Brimlow's business if he wanted to ride that way.

"When do we get to Ouray, Mr. Majors?" Brimlow asked.

This was the first time Clay had heard Brimlow speak since they had left Gunnison, and it pleased him that the man had put the question to him instead of Casteel, who lived in Ouray. Clay said, "Late tomorrow. My place towards Cimarron is an overnight stop. In the morning you'll go on to the Agency and from there to Ouray."

Brimlow opened his mouth to speak, but the words were never said. The stage stopped, Galt calling as he stepped down from his high seat,

"Clay, come out here. Rest of you stay inside."

Galt was an even-tempered man who usually took any kind of trouble in stride. Clay had never known him to get excited except when he talked about Larry Casteel, but he was excited now. As Clay got out on Pete Shannon's side, he saw that the kid's thin face was hard-set, the corners of his mouth working with nervous excitement.

Clay hesitated beside the coach, one hand on the door, his eyes sweeping the timber beside the road. Casteel asked impatiently, "What's wrong, Majors?"

"I don't know," Clay said, looking at Shannon. "What's biting you, boy?"

"Nothing," Shannon said. "I'm tired, riding in this shebang. I'll get out and stretch my legs."

"Stay inside," Clay said. "You heard what Slim told you."

Galt was striding on up the road ahead of the coach. Now he called back, "Clay, get a move on."

Suddenly uneasy, Clay ran to catch up. This was not Galt's way. Ordinarily he would no more think of stopping on Blue Mesa and taking a walk up the road than he'd think of stopping beside the Gunnison to let his passengers fish. Then, ten feet ahead of the horses, Clay saw what Galt had seen, the sight jarring an audible exclamation out of him.

The charred remains of a freight wagon stood in a small clearing to the right of the road. Reaching it, Galt stopped to stare at it, and Clay, breathing hard, came up beside him.

The contents of the wagon had been scattered on the ground: sacks of flour and sugar, canned goods, bolts of cloth, and the odds and ends that any freighter carried if he was headed for one of the small mining camps above Ouray.

Clay's first thought was that this was the work of Julio and Grat, but he knew that was foolish. They'd want money and a freighter seldom carried money. Some of the freight might have been stolen, but not much, judging from the amount that was on the ground.

Clay circled the wagon, noting that the campfire had gone cold. No smoke was rising from the wagon, either, so this must have happened hours ago, and Grat and Julio could not have been here then. Clay looked at Galt, running the tip of his tongue over dry lips. He knew what had happened, but in this first moment of shock, he could not bring himself to believe it.

Galt nodded, understanding. "Utes," he said.

"Couldn't be," Clay said. "They know a thing like this would raise hell and prop it up with a stick."

"Young bucks," Galt said. "Maybe drunk. You know how they feel. None of 'em want to be moved to Utah. They're all sore about it." He made a sweeping gesture that included the entire clearing. "You're a better tracker'n I am. I'll stay here so I won't tramp out the sign. You figger out what happened."

The horses were gone. Probably they hadn't been hooked up, for it was Clay's guess that this had happened early in the morning, perhaps at dawn. As he explored the clearing, half his mind was busy searching for the cause.

Various rumors of Ute violence had spread among the whites on the western slope since the Meeker massacre, but they had all been lies, started by newspaper editors and hack politicians hoping to hasten the exit of the Indians. But this was no lie, and Clay swore softly, thinking what the editors and politicians would do with it.

This was a common camping spot for the freighters who moved regularly between Gunnison and the Agency or the mining camps. A small spring rose in a clump of willows at the far end of the clearing and made a year-round stream that eventually reached the Blue. A few feet from the spring Clay found the bullet-riddled body of a man lying on his belly, scalped.

Clay had been reasonably sure he would find the body of the freighter, but he had kept hoping he wouldn't. Murder would be far worse on the Utes than the mere robbing and burning of a freight wagon, regardless of the cause. When he turned the body over and recognized Boone Holman, a man he had known and liked for years, he turned away, sick.

This was worse than anything he had imagined. Boone Holman had freighted across the reservation ever since the railroad had reached Gunnison. He had often brought supplies to Clay's Cimarron ranch; he was a profane, hard-drinking man like most freighters, but he hadn't hated the

Utes as so many did, and therefore had got along with them.

Clay motioned for Galt to come, then made a wide circle through the timber around the spring. When he returned, Galt was still standing there, staring at the blood-smeared body of the murdered man, his face as pale as it could be under the heavy tan that being out in the wind and sun for years had given him.

Galt wiped a hand across his face, finally turning away. He asked, "What would ever make 'em do a thing like this?"

"I wish I knew," Clay said. "There'll be hell to pay now."

"We can't leave him here," Galt said. "I'll get a canvas and we'll wrap him up and take him to your place. The eastbound stage tomorrow can take him to Gunnison. You'll probably have to talk to the sheriff."

"Wait," Clay said. "Let's figure on this a minute. You knew Boone?"

"Sure I knew him. He never had no trouble with the Indians. Hell, this would make sense if it was any of a dozen other boogers I can think of. Like Casteel who goes around blowing off about the Indians. But Holman!" Galt shook his head. "He knew 'em, and he knew how to get along with 'em."

"The way I read the sign," Clay said, "there were four of them that rode in from the south and four of them went back. The horses did, anyhow." He motioned toward the river to the north. "But there was another horse, a shod one, that took off through the trees going hell for leather. He wouldn't go far in that direction, the Black Canyon being there, so he's headed toward Gunnison or toward my place."

"Then Holman had somebody with him who got away," Galt said. "Clay, maybe we better go back. Something might have happened with the soldiers or at the Agency that's started a war. Could be they're jumping every white they can find."

Clay shook his head. "We may get a war out of this if it's handled wrong, but something happened right here that brought this on and I wish I knew what it was."

"Boone had a son," Galt said. "Called him Red. A big, loud-talking bastard. I ran into him in Ouray a couple of times."

"I was thinking of him," Clay said. "He was with Boone the last time he came through. Got drunk at my place and Boone had a hard time getting him to bed. He talked like Casteel. Hated the Utes. They'd roughed him up one time and he never forgave 'em. Could be Red that got away, all right, but he said he wasn't staying with his dad. Claimed he was going on to Silverton where he had a job."

29

"Chances are he did stay with Boone," Galt said, "and he done something that caused this. He's that kind of a huckleberry."

Clay nodded. "That's what I think, and what he did is going to tell us how bad this is." He thought of Margaret and swore. "What'll we do, Slim? We can't keep it from the passengers."

"We'll have to tell 'em," Galt agreed. "I'll get that canvas. I ain't real comfortable standing here like this. Them devils might be hiding within fifty feet of us right now."

He turned away just as Casteel and Shannon ran toward them from the road. Galt shouted angrily, "I told you to stay in the coach."

They saw the body at the same time. Shannon swung around and bent over, suddenly sick, but Casteel turned his gaze to Clay.

"Your good friends, the Utes," he said with stinging venom. "Thieving, murdering animals. You'll have a hell of a time taking their part now, Majors."

Galt had gone on toward the stage. Clay didn't feel like arguing with Casteel, so he said, "We're taking the body to my place. We don't know what brought this on, but we're on the reservation and it's possible we'll run into the bunch that did this. I've got just one thing to say: Don't start shooting if we do see any Indians, or you'll get us all killed."

"Holman was a friend of mine," Casteel snapped. "Came into the Gay Lady every time he was in Ouray. If I see any of the red devils, you can bet I'll be shooting."

Shannon had straightened up and was turning slowly, scanning the timber around them. He heard what Casteel said, and cried, "No, Majors is right."

Casteel's lips curled. "What do you know about it, kid?"

Shannon turned and lurched back across the clearing toward the road and went on to the coach.

Clay said, "Another thing. You let Margaret alone. This is going to be hard enough on her without you making it worse."

"I don't need to say anything," Casteel said. "What kind of a damned fool are you, bringing a woman like that to this country?"

Clay turned away, his hatred for Casteel brought into sharp focus by what the gambler had just said. He had never been one to think about trouble, or worry about it, confident he could handle it when it came, but now he had trouble no man could handle. Casteel was at least partly right, and that made it worse.

In almost all ways Clay was a practical man, knowing

what would work and what wouldn't, but in matters of love he felt he was the worst kind of failure. If he hadn't lost Margaret now, he surely would when she learned what had happened. Then, because frustration stretched his temper to the breaking point, he wheeled to face Casteel.

"If you treat Judy the way you have Geneva and the other women you've taken to Ouray, I'll kill you. I'm not Slim. I'll do it."

Casteel's lips curled in his hard, cynical grin. "You don't scare me much, Majors," he said. "I wonder what Miss Trent will think of your interest in women like Geneva and Judy?"

Clay stood motionless, staring at Casteel and hating him, and knowing that the man was right again. This was something else Margaret could never understand.

Galt returned with the canvas. They wrapped the body, carried it back to the coach, and lashed it on top. Casteel got in, then Clay, and Galt climbed to the box and the stage wheeled on toward the Blue.

Clay, glancing covertly at Margaret, knew that Pete Shannon had told her what had happened. He was glad she didn't look at the freight wagon as they passed it. But maybe it didn't make any difference. He had a terrible feeling that his relationship with Margaret couldn't be any worse than it was.

Five

A DISMAL SILENCE lay upon the passengers as the coach crossed the Blue and the meadow which lay beyond the creek, and slowed for the climb up the divide between the Blue and Cimarron. Clay was not a superstitious man, but he could not dispel the weird feeling that the ghost of Boone Holman rode in the stage with them.

That was crazy, of course, but Clay was certain that not one of the passengers, nor Slim Galt either, was forgetting for a moment that the stage was carrying the corpse of a murdered man. Clay reached out for one of Margaret's hands. He found it cold and limp, giving nothing back to him when he squeezed it.

Clay drew his hand away, knowing that this was an experience Margaret would always remember. He could well ask himself the question Casteel had thrown at him: what kind of a damned fool was he to bring a woman like Margaret to this country?

He could tell himself he would never have done it if he hadn't loved her and been sure she loved him; he could tell himself that he couldn't go on as he had, engaged to marry Margaret but living a long ways from her without a definite marriage date, without any mutual agreement about their future.

It was easy enough now to say he should have known Margaret would feel the way she did about this country, but it might not have been this way if Larry Casteel wasn't in the coach. Or if they hadn't found the body of Boone Holman.

Margaret wouldn't have come if she hadn't loved him. Maybe she would feel differently after she had rested and had eaten a good meal. So once more he put the doubts into the back of his mind and hope became a bright, warm glow.

Clay studied each passenger, noting that Jason Brimlow still rode with the satchel on his lap, hands clutching the sides with the same fierce grip that he had used from the moment he'd got on the stage.

Judy Allen was relaxed, her body giving with the sway of the coach, entirely free of the rigid stiffness that gripped Margaret.

Pete Shannon stared out of the window as if constantly expecting to see someone or something out there in the timber.

Larry Casteel had momentarily lost the cynical amusement which irritated Clay so much. He rode with a dead cigar gripped in one corner of his mouth, his gaze now and then coming to Margaret's face. Clay sensed what was in the man's mind, lecherous thoughts that followed a well-worn path. Suddenly it struck Clay that he would not be free of Casteel until morning, and maybe not then if there was any real threat of trouble with the Indians.

Clay tore his gaze away from Casteel's face; he tried to think about Boone Holman's killing and what it might mean, and he did not like the turn his thoughts took. He couldn't guess what had happened at the freighter's camp that had brought on the killing, but he was fully aware that the incident might be the match which would set off an explosion.

The Utes were a simple people who had a history of getting along with the whites until the Meeker massacre. Now they were sullenly resentful at being removed from their ancestral home, but it was unlikely that the older heads, chiefs like Sapinero and Santo, would resort to violence.

Trouble, if it did come, would be caused by the young warriors who refused to listen to their elders. Even a small band could reap a bloody harvest before the soldiers from the cantonment above the Agency could run them down. It was not probable, but it certainly was possible. Clay made up his mind that, even if he didn't learn what had caused Boone Holman's murder, he would keep a guard out tonight.

Suddenly Casteel, unable to stand the silence, said, "Well, Majors, what do you have to say about your red friends now?"

"Nothing," Clay answered, resolved that he would not rise to the gambler's bait. This was another item which must be added to the account that would be settled later.

"Murdering, thieving animals," Casteel said. "The soldiers ought to line every one of them up and shoot them. I'm going to see General McKenzie and tell him what happened."

"Did it ever occur to you that it might not be Indians who killed Holman?" Clay asked. "That it could have been white outlaws?"

Brimlow's head snapped around. "White outlaws? You mean road agents who might hold the stage up?"

"It's possible," Clay said. "I noticed a couple of toughs named Julio and Grat watching us when we left Gunnison."

"It wasn't them." Shannon turned to look at Clay. "It was Injuns, all right."

"How would a kid like you know?" Clay asked.

"Holman was scalped," Shannon said as if that settled it, and turned to the window again.

"Sometimes whites scalp a man they've killed to make it look like Indians did it," Clay said, but Shannon said nothing more.

Brimlow's face was whiter than ever. Saliva ran down both sides of his chin and dried there.

Amused, Casteel said, "I believe this is what you call dragging a red herring across the path, Majors. That's a good joke. Red herrings, red Indians." No one laughed, and Casteel added, "It won't do, Majors. I'd say there was a good chance we'll all be scalped before morning."

Margaret cried out.

"No," Clay said quickly. "Nothing will happen." He wasn't as sure as he hoped he sounded, but this was a time when he had to lie. He put his arm around Margaret and drew her to him, knowing she could not stand much more. He had warned Casteel, and now he had to shut him up, someway.

It was Judy who did it, her voice gently reproving. "Let's talk about something more pleasant." She made an unobtrusive gesture toward Margaret, who had closed her eyes, her head resting against Clay.

Casteel took the half-chewed cigar out of his mouth and tossed it past Shannon's head out of the window. "All right, Judy," he said. "Let's talk about all the money I'm going to make in the Gay Lady when everybody in camp comes to see you."

"You mean hear me," she said. "I don't think anyone ever comes to see me." She laughed. "If you're going to make so much money, how about giving me a raise?"

"Nothing doing," Casteel said. "I have a contract with you, signed and delivered. Remember?"

Margaret pushed Clay's arm away from her and leaned back into the corner. "How can you take danger so lightly, Miss Allen?" she said.

Judy shrugged. "I've been on the western slope before, Miss Trent. It's a rough country, but after a while you learn to live with it. I've found out that if you're afraid of it, you only make it worse."

"That's a sensible viewpoint," Casteel said, "and I admire you for taking it, but it seems to me that in the case of the savages, we would do well to consider the danger."

She gave Casteel a straight look. "I've learned something else, Mr. Casteel. I have more to fear from white men than from all the Indians on the reservation."

Clay felt like applauding. Perhaps Casteel had found his match. At least, Clay thought, she knows what she'll be up against when she gets to Ouray, for her remark was a barbed one unquestionably aimed at Casteel.

He ignored it, however, saying, "I'm afraid of savages, not civilized men," and let it drop there.

They came down off the summit, traveling against the low sharp blast of the sun, which had dropped toward the hills to the west. Below them the Gunnison glittered in the late afternoon sunlight like a silver thread.

Clay's buildings lay close to the creek, a log house much like the one where they had eaten dinner, but there the resemblance ended. Here everything was in order, neat and clean, reflecting the pride that Clay had in his place. Beyond the log barn stood a number of outbuildings and corrals. Hay meadows were located upstream, with a few weather-browned stacks from the year before, and on the slope above the house there was a fenced pasture for the horses.

Clay hoped that Margaret would see all this, and understand its cost in both money and labor, and what it meant for their future, but apparently she saw nothing. A few minutes later Galt pulled off the road into Clay's yard, calling, "Night stop."

Clay got down and gave Margaret a hand. When she was on the ground beside him, he said, "We're home, honey. Our home." But he saw that it still meant nothing to her. She only looked at him blankly.

Molly Reed, Clay's housekeeper, hurried across the yard to them. She was a big, homely woman with a loud voice and the vocabulary of a freighter. She had been with Clay from the time his ranch had become a night stop for the stage. She looked upon Clay as a son, knowing his love for Margaret, and his doubts, too.

When she came up, Clay said, "Margaret, this is my housekeeper, Molly Reed. Molly, meet Margaret."

Molly hugged the girl. "We're awfully happy you're here, honey. We've been looking forward to your visit for a long time."

Margaret murmured something that Clay didn't understand.

He said, "She's awfully tired, Molly. The train ride from Denver and then being on the stage from Gunnison. You look after her."

"Sure I will," Molly said in her overpowering voice. "You poor lamb, of course you're tired. I've got a good meal on the stove. I'll show you your room and you can rest a little before supper."

Clay climbed to the boot as Molly led Margaret into the house. Jason Brimlow scurried behind Molly, holding tightly to his satchel. Clay found the luggage that the rest needed for the night as his choreman, Bronc Pless, took care of the horses. Then, with Galt's help, he took down Boone Holman's body.

Pete Shannon stood beside the stage rolling a cigarette, his gaze on the timber through which they had just traveled.

Clay said, "Shannon, I'm asking you once more and don't lie to me. Do you know Grat and Julio?"

Shannon jumped and whirled. "No. I told you once. I never seen 'em before."

"If I find out you're lying, I'll beat the living hell out of you," Clay said, "even if you are a wet-nosed kid. We've got enough trouble without having to buck a pair of back-shooting outlaws."

35

Shannon sealed the cigarette, put it into one corner of his mouth and let it sag there, then he deliberately dropped a hand to the butt of his gun. "You're a big man here, Majors, but don't never lay a hand on me. Savvy?"

Clay stared at him for a moment, instinctively disliking the boy and yet knowing he had nothing definite to go on.

Galt said, "Come on, he's just a brat. You won't get nothing out of him."

"A brat, you think?" Shannon flared. "I'm a better man with a gun than either one of you. If you don't think so, put that carcass down and make your play."

Clay and Galt moved toward the barn with the body, leaving Shannon glaring after them, the unlighted cigarette still drooping from one corner of his mouth.

Galt said, "If tomorrow's stage comes through, you'd best send Boone into Gunnison. I'll be there the last of the week and I'll tell the sheriff what happened, but chances are you'll have to go and give your spiel, too."

They left the body in an empty granary which had been built tightly against mice and rats.

Stepping out, Clay gave the turnpin a twist. He said, "I see you said if the stage comes through tomorrow."

Galt nodded. "I've been thinking on this ever since we picked him up. I don't like it, Clay. Could be some young bucks are out gunning for all the whites they can find."

"I don't think that's it." Clay looked up the creek. "Lew's riding pretty hard. Wonder what's biting him?"

Galt turned to look at Lew Fisher, the only cowboy Clay employed, riding down the creek at a gallop. "Something's wrong, all right." Casteel came out of the house, a cigar in his mouth, and stopped, watching. Shannon still stood beside the coach.

Galt laughed shortly. "You had a hell of a bunch to ride with, didn't you?"

Clay nodded. "I did for a fact. If Casteel says one more wrong word . . ."

Galt dropped a hand on Clay's shoulder. "I've been thinking on that, too. I shouldn't have told you what I done about Geneva. It's my fight, not yours."

"Not any more it isn't. I've stood more off him today than I have any other man, but I won't stand any more."

"You've got a hell of a lot to live for," Galt said. "Don't get yourself killed by that son of a bitch."

Clay was silent, thinking of Margaret and wondering gloomily if he did have anything to live for. Lew Fisher splashed across the creek, lifting a hand in greeting to Clay and Galt as he reined up beside the corral and swung down.

Casteel strolled toward him as he called, "Hear what happened, Clay?"

He was young, not over twenty, a tall, wire-built man who had been with Clay for more than a year. He had both guts and savvy, and Clay would have trusted him with anything. Now his freckled face was flushed with excitement, and again Clay felt the familiar nag of worry as he strode toward Fisher.

"Heard what, Lew?" Clay asked.

"About Santo's son?"

"No."

"Red Holman shot and killed him," Fisher said. "I ran into three young bucks a little after noon. They told me what happened, but I knew there wasn't no use coming back then because you were gone. They were taking the kid's body to Santo. His lodge is down the river from the Agency. I reckon they'll be all around here tonight looking for Red. The three of 'em killed Boone and burned the wagon after Santo's boy was plugged, but Red got clean away. They figure he's wounded, so he probably won't go very far. But one thing's sure. Old Santo will raise Cain till he gets Red."

Clay's eyes turned to Galt. The stage driver's face was more melancholy than ever. Clay sensed that the same thought was in both of their minds. There would be hell to pay now, perhaps the same kind of bloody hell that had brought on the Thornburgh fight and the murder of Nathan Meeker and every man at the White River Agency.

And there were white women in the house to be kidnapped just as the Meeker women had been, kidnapped and perhaps raped.

Six

BOTH CASTEEL AND YOUNG SHANNON were drifting toward the corral gate and had heard what Lew Fisher had said. Shannon was visibly shaken as he made a half turn and scanned the timber to the east. Clay, noticing it, was still uncertain as to whether the boy expected a band of Indians to come riding out of the spruce trees, or whether he was looking for someone else.

Casteel's cynical grin was on his lips as he looked at Lew Fisher. He said, "So Red got old Santo's kid, did he? Too bad he didn't plug all four of 'em."

Bronc Pless had come out of the barn, and with Galt crossed the yard to stand beside Clay. Pless, like Molly Reed, had come here with Clay when he started the ranch. Now age and rheumatism had caught up with him and he wasn't able to do a full day's work, but he took care of the horses, cut stovewood for Molly, and helped with the garden.

Whether he could work or not, Pless would have a home as long as Clay could give him one. Clay was fond of him just as he was fond of Molly and young Lew Fisher, feeling he had a loyalty from all three that could not be bought.

Neither Pless nor Fisher knew anything about Casteel except that he was a sport from Ouray, and now both looked at him as if they couldn't believe they'd heard right.

Pless said, "Mister, you must have been born yesterday, talking that way. You know what this means?"

Casteel took the cigar out of his mouth and flicked off the ash. He said, "Old man, it doesn't mean a damned thing except that a young Indian buck got what was coming to him, and a freighter who was just trying to make a living got what he didn't deserve."

"The last thing you said is right," Fisher agreed. "Seems that the Indians had been camped up the Blue a piece. They were hunting but didn't find a deer, and they were hungry. They saw Holman's camp and rode up, asking for something to eat. Boone would have let 'em have something, but not Red. He cussed 'em and called 'em tramps, and told 'em to go to hell. Santo's boy understood some English and he got sore and called Red a son of a bitch, so Red shot him.

"Boone yelled for Red to git and jumped for his Winchester. He nicked a couple of the Indians, but they got him. If Red had stayed and fought, Boone might have made it, but he ran."

"Funny they didn't take after him," Clay said.

"I wondered about that, too," Fisher said, "but near as I could make out, they just got scared. They'd been told by Sapinero and Santo and some of the other chiefs not to start any trouble. With Boone dead, they knew they'd started big trouble without meaning to. Besides, Santo's boy was the leader, and with him gone the rest of 'em couldn't think of anything to do but git. They tossed most of the freight out of the wagon looking for whisky, fired the wagon, and lit out for home."

"What'll happen now?" Pete Shannon asked.

"Nothing." Casteel tossed his cigar stub toward the corral gate. "They're just a murdering, back-shooting bunch of cowards. Now that they've killed a white man, the whole tribe will head for the hills." He looked directly at Clay. "If I've learned anything since I came to this country, it's that when a white man takes the part of the Utes, he's just as yellow as they are."

Clay glanced at the house, wondering which room Molly Reed had given Margaret. He hoped it was on the other side of the building so she wouldn't see this, but the fight had to come regardless of what Margaret saw or thought. It would have come in the hotel lobby if Margaret hadn't been on the train; it would have come at the noon stop if Margaret hadn't been in the coach.

This had been waiting to be settled from the day they had fought in Ouray, the fight neither had won but that had ended in complete exhaustion on the part of both men. Today Casteel had needled Clay again and again, and now, looking at Casteel, Clay saw the bright shine of eagerness in the man's eyes. At last he had what he wanted.

Clay took off his gun belt and handed it to Slim Galt, wanting this fight as much as Casteel did. He said, "Take off your gun belt, tin horn. I'm going to give you the licking you've been asking for all day."

Casteel laughed, a sound of pure joy, as he slipped out of his corduroy coat and hung it on a corral post. "You want trouble, do you, bucko?" He unbuckled his gun belt and dropped it at the base of the post. "All right, I'll oblige you."

Casteel stood with one fist next to his chest, the other extended, waiting, on his face the superior grin that was so infuriating. Clay drove at him, swinging a fist from his knees. It missed, Casteel whirling away, and Clay was caught off balance. He never saw the blow that nailed him, but it felt like the kick of a mule and knocked him flat into the dust.

Clay lay there, staring up at Casteel, whose grin had not been disturbed; he heard Galt and Fisher and Bronc Pless begging him to get up and give Casteel some of his own medicine. But he didn't move for a time, waiting until the flashing orange lights had stopped pinwheeling before his eyes.

Then it came to him why Casteel had been so confident. He hadn't fought this way the other time. He must have taken boxing lessons since then, believing his new found skill would be the factor that would win for him. Clay learned one thing from that single punch that flattened him. He would have no chance at all if he tried to stand up to him and fight.

"You wanted some rough stuff," Casteel said. "Well, you got it. Looks like you're a one-punch man."

Clay got to his knees and shook his head. He heard Casteel's jeering laugh, then Clay came on up and drove at the gambler, bending low, both arms out. Casteel hit him again, but the blow didn't stop him.

Clay caught Casteel around the legs and brought him down into the dust. Then Clay was all over him, punishing him with fists and elbows and knees. They rolled around in the dirt like two school kids at recess; he battered Casteel in the face and they went on over, feet flailing the air.

Clay came on top again, for he was the stronger and this was his kind of fighting. He hammered Casteel in the nose and felt blood spurt into his face. Casteel drove a knee into his crotch and pain momentarily paralyzed him. His arms were slack as they went over in a half turn.

Now Casteel was on top. He sledged Clay in the face; he brought a knee down into Clay's belly, then Clay got an arm around his neck in a viselike grip, forced him around in a quarter turn and slammed him on the jaw again.

Casteel grunted an oath and clawed at Clay's face, but Clay jerked his head back so that the gambler's fingernails made nothing more than three long scratches down one cheek. Clay rolled off and got up. Casteel let out a yell of pleasure, and gained his feet, swinging a right at Clay's chin that barely missed.

Now Clay drove in, this time catching Casteel around the waist and lifting him off the ground. Casteel kicked and belabored Clay with his fists, but there was no authority in his blows, for Clay lifted him high and whirled him around and slammed him against the corral gate.

The boards squealed and gave under the weight of Casteel's body, but didn't break. He bounced off and fell hard within a foot of where he had laid his gun. He jerked it out of the holster as Clay's foot came down upon his wrist and held it there.

Clay stood looking down at Casteel, blood running into the gambler's mouth from his nose, then Clay stooped, and, twisting the pearl-handled gun from Casteel's hand, stepped back. He tossed the gun at Galt's feet, wiped a shirt sleeve across his face, and said, "Get up."

Casteel spit out a mouthful of blood, explored the interior of his mouth with his tongue, and propped himself up on an elbow. He said, "Go to hell. I'm whipped."

"All right," Clay said. "Maybe you can hear me now. Tear up that contract with Judy. Don't take her to Ouray."

"Go to hell," Casteel said again. "You don't fight like a

man. You're an animal like the Utes. Talk Judy out of going with me if you can. She'll kick you in the face and laugh while she's doing it."

"Get up," Clay said. "Go wash. Supper'll be ready pretty soon."

Casteel pulled himself upright and leaned against the corral. Blood still dribbled from his battered nose. He said, "Give me my gun."

"No," Bronc Pless said. "I know what this yahoo will do, Clay. He'll shoot you in the back."

Lew Fisher took Casteel's coat down from the corral post and searched it, then ran his hands over the man's body. "I figured he'd have a hideout," he said, "but I can't find one." He gave Casteel the coat and stepped back.

"Go on," Clay said, and motioned toward the house. "Clean up." He started toward the horse trough, then swung back. "I warned you when we picked up Boone Holman's body to keep your mouth shut, but you shot it off just the same. Don't do it again."

Casteel's mouth, bruised and swollen at one corner, held no sign of the superior grin which had been there most of the day. Neither of his eyes had been marked, and now his gaze fastened on Clay's face, his eyes holding a passionate hatred more intense than Clay had ever seen before.

"We'll see, bucko, we'll see," Casteel said, "but I'll tell you one thing. You'll never hold your girl."

He walked toward the house, lurching a little. He didn't look back once. Reaching the porch, he gripped a post, pulled himself up the steps, and, crossing the porch, disappeared inside.

Seven

CLAY TURNED TO THE HORSE TROUGH, Pete Shannon running after him. "You done good, Majors," the boy said eagerly. "You done real good. I didn't think you'd whip him after he set you down right there at first."

Clay glanced at Shannon. The same jackallike expression Clay had seen earlier in the day on the boy's thin face was there again. Shannon hadn't cared who won. He would have said the same thing to Casteel if he'd won. To him it had simply been a brutal fight he had enjoyed watching, and now it came to Clay that Shannon was the dangerous one who would have no compunction about shooting a man in the back. Clay didn't think Casteel would. Bronc Pless had been wrong about him.

Slim Galt grabbed Shannon by an arm and turned him toward the house. "Wash up for supper," he said. "Go on. Git."

Shannon jerked free, cursing, but he obeyed. Clay reached the horse trough and sloshed water over his face, then jerked his bandanna out of his pocket and dried gingerly, feeling the bruises that Casteel's fists had given him.

"How do I look?" Clay asked.

"Like hell." Galt grinned. "But better'n Casteel."

"Nothing's settled," Clay said.

"No, he'll try again," Galt agreed. "Next time with a gun if he can find one."

Clay walked to the house. He smelled Molly's supper. He paused, glancing at the door to his left that opened into the bar. Better not have any drinking tonight, he decided, and, locking the door, went on back along the hall to his room in the rear of the building. He took off his shirt, which was spattered with Casteel's blood, put on a clean one, and studied his face in the mirror of his dresser.

He had a purple bruise below one eye and the long red scratches down one cheek that Casteel had given him. Lucky, he thought, for they were the only marks he had from the fight.

He picked up a comb, tried to get some order out of his wiry hair, and gave up in disgust. He crossed the hall to the kitchen and found Judy in one of Molly's voluminous aprons standing over the stove stirring gravy.

Molly bustled in from the dining room, asking, "Ready for supper, Clay?"

"Sure I'm ready." He motioned toward Judy. "What're you working a guest for, Molly? If you need kitchen help . . ."

"Go on with you," Molly said, unperturbed. "I couldn't keep her out of the kitchen."

Judy looked over her shoulder at Clay, laughing. "I'm more than a singer, Mr. Majors. I can cook, too. The fact is I like to, so I just moved in."

"Better get Margaret up," Molly said. "She was lying down when I left her."

"Which room?"

"Front one on the east," Molly said.

Clay left the kitchen and went on through the dining room

to the parlor and climbed the stairs. If Margaret had been lying down, she probably hadn't seen the fight. He hoped she hadn't. As he made the turn at the head of the stairs, he wondered dully if Margaret would ever understand this country and the things it demanded of its people.

The door to Clay's right opened a crack. Jason Brimlow said in a low tone, "Mr. Majors, I must see you. Will you come in? Please?"

The door opened wider and Brimlow stepped back. He was hugging the satchel against his body with his left hand. The right held a short-barreled revolver. Clay hesitated, his eyes on the gun, which seemed entirely out of place in Brimlow's hand.

"Please," Brimlow begged. "I've got to talk to you."

Clay went in, as puzzled by this request as by anything that had happened all day. Brimlow closed the door and motioned to the one chair in the room. "Sit down, Mr. Majors." He sank down on the bed and laid the gun beside him.

Clay took the chair, nodding at the gun. "Who are you afraid of?"

"Casteel," Brimlow said. "I watched your fight. The way you handled him told me you were the man I need. Mr. Majors, I'll pay you a thousand dollars to go with me to Ouray tomorrow."

Clay shook his head and stood up. "I can't do it. I'm not even sure the stage will go to Ouray tomorrow."

Brimlow jumped up and grabbed Clay's arm. "It's got to," he said, more frightened than ever. "I have to be in Ouray tomorrow." He swallowed. "Why do you think the stage may not leave?"

"All depends on what the Indians do," Clay answered.

"Maybe they won't do anything. Maybe the stage will go on schedule." Brimlow swallowed again and tugged at Clay's arm. "Please sit down. Listen to what I've got to say. I didn't start out right. Let me try again."

Clay dropped back into the chair, his thoughts on Margaret. He wondered if he could get her to come downstairs for supper. She needed a good meal, for she had eaten practically nothing at noon. Then Brimlow's words caught his attention.

"I'm a desperate man, Mr. Majors," Brimlow was saying earnestly. "A scared one, too. I have $50,000 in this satchel. I know I'm a fool for bringing it this way, but I had no choice. I deal in real estate. Sometimes I buy and sell mines when I can see a quick profit. I have never made a fortune, although many of my friends have. I have a wife and three children. The oldest is a girl who is to be married next month. Her wedding will be an expensive one. If you had a wife, you would understand that, Mr. Majors. I didn't know where I would get the money, then an opportunity came along that was a godsend."

Brimlow swallowed and leaned forward. "I have a brother in New York who tipped me off about an Eastern syndicate that has been dickering for a mine near Ouray. They will go as high as $100,000 to get title to the property. Well, I have friends all over the state, men I have done favors for. One of them lived in Ouray and I had him feel the people out who own this mine.

"You see, the syndicate has been playing a cat-and-mouse game the way companies like that do, and has never made a firm offer. The point is that the owners have to sell and they will take $50,000 if it's shoved at them in cash. They've got to have it tomorrow, Mr. Majors. That's why I must be in Ouray tomorrow. I'm not familiar with the situation, but it seems that the owners are two old prospectors who got involved in too many things. They'll let this mine go to save the rest of their property."

Brimlow wiped his bald head, which glistened with beads of sweat. "So when I found this out, I mortgaged everything I had and borrowed all I could and finally succeeded in raising the $50,000. If I lose out, I'm a ruined man, but if I succeed, I'll double my money. I've got to, don't you see. I didn't really worry much until I got on the stage and learned that this man Casteel comes from Ouray. I'm sure that he knows what the deal is and may try to stop it. Or steal my money." He shook his head. "There's that awful Shannon kid. And the honky-tonk dancer who's with Casteel."

Brimlow's soft hands waved uncertainly. "If I'd had time, I wouldn't have handled it this way. But it took so long to raise the money I had no choice. That's why I need your help. I'll make it worth your while, Mr. Majors. $1000."

Clay rose and looked down at the man, a frightened human leech who was reaching for help in any direction. Clay had no sympathy for him. This country was for the strong, and the weak should never come.

"The honky-tonk dancer, as you call her, Brimlow," Clay said, "happens to be an honest woman in spite of what you think. I can't help you."

Brimlow's soft right hand grabbed Clay's arm, the other hand still clutching the satchel. "You've got to. You're the kind of man who——"

Clay jerked free. "You think you've got troubles, Brimlow? All you're worrying about is your money. Well, I've got important troubles. One of them is getting you and everybody else in this house through the night alive. I'm not sure

I can do it, and I'm not sure Slim Galt will take the stage out in the morning unless we find out what the Utes are going to do."

"But . . . but I've explained how it is, Majors. I've got to be in Ouray tomorrow."

"Come on down for supper," Clay said, and, leaving the room, walked along the hall.

Trouble, he thought bitterly, never came single. Now he had $50,000 to worry about along with everything else. The money could well be the reason Grat and Julio had left Gunnison. There could have been a leak. Pete Shannon might be in with them. Or Casteel. Judy? No, he could be sure of her.

Then, reaching Margaret's door, he put the money out of his mind. Suddenly Brimlow and his $50,000 didn't seem very important.

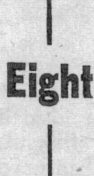

Eight

CLAY TAPPED ON MARGARET'S DOOR. When she didn't answer, he knocked again, worry a feeling that was close to physical pain. He had wanted her to come for so long, and now that she was here he was uncertain what to say and do after what had happened today.

She called wearily, "Who is it?"

"Clay."

A moment of silence, then she said, "Come in."

He opened the door and went in, finding her lying on the bed, her arms flung out on both sides of her as if they had dropped there and she lacked the strength to move them. He bent down and kissed her; she submitted, but gave nothing back.

He pulled up a chair and sat down, thinking how she had responded to his kiss that morning when she stepped off the train. That was what the day had done to her. He could not bear to think what would happen to her during the night if trouble came.

"Feel rested?" he asked.

"A little."

"Molly sent me up to fetch you down for supper."

"I don't feel like eating."

Suddenly he was impatient. He had tried to be understanding all day, but there was a limit to what any person could do for another. He said roughly, "You're coming down to eat. You didn't have anything at noon. I told you then we'd have a good supper tonight, and I'm not going to just let you lie here and say you don't feel like eating."

It was dusk now and the light here in the room was very thin. He could not see her expression clearly, but she turned her head to look at him, and finally she said, "All right, Clay," as if she had been waiting for him to start giving her orders.

She rose, and, going to the bureau, poured water from the tall pitcher into the bowl. She washed her face and hands, dried, and then stood in front of the mirror working on her hair.

"Want me to light a lamp?" he asked.

"No, Clay," she said.

Watching her, a strange sense of dissatisfaction filled him. He wanted a woman who would be a partner, not someone who must be given orders. If he had gone ahead and lighted the lamp, she would have liked it, but she couldn't face his question and give him a straightforward answer.

This was a quality he had never sensed in her before, but he hadn't seen her away from the places where she had felt at home. When he asked himself how well he had known her, he could not face an honest answer.

She kept fumbling with her hair, and finally he said, "You look fine, honey. They'll clean it all up if we don't get to the table."

"Yes, Clay," she said, and, taking his arm, went down the stairs with him.

The others had started to eat. When Molly saw them, she called in her great voice, "We waited just like a bunch of hogs at the trough. You sit right here, lamb," she said to Margaret, and pulled out a chair at one side of the table next to the corner. She motioned to the chair at the head. "Clay always sits here. Don't make no difference whether we have one of the commissioners or Agent Berry or Otto Mears eating with us. That's where Clay sits."

Judy glanced at Molly, laughing. "Or the Governor?"

"Well, the Governor ain't never been here, but if he showed up, it wouldn't make any difference. Clay would sit at the head just the same."

They began passing food and Margaret's lassitude disappeared at once. She filled her plate and ate with feverish hunger. The supper was good just as Clay had promised:

roast beef, gravy, potatoes, beans, biscuits, butter, and honey, with a three-layer cake for dessert.

As he ate, Clay studied the passengers. Casteel's face showed the battering Clay's fists had given him. No cynical smile now on his bruised lips, no air of superiority about him, and he did not once meet Clay's eyes, but in spite of his physical injuries, his appetite had not been impaired.

Brimlow sat hunched over his plate, eating with his right hand, his left on his lap. Probably holding his satchel, Clay thought.

Pete Shannon ate with the wolfish relish of a growing boy who had never quite got his stomach full. He loaded his plate three times and stopped then only because the food was gone. He seemed unaware of anyone's presence except Jason Brimlow's and when he occasionally lifted his gaze from his plate, it went to Brimlow's face with the unerring certainty of steel being drawn to a magnet.

Judy Allen seemed more at home than any of the other passengers, more relaxed at least. She still wore Molly's apron, her cheeks were flushed from being over the hot kitchen stove, and her dark hair had come loose above her forehead in curls of varied shapes and lengths.

It struck Clay that here was a girl who made a good living with her singing, who had traveled over most of Colorado, and probably knew more men of wealth and importance than all the others at the table combined, yet she was perfectly at ease sitting beside Molly and talking to her, and giving every appearance of enjoying herself.

Judy glanced at Clay's face and then at Casteel's, unquestionably knowing there had been a fight. Margaret just as certainly didn't know what had happened. Clay, seeing her now as he never had before, realized this was the real Margaret, blinded by her fears and disappointments so completely that she had no knowledge of what went on around her.

When the meal was finished, Clay said, "Breakfast at four in the morning. The stage leaves at sunup, so you'd best get to bed right away."

Molly had lighted the lamps on the table, the dusk rapidly turning to darkness. Brimlow rose and, scurrying to the stairs, went up to his room. The rest of the men drifted outside, with the exception of Casteel, who remained behind his chair after he had slid it into place.

"How about opening the bar, Majors," Casteel said.

Clay shook his head. "No drinking tonight."

Casteel's eyes briefly locked with Clay's. They were filled with brooding malice that could not be mistaken. Casteel took a cigar from his coat pocket, bit off the end, lighted it, and blew out a long plume of smoke. With this act of defiance completed, he turned and strode after the others.

Judy began clearing the table. Molly said, "You go on now. You don't have to work . . ."

"I want to, Molly," Judy said, and disappeared into the kitchen with a load of dishes.

Molly sighed as if she didn't know what to do with Judy, then looked at Margaret, who still sat at the table. "You best go to bed, lamb. After a good night's rest, you'll feel a whole lot better."

Margaret rose, and, slipping a hand under Clay's arm, went upstairs with him. He paused in the hall to light a bracket wall lamp, then went into Margaret's room and lighted the lamp that was on her bureau.

Margaret lay down on the bed, completely exhausted. Clay got out his pipe. "You don't mind if I smoke?"

She never had minded when he was in Denver. She had always told him she liked the smell of tobacco smoke, that a pipe gave a man an appearance of solid dignity. Her father smoked a pipe in the house whenever he felt like it, so Clay, knowing it was all right, had smoked in her presence without asking her permission. But now it was different, just as everything in their relationship had become different in the hours since he had met her that morning.

She was silent a moment as she looked at his high-boned face, red-bronze with the lamplight on one side and dark on the other. Then, after letting him feel the edge of her hostility for a few seconds, she said, "No, I don't mind."

He filled and lighted his pipe, wondering if he should have been more honest at the table. Brimlow was the only one to whom he had indicated the stage might not leave in the morning. Perhaps he should have told the others. Yet he had no way of being sure. He had no authority to hold the stage if Galt decided to take it out.

He shrugged, deciding that it was Galt's business to tell the passengers, not his. If Galt didn't want them to know what might happen between now and sunup, they could sleep the sleep of the ignorant for a while at least. All but Jason Brimlow, who would not sleep regardless of what Santo and his band of Utes did.

Suddenly Clay realized Margaret had been watching him, her fine-featured face filled with an expression he could not identify. Now she said, "Remember the first time I met you? It was in Dad's hotel lobby and you came in to sell him some lots in that townsite you were developing."

Her voice held no hostility now. She was reaching back into the more pleasant days of the past, he thought, trying to bridge the gap that had opened between them today. He nodded, smiling at her. He was not likely to forget the first time he had seen her.

More than five years ago. Margaret had been barely eighteen, more girl than woman, but a very lovely one. He had fallen in love with her at that moment, but he had not told her for a long time. Her father had been impressed with the prospects of the townsite, had bought some lots and later sold them for a profit, and was happy about the whole situation, although he would have made more if he had held them.

"Your dad invited me to your house that evening," Clay recalled. "After that I found some excuse to see you whenever I was in Denver. I guess I even made excuses to go to Denver so I could see you."

She sat up, her hands clasped on her lap, her face alive with memories. "I was full of dreams like any romantic girl at eighteen," she said. "I remember dreaming about you that night. When I woke up in the morning I knew I loved you and there would never be anyone but you."

"It was that way with me," he said. "Five years, and it has always been that way. That townsite was a crazy deal for me to get into. I made a little money, but I discovered I wasn't a businessman. This is what I want, Margaret. It's the only white man's ranch inside the reservation. I was Ouray's friend, or I wouldn't have got it in the first place. I put up these buildings myself, with Bronc's help. Molly's, too. My herd of cattle has doubled since I started. I've sold some steers to the Agency, too, but most of what I've made has been here, a night stop for the stage line.

"A lot of people have stayed overnight or taken meals on their way to the Agency. I'd have made a lot more if it hadn't been for the Utes who'd drop in and eat me out of house and home. They never paid, of course. I couldn't have stayed if I hadn't fed them. They knew that as well as I did, so they took advantage of me."

She was bored by this and showed it, but he went on, "Old Colorow is the worst. He's fat. I guess he'll weigh three hundred pounds or more. He'd come in with some of his band and Molly would have to feed them. She finally got enough of it and one day when he was sick and needed some 'medsin,' he said, she gave him a big dose of Epsom salts." Clay laughed. "You should have seen him the next day. He looked like a wind bag with the wind all gone."

"Clay, I talked to Dad the day I left home," Margaret said. "He wanted me to ask you how long it would take you to sell this place."

"Sell?" He wasn't sure he had heard right. "I wouldn't sell if I could. Anyhow, I'd have to wait until the Indians are moved off the reservation and the land is opened to settlement. It may be a couple of years before I get a patent on the land. It means a fortune when I do, Margaret. I wouldn't trade this place for any other site for a cattle ranch on the reservation."

She acted as if she hadn't heard. "Dad's going to build an addition onto the hotel. He needs someone to help him, a partner he can trust. He'll take you in as a full partner whether you have any money to invest or not. Can't you see what that would mean?"

"Yes, I can see all right," he said glumly. "I'd get fat and lazy standing behind a desk."

"There's a house for sale just a block from home," she hurried on. "Dad will buy it and give it to us for a wedding present."

He rose and took his pipe out of his mouth. "Margaret, you know I can't do that. I've told you. For one thing I can't live in a city. For another, I can't take something that's just handed to me whether it's given by my father-in-law or anyone else. But the main thing is that this is a home I built for you. Everything I did, every dream I had, had you right in the middle of it."

She was on her feet, her face bright with a sudden flash of anger. "Don't you think I had some dreams about you, too?" she demanded. "Why do you think I made this awful trip?"

"To see the home I built for you," he answered.

She threw her hand out in an all-inclusive gesture. "This roadhouse a home? You think I'd live in a country that has flooding rivers and roads that go up and down cliffs and where you pick up dead men who have been murdered by Indians and woods full of outlaws? You knew I couldn't stay here, Clay. You knew it all the time."

"This country isn't that bad," he said grimly. "I hoped that you would learn to love it the way I do. I thought that if you ever got here, you would see its beauty as I see it, and that you would be able to look ahead to when the railroad comes and towns will spring up and the country will be settled just like it is around Denver."

"Live here and raise my family where there are no doctors and no churches and no schools?" she cried. "Clay, are you crazy?"

"Yes, I guess I am," he said.

"I'm an old maid," she said. "Twenty-three years old. There could have been other men, but I wouldn't have anything to do with them because it was always you. You've got to marry me, Clay. You've got to go home with me."

"I'll marry you tomorrow," he said. "I wanted to marry you in Gunnison. Or I'll go back with you and have the church wedding your mother wants. But we'll live here."

The anger was gone from her face, and in its place was a hopelessness that dug at Clay's heart. "Oh, you are crazy," she breathed. "Crazy to ever think I could live in a wilderness like this." She dropped back down on the bed and began to cry.

He went to the door and opened it; he stood there looking back at her. He said, "Good night." He didn't try to kiss her. For some reason he didn't even want to.

He stepped into the hall and closed the door and went down the stairs very slowly. Yes, he was crazy, he told himself, crazy to have gone on and on month after month when even by the letters he had received from Margaret he should have known it wouldn't work out.

In most ways Clay Majors was not a visionary man. That only made it worse to have permitted himself the dreams he'd dreamed.

Nine

GLANCING BACK INTO THE KITCHEN, Clay saw that Judy was with Molly. He went on out to the front porch and found that Galt, Lew Fisher, and Bronc Pless were still there. Casteel and Shannon had apparently gone to bed.

Clay sat down on the steps and knocked the dottle from his pipe. He filled it again, asking, "What do you think, Slim?"

"I ain't sure of anything," Galt answered. "I was thinking there at the table when you said breakfast was at four that maybe I oughtta tell 'em the stage might not leave on schedule, then I decided to keep still. If nothing happens tonight, I reckon we'll be wheeling out as usual."

"Brimlow will raise hell if you don't," Clay said. "He claims he's got to be in Ouray tomorrow to wind up a big deal he's got on the fire."

"Casteel will raise more hell," Galt said sourly. "I told him to go to bed or I'd kick his butt from here to Ouray and he wouldn't have to take the stage. He went, too. I reckon you took some of the spizzerinctum out of him afore supper."

Bronc Pless sat in the grass in the fringe of light, arms around his legs, bearded face hunched forward over his knees. He had been in the country much longer than either Clay or Galt. The story was that he had taken a squaw and lived with the Uncompahgre Utes for several years until she died. He neither denied nor confirmed the story, but there was no doubt that he had spent some time at Fort Garland and had known Kit Carson, so he had been in the country as far back as the sixties at least.

"You can count on one thing, Clay," Pless said. "Santo will be around here before morning."

"He won't jump us," Galt said. "He likes Clay too well." When Pless remained silent, Galt demanded, "Well, will he?"

"No telling," Pless answered. "He won't hold off because he likes Clay. That's sure. But what we need to ask ourselves is what Red Holman's going to do. Santo will want him. You can bet your bottom dollar on that."

"Holman will head for Gunnison," Galt said.

"Or the Agency," Pless added. "Who knows what he'll do? The point is that Santo and every Ute he can get will be combing these hills to find Holman. Chances are they're at it now."

"Red's the kind who gets jumpy," Clay said. "He might not have gone anywhere. Just hid out."

"That's the way I size it up," Pless said. "If that's what he done, they'll get him on the run sooner or later. Then he'll be like any rabbit heading for the first hole he can think of, which same is right here. Then we're in trouble. Sure Santo likes Clay, but he'll take Clay's hair as soon as the next man's if Clay's standing between him and the booger who killed his son." Pless took a long breath. "What Lew should of done was to light out for the Agency as soon as he heard about it."

"I can go now," Fisher said. "Hell, I never thought twice about it. I was looking for a bunch of horses, so I kept on hunting 'em."

"No, stay here," Clay said. "Maybe we're jumping the gun. We'll wait and see what happens."

"Better do your waiting with one eye open," Pless grunted. "Just 'cause you've always been friends don't mean nothing now. The Utes are feeling mean like they was at White River when Meeker was deviling 'em about plowing up their race track. They're like kids having a temper fit. Might do something they'll be sorry for tomorrow, but meanwhile you're plumb dead."

52

Clay didn't believe it would happen like that, but then no one had believed that Nathan Meeker and the rest of the men at the White River Agency would be massacred. He thought of Margaret upstairs in her room, already badly frightened. What would she do when she found out there was threat of an Indian attack? And Clay had promised her there would be no danger from the Indians.

"We'll keep a guard out all night," Clay said. "Rest of you better get some sleep."

"I'll take it first," Lew Fisher said. "I kind of figure this is some my fault, so I oughtta stay up all night."

"Till midnight," Clay said. "Then I'll take it. Don't just sit here on the porch, Lew. Take a sashay around once in a while, but don't try to be a hero. If it comes to a fight, there's enough of us here to hold 'em off. We just don't want to be surprised."

They wandered off, Fisher towards the corrals, Galt and Pless to the bunkhouse, Pless grumbling that no one took him seriously any more. Clay thought he would probably have agreed if the old man had stayed to argue. Pless had failed a good deal in the last six months, living more and more in the past, so Clay was inclined to take his warning lightly.

Clay lit his pipe and listened to a cricket somewhere out in the grass. His mind fastened upon Margaret and would not let go. If he had been willing to wait for her to come until the Indians had been moved to Utah, then the river would have been down and Boone Holman wouldn't have been killed the day she arrived and Larry Casteel probably wouldn't have been on the stage . . .

But it was foolish to spend time on the might-have-beens, excusable only in the very young and the very old. What had happened had happened and could not be changed, and a man had to go on the basis that it was for the best.

The pipe had gone cold in his hand. He lighted it again and shook out the match, then he was aware that Judy Allen had come out of the house. He said, "Sit down, Judy."

"I don't want to disturb you," she said. "I just came out for a little fresh air. Molly's gone to bed. I guess I'd better do the same if we have to get up at four for breakfast."

"Sit down," he said. "How do you like Margaret?"

She did sit down beside him then, taking a moment before she answered. Then she said as if choosing her words carefully, "She's very pretty, Mr. Majors. She'll make you a wife that any man would be proud of."

"I don't think she'll make me any kind of a wife," he said with more bitterness than he had intended to show her. "She wants me to live in Denver and go into partnership with her father in the hotel business. I'd go crazy, standing behind a hotel desk."

"Yes, I think you would," Judy agreed.

"Looks like I made a mistake sending for her," Clay said.

"I don't think so. Isn't it better to find out now how you stand than after you're married?" He didn't answer, and presently she asked, "Mr. Majors, did you ever try to take a plant that does well in a low altitude and transplant it in the high country?"

"It works the other way, too," he said sharply.

"I know," she said. "You're both damned fools, Clay. She came to talk you into going to Denver, and you brought her here to talk her into living on your place, but neither of you can do what the other one wants."

She paused, then added, "I don't know much about love, but it seems to me it must be born of a willingness to give."

That was right, he thought. The trouble was Margaret wouldn't give and he couldn't. He knew at once he was being unfair, that Margaret looked at this situation exactly opposite to the way he did.

In spite of himself, he could not keep from comparing Margaret and Judy in his mind. Judy lacked Margaret's striking beauty and figure, she lacked Margaret's ability to wear clothes, she lacked Margaret's delicate sensitivity, which now was the very thing that was defeating Clay.

On the other hand, Judy had vitality that Clay admired, an ability to adjust herself to any situation she met, and courage, too, for that was part and parcel of the same ability. She had a tough quality about her, but that was natural, having to look out for herself the way she had. She would enjoy doing whatever she had to do, Clay thought, and suddenly it struck him that it would be fine to have her here all the time helping Molly.

"Judy, don't go with Casteel tomorrow," he said impulsively. "I know what he does to the women he takes to Ouray. I can't let it happen to you."

She laughed. "You don't have much confidence in me, Clay."

"Sure I do. It's just that I know Casteel."

"So do I. I can handle him. I've got to. If I broke my contract, I'd never get another job. Not around here, anyhow." She paused, then asked, "Would you give me a job, Clay?"

"I'd give you a job, all right," he answered, "but it wouldn't be singing."

She was silent a full minute, her eyes fixed on the creek that held a silver glint from the full moon which had come up over the eastern hills. Then she said, "Clay, I enjoyed the times you took me to supper in Gunnison more than anything else that happened to me while I was there. You remember that Sunday when you got a buggy and drove me up Tumitchi Creek, and then we came back and had dinner in the hotel?"

"I remember," he said.

"You told me about your place here," she said, "and all your plans, but the minute I met Margaret, I knew she was no good for you. Your ranch is just like you told me. I can see what it will be in five years from now, exactly what you said it would be. That is, if you don't marry Margaret."

She was right. He faced the situation honestly now, knowing he had mentally clothed Margaret with virtues and qualities she did not possess. Instead, they were qualities he had wanted her to have.

He was angry, yet he had no right to be, for Judy, with her tough directness, had a way of cutting off everything that was superfluous and false, and getting at the truth. He fussed with his pipe for a while, lighting it and getting it going again; then, his anger gone, he asked: "Judy, I don't know how you've been able to stay good, bucking men like Casteel all the time."

"Good?" Her laugh was not a pleasant sound. "You, of all men, calling me good? I guess you have a short memory. Or have you forgotten that I asked you to come to my room after the show? I haven't, Clay. I've thought of it many times. By the standard of good people, I should be ashamed, but I'm not." She stopped, as if thinking about it, then she added defiantly, "I'm not sorry, Clay. I'm not sorry at all."

"There are a lot of ways to define what's good," he said quickly, regretting he had asked the question. "I say it's what's inside people, that makes them do what they do. I still say you're good, Judy." He paused, then asked, "How'd you get into your business? After watching you give Molly a hand, seems to me you'd be married and keeping house."

"I'm still young," she said. "Twenty-one, though I've been knocking around quite a while. My mother died when I was little and my stepmother was ornery as hell, so I ran away. Funny thing, Clay. I was so damned stubborn or impatient or something that I couldn't stay at home and look after Pa. He died a year after I pulled out. I wish I had stayed. I've wished it a lot of times."

"You got what you wanted, didn't you?"

"Oh sure," she said sarcastically. "No more kitchen work. No more gathering eggs and riding after cows and splitting wood because Pa went off to work and forgot it. Now I stand up on a stage with as little on as I can keep on. I sing, which is what I wanted to do all right, and when I get done, men throw coins up on the stage and then I get down on my knees and pick them up and blow kisses to them. Sometimes I have to walk down through the tables and they reach out and pinch me when I go by, but I have to keep smiling no matter how much I want to haul off and knock their heads together."

She sighed. "Yes, I suppose it was what I wanted when I was younger. The tinsel and the glitter and the glory appealed to me, but I didn't know about the dirt, Clay, the filth I have to wade in up to my knees. No, it's not what I want. I'd rather get married and keep house."

"Clay." It was Lew Fisher running in from the darkness. "Clay, somebody's coming riding like hell. Sounds like more'n one to me."

Clay jammed his pipe into his pocket and stepped off the porch. He listened, hearing the steady drum of hoofs up the creek. More than one, all right. Nearer a dozen. He whirled to face Judy.

"Get everybody up," he said, "but no shooting unless I start it. Tell them that."

"Yes, Clay," she said, and ran into the house.

No questions, no hysterics. She simply did what she was told. Again he compared her to Margaret, and he shook his head. Margaret probably would have stood on the porch and screamed.

He wheeled toward Lew Fisher. "Get Slim and Bronc. Tell 'em to fetch their guns. You and Bronc both have rifles. Get 'em."

Fisher disappeared toward the bunkhouse. Clay moved away from the patch of lamplight that fell through the open door and, drawing his gun, stood there and waited while the sound of beating hoofs became louder and louder.

Ten

THE RIDERS BROKE INTO THE MOONLIGHT not far above the house, one man considerably ahead of the others. The one in front was lashing his horse, getting all the speed out of him that he could. Still, the pursuers were gaining steadily.

There were six or eight of them, tightly bunched. They were Indians, but the distance was too great and the light too thin for Clay to recognize any of them. He couldn't identify the man they were chasing, but he felt certain it was Red Holman.

Clay cocked his gun and ran forward, thinking bleakly that this was the worst thing that could happen. He yelled, but still the Utes came on, gradually closing the gap. If Casteel or anyone else in the house got trigger-happy and killed one of the Indians, they were all in trouble. Then Clay remembered that Casteel didn't have his gun. But it probably didn't make much difference. He could find one.

Clay threw a shot over the heads of the Indians, thinking that if Santo was leading them, they'd keep coming, but if he wasn't, they probably could be turned. He fired again. This time it worked, the Indians veering off and splashing across the creek while the man in front came thundering on past Clay toward the house.

A moment later the Indians had disappeared on the other side of the willows. Clay couldn't tell whether they had stopped to see what happened or whether they were riding upstream. He wheeled and ran to the house as the rider reined up in the pool of light falling through the front door. The man swayed in the saddle as Bronc Pless and Slim Galt ran toward him, then he swung down and stepped away from his horse. He stumbled and would have fallen if Galt hadn't caught him by an arm and steadied him.

"It's Red Holman," Galt called to Clay.

"I'm shot," Holman groaned. "Left arm."

One look at the man's face told Clay he was in bad shape, from pain and fatigue, or perhaps just panic. Clay said to Lew Fisher, who had just come up, "Take care of his horse."

Reaching for the reins, Fisher said, "This animal's about finished."

"Let's get Holman inside," Clay said.

"Throw him back to Santo's bunch," Bronc Pless growled. "He's gonna bring us nothing but a pile of trouble."

"They'll kill me," Holman said hoarsely. "You can't do that. They'll kill me."

"Come on, come on," Clay said. "Bronc, stay out here. Keep your eyes peeled."

Holman started toward the house, Galt still holding to his right arm. Clay reached for his left to steady him from that side, but dropped his hand when Holman cried out, "That arm's busted all to hell."

They went up the steps and across the porch. Casteel and Pete Shannon were there, stepping back out of the doorway.

Margaret was standing at the foot of the stairs, one hand raised to her throat. Her hair hung down her back in a yellow mass reaching below her waist. She was still wearing her gray suit. Molly came along the hall from her room, a faded and patched robe over her nightgown. Jason Brimlow was not in sight.

"Take him upstairs," Molly called. "The back room on the east side is empty. Judy, go fetch the tea kettle. Water ought to be hot yet."

She turned ponderously and tramped back to her room. Clay dropped behind Galt and Holman, the stairway too narrow for three men to go up abreast. Holman was reeling and groaning, and Clay, following a step behind, looked at his left arm with the blood-soaked sleeve, and decided that the man had a painful wound all right, but the arm was a long ways from being shot to pieces.

Casteel, standing at the foot of the stairs, stared upward, the light from a wall lamp falling across his bruised face. He called, "There's your Ute friends for you, Majors. What do you think of them now?"

Clay did not look back or bother to reply. He went on behind Galt and Holman to the room at the end of the hall and lighted a lamp on the bureau, as Galt released his grip and let Holman ease down on the bed. His feet were still on the floor, as if he lacked even the strength to lift them to the bed. Galt raised both feet and tugged off a boot, Clay removing the other one.

"You know what you've done?" Clay asked. "Coming here like this?"

Holman's eyes were closed, right arm across his chest, his wounded left arm on the bed beside him. His face was bruised and cut as if it had been slashed by the branches of trees as he bolted through the timber. He was a big man with a wiry beard and mustache, and in Clay's presence he had always been brash and loud-mouthed, but now he was thoroughly cowed.

Irritated by Holman's failure to answer his question, Clay said, "I'll tell you what you've done. You'll bring Santo and the whole Ute nation down on our heads. We've got three women here. Does that mean anything to you?"

Holman's eyes opened. They were wild and bloodshot and filled with panic. He said, "I've been running all day. I had to go somewhere."

"So you came here," Clay said sourly.

"You won't turn me over to 'em?" Holman begged. "I'm a white man. You wouldn't do that."

"No, I wouldn't do that," Clay said heavily. "But why in

hell did you have to hole up here tonight, of all nights?"

Casteel and Shannon stood in the doorway, Margaret behind them but not tall enough to see over their shoulders. Casteel said angrily, "Let him alone, Majors. Can't you see he's bad off?"

Clay wheeled away from the bed just as Molly called, "Gangway. Let us in."

Casteel and Shannon stepped out of the way, and Molly sailed in with a bottle and bundle of cloth and a pair of scissors. Judy followed with a pan of steaming water. When they were through the door, Clay said to Casteel and Shannon, "Get on back to your rooms. You'll just be in the way here."

Shannon obeyed immediately, but Casteel stood where he was, spread-legged, glaring at Clay, then, after he had made the moment one of deliberate defiance, he turned and walked away, calling back, "I'm not finished with you. Not by a damned sight."

When Casteel's door closed, Clay looked at Margaret. "I'm sorry," he said. "You'd better try to rest."

Her face was very pale, the pulse in her throat throbbing visibly. "Rest?" she whispered. "Tonight? With all these Indians around us?" She turned and fled to her room.

He stood there a moment, staring down the hall at her closed door. She was probably convinced that this kind of thing happened every day, and as he turned back into the room, he thought bleakly that there would be no use to tell her it had never happened here before. She would just think he was lying and probably tell him so.

Molly had cut the sleeve away from Holman's wounded left arm, and now was working the cloth free from where it had been stuck to the ragged flesh around the bullet hole by dried blood. Holman was groaning and crying like a child.

"You ain't bad off, son," Molly said irritably. "Don't look to me like the bone's hurt. Maybe chipped a mite, but it sure ain't broke. Don't worry none. I'm a purty fair horse doctor. Why, I remember once in the San Luis Valley I dug a slug out of a man's belly. I figured he'd cash in sure, but no sir, he made it fine."

She straightened and jerked her head at Judy. "Let's have some of that hot water. Got to clean up this hole so we can let this boy see it ain't bad."

She soaked a piece of wadded up cloth in the water, sponged away the dried blood on one side of the arm and turned it so she could examine the other opening. Holman let out a scream and twisted his head so he couldn't see the wound.

"Taking on like you had a toothache," Molly said. "You'd best see a sawbones when you get to Gunnison, but you ain't real bad off. I can tell you that. Here now, this will hurt a mite, but you just grin and bear it."

She pulled the cork from the bottle she had brought and, tipping it, dribbled some of the liquid over the wound. Holman let out another scream and jerked his arm away from Molly, the violent movement starting the wound to bleeding again.

"Now see what you done," Molly said reproachfully. "Fuming and faunching around like a baby. We'll get it all tied up again, then you'll just have to lie here and keep from moving it. I don't reckon it's gonna be long till Clay boosts you onto your horse and you can ride to hell out of here."

Watching, Clay thought that in the time she had been here, she had doctored him and Bronc Pless, and Lew Fisher during the year he had worked for Clay, through various kinds of injuries and maladies, and she had never been impatient, but she was with Red Holman for his childishness.

With Judy's help, Molly bound the wound tightly and stomped out of the room. Judy picked up the pan of water and followed, and Clay, his gaze following her until she was out of sight, thought of Margaret, who had not even offered to help.

"I need a drink," Holman begged. "Get me some whisky, Majors."

Clay hesitated, staring down at this man who, by Clay's standards, deserved nothing. Then he shrugged, and, going downstairs, unlocked the door into the bar. He found a bottle with less than a pint in it, and locked the door behind him. He put the key into his pocket, glad he had not opened the bar for business when the stage first arrived, as he ordinarily did. The night would be bad enough before it was over without whisky making it worse.

He called to Pless from the front door, "Hear anything, Bronc?"

"Nothing," Pless answered from the shadows. "Lew's here. Says Holman's horse has been pushed all day. Looks that way, anyhow."

"Probably riding in circles," Clay thought, and went back up the stairs.

He gave the bottle to Holman, who sat up and took a long drink. Clay jerked it away from him and set it on the bureau. "That's all you're getting now, Red. You may want another drink before morning. Now what happened to you?"

Holman licked his lips. He dropped flat again, rubbing his face with his right hand. For some reason he thought of his gun and reached for it, but his holster was empty. He sat up again, cursing. "Gimme my gun. God damn it, you want me to lie here and let them murdering devils come in and finish me?"

"I took your iron," Galt said. "You acted like a brat of a kid when Molly fixed your arm. I figured a boy like that didn't need no six-shooter."

Holman turned to Clay. "Make him give it back. They'll come in here and cut my heart out, and I won't have nothing to fight 'em with."

"No," Clay said. "I asked you what happened."

Holman lay back on the bed again. "We was just breaking camp. Hadn't even got hooked up. This bunch of Injuns rides up, fifteen or twenty of 'em. They said they was gonna take our outfit. They all had guns. Well, Pa got his rifle out and said they wasn't taking nothing. I was on my horse. One of 'em plugged Pa and I got him and then I ran. Been running all day. Tried to get to Gunnison, but guess I fainted and I knowed I couldn't ride that far, shot up like I was. I thought of trying to get to the Agency, but figured I couldn't get through the Injuns. So I hid. 'Bout dark I heard 'em coming after me, so I lit a shuck for here, this being the only place I could go."

Clay lifted his gaze to Galt on the other side of the bed. Galt nodded that he understood. Clay said, "You're lying, Red. There were just four of the Indians, all told. The one you shot was Santo's boy. They asked for something to eat, didn't they?"

"Hell, they wanted everything we had," Holman shouted as if he thought the loudness of his voice would make what he said sound as if it were true. "I couldn't let 'em steal us blind."

"You're still lying," Clay said. "Sure they're beggars. I ought to know, the way they've mooched off me ever since I started this place. But the trouble with you is you wouldn't let them have anything. They asked for grub, and you shot Santo's boy. If it had been one of the others, it wouldn't have been so bad, but Santo's bad medicine when he's mad, and he's likely to go out of his head when he finds out what happened. I don't blame him, either. I knew his boy. A fine kid. Now he's dead because you don't like Utes and wouldn't let them have any breakfast."

"You're a damned Ute-lover," Holman said thickly. "Everybody knows that."

"I know one thing," Clay told him. "You'll stand trial in Gunnison for murder."

"Sure, sure," Holman said eagerly. "Take me to Gunnison

and put me in jail." He licked his lips. "What are you going to do if Santo comes here and asks for me?"

Clay didn't answer for a moment. He glanced at Galt, but this time he found no help on the stage driver's angry face. At the moment all Clay could think of was the Meeker massacre. Three white women had been kidnapped, and there were three white women in this house.

Clay said, "I don't know, Holman. I just don't know." Turning, he left the room, Galt following.

Eleven

CLAY TURNED at the foot of the stairs toward the bar, feeling the need of a drink. But he realized immediately that he could hardly open the bar for himself and keep it closed to everyone else. He grimaced and swung the other way toward the parlor, where Molly and Judy sat on the sofa.

Galt, a step behind Clay, grumbled, "You had a good idea there for a minute."

Clay didn't answer. He glanced at Molly, who was still wearing her old robe over her nightgown, her usually placid face livid with anger. She asked, "What'd you do with that cry baby, tuck him into bed?"

"Yeah, and gave him a bottle." Clay looked at Judy, who was watching him with keen interest. If she was worried, it did not show in her face. Clay swung around to Galt. "What happens to these people when they're under my roof is my responsibility, but whether the stage goes out in the morning is your decision. What about it?"

"How'n hell do I know what's gonna happen tonight?"

"Suppose nothing happens?"

"Then we ain't going out," Galt said. "That'd mean old Santo was still around, like a hawk waiting for a chicken to show. He'd jump the stage the minute it moves, figuring Holman's on it. Leastwise that's my guess."

"But if he didn't find Holman on the stage . . ."

"Oh, for God's sake." Galt looked at Clay in disgust. "You're talking like a greenhorn of Brimlow's caliber, and that's about the greenest horn there is. You think maybe

Santo will ride up to me and say, 'Please, Mr. Galt, hand that murdering son of a bitch to me'? No, he won't do no such thing. They'll pile all over us, shooting as they come, and I'll be the first to get it, sitting up there like a pigeon on a ridgepole."

Clay nodded, grinning a little. "It's pretty bad if I'm talking like Brimlow. I was thinking same as you, but I wanted to be sure you were figuring the same way. I think we'd better tell them. They've got to get used to the idea. Besides, we may need all the guns we've got before morning."

"I'll ask them to come down," Judy said, and went up the stairs.

Clay filled his pipe and walked to the door, standing with his back to the casing as he lighted it. Bronc Pless was still sitting on the porch. Clay asked, "Hear anything?"

"Nothing," Pless said. "That's worse than hearing something at a time like this."

That, Clay knew, was true. There could be a hundred Indians within fifty yards of the house and not make a sound that would give away their presence. He asked, "Where's Lew?"

"Prowling," the old man said.

"Fetch him in," Clay said.

Pless disappeared across the yard. Clay watched him until he was lost to sight, the moon covered by clouds so that for the moment the light was not as strong as it had been when Holman had ridden in.

He thought of Red Holman lying in bed. Sooner or later Santo would demand the murderer of his son. Clay didn't know what he would say or do, but he did know he could not hand Holman over to the Indian chief to be killed no matter how much Holman deserved it. Any man had the right of a trial by jury regardless of what his crime had been.

Clay, trying to be objective about it, realized that his decision was irrevocable because it was based on more than a conviction about law and the rights of man. He simply knew that if he yielded to Santo's threats, he would never be able to live with himself.

He was not aware that they had all come downstairs until Judy appeared at his elbow, saying, "They're here, Clay."

He nodded, knocked his pipe out against his boot heel, and followed Judy into the parlor. Margaret sat beside Molly on the couch. Brimlow occupied a chair near the couch, sitting toadlike, the satchel in his hands, and Clay came close to smiling when he glanced at the man, wondering what he would look like without the satchel.

Casteel stood with his hands jammed into his pockets, not deigning to sit down. He had taken off his coat, and now, standing there in his shirt sleeves glaring at Clay, he lacked the dignity and air of superiority in which he had been clothed most of the day.

Shannon slouched beside him, his eyes flicking restlessly around the room, as tense as a wild animal that finds itself unexpectedly caged.

Margaret surprised Clay more than the others. She was very pale, but she had complete control of herself. With her hands folded on her lap, and her gaze on Clay's face, she seemed cool and withdrawn, and very much the lady.

"We're in a tight corner," Clay said frankly. "It's only fair that you know what the situation is. We may need a gun in every hand before this is over."

"I have no gun," Casteel said sourly.

"You'll have one if it comes to that," Clay said.

"Aren't you scared I'll use it on you?"

"Not till this is over," Clay said. "Then I'll be ready for you."

"I'll get a gun whether we have Indian trouble or not," Casteel said, "and I'll use it on you. You can count on it."

"You willing to wait till we're sure this is over?" Clay asked.

"I'm in no hurry." Casteel's lips curled into something like his familiar cynical smile. "But there won't be any trouble with the Indians, if that's what you've got us down here to say. Cowards like these Utes won't attack us."

"You're loco——" Galt began, but Clay motioned him into silence.

"I didn't have Judy fetch you down here for an argument," Clay said. "I just wanted you to know what me and Slim had been thinking. When you're in the stage, he runs the show. While you're staying here, I do. Let's understand that."

Shannon's eyes had been switching to the door and back to Clay's face. Now he said rudely, "Get your gabbing over with, Majors, so we can go to bed."

"All right, I'll get it over with," Clay said. "Red Holman shot and killed Santo's son early this morning and then ran. His father held off the other three Utes long enough for Red to make his getaway, then he got plugged. The three Ute boys took the body of Santo's son to Santo's lodge, but it's my guess he was out hunting, or maybe down to the Agency. I'm pretty sure he wasn't in the bunch that was chasing Holman while ago."

"Why not?" Casteel demanded.

"They turned back when I threw a couple of shots at

64

them," Clay said. "If Santo had been leading them, they'd have kept on coming."

Casteel's lips curled in derision. "I told you they're cowards. They won't stand up against a gun, Santo or none of them."

"I know better," Clay said. "Santo was a great warrior with Ouray twenty years ago. He's middle-aged now, but he's no more coward than he was then. Sooner or later he'll come here demanding that we turn Holman over to him. Well, I won't do it. I don't know what he'll do then. Probably wait till sunup, but he'll make trouble one way or another."

"Now can we go to bed?" Shannon asked impatiently.

"One more thing," Clay said. "If nothing happens during the night, the stage won't go out in the morning. You may be here all day. And the day after that. All I can say now is that until Slim knows it's safe to travel, you're staying here."

"So you can make more money out of us," Casteel said. "Renting your rooms and selling us meals. There's nothing to this scare talk, I tell you. I've got to be in Ouray tomorrow. So has Miss Judy. I've advertised her initial performance for tomorrow night, and she'll pack the house. If you think we're staying in this rathole because you're scared of a few cowardly Indians, you are crazy."

"It's a long walk to Ouray," Galt said. "I don't think Miss Judy can make it."

"There isn't any problem the way I see it," Brimlow said. "Holman is a murderer who should be executed. The manner of his death is not important since he deserves to die anyhow. Hand him over to Santo, Majors. Then we can all go in the morning and be safe."

"No," Clay said. "It is important how Holman dies, Brimlow. I won't turn him over to them."

"You mean you'll risk our lives because of him?" Brimlow asked incredulously. "You say he's a murderer, yet you'll protect him and maybe start an Indian war when all you've got to do is to turn him over to them. That's insane, Majors, completely insane."

"But it's the road to honor, isn't it, Majors?" Casteel asked sarcastically. "I've never heard so much scare talk over nothing in my life. I'm going to bed. Galt, you'll take the stage out of here on schedule or I'll see you're fired. I'm not without influence, you know."

He stomped out of the room and up the stairs, Brimlow and Shannon following. Margaret remained on the couch, her hands clasped on her lap. Clay said, "Someone should sit up with Holman. He may get a fever out of that bullet wound."

His gaze was on Margaret, and suddenly he realized

65

how much he wanted her to volunteer to do this simple thing. Not until that moment did he understand how hope lingered stubbornly in him, the hope that the Margaret he had seen today was not the real Margaret, stripped of all the parlor, tea-and-cake niceties she had assumed in Denver when nothing else was demanded of her.

"Don't look at me," Margaret said. "I need all the sleep I can get, although I don't suppose I'll sleep a wink."

"I'll sit up with Holman," Judy said, and rose and left the room.

Molly yawned loudly. "I'll go try my bed again. Wake me up when the shooting starts, Clay. I'm a pretty good hand with that old Sharps."

She tramped heavily out of the room, yawning again. When Clay glanced around, he saw that Galt was gone, too. He brought his gaze back to Margaret's face. He said wearily, "I'm sorry, Margaret. You don't need to remind me that I promised you there would be no danger. All I can tell you is that nothing like this ever happened before. If I had known, or even suspected . . ."

"Of course not, Clay."

She rose and walked to him, her hips weaving seductively in a way he had never seen before. She wouldn't have moved in that manner in Denver, and he would have considered it highly improper if she had. She put her hands on his shoulders and lifted her face to his. When he did not try to kiss her, she stood on tiptoes and brought his head down and kissed him. It was not like any other kiss she had ever given him, but passionately fierce, her lips pulling at his, a wanton's kiss who was hungry for him and wanted him to know it.

She drew her lips back from his and lowered her heels to the floor. She whispered, "I'm going to bed now."

He felt the pressure of her body against his, exciting and titilating, and he knew an overpowering desire for her, yet with it was the inhibiting knowledge that it was false, a trap, that she would demand a price he could not pay.

When he simply stood there doing nothing, she said, "You've told me many times you love me. Prove it, Clay."

"How?"

"Do what Brimlow said. Let the Indians have Holman. You've said he was a murderer, that he deserved to die for what he did. Why should you protect him and risk all of our lives?" She pressed harder against him, arousing him and stirring him as she had never done before. "Clay, it's my life you're risking. If you ever loved me, you won't throw my life away or make me go through what the Meeker women did just to protect a man like Red Holman."

He pulled her arms away from his neck, feeling the sour run of disappointment poisoning his mind. This was the proper Margaret Trent who had let him hold her hand or kiss her upon occasion, but only with decorum and with no hint of passion.

Yet now, in exchange for his promise to turn Red Holman over to Santo, he could go upstairs with her. He could not keep the thought from embittering his mind that she must have known men in spite of all her pretenses of innocence, or she could not have done what she had so perfectly and so well timed.

"I can't give Holman to them," he said as he walked to the door.

He heard her gasp, heard her run up the stairs, heels cracking noisily on the steps, and he heard her sobs. Perhaps she was disappointed that he had not accepted her invitation, he thought harshly.

Now all the bonds between them had been cut, and she could go back to Denver, hating him as any woman would who had thrown herself at a man and been turned down. More than that, he was glad he would never have her for a wife. He knew now that she wasn't the thoroughbred Larry Casteel had taken her for, and he knew, too, he would never have any regrets for losing her.

Twelve

CLAY FOUND Galt and Lew Fisher sitting on the porch, smoking. Bronc Pless hunkered in the yard at the edge of the pool of light falling through the front door. Galt glanced up at Clay, asking, "Everything fixed?"

"Yeah," Clay said heavily. "All fixed."

He stood there motionless and tense, but no sound came to him that was alarming. The moon, well up in the east now, was almost full. The ridge lines were dark against the sky, but the yellow moonlight was bright here in the valley, bright enough for Clay to be confident he could see anything that moved. Even the air seemed close and stifling and unusually warm.

Clay remained that way for a long moment, listening carefully, eyes searching the valley, and although he could not see or hear anything that was out of the ordinary, he felt a prickle run down his back, a definite tightening of his stomach muscles. This was not a new feeling to him. Still, he could not identify it exactly beyond knowing that it wasn't fear, but rather a warning triggered off by some sixth sense which a man must develop in this country if he survived.

"Bronc said you were prowling around, Lew," Clay said. "Find anything?"

"No," Fisher said, "but I got a hell of a scare. I thought I heard a man cough. I was on the other side of the woodpile when I heard it. Sounded like it came from the barn."

"You take a look?" Clay asked.

"Sure, but I didn't find nothing. The inside of the barn is as black as a bull's gut. Santo and fifty bucks could be hiding inside and I couldn't have seen 'em. I thought the four of us ought to take lanterns and look good."

"They ain't in the barn," Pless said a little irritably. "They're out yonder. A hundred of 'em, I'd guess, and they've got us surrounded. You can count on that."

"Figger they'll be moving in on us?" Fisher asked.

"Not now," Pless said. "The Utes ain't much for moving in and getting a bellyful of lead if they can work it some other way. They won't make a move till Santo gets here. Depends on how much whisky they got their hands on, too. If they get drunk enough, some of 'em will start shooting. After that anything can happen."

"We oughtta put the lights out," Fisher said. "We're sitting ducks this way."

"No," Clay said. "They know somebody's awake long as the place has got lights. If they do come after Holman, it'll probably be after they figure we're asleep."

That wasn't Clay's real reason for keeping the house lighted. Rather, it was the simple fact that darkness bred trouble at a time like this. He considered the people in the house.

He had no trust whatever in the kid, Pete Shannon. He probably didn't know what was in Brimlow's satchel, but he had shown too much interest in it all day.

Brimlow was a coward, the kind who might blow up completely if he had to spend the rest of the night in darkness.

Casteel was the most dangerous of any of them because he was smart, sly, and unscrupulous, and he hated the Utes.

Still, the way things were now, Clay didn't see what harm Casteel could do.

Judy would be all right, except that it would be difficult for her to take care of Holman in the darkness if he needed any care.

Clay's thoughts turned briefly to Margaret. It would be impossible for her to keep her sanity until morning without the assurance of a lighted lamp in her room. Five minutes of darkness and the walls would be crawling with Indians, and she'd have hysterics. Clay knew he couldn't stand it, and neither could the others.

A moment of uneasy silence, then Fisher asked, "Want me to get a lantern? The truth is I got boogery and didn't give the barn a good looking over."

"No," Clay said. "Bronc knows what he's talking about. They wouldn't be in the barn."

"Damn it, I heard a man cough," Fisher said stubbornly. "Wasn't any of us. You and Slim were in the house, and Bronc says he stuck right here till you sent him after me."

"You said you *thought* you heard a man cough," Clay said. "Chances are it was one of the horses in the corral. Or maybe the wind knocking something over."

"Wasn't no wind blowing then," Fisher said. "Hell, you think I dreamed it up. Well, I didn't. I heard something."

"I'm not denying you heard something," Clay said, "but I don't think you heard a man cough. You don't hear Indians, Lew. Take Bronc here. He hasn't heard anything, but he knows they're out there. A lot of them. I doubt that he knows how he can tell, but he knows, all right."

"His nose knows," Fisher said irritably. "He smells 'em."

"No," Pless said. "Ain't nothing you can hear or smell or see, Lew. Just a feeling you get. I wouldn't have had it when I was twenty."

Fisher lapsed into sullen silence, insulted because no one believed he had actually heard a man cough. Presently Pless said, "Only one thing you can be sure of, Clay. Santo ain't gonna let Holman get away. Or if he makes a break, the Indians will be right along behind him. The thing is they know for sure he's here. I dunno how Santo will get him, or when, but sure as I'm sitting here, Red Holman is a dead man."

"All of us, too," Galt said.

"Maybe," Pless said. "If Santo comes in here after Holman, and we start shooting, we are dead. But then he may hold off and give Clay a chance to hand Holman over. I don't figger we'll get hurt none if Clay lets him have Holman."

"I won't," Clay said.

"Then you'd better get fixed for a fight," Pless said.

Clay had been sure of that from the first. Nothing had happened to make him change his mind and he was sure nothing would. The bitter part of it was that probably no one, unless it was Slim Galt, would understand why that was the way it must be.

"Santo is a pretty level-headed Indian," Clay said thoughtfully. "I don't think he'll attack the house and wipe us out."

"What makes you think that?" Pless asked.

"I've always been his friend," Clay said. "He's not one to forget it. Besides, he knows what will happen to the whole tribe if there's another massacre like there was on White River."

Pless made a snorting sound of derision. "Remember three things, Clay. Santo's son was murdered, Holman done it, and Santo knows Holman is right here in this house."

"Sure," Clay said impatiently, "but I don't think Santo's going to start anything. He'll just keep us surrounded, so maybe we could get a rider through to the Agency."

"The agent can't stop 'em," Pless grunted.

"To the cantonment, then," Clay said. "The cavalry will."

"You won't get a man through," Pless said. "If I could ride, I might have a chance, but I can't hack it."

"I'll go," Fisher said eagerly. "Put me on Diamond and there's no Ute buck living that can outrun me. He ain't been rode for two, three days. He'll go out of here like a streak."

Fisher was young and might panic, Clay thought. Bronc Pless had savvy, but age and a hard life had caught up with him. He wasn't physically able to make the ride. Galt couldn't go because his first responsibility was to his passengers. He had to be here to take the stage out in the morning if he could.

"I'd better go," Clay said.

"I can ride as well as you can," Fisher urged. "Better maybe, 'cause I'm twenty pounds lighter. Besides, this is your place and you've got to stay. You're the one Santo will want to dicker with."

"That's right," Pless said. "The only thing wrong with Lew is that he's young. If he tried to run after they jump him, or if he fights 'em, they'll kill him."

"I won't," Fisher said. "I don't want to lose my hair no more'n any of you. I'll keep in the timber and take it slow for a spell, then I'll swing back on the road and go like hell. With this moon, I can let Diamond out."

Clay turned it over in his mind. If Fisher could get two miles away, he might make it. A slim chance, but the only chance they had, the way Clay saw it. Whatever was done had to be done now, for if they waited until daylight, there would be no chance whatever. Diamond was a black gelding that was unquestionably faster than any horse the Utes had. Fisher had run him in enough races against the Ute ponies to prove that.

The trick would be to reach the fringe of timber to the north and use it for cover until Fisher could make the wide swing to the west. Clay glanced up at the sky. The moon was a nearly perfect ball which had been moving steadily upward without the slightest stain of a cloud across its face, but now Clay saw that the first filmy fingers of a cloud were touching the moon.

To the west the sky had become darkly menacing, with now and then a flash of lightning striking downward toward the crest of the hills. For the first time the sound of thunder came to Clay. He had no way of knowing whether a bad storm was developing or not. The chances were good that one was, for summer storms had come early this year. If the clouds hid the moon long enough for Fisher to swing around the Ute guards, he might make it.

"All right," Clay said reluctantly. "Saddle Diamond and make a stab at it. Just remember that if they stop you, don't fight them. They may turn you back, or they might hold you prisoner until this is over. Most of them know you, so if you play it right, I don't think they'll hurt you. But if you make a run for it, or fight, you're a goner."

"Sure, sure," Fisher said, eager to be gone.

"Damn-fool business," Pless grumbled. "He ain't got no show."

Fisher had already started toward the corral, Galt a step behind him. Clay glanced at Pless, who still sat hunkered on the grass. The sharp fingers of fear clawed up through Clay. He wasn't sure what he feared, but in spite of himself he was beset by a premonition of disaster. If Fisher was killed Clay would never forgive himself, but he had considered the alternatives as closely as he could and this seemed the only thing that could be done.

"They won't kill him, Bronc," Clay said as he knocked his pipe against his boot heel and slipped it into his pocket.

He said it as more of a question than a statement. Pless grunted something, then said, "Not if he keeps his head, but it's like you told him. If he gets boogery, they'll beef him sure."

"Stay here," Clay said. "Don't let anyone leave the house."

Pless cackled. "You think any of them greenhorns want

to get out of the house? No sir, they know when they're well off."

Clay crossed the yard to the corral, thinking that Pless was getting old and maybe turning a little crazy as old men do who know they've lived their lives out and all the good days are behind them, but still he had more savvy than any other white man on the reservation.

Clay stood beside Galt while Fisher led Diamond out of the corral. The moonlight had faded as the dark clouds moved eastward, and the thunder was louder now. Clay said, "You're lucky. Another two, three minutes and the moon will be pretty well covered. Take it easy to the timber."

"I know what to do," Fisher said impatiently, and swung into the saddle.

"Good luck," Clay said worriedly. "Remember what I told you. Come back if you have to."

"Sure," Fisher said, and rode around the barn.

"He's young and full of vinegar," Galt said, "but he'll be back."

"I hope so," Clay said. "If he doesn't . . ."

"Don't blame yourself," Galt said sternly. "You've done all you could. It's up to him now."

The minutes dragged. No sound except the heavy roll of distant thunder, no light except that of the lamps in the house and the lightning which threw a sudden burst of flame upon the earth and was gone.

Clay began to breathe easier, thinking Fisher had made it. At least he had kept his horse to a slow pace, for they had not heard Diamond's hoofs. That had been Clay's greatest fear, that Fisher would forget everything he had been told and make a run for it before he had threaded his way through the Indian cordon.

Then, between rumbles of thunder, Clay distinctly heard the sound of a man's cough from the barn, a choking sound as if he had tried to smother it and failed.

Clay gripped Galt's arm. "Hear that?"

"Yeah, I heard it," Galt said. "It sure as hell wasn't no horse and it wasn't the wind. It's what Lew heard while ago. We've got company."

"And I figured Lew was just jumpy and dreaming it up," Clay said.

"So'd I," Galt admitted. "Well, let's go find out what color this yahoo is, but I'll bet my bottom dollar he ain't red."

They started toward the barn, Clay lifting his gun from leather, but they had not taken more than three steps when they heard Pless yell, "Stay inside, Shannon."

They wheeled toward the house as a revolver shot blasted

the silence. Pless, who had just stepped up on the porch, fell back and went down. Pete Shannon lunged through the door and crossed the porch in two long strides.

Molly Reed yelled, "He got Bronc," and fired the Sharps, the old gun sounding cannon-loud between rolls of thunder. Briefly the clouds broke and moonlight came again, and by its light Clay saw that Shannon was carrying Brimlow's satchel.

Clay yelled, "Stop."

Shannon didn't even pause in his headlong run toward the barn. Clay raised his gun and fired. Shannon went down as cleanly as if he had been tripped by an invisible wire. Clay heard his yell of pain, then the explosion of a shot from the barn, the slug passing so close to Clay's head that he heard its ugly, snapping sound. He dropped and rolled toward the horse trough, expecting a bullet to tear into his body every second.

Thirteen

GALT REACHED THE HORSE TROUGH almost the same instant Clay did. They dropped belly flat into the mud where the water had lapped over the sides of the trough. Now two guns were talking from the barn, slugs slapping into the thick sides of the pine log from which the trough was made, or kicking up geysers of water or passing overhead to be lost in the far darkness.

For a time Clay was silent and motionless as he considered what he should do. He didn't have the slightest intention of staying pinned down here in the mud. Clouds had covered the moon again and he couldn't see what had happened to Pete Shannon. The boy might be dead. If so, he wouldn't be going anywhere with Brimlow's satchel, but, on the other hand, he might be only wounded and be crawling to the barn where he'd give the satchel to the men who had been hiding there.

Clay didn't feel any personal responsibility for Brimlow's money and the pending deal in Ouray which meant so much to the man. But Brimlow was a stage passenger and Clay's place was an official night stop on the stage run to the Agency.

So, in that way, both Clay and Galt were responsible for Brimlow and his property. More than that, there had never been a stage holdup or robbery since Clay had been here. If Shannon and his partners succeeded, others would be encouraged to try.

"Can you see the kid?" Clay asked between bursts of firing from the barn.

"No," Galt answered. "I saw where he went down, but he ain't there now, near as I can tell."

"He's been scared of the Indians all day," Clay said. "He wouldn't have headed for the barn if he figured that's who was out there."

"Then who is it? And how would he know?"

"Could be Grat and Julio. Shannon must have been mighty damned sure they'd be on hand to help him if he needed help or he wouldn't have made his move."

"Well, we've got to dig them two badgers out of their hole," Galt said, "whoever they are."

"Yeah," Clay said, "and I'll bet old Santo's listening and wondering what kind of war we've got going."

For the moment Clay had forgotten that Bronc Pless had gone down and Molly had yelled that Shannon had got him. Now Molly stepped out of the house and let go with the Sharps again, the booming explosion making the shots of the six-shooters in the barn sound like popguns.

Molly had often scolded Bronc in her loud, overbearing voice for his failings of one kind or another, but she had loved him, too. Now he was dead, Clay thought, or Molly wouldn't be using the Sharps. She'd be looking after Bronc if he were alive instead of wasting ammunition. All she was doing was getting rid of her hate.

The suddenness of what Shannon had done combined with the attack from the barn had momentarily shocked Clay into getting under cover. But now the shock passed and the same cold fury that was in Molly took hold of Clay.

"I'm going in after them," Clay said.

Galt grabbed his arm. "Don't be a fool. Let's figure this out."

"I'd be a bigger fool to let them keep us pinned down until Santo decided to horn in. We'd be in a hell of a fix then."

Galt grunted something, and Clay went on, "Another thing. If Shannon can make it to the barn and they get the satchel, they'll be gone. If Shannon can't get to the barn, one of them will be out looking for it. If he finds it, they'll be on their way."

"The moon will be in and out for quite a while," Galt said, "the way the clouds are. If we get a storm, it'll be later. Right now we're getting enough light so that if one of them boogers pokes his head out of the barn, I'll blow it off."

But impatience was in Clay now, aggravated by the knowledge that Santo might take advantage of this dissension among the whites to come after Holman. "I'm going in after them," Clay said again. "Keep shooting. Go back and forth from one end of the trough to the other so they'll think we're both still here."

He didn't wait to argue with Galt, but slid into the open, staying as flat on his belly as he could. The moon was still under a cloud, but there was enough light so that Clay could have been seen if he had got to his feet and made a run for it across the yard where any movements would be detected. The men in the barn would naturally expect Clay and Galt to stay pinned down, so if Clay could get into the barn without being discovered, he had a chance. At least that was the way he saw it.

Galt cut loose when Clay left, rushing from one end of the trough to the other. Clay wormed his way to the shadow of the corral. He moved as fast as he could, but still it took him what seemed an eternity to cover the few feet.

Molly banged away with the Sharps again, and Clay, reaching the corral, got to his feet and sprinted toward the corner of the barn, keeping close to the corral as long as he could. He reached the barn and went on along its south side, panting hard, not sure he hadn't been seen, but believing he'd made it.

Molly had done some good, he thought grimly. At least she'd make the outlaws keep their heads down. Her heavy slugs wouldn't go through the logs, but they would slice through the door like paper, or through the chinking between the logs. Just the sound of the booming Sharps was enough to worry a man.

Clay eased around the back of the barn. The south half along whose side he had just moved held a long row of stalls. During cold weather the stage horses were often kept there, but they were in the pasture now, and the stalls were empty.

There was a back door on that side, but Clay decided against using it. The slightest squeak of hinges would warn the outlaws and for an instant at least Clay would be silhouetted against the greater light of the outside. If the moon happened to break free at that exact moment, they'd have a perfect target.

So Clay took the additional time to go on around the barn to the door on the north side. Here was his work bench, the granary that held Boone Holman's body, and the odds and ends that didn't seem to fit anywhere else. Here, too, was a storage space where he kept the new buggy he had driven from Gunnison only a few weeks before. He had bought it to have a rig to take Margaret riding when she came. His thoughts touched briefly on Margaret and then he forgot her. He had no time for contemplation of the mental debris that had once been his dreams.

He threw the bar and opened the door, waiting until a burst of gunfire would cover any noise he might make, slipped inside, and closed the door again. He stood motionless for a time, his breathing very loud in the silence that followed the last fusillade, then he felt his way around the buggy and on to the west wall and along it to the vacant stalls.

Molly banged away with the Sharps again, and Clay heard a man curse and say, "Who the hell is shooting that Sharps? Fisher's gone, and we've got Galt and Majors nailed down behind the horse trough. Pete put the old man down. Who's left?"

"Some of the passengers," the other man said. "Can you see Pete?"

"He's twenty feet from the door and he ain't moved for five minutes," the first said. "He's still got the satchel. I can see it."

Clay eased over a manger into a stall near the back. There he stood motionless, debating what his next move should be. Apparently the moon had come out, or the men couldn't have seen Shannon and the satchel. Clay wondered if Shannon was dead. The bullet that had put him down hadn't killed him immediately, or he couldn't have crawled to within twenty feet of the barn.

Here inside the barn the darkness was absolute. Clay remembered Fisher saying it was as black as the inside of a bull's gut. Clay knew exactly how the young cowboy had felt when he'd opened a door and looked inside. Fisher had promptly shut the door and left, momentarily content to let whoever was there remain undisturbed. Now Clay was thankful they hadn't taken lanterns and explored the barn as Fisher had suggested. They would probably all have been dead if they had.

Carefully Clay slipped out of the stall he occupied into the next one. At once he knew he had been foolish. He should have waited for another burst of gunfire. Instead, he had moved during a moment of silence, and his feet had made a faint rustling in the barn litter.

"What's that?" one of the men asked.

"Rats, maybe. Nothing to worry about. You're jumpy."

"Sure I'm jumpy," the first said. "I've got a right to be. This job didn't work right. Pete went loco or he wouldn't have been the damn fool he was." A pause, then the man asked, "What do you suppose is in that satchel?"

"Dinero, or he wouldn't have performed like he done. A lot of it, I'd say. He's never missed yet, Grat."

"He ain't moving, so I'm going out after it. Then we're drifting. We've been here too long now."

"Wait till the moon goes under and I'll cover you."

Silence then, Galt holding his fire. Clay wondered if the driver had emptied his cartridge belt. Clay stood with one foot in the runway, his back to the side of the stall. He could see nothing. He couldn't tell from the sound of the voice exactly where the two men were, but he thought they were crouched close to the wall just to the left of the door.

Clay was goaded by a feeling of urgency, the necessity of closing this out before Santo made a move, and yet he knew he couldn't risk any precipitate action yet. He should wait until they opened the door and went after the satchel, and then, if Galt was alert, they could finish it.

The Sharps again, the heavy slug slapping through the door and screaming past Clay and going *thwack* into the west wall. One of the men cursed bitterly. "That gun would knock a buffalo down. I'd like to know who the hell's shooting it."

Silence again that seemed to run on and on, stretching Clay's nerves to the breaking point. He knew he couldn't wait for the moon to come out. He inched out of his stall and into the next one, thinking he had made no sound, but one of the men said, "I heard it again. We've got somebody in here with us. I'm going after that satchel."

"And get plugged," the other snapped. "Galt and Majors are out there watching. With the moon as bright as it is, you wouldn't get halfway to where Pete's lying."

A stubborn, impelling anger had taken hold of Clay. He knew he couldn't wait. If Bronc Pless was dead, and he undoubtedly was, these men were to blame. Shannon's finger had pulled the trigger, but back of Shannon were the two men standing within fifteen or twenty feet of Clay.

The darkness pressing against Clay seemed to be alive and breathing. He had to do something to end the tension that had built in him, tightening his nerves until they seemed to sing. He took two careful steps into the runway so the wall was within reach of his right hand. He tried to bring into his mind the exact picture of the wall and the harness that hung there, tried to place where Bronc Pless, a methodical man, had always left the manure fork.

He eased forward another step, changing the gun to his left hand. He searched the wall with his right, thinking that this was where the fork should be. He touched some harness just as Galt broke his silence with three quick shots, and Clay, taking advantage of the gunfire, moved ahead, raking the wall with his right hand.

His fingers found the smooth handle of the fork; he gripped it in the middle and threw it, spearlike, at the spot where he thought the men were standing, hoping that Molly wouldn't put another slug through the door while he stood in the runway, then he changed his gun back to his right hand.

He heard a yelp of pain and the clatter of the fork handle hitting the wall. Instantly the barn was filled with the explosions of shots as both men whirled and fired blindly in the direction from which the fork had come. Clay plunged forward and dropped belly flat in the runway close to the wall. He opened up, keeping his bullets low and laying four of them in a line, sweeping the wall from the corner of the door to the manger end of the stall which held the two outlaws.

Holding one shell back, Clay dived forward so he wouldn't be in the same position if either of them was still alive. He listened, but heard nothing except the heavy breathing of a man hard hit. He fished a match out of his vest pocket, and crawling forward, lighted it, the gun held on the ready.

Both men were dead, their shirt fronts dark with blood. Grat's hand, thrown out at his side in the straw, was twitching in the last agony of death. His gun lay inches from his finger tips. Julio had a slug squarely through his chest. It must have hit his heart and he had probably died the instant Clay had fired.

Clay opened the door, calling, "Slim, I got 'em. Molly, don't shoot any more. Get a lantern and come out here."

He heard Molly whoop. Galt ran toward him as he left the barn. Clay knelt beside Shannon, the gun with the one bullet in it still in his hand. His left, feeling on the ground, found the satchel. He handed it to Galt, saying, "Here, Slim, want to hold $50,000?"

"The hell," Galt said, and took the satchel.

Clay's fingers felt along Shannon's arm until they reached the wrist. He searched for the boy's pulse and found it, weak, but still a pulse. He said, "This son of a bitch is alive." He rose and stood over Shannon, feeling an almost compulsive urge to fire the last bullet that his gun held into Shannon's body.

Molly, coming across the yard with a lantern, called, "Clay, he killed Bronc."

Clay holstered his gun. For some perverse reason Molly's words shattered the wild hunger that had been in him to destroy the flicker of life that was left in Pete Shannon. The boy would probably die from the bullet wound. If he didn't, he would surely hang. Even an outlaw had a right to a trial just as Red Holman had.

"Better move the men in the barn, Slim," Clay said. "Put them in the granary with Boone. Give him your lantern, Molly."

Then he stooped, and, picking up Shannon's scrawny body, carried him toward the house.

Fourteen

CLAY HAD NOT REALIZED until Shannon's limp body was in his arms that the boy was so light. Undernourished, kicked around, probably without parents or a home . . . But there was no reason for Clay to feel sorry for him. If a boy insisted on being a man, he had to take a man's responsibility. A bullet was his just due, and he'd got it.

"How'd he get the satchel from Brimlow?" Clay asked. "I didn't hear a shot until he plugged Bronc."

"Must have knocked him on the head with his gun barrel," Molly said. "I didn't go up to see. I was in the hall when I seen him come down the stairs and I heard Bronc tell him to stop. He shot Bronc and kept going. I grabbed the Sharps off the wall and took a shot at him, then I got Bronc inside and seen he was dead. After that I just kept shooting."

As Clay crossed the porch, he saw that Molly had dragged Bronc's body through the door and covered it with a blanket. He went on into the parlor and laid Shannon down on the couch. Examining the boy, he found that the bullet had ripped through his belly below his ribs. He must have bled a great deal internally. He would die from the wound, but perhaps not immediately. Clay had seen gut-shot men linger for days, but he didn't think Shannon would, the boy was so frail.

"Let him die," Molly said. "The spalpeen! He don't deserve nothing from nobody. All Bronc did was try to keep him from going outside."

"We can't keep him from dying," Clay said. "Nothing we can do for him."

"I wouldn't if he had a chance, the dirty booger."

Clay was silent, looking down at the boy's slack face, his eyes closed, his parted lips showing his yellow teeth. He had been a vicious little animal of the forest, a weasel preying on anyone he could find who was weaker. But now he was just a boy, helpless and dying. Clay discovered he could not hate Shannon; he could only pity him.

Molly crossed the room and sat down in a rocking chair. Clay glanced at her, saying, "You don't mean that, Molly. If there was anything you could do for him, you'd do it."

"I dunno 'bout that," she snapped. "Sure sets you back, the way things have been happening. I thought supper was real nice, with Judy helping me and everybody eating like they enjoyed their grub. But hell's been breaking loose ever since, with that Red Holman coming here and them outlaws in the barn and Shannon beefing Bronc." She looked up at Clay, chewing on her lower lip. "I guess the worst is that there Margaret you fetched here. You know what kind of woman she is? Do you, Clay?"

"What did she do to you?"

Molly glanced away. "Never mind. It's poor old Bronc I keep thinking about. I'm ashamed of the way I treated him. I'd cuss him something fierce because he didn't cut my stovewood fine enough or didn't keep the box filled or didn't hoe my garden right, and all the time he was so boogered up by rheumatism he couldn't hardly move."

Molly dabbed at her eyes. It was the first time Clay had ever seen her cry, the first time he had seen her really bothered by anything. He wanted to comfort her, but he didn't know how to do it. She was not one to want or need sympathy, and she was more likely than not to resent it.

"Bronc didn't care, Molly," was all Clay said. "Fetch a lamp. I'm going to take him back to his room."

He lifted the old man's body from the floor and followed Molly down the hall and into Bronc's room and laid the body on the bed. He lighted the lamp on the bureau, then said, "Go back and sit with Shannon. If he comes around, I want to hear what he's got to say."

She obeyed reluctantly, finding it distasteful even to be in the same room with the boy, Clay thought. For a time he stood looking down at Bronc's lined, leathery face, serene now in death. He had been the kind who wouldn't want any tears shed for him. And none should be, Clay thought. He had lived his normal span of years; he'd had a good free life, the sort he had wanted.

It was different with a young man like Lew Fisher, exuberant and vital, who had, or should have, most of his life before him. If he didn't come back, Clay knew he would never forgive himself for letting him go. But he would come back. The Utes knew him and liked him. They wouldn't kill him.

Clay shook his head, realizing he was like a small boy trying to whistle away his fears of the dark. Now, honest with himself, he knew the chances of Fisher's coming back were slim. The danger was that the Utes might mistake him for Red Holman trying to make a run for it. If they made that mistake, they'd kill him.

But Fisher might be as safe out there on Diamond as he would have been if he'd stayed here. Bronc was dead. Shannon soon would be. Brimlow would be only a liability if it came to a fight. Holman would be the same or worse, wounded, and a coward to start with. That left Molly, who would handle the Sharps, Slim Galt, maybe Casteel, and Clay. He didn't know whether Judy could use a gun or not. And Margaret?

He wiped a hand across his face. He didn't fully understand what had happened, or how or why it had happened. He was puzzled how a feeling he had nourished for so long, a feeling he had thought was love, could be so completely burned out.

He had promised Margaret safety, but how was he to keep that promise, with Red Holman here in the house and Santo and his Utes outside, like great hungry cats waiting to spring, but not telling their victims how or when they would come?

Clay heard Molly's heavy steps in the hall and turned to the door.

"He's coming around, Clay," Molly said when she saw him, "but don't look to me like he's gonna last very long."

He hurried down the hall and into the parlor to find Shannon's eyes open.

The boy asked in a whisper, "I didn't make it, did I, Majors?"

"No. But you killed Bronc Pless."

"Had to do it. He was aiming to make me stay in the house. I couldn't do it."

"Grat and Julio are dead, Shannon."

If he felt any sorrow, or even a hint of regret, he didn't show it. He asked, "Have I got any chance, Majors?"

"None. But it doesn't make any difference. You'd hang anyhow."

"Pa told me I would someday. That was a long time ago. Before I ran away from home."

"You were working with Grat and Julio all the time, weren't you?"

"Sure. I was their eyes. Nobody suspected me 'cause I was a kid. I rode the train picking out the suckers. I never missed. I had a nose for money, they said. I saw Brimlow on the train. I knew he was a fat goose, so I got on the stage when I saw where he was going."

"And tipped Grat and Julio off before we left Gunnison, didn't you?"

"Yeah. It would have worked all right if it hadn't been for the damned Indians. Grat and Julio must have got scared when they seen the freight wagon and Holman's body. They would have held the stage up on Blue Mesa if it hadn't been for that."

Shannon shut his eyes as a spasm of pain shot through his body. Clay thought he was gone, but a moment later he opened his eyes. He went on, "They'd been here once when you were gone. They knew the lay of the land, so I was purty sure they'd be in the barn waiting for me to start the ball. Trouble was, I lost my head. Should have waited. But I couldn't. I got scared, thinking about the damned Indians."

He licked parched lips, straining to say something more, but all he could manage was, "I'll see you . . . in . . . hell." Then he died.

Clay turned to see Slim Galt standing behind him, Brimlow's satchel in his hand. "Might as well tote him out to the granary," Galt said as he tossed the satchel into the corner. "We'll have 'em piled up like cordwood purty soon." He picked Shannon up. "Hell, he's lighter'n a feather. But maybe the devil don't weigh much neither."

He picked the lantern up and went outside. Molly was sitting in the rocking chair again, her big-knuckled hands clasped on her lap. Clay pulled up a chair and sat down beside her. "What were you going to tell me about Margaret?"

"Don't make no difference." Molly refused to look at him. "Marry whoever you damn please."

"It won't be Margaret," Clay told her.

Molly straightened her slumped shoulders and looked at him sharply. "Well now, that's more sense than I allowed I'd hear from you. I figured she was winding you around one of her purty little fingers."

Clay shook his head. "Not any more. I guess I don't savvy women."

Molly sniffed. "The man who says he does is a fool or a liar. But then there's women and there's women. Take that Judy. She don't hide nothing. Margaret now, she's the other kind. She'd never tell you where she was taking you or what she was fixing to do till it was too late, then she'd have you all tied up, boxed, and delivered."

"What did she do?"

Molly fidgeted and stared at the wall above Clay's head. "I guess it was mostly that you kept telling me how purty she was, and good and all, so I started trying to see the angel's wings she was sprouting, but all I've been able to see is a tail and two horns right from the minute she stepped out of the stage. She's a bitch, Clay, a damned, no-good bitch."

"What did she do?" Clay asked again, irritated by the way Molly avoided answering his question.

Molly began to rock, the chair squeaking dismally. A full minute passed before she said, "Well, the first thing was when she got here and I took her to her room. She wanted to know if it was the best we had. Then she starts in on you, how you was lying about how peaceful the country was and she'd be safe and all. I just walked out, leaving her on the bed. I could have forgiven her that, tired and scared and jumpy like she was."

She stopped talking, more nervous than Clay had ever seen her. He said, "Go on."

"You'll think I'm lying, Clay. So help me, you will, but I ain't just trying to bust you up with her. I ain't no blue-nosed old gossip, neither."

Impatient with her, Clay said, "Go on. Go on."

She spread her hands and laid them on her fat thighs. "It was like this. I was fixing to go to bed when you and Slim and Lew went to the corral and left Bronc outside. Then I got to thinking about Judy sitting up with that no-good Holman, so I went upstairs and told her I'd sleep a wink or two, then I'd come up and spell her off. She said she'd like that 'cause she was purty tired."

Molly cleared her throat and looked at Clay uneasily, then plowed ahead. "Well, I came back along the hall. When I passed Casteel's room, I heard Margaret talking to him. Been bad enough for any woman to be in his room, but Margaret!" Molly shook her head. "I listened, and you know what she was saying? She wanted Casteel to do something to you. Beat hell out of you or something so Casteel could start giving orders and they could turn Holman over to the Indians. Then the stage could go out in the morning and Casteel could go to Ouray and Margaret could catch the eastbound and head for the railroad. Can you imagine her doing a thing like that?"

He nodded. "Yes, I can imagine it. She thinks Casteel is a gentleman."

Molly snorted in disgust. "The worst of it was that Casteel said you had his gun. She promised to get him one. Then Casteel got to playing it real cozy, so she offered to give him money. I couldn't stand it no longer. Next thing she'd have got into bed with him. I went banging into his room and yanked her into the hall and told her to git into her room and stay there. Casteel didn't budge. After she left, I told him I didn't figger he'd ever get Judy to Ouray. He'd better take Margaret, I says. They'd make a good pair. Then I slammed the door and came downstairs, so mad I couldn't see straight. Shannon must have been in Brimlow's room all that time 'cause he came piling down the stairs a little after I did."

Clay rose and walked to the door and stood leaning against the casing staring into the night. The moon was breaking through the clouds, for the moment throwing its bright light upon the valley. He stiffened, hearing horses up the creek. He saw them then, for a moment, a dozen or more Indians, then they disappeared into the willows.

He wished they'd do whatever they were going to do. A man can stand so much, and he'd stood about all he could. Perhaps that was what Santo was gambling on, hoping that the suspense of waiting would be more than Clay could bear and he would offer Holman to them.

Silence again, except for Galt's movements in the yard. Slowly, because it was a painful thing, Clay's thoughts focused on Margaret and what Molly had said about her. No doubt Molly had exaggerated, but Clay didn't doubt that in the essentials her story was true. Then he thought he knew what had happened to Margaret. She had buckled under the danger or imagined danger, doing and saying things she would not have done . . .

A woman screamed from upstairs. In the back of the house. Judy, Clay thought, as he wheeled from the door and took the stairs three at a time. Molly followed as fast as she could. When Clay reached the upstairs hall, he heard someone fall, and heard Judy cry out again.

Clay ran down the hall and jerked open the door of Holman's room. He was in bed, propped up on his right elbow, a scared expression on his face. Judy lay on the floor next to the wall, blood running down one cheek from a cut. Casteel stood over her, his fists clenched. When he heard the door open, he swung around to face Clay, his eyes those of a wild man.

Fifteen

FOR A MOMENT Clay stood stunned by what he saw. He had expected anything but this, for Casteel to strike Judy and disfigure her face before he even got her to Ouray. After he had possessed her and tired of her, but not now.

Clay had no time to consider Casteel's motives. The instant he recovered from the shock of seeing Judy on the floor, he was filled with the most overpowering rage he had ever experienced. Casteel rushed at him and Clay met him, the sound of their coming together like that of two great bulls, the impact shaking the rooms.

Whatever Casteel had learned about boxing was forgotten. He swung a looping left from his boot tops that missed. Clay hit him solidly in the stomach, but the gambler acted as if he didn't feel it. He threw a right that caught Clay on the chin and snapped his head back, then for a time they stood in the middle of the room, trading blows, each willing to be hurt in order to hurt the other.

But Casteel wasn't getting the best of it, so he wasn't satisfied. He wanted to kill, to maim, and he had learned from his previous fights with Clay that he could not do this with his fists. Suddenly he backed up and whirled away, and Clay was turned half around by a powerful blow he had already started that met nothing more solid than air. He heard Judy scream a warning and he backed toward the far wall.

From a bureau Casteel had grabbed the whisky bottle that Clay had brought up from the bar for Holman earlier in the evening. Now he moved toward Clay, the bottle held over his right shoulder like a club. Clay retreated before him, knowing that the bottle in Casteel's hand was a lethal weapon that could split his head open.

There was a moment of savage stalking, Casteel's intentions written clearly on his battered face. His nose was bleeding again and one eye was almost closed, but the bitter memory of his first defeat must have been a constant prod goading him forward. Ordinarily he was a careful, calculating man, but now the thought that he might hang if he killed Clay apparently did not register in his mind. He wanted to kill; beyond that there was nothing.

This much Clay knew as he circled the room, keeping away from Casteel. He heard Judy screaming something at him and Molly yelling that she'd get the Sharps, then Casteel rushed him. Clay had gone once and a half around the room, widening the circle so that now he was behind the rawhide-bottom chair in which Judy had sat beside Holman's bed. He hooked the chair with his right foot and brought it up, sending it flying at Casteel.

Casteel batted it away with his left hand, but Clay was right behind it, charging headlong. He had only a moment's respite while Casteel's attention was fixed on the chair, but it was enough, his left hand catching Casteel's right wrist as it started down with the bottle.

Clay got his right arm around Casteel's waist, hugging him so hard he couldn't get the freedom of movement he needed for a blow with his left fist, and, in spite of all Casteel could do, Clay succeeded in forcing his right arm down. He twisted the gambler's wrist until he loosened his hold on the bottle. It struck the floor and rolled under the bed.

Clay released his grip around Casteel's waist, shocked by the murderous fury that he felt, the same desire to maim and kill that was in Casteel. Yet, recognizing it, he could not control it. He slammed Casteel's head from side to side with rights and lefts, giving way to the maniacal desire to smash this man who had insulted and belittled him and even tried to kill him. He had dammed all this up because of Margaret, but now there was no reason to hold back, and the self-control that had restrained him in the first fight tonight was gone. He was no better than Larry Casteel.

He hammered the man savagely, driving him back the length of the room. He heard Molly yell, "I've got the Sharps. Stand away and I'll shoot the son of a bitch." But Clay had no desire to stand away. He forced Casteel against the wall, and Casteel, unable to stand up under this beating, dodged to one side and fell forward, clinging to Clay in a desperate effort to smother his punches.

Casteel grabbed a fistful of Clay's hair and yanked. He lifted his head and butted Clay under the chin, cutting his lower lip as his teeth snapped together. Clay hit him in the side; he backed off and ducked a wild swing, and Casteel, thrown off balance, was wide open.

Clay brought his right through in a sledging blow squarely to the jaw. Casteel's knees folded and he toppled forward, hands grabbing Clay's shirt, but there was no strength in his fingers and his grip loosened and he went on down to the floor.

Clay lunged toward him, bringing a boot back to kick him in the face, but Galt had him by the shoulder and pulled him away from Casteel.

"All right, Clay, all right," Galt said. "Take your gun and kill him, but don't kick him to death."

Clay stumbled back against the wall, some semblance of sanity taking hold of him. He was weak and a little sick now that the crazy demon of rage and hate was dying in him. He bowed his head, struggling to suck air into his tortured lungs. He felt blood dribble down his face and wiped it away with a sweep of his shirt sleeve.

Realizing how close he had come to murder, he looked at Galt, who stood over Casteel's motionless body. He knew that Judy was staring at him, too. Then Molly had him by the arm and said, "Come down to the kitchen. Maybe I can patch your face up a little."

He jerked away from her and staggered out of the room and along the hall, still breathing hard. He went down the stairs and on back to the kitchen, where he dropped into a chair at the table and lowered his head into his arms. He heard Molly bustling around the room, and presently she put a pan of hot water and a rag on the table, and a jar of salve.

She tugged at his shoulder. "Let me get to work on it, Clay. You ain't gonna get no better that way."

When he lifted his head and leaned back, the room seemed to turn and tip crazily, and he had a weird feeling that he could not keep from pitching out of the chair to the floor. He reached out and gripped the edge of the table as Molly washed his face with the cloth she'd dipped into the hot water.

"You got some bad bruises," Molly said, "but this here cut on your cheek is the only scar you'll get." She gently applied the salve to his face, adding, "I've got that bottle of horse liniment in the pantry. Maybe you oughtta take your clothes off and let me rub you good with it."

Suddenly he was aware that Judy was standing on the other side of the table, holding a handkerchief to the side of her face. He pushed Molly away, saying, "To hell with it. Go to work on Judy." He got up, and at once the room began to turn and tip and he promptly sat down.

"All right," Molly said caustically. "Maybe you know now you ain't as skookum as you think you are. Stay sat for a while."

Molly looked at the cut on Judy's face and clucked sympathetically. "That's purty deep, honey. He must have caught you with that ring he wears. I'll get some cobwebs and stop the bleeding, but I'm awful afraid you'll have a scar there. It ain't gonna help your looks none."

Judy sat down across the table from Clay. "Looks?" she asked bitterly. "You can't lose what you don't have."

"What're you talking that way for?" Molly asked angrily. "You're a fine-looking woman, with real good coloring that don't need no paint and powder like most entertainers do. And I'll tell you something else. You're attractive to men, or you wouldn't be where you are."

"Oh, hush up," Judy said irritably, and at once was contrite. "I'm sorry, Molly. I know I'm attractive to men. Some men, I mean, but it's just because I'm a woman, not because of my looks."

Molly sighed. "You're all mixed up, honey, and that's too bad 'cause you just ain't found the right place and the right man, so I reckon you'll go on singing——"

"No," Judy said. "I'm done singing. I told Casteel I wasn't going to Ouray with him. That's why he hit me."

"Why did he go into Holman's room?" Molly asked. "Or did you go to him first?"

"No." She shook her head, then looked at Clay. "Oh Clay, I didn't intend to bring this onto you."

"I whipped him before supper," Clay said, "but I guess he had to have it again. It wasn't just you anyhow. It goes back for a long time."

And it would keep on going on until one of them was dead. Clay had known that before, but he felt it now more keenly than ever. Casteel would never forget he had been beaten twice tonight. He wouldn't try with his fists again. He probably wouldn't have tried this time if he could have avoided it. Next time it would be with a gun.

"You asked me why he came into my room," Judy said to Molly. "You told him not to take me to Ouray or something like that. I guess Clay had said about the same thing. He got to brooding over it. He had a bottle in his suitcase and he started drinking. He came in and told me I couldn't get out of my contract. He said no woman ever made a fool out of him and he wasn't going to let me do it, either."

Clay nodded, understanding this. Casteel had an inordinate pride about many things, but he found his greatest satisfaction in his appeal to women, a vanity that, if destroyed, left him without a shred of self-respect.

"I hadn't intended to tear up my contract," Judy went on. "Not that I ever had any use for him. I knew what he was when I signed the contract, but I never had the least doubt I

88

could handle him. I've handled a lot of men just like him in the last six years. But when he came in, drunk and mean like he was, and started to bully me just to prove how big he was, I knew you were right, Clay. About me not going with him. I made up my mind right then and I told him I wouldn't go."

She shrugged. "So he got mad and hit me, and I guess I yelled. The next thing I knew you were there." She tried to smile. "Oh well, maybe it's time I was getting out of Colorado. He'll see to it I don't get another job around here. I can go to the Black Hills. Or to California."

Clay rose and stood there a moment, finding that he wasn't dizzy, but he felt as if every muscle in his body had been battered by a hammer. He said, "Think it over for a while, Judy. Stay here while you're thinking."

He went into his room and took off his shirt, which was spotted with blood—his own, this time—and put on a clean one. He started up the stairs, then remembered Brimlow's satchel, which was still in the parlor. He got it and took it to Brimlow's room and went in.

Brimlow was in bed, a wet towel held to his head. When he saw the satchel, he sat up and reached for it, grimacing as pain shot through his head. He hugged it to his chest, an expression of groveling gratitude on his face.

"Thank you, Majors. I didn't know what to do. I thought it was gone." He put his hand out to the pistol that was on the bed beside him. "With my money gone, I just couldn't face the future. How did you get it?"

Clay told him, and added, "You'd better save your bullets for the Utes if it comes to that. How'd Shannon get the satchel?"

"He knocked on the door and I opened it a crack to see who it was," Brimlow said. "I had the gun in my hand, but I didn't have any chance to use it. He slammed the door open, knocked my right hand aside and slugged me with the barrel of his gun. I guess that's what he did, although I don't actually remember seeing him do it." He felt gingerly of the top of his head where a long, red welt was visible evidence of what had happened. "When I came to, I was on the floor and the money was gone."

As Clay turned to the door, Brimlow asked in a shaky voice, "We've had more than enough trouble, Majors. You don't really think we'll have some with the Indians, do you?"

"A thing doesn't go away just because you want it to," Clay said. "We'll have trouble with the Indians, all right, if that's any help to you."

He stepped into the hall and went into Casteel's room, not

wanting to see the man, but knowing he had to. Casteel was on his back in bed, his face as bloody as a piece of freshly cut beefsteak. He was conscious, but he said nothing when Clay reached the side of his bed and looked down at him. He had no need to. One eye was closed, but the other was virulent with his hatred for Clay.

"I know what will happen if you get your hands on a gun," Clay said. "It's all right with me, and maybe you'll find one before you leave, but I'm asking one thing. Hold off until we get this business with Santo settled."

Casteel said nothing, but his one good eye did not change expression. Clay turned away, knowing there was nothing he could say that would touch Casteel.

Reaching the door, Clay paused to look back. He thought of how Casteel had looked in the hotel lobby in Gunnison: impeccable, dignified, coldly superior, as he had tried to maneuver the crowd into mob frenzy. He was none of those things now. He was dirty, his shirt was soiled, his bruised face would carry the marks of Clay's fist to his grave, and his puffy lips could not manage even a ghost of the cynical smile that had been on them most of the day. Only his one good eye gave expression to his feeling.

Clay went on, forgetting his own aches and pains for the moment. Physically, Casteel was far worse off than he was, but the gambler was all the more dangerous because of his injuries.

Margaret's door banged open. She saw Clay and cried out, "Someone's coming. Is it the Indians?"

He saw that she was almost hysterical. That would be more than any of them could stand, to have a screaming woman on their hands. He said curtly, "No," and went down the stairs.

When he reached the front door, Galt called from the hitch rail: "Lew's back, Clay. He didn't get through."

Clay walked toward them, his thoughts bleak and depressing. He had the weird sensation of standing apart from this and watching one scene after another as they developed, and all the time he had an even more weird sense of being able to look ahead and see that disaster waited for them, that there was nothing he or anyone could do.

He had not really counted on Fisher's getting through, but there had been a chance. Now he recognized the dismal truth. The last hope was gone.

Sixteen

THE INSTANT FISHER SAW CLAY, he started babbling. "I couldn't make it, Clay. God, there's a thousand of 'em out there. Nobody could have got through. Old Bronc can try if he wants to, but he won't make it, neither."

"Bronc's dead," Clay said. "Pete Shannon shot and killed him after you left. Come inside and tell us what happened."

Clay turned on his heel and strode toward the house, thinking that the news of Bronc's killing might shock some sense back into Fisher. The cowboy had always been far more level-headed than most men his age, and Clay had never seen him really terrified before, but he was now. Clay recognized the bitter truth. If it came to a fight, Slim Galt was the only man here he could count on.

Clay walked into the parlor and sat down. Judy and Molly were already there, having been in the kitchen until Galt shouted that Lew was back. Margaret, Brimlow, and Casteel were on the stairs. Now they came on into the parlor, too.

Margaret was wearing a blue velvet robe over her nightgown. She seemed composed, exactly opposite to the nearly hysterical girl who had rushed out of her room a few minutes before and asked if it was the Indians who were coming. Suddenly it struck Clay that Margaret, chameleonlike, had changed repeatedly from one kind of person to another since he had met her at the train, and he asked himself if he had ever seen the real Margaret, or even if there was such a woman.

Brimlow scuttled across the room and sat down in a corner, one hand clutching the satchel, the other holding the wet towel to his head. Casteel stood with his back to the wall near the hall door, his face a horrible mask of dirt and dried blood. His puffy lips and black eye distorted his face so he looked like something less than human.

Casteel must, Clay knew, be suffering a great deal of pain, but he was a stubborn man as well as a proud one, holding himself upright by sheer power of will because to sit down would have been a mark of weakness. Clay could not keep from feeling a grudging respect for the man. He would be dangerous as long as he drew a breath.

Fisher had taken time to tie Diamond to the hitch rail in front of the house. When he came in with Galt, Clay saw that the right side of his face was raw as if he'd been scratched with a kitchen grater. His clothes on the same side were ripped into shreds from the point of his shoulder down to his knees.

Fisher picked up a rawhide-bottom chair, whirled it around and straddled it. He dropped a hand on the back, and motioned nervously with the other from Casteel by the door on around to Brimlow who sat behind Clay.

"Thought I was going to tell you about it, Clay," Fisher said. "What's the audience for?"

"They've got a right to hear what happened to you," Clay said. "We're all in this together."

"Yeah, I guess so." Fisher glanced at Galt, who had come in with him and now stood in the doorway. "Well, I done like you said, Clay." He wet dry lips with the tip of his tongue, looking at Clay uneasily and then shifting his gaze to the others. "I circled through the timber, taking it real easy. I didn't hear nothing or see nothing, so I figured there wasn't no Indians around and all I had to do was to get on the road and let Diamond out."

He cleared his throat, and Clay said, "You mean you didn't hear anything except maybe a coyote yapping. Or a hoot owl."

"Hell yes," Fisher said, visibly surprised, "but that's nothing. You can hear sounds like that any night just sitting on your front porch. Well, I got on the road finally about the time the moon came out good, so I let Diamond have his head. He was fresh and wanted to run, and I figured I'd get to the cantonment before sunup when all of a sudden a rope was around my shoulders and I was flying clean out of my saddle.

"I hit the ground like ten tons of ore and got dragged some before they got Diamond stopped. I didn't have a chance to fight or nothing. They piled all over me, took my gun, yanked me to my feet, and pulled the rope off me. One of 'em fetched Diamond back, and Kuero, he seemed to be running the show, told me to climb back on."

Fisher looked at Clay. "You remember Kuero? He's the tall one, about the tallest Ute I ever seen. He's young and ornery. He missed out on the Thornburgh fracas and he's been aching for another one ever since, him and old Colorow. Well, there wasn't much I could do except get back in the saddle. Kuero led out, the rest of 'em crowded behind me and on both sides. They didn't say a word, but they acted plumb ornery. I guess my hair ain't laying down good yet."

He had no reason to be apologetic, Clay thought, and he said impatiently, "I told you not to fight. I was worried they might mistake you for Holman and kill you before they found out different."

"Some of 'em thought I was Holman till Kuero recognized me," Fisher said. "But I don't think they would have killed me. Looked to me like Santo's aiming to fix Holman's clock himself. Anyhow, they took me upstream maybe a mile above the house, going on the other side of the creek most of the time. I guess they didn't want me to see 'em. The moon was shining pretty good right then."

Fisher glanced around the room, still nervous but plainly enjoying the attention he was getting. His gaze returned to Clay. "Santo was waiting for me. Leastwise he was there with more damned Indians than I ever saw in my life before in one place. Must have been two, three hundred. I didn't know many of 'em. I'd say all the Uncompahgre bucks were there and a bunch of the White River ones, too.

"I didn't see Sapinero or Colorow, though. I don't think Piah was there, either. Santo was running things. He didn't leave no doubt about that. He was the only one who said a word. The others were mostly young bucks, all of 'em itching to hang my hair in his lodge. I thought I'd been scared a time or two before in my life, but I hadn't been. Not till tonight, and I'm still scared. I ain't ashamed to say so."

"What did Santo say?" Margaret asked.

Fisher glanced at her, surprised that she was the only one to press him. "Not much," he said. "Wanted to know if Holman was here in the house. Finally he said for me to come back and tell Clay he wanted to talk to him. They let me go then. Santo speaks good English. Most of 'em do better with Spanish than English, but he didn't talk anything but English to me. I didn't have no trouble understanding him."

"He didn't say what he wanted of Clay?" Margaret asked.

"No, but I can tell you," Fisher said. "I'm guessing, but I know I'm guessing right. He'll tell Clay to go fetch Holman and turn him over to 'em, and that'll be the end of the whole business."

"I reckon that's right," Galt said from the doorway. "If they were fixing to make real trouble, they wouldn't be performing this way."

"Real trouble," Molly bellowed. "What'n hell do you think

we've got already? That ornery Red Holman moves in on us and that's trouble, mister, any way you cut it."

"Sure is," Fisher said. "They're feeling mean. I've been with 'em plenty. Rode Diamond in their races. I've seen 'em hang around the Agency. Ordinarily they'll talk your leg off, friendly as all hell, but they ain't that way now. I tell you they're mean."

"They want Holman," Molly said. "That's the nub of the whole thing, and I'd say they had reason to feel mean on account of him."

"I reckon they have at that," Fisher agreed, and turned to Clay. "You're running the shebang and maybe you know them boogers better'n I do, but was I you, I'd take Holman with me and Santo will send you back in one piece and ride off."

"That's what I was thinking," Brimlow said. "It seems simple enough to me. Don't wait for them to ask for Holman. Just take him."

Fisher was staring at Margaret. He said, "Ma'am, your yellow hair would sure look good to 'em. Whoever takes it will hang it up in his lodge and the others will all come in and admire it."

If he had been closer, Clay would have kicked him. Fisher was panicky or he wouldn't have said it. Perhaps he had a right to be, having been roughed up and certainly believing he was going to be killed. But to use Margaret to force Clay's hand was too much, and Clay rose, his hands fisted.

"Shut that kind of talk up, Lew," Clay said. "You hear?"

"Yeah, I hear," Fisher shot back. "Maybe I'm different from everybody else here, but I ain't one to die from bravery. I've seen 'em and I know how they feel and how many of 'em are out there. It would be different if Holman was any damned good, but he ain't. Why should we get murdered because of him?"

"I was thinking that, too," Molly agreed. "I dunno what's got into you, Clay. We can put up a fight if we have to and do a better job than Meeker and his men done, but it don't make sense that we've got to fight. I had my belly full of Holman when I patched him up. Yelled like a baby. If I've got to die fighting Indians, I don't want it to be for Red Holman."

"That's right," Brimlow said eagerly. "No sense dying for a man like him."

They were all against him, Clay knew. He could feel their antagonism. He glanced at Judy and saw at once she was the exception. She was frightened, too, but she hadn't said

94

anything. He looked at Brimlow, his anger growing until he could not control it.

"You're all making an excuse out of what Holman is," he said. "Would you feel any better about dying for Brimlow?"

The man lowered his head to stare at the satchel on his lap, his face turning brick red. Clay heard his own breath sawing in and out of his lungs. He had seen panic spread from Fisher to everyone in the room except Judy; he had seen it spread and grow until now it was a tangible force pressing against him. Even Slim Galt was no better than the others. He stood in the doorway, trimming his fingernails with a pocketknife, but from the expression on his face, Clay knew he agreed with those who had spoken.

Clay could not bring himself to look at Molly, but she hurt him more than anyone else, hurt him and disillusioned him. Many times he had seen her feed Santo and Colorow and Kuero and other Utes right in this room, and she had never, to Clay's knowledge, been frightened by them.

Colorow, more of a scavenger than the others, had been the most obnoxious. One day, Molly, having been driven beyond endurance, picked up a frying pan and ran him out of the house. Now, after listening to Fisher, she was as bad as any of them.

One thing Clay did not understand was the fact that Margaret had retained her composure after Fisher had said her hair would make a fine scalp. She sat with her hands tightly clasped, the knuckles white, a pulse beat throbbing in her forehead. She looked at Clay, hating him, he thought, but still not giving way to the terror that must be in her.

There was this long moment of silence, finally broken by Margaret, who said, "You aren't being fair to Brimlow, Clay. He didn't kill Santo's son. Neither did I, or anyone else in this room, but we'll be the ones to die because of Holman's crime if you don't give him to them."

Galt snapped his knife shut and jammed it into his pocket. He said, "She's right, Clay. You ain't looking at this the way I do. If it was just me'n you, I'd say board up the windows and bar the door and fight 'em. But there's more'n me and you. We've got three women to think of. We've got stage passengers we're responsible for. If Holman's life is the price we've got to pay to get our passengers to where they're going, then let's pay it."

Clay took a long breath, knowing he had read Galt's expression correctly. Finally he looked at Molly who was scowling at him, at Margaret, who cried out, "I know I don't mean anything to you any more, but these others must. Are you human, Clay? Do you have any decent human instincts left in you any more, or have you become like those savages out there?"

He said nothing. There was no use to say anything. His gaze traveled to Brimlow, who still stared at his satchel, to Galt, who was frowning, his usual melancholy face resentful and bitter, to Fisher, who was shaking as if he had a chill, to Judy, who plainly showed her worry but held her fear under strict control, and last to Casteel, who still stood braced against the wall.

"By God, you're a man," Casteel said reluctantly and unexpectedly. "It gravels me to agree with you on anything, Majors, but you're right on this. Never give a white man to the damned Indians."

"Thanks, Casteel," Clay said dryly, and started towards the door.

Galt stepped aside as if realizing Clay's mind could not be changed. Molly shouted, "What're you going to do, Clay?"

"Talk to Santo," Clay said.

"Don't go," Molly urged. "They may be cowards, but even cowards will kill a brave man when they outnumber him like this."

Judy ran across the room to him and gripped his arms. "They'll kill you if you go out there to them alone. Stay here. We'll fight if that's what we've got to do."

He looked down at her, smiling a little. It warmed him that at least she was interested in his safety. Molly, too, which surprised him after what she had said. "I'll be back," he said.

"She's right," Galt said. "I never knew you to be so damned bullheaded when you're wrong. You're figuring we've all turned yellow. It ain't that. A lot of these same Indians were at the White River Agency being friendly one minute and turning into yelling, murdering devils the next. They killed Meeker and took off his clothes and pounded a stake down his throat. We all know that. What they done up there they can do here if they're feeling mean as Lew says."

"Oh Clay, Clay," Molly said with great feeling. "We ain't cowards. It's just that we're a handful and there's a whole passel of the ornery devils out there. They know you're a fighter and you'd make it tough on 'em if you were inside the house, so they won't let you come back. Then they know they'll have an easy time of it."

"Be a damned sight easier for 'em to get Holman with you dead, all right," Galt said. "Santo knows it, too."

Judy began to cry and turned away. Fisher started to get up and sat down again. Margaret demanded in a strident voice, "Why did you have me come here, Clay? So my scalp would hang in a lodge? So I'd be treated the way the Meeker women were?"

Clay took off his gun belt and handed it to Galt. He would be safer if he went to Santo unarmed. He went out then, thinking that no one, unless it was Judy, understood why he could not turn a man like Red Holman over to the Indians. No, he told himself, even Judy didn't understand.

He untied Diamond and mounted, and suddenly the irony of it struck him, that of all the people in the house, Larry Casteel came nearer understanding than any of the others. Then he turned his black gelding and rode away into the darkness, toward Santo and his Utes.

Seventeen

THE NIGHT had been one of alternating spells of moonlight and darkness. Now the moon was well over toward the west, and the clouds, at one time threatening to clear away, had gathered again and were moving eastward, the lightning still flickering above the western hills.

As Clay rode through the blackness, the night seemed to have a thousand eyes and a thousand perils. He expected the Utes to rush at him and surround him every step Diamond took. Bronc Pless had been right when he'd said earlier in the evening that Santo would not hold back because of any friendship he and Clay had once shared. Galt and Molly had been right, too, in saying that Santo knew Holman would be easier to take if he kept Clay, or killed him.

As he rode, the left side of Clay's chest began to ache with nervous pressure. The muscles of his neck started to tighten, and his spine felt as if a thousand vicious little animals were clawing up his backbone. He had seen the Ute scalp dance, and he wondered if one would be held to celebrate the taking of his scalp.

There would be the red tepee which was the medicine lodge, the medicine and scalp poles over the fire, the medicine men wearing bear's-head masks, and the eight young women, their faces painted black, singing praises of the warriors who had taken the scalps.

97

They would leave the circle and the brave would ride forward, the scalps dangling from his lance. After reciting what he had done in a great voice, he would whirl his horse and ride away at a hard run, pretending his modesty had suddenly become too much to bear. Clay's scalp could be the one that hung from the warrior's lance. And Margaret's. Lew Fisher had been right. Her long yellow hair would make a much-admired trophy. And Kuero's lance could well be the one from which the scalps dangled.

Clay had felt this way twice before since he had moved into the reservation. Once had been when he had ridden into the Ute camp on Grand Mesa with General Adams and had helped rescue the Meeker women; the other time at the Agency in December following the rescue, when the commission had been having a conference with the Ute chiefs. Even Ouray had become angry and bitter with the whites and announced that none were his friends, and finally old Colorow had thrown his knife into the ground in front of him.

It had been touch and go on both occasions, taking only some small incident to set the Utes off. Outnumbering the whites as they had, the fight in either case wouldn't have lasted long. If the Indians had exploded, Clay Majors, Ouray's and Santo's friend, would have died with the others. As Lew Fisher had pointed out, the same Indians who were waiting for Clay now could be as gossipy as old women, but a few hours later turn mean and vindictive, and capable of repeating the Meeker murders.

Clay was a man who had known fear, but he was never one to let it overcome him as it had Red Holman, or Lew Fisher. Now, as he rode, he thought of what he would say to Santo, and he considered, too, how much depended on handling this right.

The whites all along the edge of the reservation, particularly in towns like Gunnison and Ouray, had been bitter against the Indians for months. They had accused the Utes of starting forest fires, and of murdering trespassing miners they found on the reservation, reports which had never been substantiated, but had probably been lies made up by mining-camp newspapermen to fan the fire of fury and hasten the day when the Indians would be moved out of Colorado.

The cold fact was that if Clay and the people he had left in his house were massacred tonight, there would be no holding back the whites who would force the Utes to go to war. Even though troops were stationed at the cantonment near the Los Pinos Agency, they could not prevent a blood bath all along the edge of the reservation. Small bands led by warriors like Santo and Kuero could strike and retreat and hide in the mountains that had been their ancestral home, mountains they knew better than anyone else.

More than that, there had been talk of a general Indian uprising if one started here, of Navahos and Apaches and Piutes going on the war path so that the entire mountain area and the southwest would be drenched with blood. No, there was far more at stake tonight than the life of Red Holman, or of Clay and those he had left in his house.

Earlier this month the Utes had met at the Agency and showed their reluctance to leave the reservation. Again it was a case of the white man breaking his word and interpreting the treaty to suit himself that had turned the Indians sullen. This was the reason that nearly all the Ute braves would be willing to follow Santo if he decided to lead them to war. It was a combination of events, Clay thought bitterly, that made this as serious as it was. If Red Holman had killed any other Indian than Santo's son . . .

Then they were all around Clay as he had known they would be sooner or later, a dozen or more braves who suddenly materialized from the willows along the creek. Kuero said, "Come." That was all. They pressed against him from both sides and the rear, and at once Clay had the feeling Fisher had mentioned, of the sullenness and meanness and the hunger for violence that was throbbing in the veins of Kuero and the braves who were with him.

A few minutes later Kuero said, "Stop," and Clay reined up, knowing that Santo and his band were directly ahead. He could not make them out clearly, the darkness as complete as it was now, and he could not tell how many warriors were behind Santo. Certainly not the two or three hundred that Fisher's fears had conjured up for him. More likely fifty or sixty, but with Kuero's bunch and the others who undoubtedly still surrounded the house to prevent Holman's escape, there were too many to make resistance practical.

Kuero sat his horse beside Clay, and now the Indian's knife point was pressed against his side. They had not searched him for a gun, and Kuero's action made one thing clear. Any fast move on Clay's part would cause the knife to be buried to the hilt in his side.

"Holman killed my son," Santo said. "I want him."

"I can't give him to you," Clay said, "but I will take him to the Agency where he will be arrested. Later he will be moved to the jail in Gunnison and tried for murder."

"We will take him," Santo said.

"If you do, you'll kill him," Clay said. "I don't blame you

for feeling like you do, but he's got to be tried by a white man's court and punished in the white man's way."

"White man's law is for white men," Santo said. "Holman would not be punished."

"There's more to it than you and me and Holman," Clay said. "You know that. If you kill him, you will bring death to your people. You know how the whites feel because of the trouble at White River. Boone Holman is already dead. Let that be enough for the death of your son."

"No," Santo said. "We take Red Holman."

Clay had a feeling he might as well butt his head against the trunk of a big spruce. He could not tell how Santo was dressed, or if he and the others wore the black and yellow war paint of the Utes. All he could see was Santo's square shape on his horse.

The chief was middle-aged, a squat man who, when he was younger, had ridden with Ouray, and had the reputation of being the best war chief among the Utes and of having killed more whites than any other Uncompahgre. It might be true, but now, with those days behind him, Clay knew him as a reasonable man, although a stubborn one. His mind was made up. He cared nothing about what happened to him or his people. Only Red Holman's death would satisfy him.

"I won't let you have him," Clay said, the knowledge that anything he said was useless turning his voice harsh. "Whatever you do to punish him will lead to greater punishment of you and your people."

"We take him," Santo said. "If we do, you die, and so will the people in your house."

"Let me send the women on to the Agency in the stage," Clay said. "They have done nothing to hurt you."

"No," Santo said. "They would send the troops. We take Holman."

"Then the troops will come," Clay said. "You know that."

"Holman will be dead," Santo said, his tone decisive.

That was as far as the chief's reasoning went, Clay knew. He didn't care about what happened, once Red Holman was dead. Now Clay realized the Indians had no intentions of either holding him or killing him. Some of them, like Kuero, might have held such a notion, but not Santo. He only wanted to tell Clay what he must do.

"I can't give him to you," Clay said doggedly.

There was nothing to be gained by argument, and no amount of explanation about the right of a trial by jury would be understood by Santo. The truth was, and Clay would not deny it to himself, that Santo was right when he said white man's law was for white men and Holman would not be punished by it.

The braves behind Santo and the ones with Kuero had been motionless and silent, although Kuero's knife point had kept a steady pressure against Clay's side just under his ribs. Now one of the Indians behind Santo, it might have been Piah from his voice, but Clay wasn't sure, shouted, "White man heap no good. Heap lie like son of a bitch. Holman die."

Santo spoke to him in the Ute tongue, a curt order, and the man was silent.

"Ouray would want you to stay peaceful," Clay said. "What you're asking will destroy you."

"Ouray Apache papoose." Kuero spat the words. "Holman die."

Clay shouldn't have mentioned Ouray's name and he knew it the instant he'd said the words. Ouray had been half Apache, and there were many of the Utes, even some of his own Uncompahgres, who had hated him as long as he was alive, and had never fully accepted his leadership. This was particularly true of the White River Utes, who had lived in the northwestern part of the state and had drifted south after the trouble at the White River Agency.

Again Santo spoke a curt order in the Ute tongue, but Kuero was not as easily silenced as the first one who had spoken out. For Clay's benefit, Kuero said, "Majors has two tongues. Friendly one now, but with his friends he speaks with a brass tongue."

The knife point pressed harder into Clay's side, pricking the skin, but Clay did not flinch. That, he well knew, would have been fatal. Kuero added, his voice filled with violence, "White men die. Maybe Majors die, too."

Now the other who had spoken, emboldened by Kuero's talk, said, "No afraid. Utes heap fight."

This time Santo left no doubt in anyone's mind who was running the parley. Clay could not understand all of it, but he knew enough of the Ute tongue to make out the essence of what Santo said. It was, in effect, that it was his son who had been murdered, that both men would remain silent and let him do the talking or he'd kill the two of them.

Then Santo said to Clay, "Go home. Bring Holman to us and no one else will be hurt. One sleep. No more."

Kuero's knife was withdrawn and the warriors behind Clay fell back. He turned Diamond and rode away, knowing he had until sunup. Not long, he thought dismally. Not long enough to decide what to do, for this was a situation which had no solution that would be the right one.

At least Clay knew how he and the rest in the house stood with Santo. The Utes would not attack during the night. He had been reasonably sure they wouldn't, but he'd held a small hope that they would not do anything worse than maintain a siege of sorts even after the sun was up. He could no longer hold to that hope, for Santo would keep his word. If he didn't have Holman by sunup, they would sweep in and seize Holman, killing the white men and taking the women.

It would be the Meeker massacre all over again, the Utes taking out on this small party of whites their revenge for all the injuries and broken promises that had been given them for close to a generation.

Clay rode back slowly, the storm clouds moving steadily eastward, the lightning crackling in great sweeps across the sky, the thunder louder and coming more quickly after the lightning than it had earlier in the evening. The storm which had been playing a cat-and-mouse game from the western sky was going to materialize before dawn. Morning would be slower coming than on a clear day.

Clay thought about this absently, then tried to fix his mind on his problem. The fear which had been in him when he'd ridden out a few minutes before had not entirely left him. His chest still hurt, the ache of tense muscles remained in the back of his neck, but his immediate danger had been removed and he was thinking clearly.

It was a weakness in Clay that he could see the Ute side of this trouble. They were a small mountain tribe that the Plains Indians held in contempt when they fought east of the Rockies, but in their own environment they were invincible and the Plains Indians were in terror of them. Kit Carson, who had known the Utes well, had spoken highly of them. They had good reason to say the white men lied, and Santo, from long experience, knew what a white man's court would do to Red Holman.

So Clay, in all fairness, could not blame them. If the old law of an eye for an eye and a tooth for a tooth was to be obeyed, Santo, by his lights, had every right to take Holman's life. But Clay, by his standards, could not deliver Holman into Santo's hands. He had known that from the first, and nothing had happened to change his conviction.

He dismounted in front of the house and went in. They were all in the parlor much as he had left them except that Casteel was sitting down. Clay stood in the doorway looking at them for a moment, then put a hand out to Galt and took his gun belt from him. Most of them had not expected him to come back, he saw, and he thought that Judy's face was the only one which showed relief.

At least Judy was the one who expressed it, and when she said, "Clay, I'm so glad you're back," she left no doubt from her tone that she meant it.

Margaret asked, "What did they say?"

"We've got till sunup," Clay answered. "I told them I'd turn Holman over to the law, but Santo said he wouldn't be punished, that the white man's law was for the white man."

"Well, you sure can't argue about that," Galt said.

"My God," Margaret cried in sheer anguish, "will you let us all die for the life of a man who will probably die anyway?"

They nodded agreement—even Casteel, whose courage had leaked out of him while Clay was gone. Clay was alone more than ever, not even sure of Judy's backing now as his gaze moved from one to the other. Not Molly's. Or Lew Fisher's. Or Slim Galt's. He realized it was within the realm of possibility that some of them might try to throw a gun on him and keep him covered while they took Holman from his room and delivered him to Santo.

"I'm not sure what I'm going to do," he said, his eyes meeting Margaret's. "But you won't die. We'll figure something out."

"Figure something out of nothing," Fisher said hotly. "You've gone clean crazy, Clay."

Brimlow, trembling as if he had the ague, whispered, "He is crazy. Completely crazy."

"I may be crazy, but crazy or not, I'm disappointed in you," Clay said, more angry than miserable. "The lot of you. I know one thing, and you'll do well to think about it. We know it's wrong to turn Holman over to Santo even if he does deserve to die. If I did it to save my own hide, I'd hate myself as long as I live."

"I reckon that's right," Galt said, "But we've all got something to live for. A duty to do, too, if you want to think along that line. My job is to get my passengers through safely. I've been on this run since the railroad got to Gunnison, and I've never lost a passenger yet. I don't aim to break my record because of Red Holman."

"You've got the same duty as long as these passengers are under your roof," Molly said, "and don't you forget it for a minute, Clay Majors."

Clay turned and went outside, realizing there was truth in what Galt and Molly had said, but it only pointed up the fact that right and wrong were never absolute. But such a philosophical consideration was of no help in solving a problem of grim reality such as the one he faced.

He wished it wasn't his responsibility to face it, but it was, and he wasn't a man to push that responsibility off on someone else. Not even Slim Galt.

Eighteen

CLAY CROSSED THE YARD to where the stagecoach stood, in the exact spot where it had stopped when Galt had brought it in. He filled his pipe and, lighting it, glanced up at the sky. It was completely covered by clouds and he could not see the stars, so he was unable to tell how late it was. But he did know it was long after midnight, and that he had to make his mind up soon, that time was running out on him.

He heard someone leave the house and come toward him, then Judy called, "Clay?"

"Here," he said, and a moment later she stood beside him.

"I thought you'd want to talk to someone," she said simply.

He was grateful, thinking that this was consideration which he would never have received from Margaret. "I guess I do," he said, "but even talking isn't going to answer some questions which can't be answered."

He felt her hand on his arm. She said, "Clay, I have never met a man I admire more than you. You have courage or you wouldn't have gone to Santo tonight. But lots of men have courage. You have something else. It sets you apart from even a man like Slim Galt. I guess you'd call it integrity."

For a moment he was too choked up to say anything. He put an arm around her and held her hard against him, thinking he had not felt this way since he'd been a boy. She had said what he needed to hear, she had given him an expression of confidence. Of all the people who were here, it could have come only from her.

"Thanks, Judy," he said finally.

"There's always an easy way out," she said, "but you couldn't take it. That's why I said what I did about integrity. The other men, including Slim, would have let the Indians have Holman, and then excused themselves by talking about other duties. That would have been the end of it, although I suppose it's like you said. They'd never forgive themselves for it afterwards."

"Casteel?"

She laughed shortly. "I think you beat all his courage out of him. After you left, he changed his tune. If you came back, you'd be unarmed, with Slim holding your gun, so Casteel and Brimlow wanted to make you a prisoner and let Santo have Holman. Even Fisher sided with them."

"And Margaret," Clay added.

"Of course," Judy admitted. "But Molly and Galt wouldn't stand for it. They'd argue with you if they disagreed, they said, but you were the boss, and they'd back you even if they thought you were wrong."

He was silent, thankful for that much support. After a time he said, "It's strange, the way I drifted around before I came here, working on ranches or in mines or anything I could find. Helped develop a townsite and made a little money. Then I got this ranch because Ouray liked me and he knew someone had to operate a stage stop. He'd rather have me than someone who hated his people. Casteel tried to get it, but Ouray wouldn't let him have it. I took it because I knew that sooner or later the Utes would have to go and the whites would settle the reservation. Now it'll happen, probably within a month or two, but chances are I won't be here."

"Maybe you will," she said.

"What you called integrity might just be stubbornness," he said. "I got that from my dad. He was a blacksmith. Never said much, but he turned down a lot of deals that would have been profitable because they went against his beliefs. Ma was the one who made me read a lot. Old classics, mostly. She'd been a teacher and had saved most of her books. She used to talk to me about right and wrong, and how a man had to decide for himself and not let others decide for him. She was right. Didn't take me long to find that out. If I make a mistake, at least it's mine and I can't blame anybody else for it."

"Where are your folks?"

"Dead," he said. "A typhoid epidemic took them when I was fifteen. It was just after the war was over. I've been on my own ever since." He took the pipe from his mouth, knocked out the dottle against a wheel of the coach, and slipped the pipe into his pocket. "I've never talked to anyone like this before, Judy. I guess it's because you're like you are. With most people, I always figured that what was behind me was my business." He hesitated, then added, "And Margaret never seemed interested."

"I wish we'd met sooner," she said softly. "Before you knew Margaret."

"It's all over between Margaret and me if we get out of

this alive," he said. "She'll take the next stage to Gunnison. It's just as well because it wouldn't have worked out."

He felt something for Judy he had never felt for Margaret. He wasn't sure he loved her, for it seemed unreasonable that a man could be with a woman less than twenty-four hours and fall in love with her. Then he remembered how much he had liked her when he had been with her in Gunnison, the two evenings he had spent with her, how real and unaffected she had been.

What he had seen of her since he had met the train in Gunnison simply proved what he had sensed in her before, that there was only one Judy Allen, and that she was not ashamed of what she was and what she had done. She made no pretenses, therefore she had no need to resort to playing a dozen roles to match the demands of the moment.

"No," Judy agreed after a moment of silence, "it wouldn't have worked out. She's so damned selfish nothing would work out with her."

"Funny how everything happens in a few hours," he mused. "Seems like the Lord arranges things and you have the experiences of a lifetime jammed into a few hours."

"Yes," she said. "I know."

He was silent again, conscious of passing time, that he must do what he had to do. He said, "I've been trying to sort out the alternatives. First, there's the idea of giving Holman up. I liked Red's dad. He threw his life away for a no-good son, but I suppose a lot of fathers would do that. It's the same thing that makes Santo come after Red. If it had been the other way around, Boone would probably be doing the same thing Santo is. But that's not important. No matter what I thought of Boone, I couldn't give Red to Santo."

"Go on," she urged. "Keep talking, Clay. This is a hell of a mess, but you'll find a way out of it."

"The second thing we can do is to bar the doors and windows and fight," he said. "That was what I thought we'd do, but we'll throw that out, too. I can't stand Margaret looking at me the way she does and asking me why I brought her here. And the way everybody else feels. We'd die, all right, if the shooting starts. I know that, after talking to Santo. Too many of them are like Kuero. They just want trouble."

"That doesn't leave anything else to do," she said, "unless you have Slim hook the team to the stage and put us on it and start for the Agency. At least our lives wouldn't be on your conscience."

"Slim wouldn't do it. Anyhow, you wouldn't get half a mile." Clay paused, then added, "There is one other alternative. I can get Holman out of the house and take him to jail."

106

"You can't do that, Clay," she whispered. "You couldn't get through. They'll kill you."

"Maybe."

"Fisher couldn't make it. How could you?"

"Just because Lew didn't make it doesn't prove I can't," he said. "Looks to me like it's the only thing I can do."

It was that simple. He had a feeling he had known for hours that in the end that was what he would do. He had no illusions about his chances of getting through alive, or what Kuero would do to him after they caught him, so he had refused to recognize the one choice he had. The truth was he had no more desire to die than anyone else.

For all of Santo's tough talk, Clay had little confidence the old chief could handle the young men like Kuero. Maybe even Santo wouldn't try to save him after giving him the warning he had. Still, it was the only action Clay could take which might save the lives of Judy and the others in the house. He wasn't sure it would, once the Indians learned that Holman was gone.

Suddenly restless, now that his mind was made up, he said, "I want you to stay here, Judy. If I get back."

"I'll be here, Clay," she said.

He put both arms around her, and bringing her to him, kissed her. He knew then that he loved her, and that she loved him. It was not the kind of kiss Margaret had given him when he had seen her in Denver, very proper and chaste, or one designed by passion to buy a promise from him, such as Margaret had given him in the house earlier in the night. It was simply Judy's kiss, one filled with promise, one he would never forget.

Then, her lips drawn back from his, she said firmly, "You'll come back. I know you will."

For a moment he wanted mightily to tell her he loved her, but he didn't. She would forget him more easily if he didn't tell her, and forget him she must if he didn't come back. The last thing he wanted was for her to be tied to his memory.

"I've got to go," he said. "It's going to rain. That might give us a chance."

She was in his arms again briefly, her lips pressed against his, then she whispered, "I felt a drop just now. It'll pour before long. You'll have to hurry." Still she couldn't bring herself to let him go. He felt her strong arms around him, the pressure of her body against his, and heard her whisper, "God go with you, Clay. Please come back."

Then she stepped away from him and he strode to the house, Judy running to keep up with him.

Nineteen

WHEN CLAY RETURNED TO THE PARLOR, he had the feeling they had been arguing about him and what should be done. He said, giving them no chance to argue with him, "I'm going to take Holman and make a run for the Agency. It's closer than Gunnison, so I figure there's a better chance for me that way than the other."

"They'll skin you alive, Clay," Fisher said.

"Maybe, but it's the only thing I can do. They won't harm any of you if they know Holman's gone. Lew, bring Diamond around to the back of the house. Saddle Pronto for Holman. You said his horse was beat. Saddle another horse for you. Be sure to keep out of the light. They're watching us all the time."

"What do I need a horse for?" Fisher demanded.

"Just do what I tell you," Clay said irritably. "You're not going with me."

Still Fisher hesitated, then he blurted, "I don't like it, Clay. Even if I ain't going with you, you're taking two guns out of the house. Looks to me like we oughtta stick together."

"That's not the way you've been talking," Clay said. "Now move."

Fisher glanced at Galt, but found no help there. Reluctantly he rose and started toward the door. Clay said, "Fetch them around to the back and keep out of the light. You hear?" Fisher grunted something and went out. Clay turned to Galt. "Give me an hour, then you ride out and tell Santo what I've done."

"He won't believe Galt," Casteel said. "It's like Fisher says. You're leaving us with two less guns."

"Santo knows Slim," Clay said. "He'll believe him. I've got a hunch that's what Santo expects me to do because I told him I wouldn't give Holman to him."

He saw the glance Casteel exchanged with Margaret, and he thought Brimlow brightened as if he had suddenly caught a glimmer of hope. Judy said sharply, "Clay, they don't intend to give you an hour."

"I was thinking that," Clay said. "The minute I step out the back door, Casteel will go high-tailing to tell Santo what I've done, and my goose will be cooked quick and sudden."

He looked at Molly, measuring her. She had been watching him intently, bent forward a little, her hands spread over her big thighs. She had been against him earlier in the night, but now he thought he caught a hint of admiration on her homely face. He had to gamble on someone, and Judy was not familiar enough with guns to do the job that had to be done.

"Molly, can I count on you?" Clay asked.

"You know you can," she said. "I was agin' you awhile ago because I thought you were talking silly, but if it had come to a showdown, I'd have gone down the line for you and you damn well knew it."

He gave her a tight grin. "I wasn't so sure from the way you talked. Get your Sharps. Keep them right here where they're sitting for an hour. Then I don't care what they do."

"I'll get it," she said, "and I'll guarantee they won't budge."

She left the room. Margaret's face had been getting red, her hands fisted on her lap. Now, her lips twisted in a hateful grimace, she said in a voice that was not at all ladylike, "You bastard! You brought me here with a lot of promises, and now you ride off and leave me with this . . . this scum. If you were any part of a man, you'd stay here and protect me."

She was a vixen. He pictured himself married to her, and the first time something went wrong, she'd curse him with a mule skinner's vocabulary. The word "bastard" slipped off her tongue as if it were a familiar one, and the thought came to him that danger such as they faced now brought out qualities in people that lay dormant in different circumstances.

Clay looked at Casteel. "There's your thoroughbred," he said, and, turning, left the room and climbed the stairs. Casteel, he thought, had been as shocked as he was.

Holman was flat on his back, his eyes closed. When Clay stepped into the room, he heard the clatter of big raindrops on the roof. It would come down hard now, he thought, so this was the time to move. The storm might last a few minutes, or a few hours, but it would give him the cover he needed when he left the house, and he had to get away before it stopped.

"On your feet, Holman." Clay picked up Holman's hat and tossed it on the bed. "We're making a run for it."

Holman's eyes snapped open and he cowered against the wall. Clay saw craven fear in his face as he whispered, "I ain't going. I can't. I'm shot."

109

"Get on your feet and pull your boots on," Clay said, "or I'll give you the damnedest beating you ever had, even if you are shot. I'm not going to throw away the lives of everybody in this house because of you."

"We can't get away," Holman whined. "They'll kill both of us."

"I figure they will," Clay said. "We're making a gamble with about one chance in a hundred of pulling in the chips, but it's the best bet we've got. You coming, or do I drag you down the stairs by your left arm?"

"I'll come." Holman sat up and pulled his boots on, then he rose and grabbed the head of the bed to keep from falling. "Gimme a drink before we start."

"No."

"Gimme my gun, damn it. You want 'em to kill me without having no chance to fight back?"

"You didn't give Santo's boy a chance to fight back. Come on."

"I'm a white man. I ain't no goddamned Injun!"

Clay walked to the door. He said thinly, "You'll get no gun. There's a slim chance I can get you through. If you had a gun and they spotted us, we wouldn't have any."

Clay motioned for Holman to follow. He did, reluctantly. When they reached the parlor, Molly sat in a rocking chair near the doorway, the Sharps across her lap.

She said, "Good luck, son. Takes a man with guts to try what you're trying, but you'll have your hour, if that's any consolation. The first one to make a move will get it, and at this range, this here cannon will blow their heads off."

He looked down at her, knowing she would do exactly what she said. "Thanks. It's about twenty-six miles to the Agency. With an hour's start and a rain coming, I figure we can make it."

Casteel said, "Majors."

Clay turned to him. "Well?"

"Looks like we won't get a chance to settle our trouble," he said, his battered, puffy lips slurring the words. A dark clot of blood had dried on one end of his mustache, giving it a queer, unbalanced look. "Providing you're really going to try to get through."

"I'll try, all right," Clay said.

"I doubt like hell that you will," Casteel said. "I figure you'll get out there a piece and see that Santo gets Holman and you'll come back as healthy as you are right now. If you do, I'll see that everybody on the western slope knows you're a Ute-lover and that you're responsible for the death

110

of a white man. Then this country won't be big enough to hold you."

"Yes, I think you'd do that if you were alive to talk," Clay said, "but if I do come back and find you here, I'll see you have a gun." He nodded at Galt. "Take Holman out through the back door. Shut the kitchen door when you go through. I don't want any light showing back there."

He turned and, leaving the parlor, strode along the hall to his room. He lighted a lamp on the bureau, picked up his Winchester, and took some shells from the top drawer. He filled the magazine, then dropped a handful into his coat pocket.

He looked around, thinking this had been his home for more than four years. The house, the barn, the hay meadows, his herd of cattle: all his work would go to someone else. He didn't believe he would return. Even if he did, he still had to face Larry Casteel.

A thought occurred to him. He found a piece of paper and a pencil, and scribbled out a will leaving everything to Judy. He wasn't sure it would hold up in court, but it was the best he could do. Then he blew out the lamp and walked toward the back where Fisher was waiting in the rain with the horses.

Twenty

CLAY PAUSED ON THE BACK PORCH long enough to take a slicker off the wall and slip into it, then took down a second one for Holman. The night was black dark now, the rain a rushing downpour that blotted out all other sound.

It seemed to Clay that this was the first time grudging luck had smiled on him since early morning almost twenty-four hours ago. If the rain kept up, he and Holman would be able to pass within a few feet of the Indian guards and not be seen or heard.

Clay handed the extra slicker to Galt. "Put this on Holman."

"He's got one," Galt said. "I helped myself as I went past."

Clay tossed the slicker back onto the porch. He said, "Watch out for Judy, Slim."

"I thought it was working that way," Galt said. "I will, Clay. I sure will."

No falseness about Slim Galt, no sentimental assurance that Clay would be back and could look after his own girl. Galt knew the odds as well as Clay did.

"Holman, I don't want a sound out of you," Clay said. "Not a sneeze or a cough or a grunt. No talking, either. This rain might drive whites to cover, but not the Utes. They're out there just like they were a couple of hours ago. If we're lucky, we'll get through. If we tip our hand, we won't be lucky. We'll be dead."

"Lucky?" Holman groaned. "Luck won't do it. My arm hurts like hell . . ."

"It doesn't hurt as much as a head without a scalp," Clay said. "I'm not going to tie you or lead your horse. It's up to you to keep up with me, but I'll tell you this. If you make a run for it, I'm not chasing you. I'll leave you to Santo and he'll find you. Your only chance is to stick close to me."

"I'll stick," Holman said.

"All right, we'll ride," Clay said, and, moving to where Fisher held Diamond, he slipped the rifle into the scabbard and stepped into the saddle. "Lew, you're our decoy."

"I ain't going out there again," Fisher said sullenly.

"I didn't figure on you going back to Santo," Clay said. "Just head west. Ride hard so they can hear you. We know damned well there's a guard, maybe two or three of 'em, out north of the house. If you can pull them out of position, we can slip through."

Fisher hesitated, then Galt said, "I'll do it."

"No," Fisher said, still sullen. "I'll try."

"Don't go far," Clay said, "and then swing back. If we can get into the timber, I think we'll be all right."

He waited until Fisher was in the saddle, then he said, "Ready, Holman?"

He heard a groan. Finally Holman grunted, "Yeah, I'm ready."

"Good luck, Clay," Galt said.

"Thanks, Slim," Clay said, and rode north slowly, skirting the horse pasture, and angled northeast toward the timber.

There had been a lull in the rain. In the sudden quiet Clay heard Fisher's horse. Another horse took off in pursuit, then the rain came down harder than ever and he lost the sound of hoofs.

Clay had never seen a night as black as this one, or so it seemed. He had to depend upon an instinctive sense of direction because he could see nothing. Holman, burdened by his fears and pain, did not realize for a time that they had turned east instead of west. When he did, he called, "This ain't the way to the Agency."

Clay swore under his breath at Holman's stupidity. He reined up, listening. No sound but the wind screaming through the pines and the steady hammering of the rain.

Santo, Clay knew, would block the east road to Gunnison and the west road to the Agency. Traveling on a night as black as this, over rough country and through timber, was slow and dangerous, so Clay was convinced that Santo would concentrate on the road.

Still, he would not have left the house unguarded. If Fisher had been successful, there was a hole here and Clay and Holman had slid through it. If Fisher had failed, they might be sitting their saddles within ten feet of a Ute brave.

The wicked little animals began working along Clay's spine again, and the hot spot appeared between his shoulder blades. If a guard was still here and had heard Holman, he'd cut loose. Even if neither Clay nor Holman was hit, the sound of a gunshot would bring the Indians swarming around them within a matter of minutes like angry bees from an overturned hive.

But the minutes passed and nothing happened. Clay said in a low tone that barely reached the other man, "Holman, you'll keep your mouth shut from now on or I'll knock you in the head and tie you across your saddle. Savvy?"

"Yeah," Holman groaned. "God, my arm hurts."

"Let's ride," Clay said. "Remember. Keep your mouth shut.

They were in the pines now, wet branches slapping them in the face as they rode. Clay didn't know the time, but he thought that dawn was about an hour away. The big question in his mind was whether Santo would have guards scattered through the timber. If so, was this hour of darkness long enough to get past them?

Time would give him the answer to that. Clay was sure of only one thing. They had to stay in the timber for that hour at least. After that they could likely swing back to the road and be reasonably sure they were safe. The thing to do then was to get across the reservation line as soon as they could.

Holman was probably a little feverish, and certainly scared, so scared he was panicky. A panicky man was never a rational one. If they ran into a drifting band of Utes, the chances were Holman would do something foolish and get himself and Clay killed. But that was the chance Clay had taken when he'd left the roadhouse. He could do nothing except try to meet the emergency when it came.

The Black Canyon of the Gunnison was not far to the north. The country between here and there was deeply furrowed by washes and gullies that could not be seen on a night like this, so Clay gave Diamond his head, holding only to a general easterly direction. They angled through spruce, across small meadows, hoofs making a squishing sound in the mud, and through quaky pockets, the aspens growing so close that Clay felt the trunks rub his legs.

He was afraid Holman would drop behind, but he didn't. Now and then a groan of pain reached Clay's ears. The rain slacked off some, but the wind increased until it was a gale, occasionally snapping a limb and sending it crashing to the ground, or uprooting a tree.

Once a pine limb fell so close to Clay that the needles scraped the side of his face. A few feet closer and he'd have been struck on the head and knocked cold. But he was thankful for the noise and fury of the storm. It smothered the sounds of their passage from scouting parties that Santo might have sent out, and drowned out Holman's groans, which seemed to be louder than they were and coming more often.

So the long hour dragged by. They traveled slowly because they could do nothing else, through brush pockets, over windfalls and tangles of interlaced limbs, Diamond moving cautiously along the edge of gullies with steep walls that would have brought horse and rider down in a leg-breaking fall if Diamond had made a misstep. Holman's mount Pronto followed Diamond like a sure-footed dog not more than a step behind.

The moon must have been down for some time, or so completely covered by thick clouds that it gave no light. The first hint of dawn crept out over a sodden earth so slowly that Clay was not immediately aware of its coming, or that the clouds had begun to break away overhead. He was not even aware that the rain had stopped, for each time they touched a limb or jammed through a brush thicket they brought a cold shower down upon them.

This was the world's ebb time when it is said that the forces of life are at their lowest point. So it was with Clay. He hated Holman, hated him for not staying with his father once he had provoked the fight, hated him for killing Santo's son, hated him for coming to the roadhouse last night and dragging the threat of death with him. And he hated Holman, perhaps more than for the other reasons, because he had taken Clay from Judy at a time when life was filled with promise.

Now Clay knew he wanted to live as he never had before.

114

Regardless of Judy's past, and regardless of what the gossips said about her, she would enjoy living at Cimarron just as he did, and it would be a pleasure to live there with her. And if he didn't survive? All he could hope for, then, was that the will he'd left would be recognized and the ranch would be hers.

The weight of the night and the timber through which they'd passed pressed heavily upon them, but now Clay was aware that the earth was beginning to come to life with the day, that color was brightening the sky ahead of them. This was new country to Clay, but he knew they were still inside the reservation, the line a long ways ahead of them.

The road was somewhere to their right and they angled toward it, Clay realizing that speed was essential now. He felt certain they had gone well beyond the line of Ute guards. Santo would know they had left the house and he would be on his way to the Agency to overtake them. In that regard, the rain had been a lifesaver again, for it would have washed out their tracks, and Santo would probably go halfway to the Agency before he gave them up and realized they had not gone that way. By that time Clay should have Holman across the line.

Santo would not leave the reservation. Or would he? Clay couldn't be sure, now that he thought about it, knowing how passionately Santo felt about taking Holman. The chase, once they were in the open and along the river, might last almost to Gunnison.

The air was cold and damp and heavy with mountain smells. Mountain sounds, too. A deer, spooked by their coming, crashed away to the south. From some high point a lonely coyote lifted his voice and was silent, for now day was at hand, the sullen gray of dawn giving way to full light, and then the sun was touching the sky with a long sweep of gold and scarlet far to the east beyond the divide above the Blue.

They reached the road and Clay pulled up, motioning for Holman to do the same. He sat there a long moment studying the soaked earth. No one had passed this way since the rain had stopped. Even with good luck and accurate guessing on Santo's part, Clay didn't believe the Indians could have come this far during the rain, if Galt had waited a full hour before telling them what Clay had done.

He went on, lifting Diamond to a faster pace. Holman caught up and rode beside him. His teeth were chattering and his face was gray and tortured by pain, but he hadn't changed and he wouldn't change. He said callously, "If Pa had been worth a damn, he'd have got them three Injun kids, and old Santo wouldn't have knowed what happened. Then we wouldn't be in this jam."

Clay looked at him, despising him as he had never despised another human being in his life. He said, "I suppose it never occurs to you that if you hadn't shot Santo's boy, we wouldn't be in this jam, either."

"What's one Injun brat, one way or the other?" Holman said. "Started begging and I told him to git. He called me a son-of-a-bitch, and I shot him. Nobody calls me that." He grimaced. "Hell, this was the last trip I was gonna make. I was going on to Silverton from Ouray. Had a job waiting for me there. A woman, too. By God, she can do more for a man in bed than any other woman I ever slept with."

Clay looked briefly at Holman and turned his gaze away. This was the man he was risking his life for.

Holman said harshly, "I figured you had some kind of trick up your sleeve, but you'd better be sure you get me to Gunnison. You better be goddamned sure."

"Shut up."

"Hell, you don't need to get proddy. We're in the clear, ain't we? Just like cutting butter with a hot knife from now on, ain't it?"

"I don't know," Clay said. "Just shut up."

The sun rose higher, turning the morning hot and lifting steam from the sodden earth. Now the Blue was directly ahead of them, and Clay took a long breath of relief. They had made it, he thought. On beyond the Blue was the ridge that was the divide between it and the Lake Fork, and they'd soon be off the reservation. For the first time he believed he would live.

He didn't know what Santo would do to him for getting Holman out of the house and to safety, especially after a court turned him loose, which it probably would. It was hard to tell what kind of lie Holman would tell in Gunnison, being the kind of man he was. With the people there feeling as they did, the lie would be believed whatever it was.

But somehow, now that it was day and the wind had died, and the reservation line was just a few miles farther east, all of these dangers suddenly seemed trivial ones compared to that from which they had escaped.

They reached the Blue and reined up. Clay said, "Better get down and stretch. Let Pronto have a drink."

Clay took off his slicker and tied it behind the saddle, let Diamond drink, and then bellied down and had his drink upstream from the horse. He rose, wiping his mouth with his sleeve, then he glanced at Holman and his heart leaped into his throat, his stomach muscles tightening so that for a moment he could not breathe.

He had never before seen an expression of such abject terror on the face of any human as he saw now on the face of Red Holman. Clay made a slow turn, right hand dropping to the butt of his gun; then it fell away.

There, on the other side of the creek, was Santo, his rifle lined on Clay's chest, a dozen Ute braves behind him.

Twenty-One

THE UTES WERE A FREEDOM-LOVING, MOUNTAIN PEOPLE who had been called the Switzers of America. They were not, contrary to a popular conception among the whites, a stoical, humorless people. They loved horse racing. They were habitual gamblers. They liked to dance. On several occasions Clay had watched their Bear Dance which was held each spring, a celebration that lasted for three days and three nights, the oldest and most typical of their many dances.

Clay had sat with them around the Agency buildings, laughing and gossiping for an hour at a time. Even Ouray, a serious-minded man, had been something of a prankster. Clay remembered one occasion when he was eating at a table with Ouray and Buckskin Charley. A dish of olives was passed. Ouray had tasted them, but Buckskin Charley hadn't, so Ouray took one and gave the dish to Charley, blandly saying they were good. Charley popped one into his mouth, got the taste of it, and promptly spit it out, the olive bouncing off the opposite wall. Charley sputtered and grimaced, looking as if he thought he'd never get the taste out of his mouth, and Ouray laughed so hard he almost fell out of his chair.

All of this flashed through Clay's mind in the few seconds he stood frozen, his gaze on Santo's expressionless face, a rush of thoughts similar to the thoughts that come to a drowning man in the brief interval of time before he dies when he knows he must. Those were good memories, pleasant ones, and Clay had unconsciously based his hope of survival upon the good nature of the Utes and his friendship with Santo, a friendship which Bronc Pless had said would mean nothing.

Now, in these horrible and terrifying seconds, the scene a tableau of motionless players, Clay knew Bronc had been right. Santo's face was the inscrutable face of fate that could not be altered. He said something in the Ute tongue to one of the braves, and splashed across the creek, his rifle barrel swinging in his hands so that Clay was covered. Santo didn't need to say a word. Clay didn't have to be told that any move on his part would bring a bullet smashing into his chest.

"Don't move," Clay said softly to Holman.

Even as he said it, he sensed that anything he said would be wasted words. Knowing Holman, he realized that the man was caught in a flood of panic that would make his behavior completely irrational. More than that, Clay sensed that Holman would die regardless of anything Clay could say or do. Bronc Pless had said Holman was a dead man. The old man had been right in that, too.

One young Ute rode downstream, probably to bring in guards who had been posted along the creek. The rest followed Santo. Last night in the darkness Clay had been unable to see their faces, but now he saw that all of them wore the yellow and black war paint of the Utes.

Santo's coarse black hair, slightly touched by gray, hung down his chest in two long braids, colored beads woven through them. The others wore buckskin, but Santo was clad in an officer's dark blue uniform which had been given to him years ago by someone at Fort Garland. He had taken the best possible care of it, wearing it only on special occasions, and this, the avenging of the murder of his son, would be such an occasion. A big silver medal, probably presented to him at the signing of some treaty, hung from a buckskin thong around his neck.

Several of the Utes dismounted and moved in behind Clay and Holman, and Holman, making whimpering sounds, crowded against Clay, who kept turning slowly so that he faced Santo.

"Don't do this, Santo," Clay said. "For your sake and the sake of your people. After what happened on White River, you will only bring great trouble upon your whole nation. On you, too."

Santo's expression did not change. Clay saw that the chief didn't believe him. Perhaps he had logical reason not to believe, for none of the murders committed by Meeker and his men at the White River Agency had been punished except that Douglas had been imprisoned for a year in Fort Leavenworth. Santo doubtless thought the same laxity would be demonstrated by the whites again. Or maybe he didn't care. This was something he must do, just as Clay could not have handed Holman over to him last night when Santo demanded him.

"Galt lied," Santo said. "He told me you take Holman to Agency."

"I lied to him," Clay said. "I thought I could trick you so I could come this way and take Holman to jail in Gunnison."

One of the older men beside Santo snarled, "White men heap big liars."

Clay knew some of the Indians were still behind him, but he couldn't risk looking around. That would have indicated fear, the one emotion he must not show. He felt Holman's breath on the back of his neck, heard the whimpering sounds that the pressure of panic forced out of him.

"I promised you I would take him to jail and he'll be tried," Clay said. "It will be best for all of you if I do that."

"I did not believe Galt," Santo said, "But I sent Kuero to watch the Agency road. I came here to watch for you. You lied. Why should I believe you now?"

"It was my job to take Holman to jail," Clay said. "I thought I could do it by getting you to watch the Agency road. I will take him to jail. I will promise that."

"You talk of white man's law and white man's trial." Santo spat in the mud at Clay's feet. "Holman killed my son. You know that."

"I know he did," Clay said. "He told me himself, and I'll swear to that in court."

"Nolo saw it," Santo said. "Tell Majors."

Nolo was one of the Ute boys who had been in the party that had asked the Holmans for breakfast. He could not speak English, but, like most Utes, he knew Spanish, and Clay was able to follow his story, which agreed with what Lew Fisher had told the evening before, and what Holman had practically admitted this morning.

When Nolo finished, Santo said, "You promise they let Nolo talk? You promise they listen to him and hang Holman?"

This was the weakness of Clay's position and Santo knew it. He had lived too long next to the fringe of white settlement to believe a white man's court would punish any white man who had injured an Indian. All Clay could say was, "I can't promise that, but I'll do all I can."

A moment of silence then, with no change in Santo's inscrutable expression, silence except for the whisper of the creek and the increasingly louder sounds of Holman's whimpers. Clay didn't know what they were waiting for, but every instant he expected to feel a knife driven into his back, or a bullet slamming into his spine. Now Santo's rifle turned from Clay to cover Holman, who had begun to edge toward Clay's horse.

Clay fully expected to receive the same treatment Holman did because he had tried to trick Santo by having Galt say he was taking Holman to the Agency. So, expecting to die, Clay would have welcomed any quick death that the Indians wanted to give him. Otherwise it would be torture, for the Utes knew the Apaches, and the Apaches knew every trick in the book.

But apparently Santo found pleasure in prolonging the tension, the waiting which was designed to break Holman. Clay knew that it would if it continued, so he tried to think of something to say, some new argument which might touch Santo, but he could think of nothing, perhaps because he knew there was no use, that what was destined to happen would happen.

Holman was sobbing now. Suddenly he screamed an oath and lunged toward Diamond, perhaps to get into the saddle and make a run for it, or perhaps to yank the rifle from the scabbard and kill Santo. Clay tried to get his revolver clear of the holster, thinking bleakly that, like Boone Holman, he would die for no good reason.

His hands closed over the butt of the .45 as Santo's Henry cracked twice. Clay had his gun barrel clear of leather when one of the Indians behind him struck him on the head with a rifle barrel, the blow driving him to his knees. The earth tipped and spun crazily before Clay as the revolver was snatched out of his hand.

From a great distance Santo's words beat against his ears, "You get guns at ranch." Blood ran down his forehead as he tried to struggle to his feet, then daylight became night and he toppled forward on his face.

When he came to, the sun was higher in the sky and the morning was very hot. His first awareness was that of a thundering headache. It took time to remember what had happened, to realize how close he had been to death and how grateful he was to be alive. He crawled to the creek and washed his face in the cold water. Blood from his head wound had clotted around the edge of one eye and along his nose and over part of his upper lip.

Later, revived by the cold water and his face clean, he sat up and looked at Holman, who lay on his back, two bullet holes in his chest, his sightless eyes staring at the sky. Clay went to him and felt for a pulse. He was dead, as Clay knew he would be. Probably he had been killed instantly.

Clay's revolver was gone and his rifle wasn't in the scabbard. He remembered the last thing Santo had said. The chief apparently had been afraid he might recover consciousness and shoot at them before they were out of sight, or pursue them, and, not wanting to kill Clay, he had taken the guns.

There would be no more trouble, now that Holman was dead, unless the whites forced it by trying to punish the Utes for Holman's killing. Clay staggered to an aspen and leaned against the trunk, waiting for the dizziness to pass, all the time blaming himself for failure. Yet, thinking back over what had happened, he knew he could not have done anything more than he had.

At least he had prevented the massacre of those who were in the house, a massacre that would certainly have brought the red flame of war to the entire Colorado frontier and probably beyond it, and have ended in terrible punishment to the Utes. Compared to that, Holman's death was insignificant.

Clay had been foolish to try to draw his gun, and only Santo's forebearance had kept him from being killed along with Holman. Yet, considering it, he knew the action was one for which he should not be ashamed. It was an act he had been compelled to make just as he had been driven by his conscience to try to take Holman to Gunnison.

He lifted Holman's body and laid it across the saddle on Pronto and tied it down, then, mounting Diamond, he took Pronto's reins and started home. Every step Diamond took sent racking pain through his head. For a time he thought he would faint, but he never quite lost consciousness. Then the worst of it passed. He crossed the divide and started down the long slope toward Cimarron as the east-bound stage left his ranch.

When the coach reached him, he raised a hand. The driver, Howard Negly, knew him almost as well as Galt. Negly stopped, asking as he nodded at Pronto, "Holman?"

"Yeah, it's Holman," Clay said, stepping down. "I want you to take him to Gunnison."

Margaret was in the coach, sitting beside a young lieutenant from the cantonment. He spoke to Clay and Clay returned the greeting, his gaze on Margaret. She was wearing the same gray traveling suit she'd worn the morning before when she'd stepped down from the train, the same chic straw hat.

It came as a shock to see that she was quite composed; her eyes were on him briefly and impersonally as if he were a

121

complete stranger. Then she turned her head and looked away. There were a thousand Margarets, he thought, with more detachment than he had imagined he could think of her; which Margaret made her appearance depended upon the occasion and circumstances.

Clay decided he liked none of them, and he could only wonder why he had ever thought he loved her. He hadn't, of course, and he saw the truth fully and realistically. He'd had to have a woman to work for and build for and dream about. Actually, he had been a lonely man who had loved a dream woman and he had named her Margaret.

The lieutenant said, as if surprised at her lack of recognition, "That's Clay Majors. You know him, of course. You stayed at his roadhouse last night."

"I thought I knew him," she said quite coolly, "but I found I didn't know him at all."

Clay walked to Pronto, thinking, *I found I didn't know you, either, Margaret, and maybe this has been worth it to discover that I didn't.*

"I'm driving a hearse today," Negly said as he swung down. "Not a stage. Damned if you don't have your killings in wholesale lots."

"Something like that," Clay said.

He helped Negly lift the body to the top of the stage and lash it into place, then he said, "I'll be in town one of these days and tell the sheriff what happened."

"Or he'll be out here asking," Negly said, "along with a U.S. Marshal."

Negly climbed back to the high seat. Then he said, "Santo rode by your place with some of his bucks while ago and left your revolver and rifle. He gave the peace sign to Slim or there'd have been some shooting. Anyhow, he said he'd got Holman and that was the end of the ruckus. He promised to take care of Kuero and the rest of them. Slim's gonna be wheeling out purty quick now. Good thing I didn't know what kind of a fracas you were having or I'd never have started."

The stage rolled on up the slope, wheels and hoofs squishing in the mud. Clay mounted, and, leading Pronto with his empty saddle, rode on toward the ranch.

Twenty-Two

As CLAY RODE INTO THE YARD, Jason Brimlow scuttled across the space between the front door and the stagecoach, his satchel in his hand. He climbed in and closed the door. Lew Fisher had just finished hooking up. Galt climbed to the box, waved at Clay, cracked his whip, and the stage rumbled down the Agency road.

Clay dismounted stiffly. Fisher walked toward him, a little warily and certainly fearfully. He said, "We figured you'd be along." He motioned toward the corral, where Clay's rifle leaned against the bars. His gun belt hung from a post beside it. "Santo left 'em here while ago. . . .

"About last night. Maybe I'd best ride on. I ain't real proud of myself, now that I think about it."

Clay expected loyalty from a man and he hadn't received it from Lew Fisher, but when he looked at the boy's face, he saw shame there. He could not fully condemn him, for he knew how Fisher had felt when he'd talked to Santo. Any man had a right to be afraid. The trick was to control the fear instead of letting the fear control you as Fisher had done. But maybe it was excusable, as young as Fisher was.

"You're entitled to one mistake," Clay said. "Besides, I didn't save Holman."

"But you tried," Fisher said. "You tried like hell. I wish I had half your guts, but last night I . . . I . . ." He couldn't finish, and turned away, calling back, "I guess I'd better get my war sack."

"I'm short-handed, with Bronc gone," Clay said. "I wouldn't take it kindly if you pulled out now."

"You mean you want me to stay?" Fisher wheeled to face him, his freckled face eager.

"Unless you want to ride on."

"No, I sure don't," Fisher said. "I'm proud to work for you. I'll take care of the horses."

Clay walked slowly toward the corral, so tired he couldn't walk straight. His head was pounding again, but there would be no rest. Bronc Pless had to be made ready for burial and there was a coffin to be made and a grave to dig.

"Clay, Clay."

It was Judy running toward him from the house, her face showing her pleasure at seeing him. Molly ambled along behind, grinning broadly. Clay took Judy into his arms and hugged her hard, then Molly was there and Clay put an arm around her ample waist.

"Oh Clay," Judy said. "You don't know how good it was to look out there and see you, alive and well. I didn't think I'd ever see you again when you left with Holman."

"Neither did I." Molly looked Clay in the eyes, not backing up an inch. "You'n me didn't see things alike last night. I ain't real sure yet you were right, but Judy says you were. If I was wrong, I'll sure as hell admit it, and I'll go pack my bag. If I wasn't, I'll stay right here and keep on taking care of things like I have been."

"You stay," Clay said. "It isn't just a proposition of being right or wrong. When I left, you were sitting in the door with the Sharps on your lap, and I didn't have any worry about not getting the hour I needed."

Molly's leathery face broke into a grin. "Why sure, you knew I'd do what you asked me to. If we'd fought them devils, I'd have cracked my share of caps, too."

"I know you would," Clay said.

"I'll go get your breakfast. Or dinner, I guess we'd best call it now." She started toward the house, then turned back. "There's something you've got to know and I don't figure Judy will tell you."

"Molly," Judy said sharply.

"I'm going to tell him," Molly said. "He ought to know it. After you started off with Holman, Margaret got madder'n madder. She got to calling you names. I use them kind of words, but hell, I ain't supposed to be a lady. And I wouldn't use 'em on the man I'd come here to marry."

"I'll tell him, Molly," Judy said. "You go get dinner."

"No, I'm goin' to tell him," Molly said doggedly. "She's nothing but a bitch and he might as well know it. I kept wondering why she came here in the first place. I wondered that as soon as she got off the stage and I took her to her room. Well, purty soon it all came out. She couldn't do nothing but sit there and talk, and when she got started, she couldn't quit.

"Seems like her dad's in bad trouble. Gambling, maybe. Or buying worthless mines like a lot of men do. She never said. Anyhow, he's got his house and hotel mortgaged, so Margaret figured you'd throw in with him and save his hide.

I guess she thought you had a lot of money, this ranch and all. Then when you told her you didn't own the land and wouldn't till after the reservation was open, she didn't have no more use for you. After that she couldn't think of nothing except saving her purty hide."

Molly turned and walked to the house, her expression one of a woman who had done her duty. Clay backed up to the corral and leaned against it, watching her, surprised that he had no strong feeling about what Molly had said.

Judy said, "I'm sorry, Clay."

"It's all right." He looked at her, seeing a beauty of expression on her face he had never noticed before, a beauty that came from the genuine goodness of spirit which was hers. "I'm glad it's over. I feel like I've lived ten years in the last twenty-four hours. I've been thinking about what it's done to all of us. I don't think any of us will be the same as we were."

Lew Fisher came out of the corral, leading his horse. "I didn't find them ponies I was hunting yesterday. I'm gonna have another look."

Clay started to tell him to stay here, that they had to dig a grave, but decided against it. Probably Fisher needed to ride, needed to feel the wind in his face. He still had the embarrassed look of a boy who had done something wrong and been forgiven, and didn't know how to express his gratitude. He rode away, Clay watching until he crossed the creek.

Judy laid a hand on his arm. "I don't think you've changed, Clay, unless you'd discovered something in you that you didn't know you had. Everybody respected you, even Brimlow, who is such a despicable coward."

Clay grinned. "I wonder if he'll get to Ouray in time with that satchel full of money." Then the grin faded and he shook his head. "It isn't over. I'll have to go to Gunnison. They'll fry me with questions and the newspapers will call me a Ute-lover and claim I could have saved Holman's life if I'd wanted to." He spread his hands. "I failed, Judy, and I'll have to pay for my failure."

"You failed?" she asked as if she couldn't believe what she'd heard. "Oh Clay, you didn't fail at all. Don't you know you prevented something that would have been far worse than Holman's death?"

"I know," he said, "and I'm glad you do, but not many people will. At least the Indian-haters won't."

"And you could have been killed."

He nodded. "It was close. I thought I was going to get it."

"You tried, and did the best you could," she said. "That's

what's important. You didn't take the easy way like the rest wanted to do. Even Slim Galt."

"I'll tell you what happened," he said. "I . . ."

"You don't have to explain anything to me," she said. "Come into the house and get your dinner."

He took a long breath. "All right, I'll tell you later. But there is something I've got to say. I guess it's pretty presumptuous to ask a woman who has made a fine living the way you have to marry me when all I have to offer is hard work . . ."

"Clay, don't talk that way." Her hands squeezed his arm. "A woman only wants to know one thing from a man. Does he love her?"

"I love you," he said quickly. "Maybe it seems funny after bringing Margaret here, but I think I've loved you ever since I met you. At least it seems that way now. You see, I built up in my mind a woman I loved, but it wasn't Margaret. The woman was you, Judy. I realized it yesterday. From the things you said on the stage. The way you jumped in and helped Molly. The way you offered to take care of Holman. You're real, Judy. You never have to pretend you're something you're not."

She was smiling at him. "Clay, I like to hear you talk."

He put his arms out for her, but she didn't move. He heard the stable door slam open; he saw the look of terror on Judy's face, and heard her whisper incredulously, "It can't be him. It just can't be."

He turned. Larry Casteel stood looking at them, one eye swollen shut, his face splotched with bruises, the clot of blood on his mustache still giving it that strange, unbalanced look. He had a gun in his hand, he wore neither his coat nor his hat, and his shirt was soiled by dirt and blood spots. He bore little resemblance to the confident and immaculate Larry Casteel that Clay had met in the hotel lobby in Gunnison a little more than twenty-four hours before.

"I thought he left on the stage with Brimlow," Judy said as if she still could not believe what she was seeing. "He left the house before Brimlow did."

Casteel took a step forward, his good eye pinned on Clay. "Move away," Clay whispered. "Quick."

She didn't move. Casteel took another step. He said, his speech still thick because of his bruised lips, "I'm going to kill you, Majors."

"He doesn't have his gun," Judy cried. "You can see that. He doesn't have a chance."

But Casteel plainly had no intention of giving Clay a chance. He took another step, the gun still held at his side.

126

He was playing this out just as Santo had stretched out the time on the Blue before he'd killed Holman. Like Santo, Casteel wanted his man to break and run.

But running was one thing Clay would not do. He couldn't reach his revolver, which was in the holster, the belt still hanging from the corral post. His rifle was closer, but it was a long reach. The instant Clay moved toward it, Casteel would fire.

"No man ever whipped me twice before in my life," Casteel said. "No man ever took a woman away from me before. I told you I'd kill you. Now I'm going to do it."

"This is murder," Judy screamed. "They'll hang you."

Casteel didn't take his gaze from Clay. He said, "Who'll tell them? They'll think it was the Indians. Like Fisher said, your hair will make a fine trophy to hang in a Ute lodge. It will be gone when they find you. I've lifted scalps before."

A chill raced down Clay's spine. He could not believe Casteel would do what he had just threatened, and yet he did believe it. Pride overshadowed everything else in Casteel's make-up, and it has been smashed and battered until nothing was left of it. Now Casteel was conscious only of the maniacal urge to kill the two people who had done this to him.

Casteel took another step and slowly began to raise his gun. Clay's muscles tensed. He'd try for his rifle. It was the only chance he had, and that wasn't a chance, with the distance it was from him and the time it would take him to get it into action.

"I'll go with you to Ouray," Judy cried. "I'll do anything you——"

"You're too late," Casteel said. "Too damn late." His gun was coming up.

"Drop it, Casteel," Molly shouted from the front porch. "I've got my Sharps. Damned if I won't blow your head off if you don't drop that gun."

Casteel's head turned just as Clay jumped. He grabbed the rifle, levered a shell into the chamber as he whirled toward Casteel. The man fired, the bullet splintering a corral bar inches from Clay. He fired again before Clay got off his first shot, this one thudding into a post. He was hurrying too fast to be accurate, and he was handicapped with only one good eye. Apparently he realized this, for he started running toward Clay, bringing his gun down for a third shot when Clay squeezed trigger.

Casteel kept on coming, lurching as he tried to raise his gun, then his knees buckled and he spilled forward into the dirt, his gun falling from lax fingers. He reached for it blindly, cursing as his hand searched for the gun. He started to crawl, leaving a bloody path behind him. Then strength was gone from him, and he dropped to the ground.

Clay strode forward, the rifle covering Casteel, but the gambler was dead. For a moment Clay stood over him, sweat running down his face as he felt his blood pounding in his temples. He was trembling, his knees weak, and he could not believe, even now, that Casteel was really dead, that the last danger which had threatened him was finally gone.

Molly ran across the yard to him, shouting, "The ornery spalpeen! The lowdown killin' whelp. He aimed to gun you down without no show."

She wasn't carrying the Sharps, and Clay, glancing back at the house, couldn't see it leaning against the wall. He asked, "Where's the Sharps?"

"I didn't have it," she said. "I came out to call you to dinner, and I saw him. All I could think to do was to yell. I knowed I didn't have time to go back inside and get the Sharps."

He shook his head, thinking how she had risked her life, for Casteel would have killed her as surely as he would have killed Clay and Judy. He would not have left a witness.

Clay said simply, "Thanks, Molly."

He could not say the words that should be said, about Molly's loyalty and courage and his debt to her for saving his life, but he knew she didn't expect to hear them. He knew, too, that his troubles were not over, but he was alive, and he could handle troubles when they came. There was a lot of work ahead of him, a lot of living to do, and when he turned his gaze to Judy, he knew that the years ahead would be the best years.

He said, "Let's go inside, Judy," and, putting an arm around her, led her toward the house.

Big Bestsellers from SIGNET

☐ **HOW TO SAVE YOUR OWN LIFE** by Erica Jong.
(#E7959—$2.50)

☐ **FEAR OF FLYING** by Erica Jong. (#E7970—$2.25)

☐ **WHITEY AND MICKEY** by Whitey Ford, Mickey Mantle and Joseph Durso. (#J7963—$1.95)

☐ **MISTRESS OF DESIRE** by Rochelle Larkin.
(#E7964—$2.25)

☐ **THE QUEEN AND THE GYPSY** by Constance Heaven.
(#J7965—$1.95)

☐ **TORCH SONG** by Anne Roiphe. (#J7901—$1.95)

☐ **ISLAND OF THE WINDS** by Athena Dallas-Damis.
(#J7905—$1.95)

☐ **THE SHINING** by Stephen King. (#E7872—$2.50)

☐ **CARRIE** by Stephen King. (#J7280—$1.95)

☐ **'SALEM'S LOT** by Stephen King. (#E8000—$2.25)

☐ **OAKHURST** by Walter Reed Johnson. (#J7874—$1.95)

☐ **FRENCH KISS** by Mark Logan. (#J7876—$1.95)

☐ **COMA** by Robin Cook. (#E7881—$2.50)

☐ **THE YEAR OF THE INTERN** by Robin Cook.
(#E7674—$1.75)

☐ **NOT AS A STRANGER** by Morton Thompson.
(#E7786—$2.25)

THE NEW AMERICAN LIBRARY, INC.,
P.O. Box 999, Bergenfield, New Jersey 07621

Please send me the SIGNET BOOKS I have checked above. I am enclosing $_____(check or money order—no currency or C.O.D.'s). Please include the list price plus 35¢ a copy to cover handling and mailing costs. (Prices and numbers are subject to change without notice.)

Name_____

Address_____

City_____State_____Zip Code_____
Allow at least 4 weeks for delivery

More Big Bestsellers from SIGNET

- ☐ **MISTRESS OF DARKNESS** by Christopher Nicole. (#J7782—$1.95)
- ☐ **SOHO SQUARE** by Clare Rayner. (#J7783—$1.95)
- ☐ **CALDO LARGO** by Earl Thompson. (#E7737—$2.25)
- ☐ **TATTOO** by Earl Thompson. (#E8038—$2.50)
- ☐ **A GARDEN OF SAND** by Earl Thompson. (#E8039—$2.50)
- ☐ **DESIRES OF THY HEART** by Joan Carroll Cruz. (#J7738—$1.95)
- ☐ **THE RICH ARE WITH YOU ALWAYS** by Malcolm Macdonald. (#E7682—$2.25)
- ☐ **THE WORLD FROM ROUGH STONES** by Malcolm Macdonald. (#J6891—$1.95)
- ☐ **THE FRENCH BRIDE** by Evelyn Anthony. (#J7683—$1.95)
- ☐ **TELL ME EVERYTHING** by Marie Brenner. (#J7685—$1.95)
- ☐ **ALYX** by Lolah Burford. (#J7640—$1.95)
- ☐ **MACLYON** by Lolah Burford. (#J7773—$1.95)
- ☐ **FIRST, YOU CRY** by Betty Rollin. (#J7641—$1.95)
- ☐ **THE DEVIL IN CRYSTAL** by Erica Lindley. (#E7643—$1.75)
- ☐ **THE BRACKENROYD INHERITANCE** by Erica Lindley. (#W6795—$1.50)

THE NEW AMERICAN LIBRARY, INC.,
P.O. Box 999, Bergenfield, New Jersey 07621

Please send me the SIGNET BOOKS I have checked above. I am enclosing $_____(check or money order—no currency or C.O.D.'s). Please include the list price plus 35¢ a copy to cover handling and mailing costs. (Prices and numbers are subject to change without notice.)

Name_____

Address_____

City_____State_____Zip Code_____

Allow at least 4 weeks for delivery

Have You Read These Big Bestsellers from SIGNET?

☐ **LYNDON JOHNSON AND THE AMERICAN DREAM** by Doris Kearns. (#E7609—$2.50)

☐ **THIS IS THE HOUSE** by Deborah Hill. (#J7610—$1.95)

☐ **THE DEMON** by Hubert Selby, Jr. (#J7611—$1.95)

☐ **LORD RIVINGTON'S LADY** by Eileen Jackson. (#W7612—$1.50)

☐ **ROGUE'S MISTRESS** by Constance Gluyas. (#J7533—$1.95)

☐ **SAVAGE EDEN** by Constance Gluyas. (#J7681—$1.95)

☐ **LOVE SONG** by Adam Kennedy. (#E7535—$1.75)

☐ **THE DREAM'S ON ME** by Dotson Rader. (#E7536—$1.75)

☐ **SINATRA** by Earl Wilson. (#E7487—$2.25)

☐ **SUMMER STATION** by Maud Lang. (#E7489—$1.75)

☐ **THE WATSONS** by Jane Austen and John Coates. (#J7522—$1.95)

☐ **SANDITON** by Jane Austen and Another Lady. (#J6945—$1.95)

☐ **THE FIRES OF GLENLOCHY** by Constance Heaven. (#E7452—$1.75)

☐ **A PLACE OF STONES** by Constance Heaven. (#W7046—$1.50)

☐ **THE ROCKEFELLERS** by Peter Collier and David Horowitz. (#E7451—$2.75)

THE NEW AMERICAN LIBRARY, INC.,
P.O. Box 999, Bergenfield, New Jersey 07621

Please send me the SIGNET BOOKS I have checked above. I am enclosing $_____ (check or money order—no currency or C.O.D.'s). Please include the list price plus 35¢ a copy to cover handling and mailing costs. (Prices and numbers are subject to change without notice.)

Name_____

Address_____

City_____ State_____ Zip Code_____

Allow at least 4 weeks for delivery

Other SIGNET Bestsellers You'll Enjoy

- ☐ **THE HAZARDS OF BEING MALE** by Herb Goldberg.
  (#E7359—$1.75)
- ☐ **COME LIVE MY LIFE** by Robert H. Rimmer.
  (#J7421—$1.95)
- ☐ **THE FRENCHMAN** by Velda Johnston.
  (#W7519—$1.50)
- ☐ **THE HOUSE ON THE LEFT BANK** by Velda Johnston.
  (#W7279—$1.50)
- ☐ **A ROOM WITH DARK MIRRORS** by Velda Johnston.
  (#W7143—$1.50)
- ☐ **KINFLICKS** by Lisa Alther. (#E7390—$2.25)
- ☐ **RIVER RISING** by Jessica North. (#E7391—$1.75)
- ☐ **THE HIGH VALLEY** by Jessica North. (#W5929—$1.50)
- ☐ **LOVER: CONFESSIONS OF A ONE NIGHT STAND** by Lawrence Edwards. (#J7392—$1.95)
- ☐ **THE SURVIVOR** by James Herbert. (#E7393—$1.75)
- ☐ **THE KILLING GIFT** by Bari Wood. (#J7350—$1.95)
- ☐ **WHITE FIRES BURNING** by Catherine Dillon.
  (#E7351—$1.75)
- ☐ **CONSTANTINE CAY** by Catherine Dillon.
  (#E7583—$1.75)
- ☐ **FOREVER AMBER** by Kathleen Winsor.
  (#E7675—$2.25)
- ☐ **SMOULDERING FIRES** by Anya Seton.
  (#J7276—$1.95)

THE NEW AMERICAN LIBRARY, INC.,
P.O. Box 999, Bergenfield, New Jersey 07621

Please send me the SIGNET BOOKS I have checked above. I am enclosing $_____(check or money order—no currency or C.O.D.'s). Please include the list price plus 35¢ a copy to cover handling and mailing costs. (Prices and numbers are subject to change without notice.)

Name_____

Address_____

City_____State_____Zip Code_____

Allow at least 4 weeks for delivery